A BRIDE'S STORY

3

Kaoru Mori

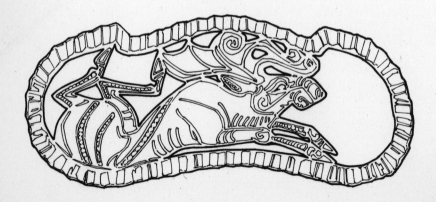

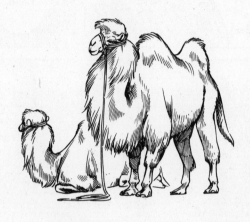

TABLE OF CONTENTS

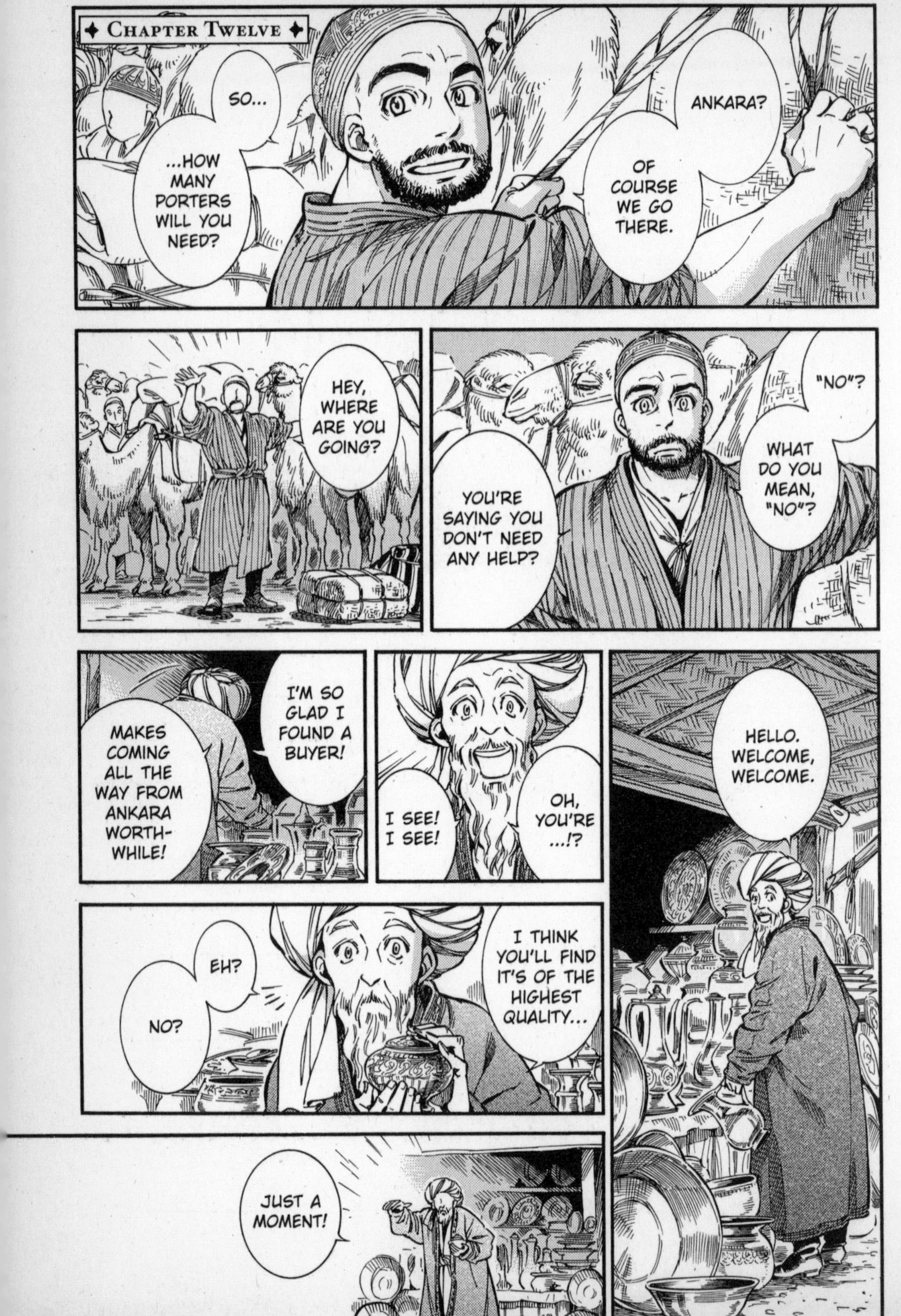
CHAPTER TWELVE
ANKARA?
OF COURSE WE GO THERE.
SO...
...HOW MANY PORTERS WILL YOU NEED?
"NO"?
WHAT DO YOU MEAN, "NO"?
YOU'RE SAYING YOU DON'T NEED ANY HELP?
HEY, WHERE ARE YOU GOING?
HELLO. WELCOME, WELCOME.
OH, YOU'RE ...!?
I SEE! I SEE!
I'M SO GLAD I FOUND A BUYER!
MAKES COMING ALL THE WAY FROM ANKARA WORTH-WHILE!
I THINK YOU'LL FIND IT'S OF THE HIGHEST QUALITY...
EH?
NO?
JUST A MOMENT!

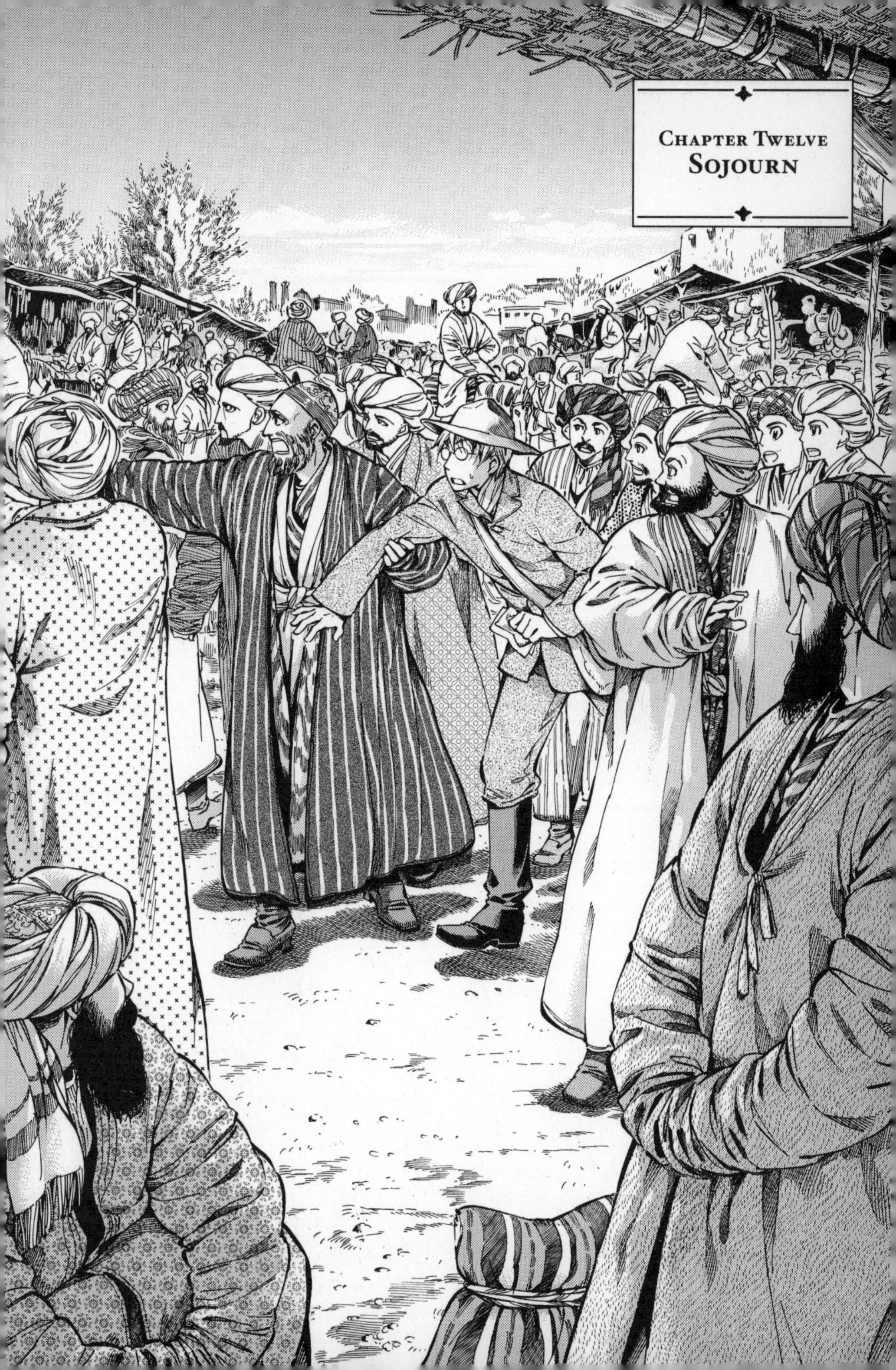
CHAPTER TWELVE
SOJOURN

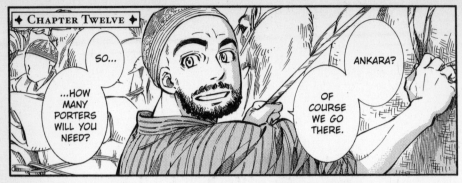

SO...

...HOW MANY PORTERS WILL YOU NEED?

ANKARA?

OF COURSE WE GO THERE.

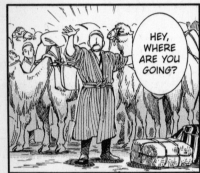

HEY, WHERE ARE YOU GOING?

YOU'RE SAYING YOU DON'T NEED ANY HELP?

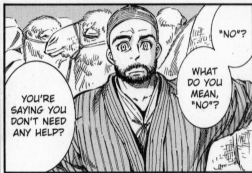

"NO"?

WHAT DO YOU MEAN, "NO"?

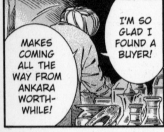

MAKES COMING ALL THE WAY FROM ANKARA WORTH-WHILE!

I'M SO GLAD I FOUND A BUYER!

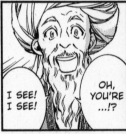

I SEE! I SEE!

OH, YOU'RE ...!?

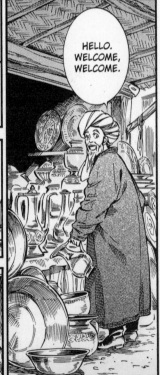

HELLO. WELCOME, WELCOME.

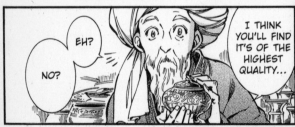

EH?

NO?

I THINK YOU'LL FIND IT'S OF THE HIGHEST QUALITY...

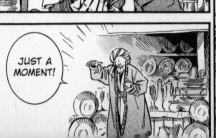

JUST A MOMENT!

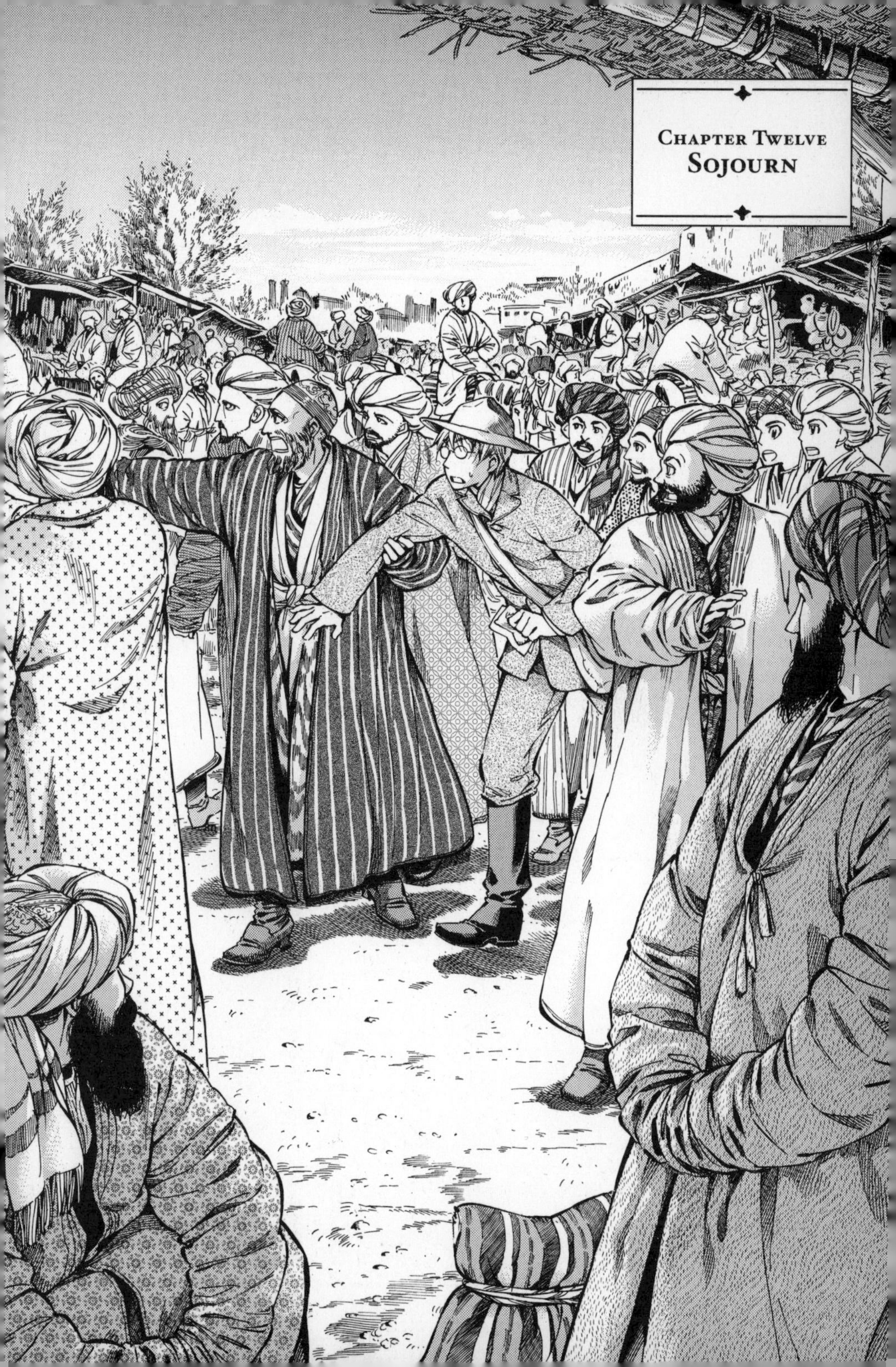
Chapter Twelve
Sojourn

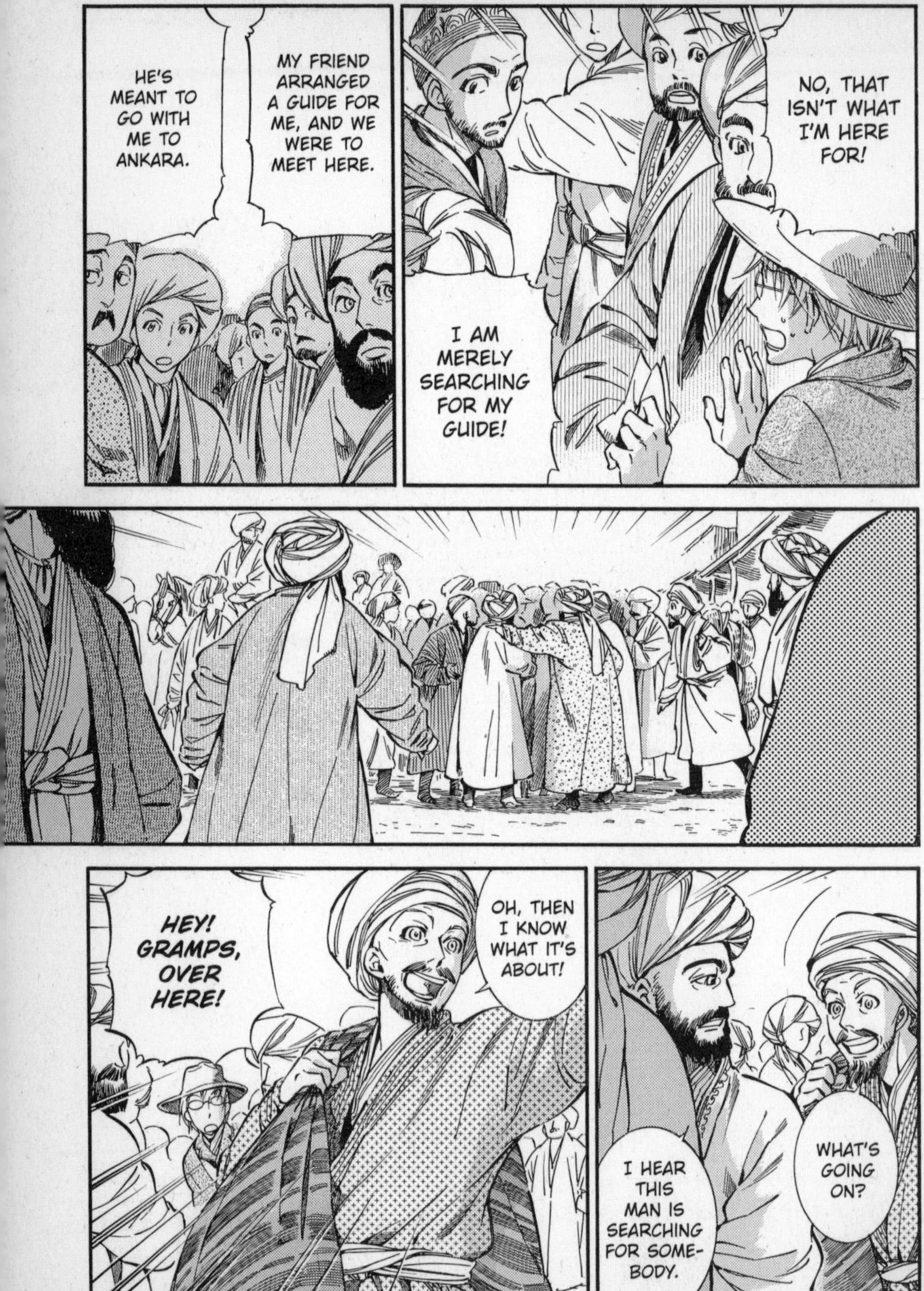
NO, THAT ISN'T WHAT I'M HERE FOR!
I AM MERELY SEARCHING FOR MY GUIDE!
MY FRIEND ARRANGED A GUIDE FOR ME, AND WE WERE TO MEET HERE.
HE'S MEANT TO GO WITH ME TO ANKARA.
WHAT'S GOING ON?
I HEAR THIS MAN IS SEARCHING FOR SOME-BODY.
OH, THEN I KNOW WHAT IT'S ABOUT!
HEY! GRAMPS, OVER HERE!

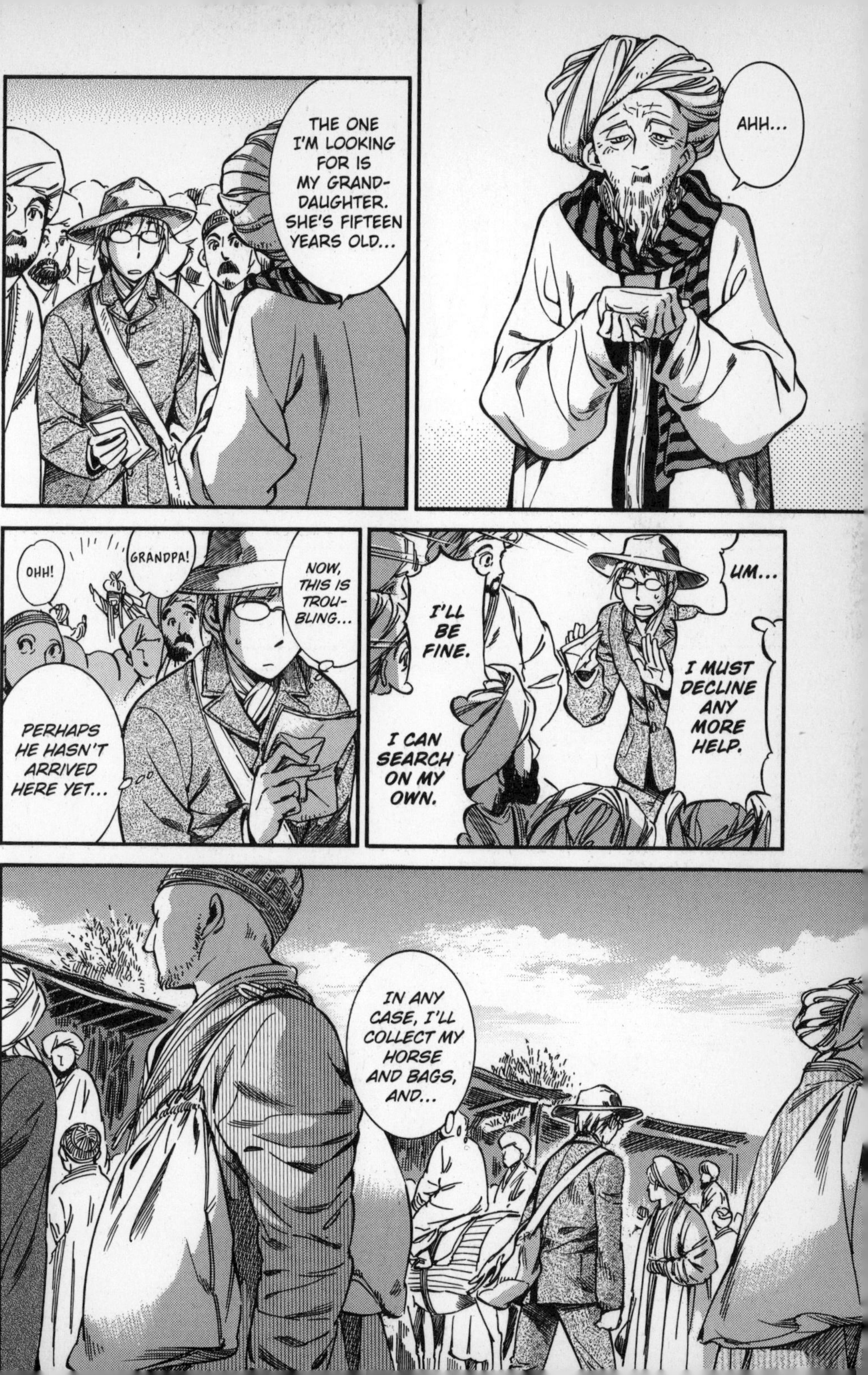
AHH...
THE ONE I'M LOOKING FOR IS MY GRAND-DAUGHTER. SHE'S FIFTEEN YEARS OLD...
UM...
I MUST DECLINE ANY MORE HELP.
I'LL BE FINE.
I CAN SEARCH ON MY OWN.
NOW, THIS IS TROUBLING...
GRANDPA!
OHH!
PERHAPS HE HASN'T ARRIVED HERE YET...
IN ANY CASE, I'LL COLLECT MY HORSE AND BAGS, AND...

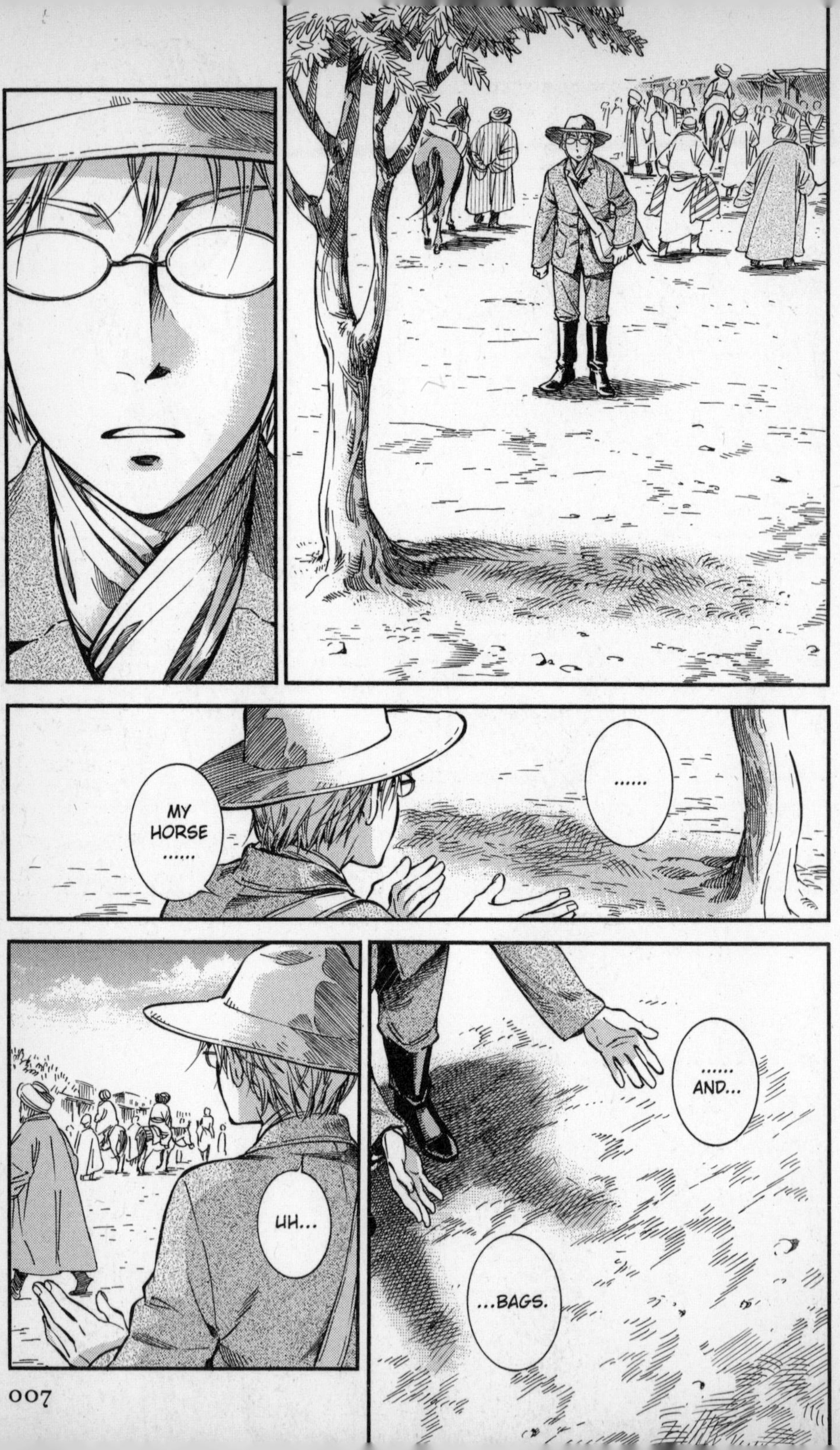
......
MY HORSE ......
...... AND...
...BAGS.
UH...

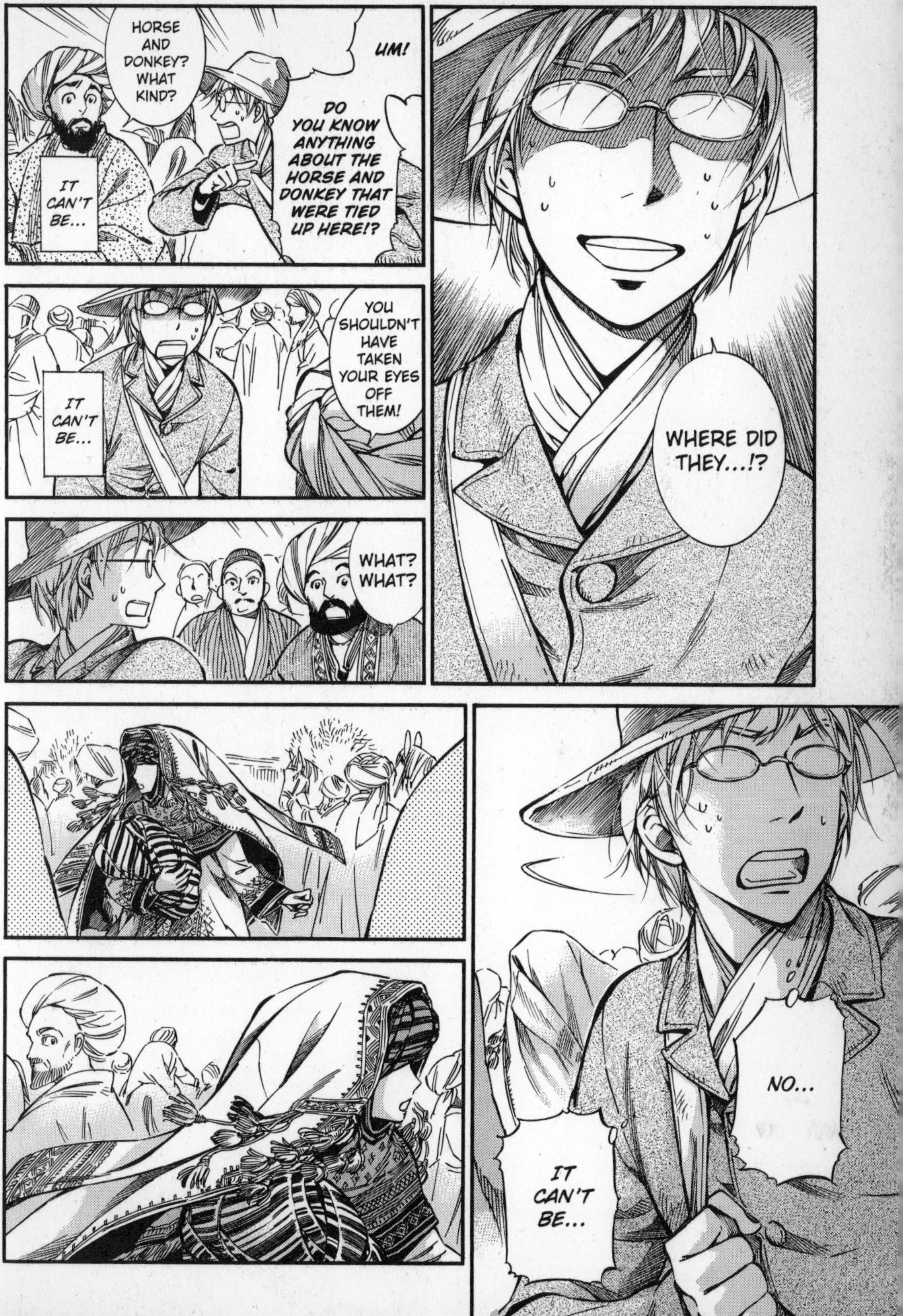
WHERE DID THEY...!?
UM!
DO YOU KNOW ANYTHING ABOUT THE HORSE AND DONKEY THAT WERE TIED UP HERE!?
HORSE AND DONKEY? WHAT KIND?
IT CAN'T BE...
YOU SHOULDN'T HAVE TAKEN YOUR EYES OFF THEM!
IT CAN'T BE...
WHAT? WHAT?
NO...
IT CAN'T BE...

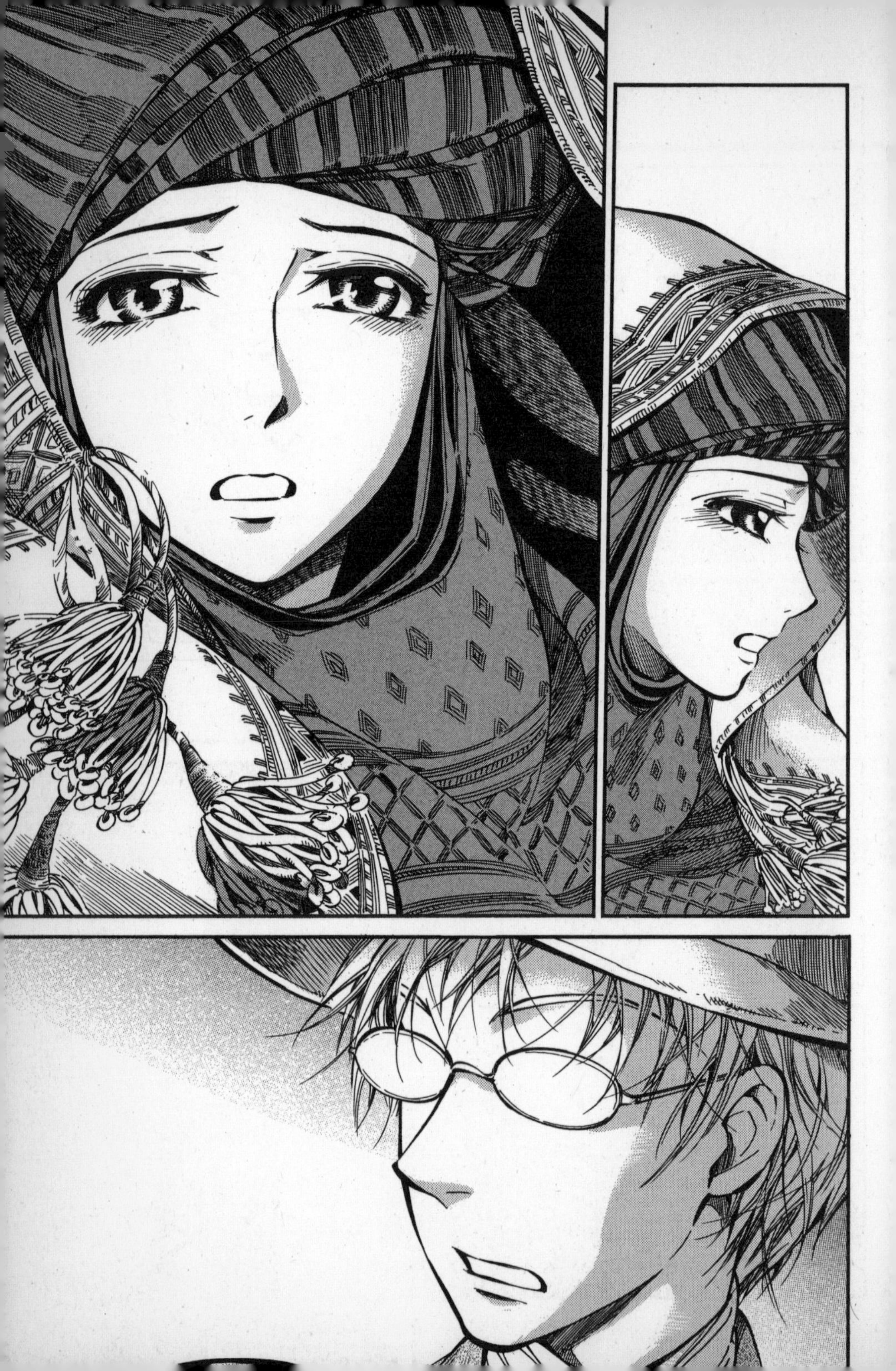

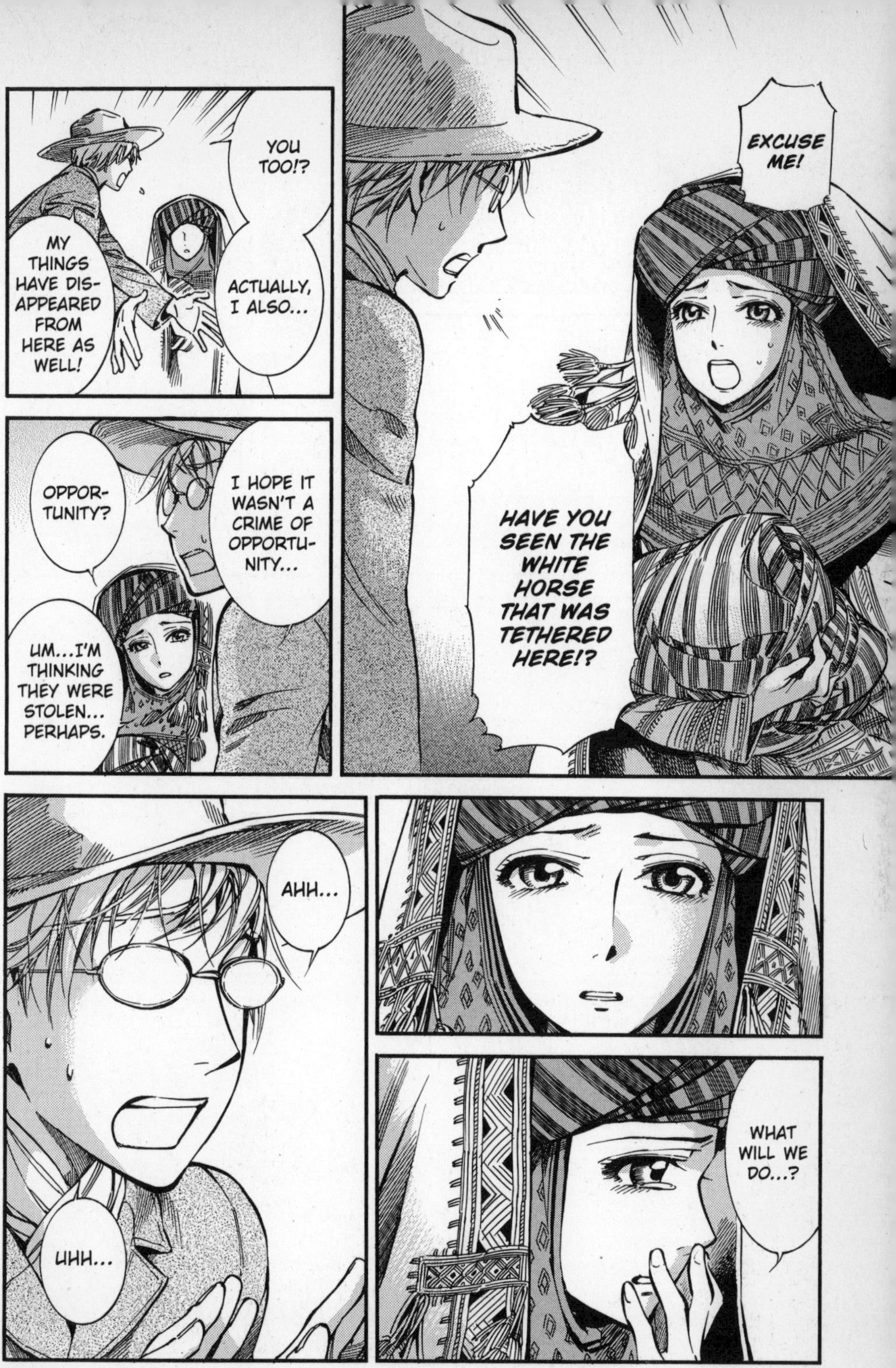
EXCUSE ME!
HAVE YOU SEEN THE WHITE HORSE THAT WAS TETHERED HERE!?
YOU TOO!?
ACTUALLY, I ALSO...
MY THINGS HAVE DIS-APPEARED FROM HERE AS WELL!
I HOPE IT WASN'T A CRIME OF OPPORTU-NITY...
OPPOR-TUNITY?
UM...I'M THINKING THEY WERE STOLEN... PERHAPS.
WHAT WILL WE DO...?
AHH...
UHH...

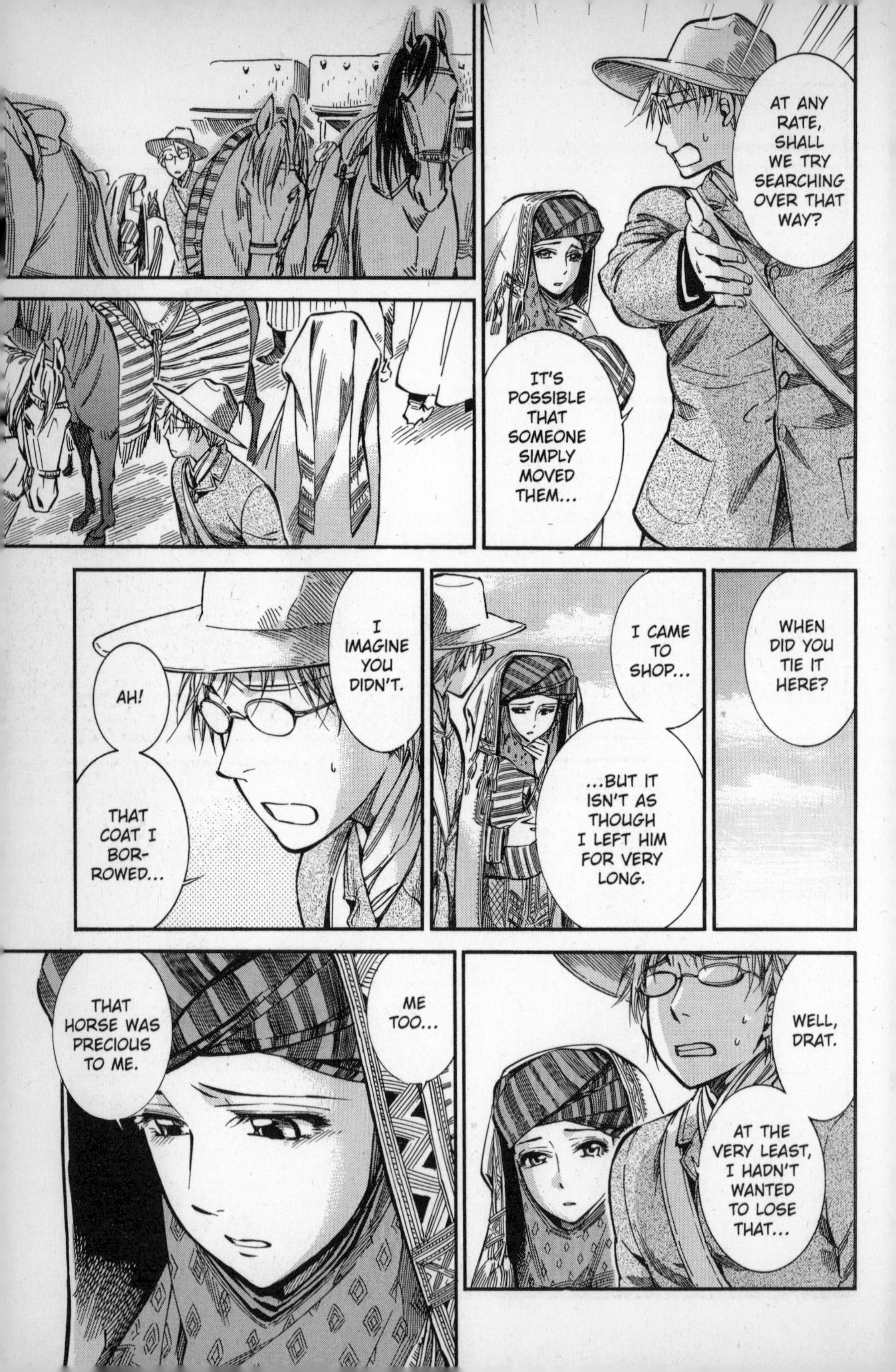
AT ANY RATE, SHALL WE TRY SEARCHING OVER THAT WAY?
IT'S POSSIBLE THAT SOMEONE SIMPLY MOVED THEM...
WHEN DID YOU TIE IT HERE?
I CAME TO SHOP...
...BUT IT ISN'T AS THOUGH I LEFT HIM FOR VERY LONG.
I IMAGINE YOU DIDN'T.
AH!
THAT COAT I BOR-ROWED...
WELL, DRAT.
AT THE VERY LEAST, I HADN'T WANTED TO LOSE THAT...
ME TOO...
THAT HORSE WAS PRECIOUS TO ME.

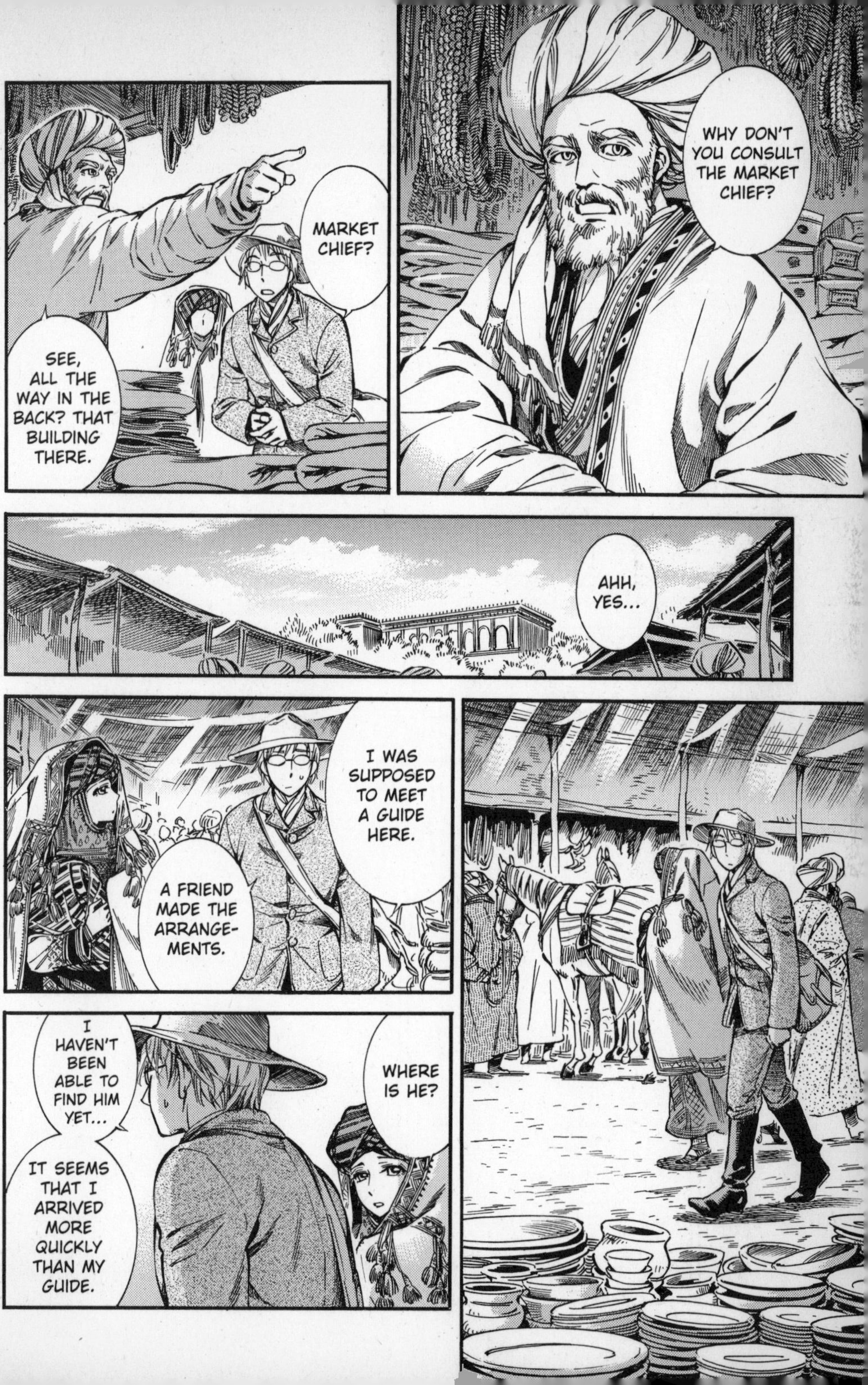
WHY DON'T YOU CONSULT THE MARKET CHIEF?
MARKET CHIEF?
SEE, ALL THE WAY IN THE BACK? THAT BUILDING THERE.
AHH, YES...
I WAS SUPPOSED TO MEET A GUIDE HERE.
A FRIEND MADE THE ARRANGE-MENTS.
WHERE IS HE?
I HAVEN'T BEEN ABLE TO FIND HIM YET...
IT SEEMS THAT I ARRIVED MORE QUICKLY THAN MY GUIDE.

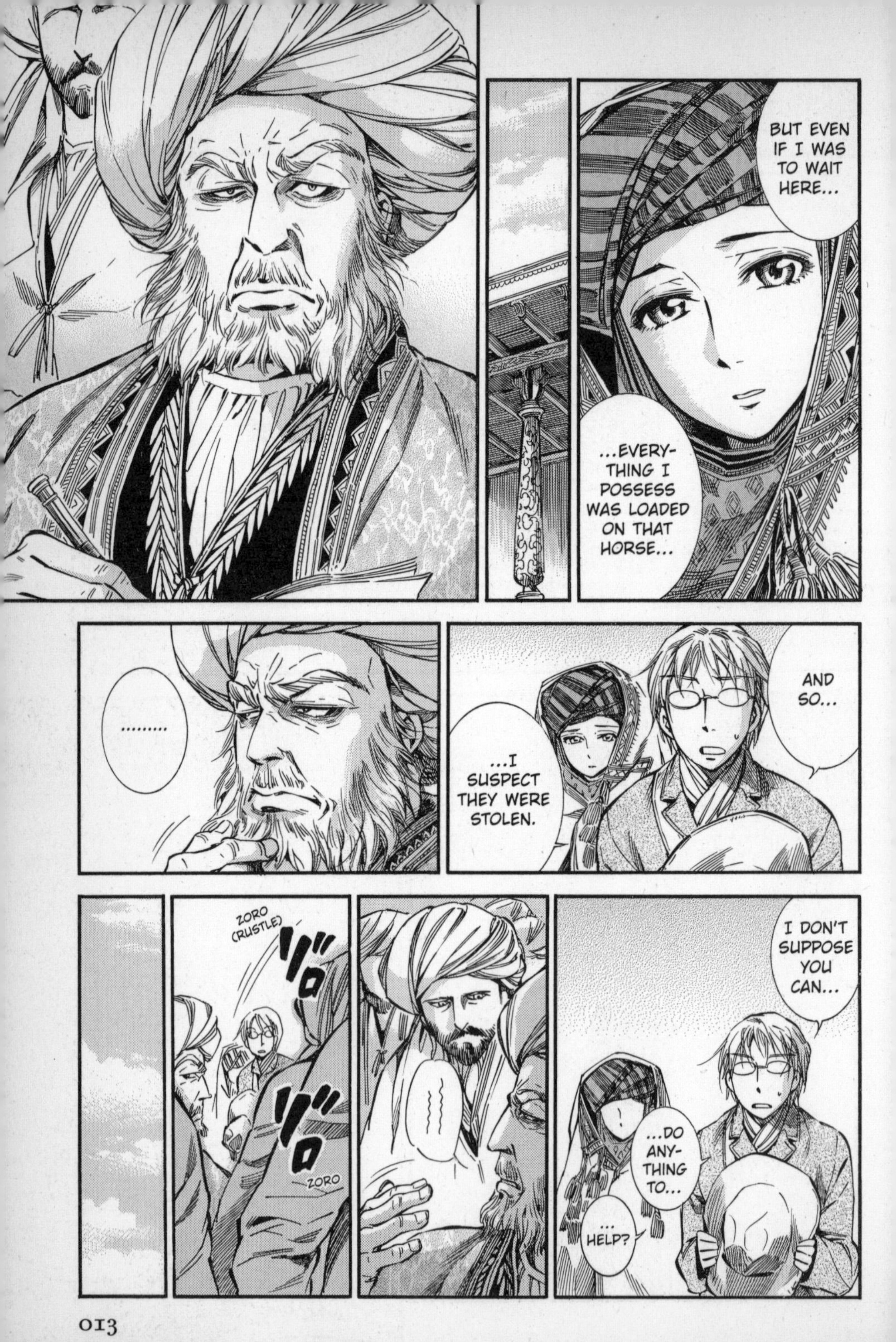
BUT EVEN IF I WAS TO WAIT HERE...
...EVERY-THING I POSSESS WAS LOADED ON THAT HORSE...
AND SO...
...I SUSPECT THEY WERE STOLEN.
....
I DON'T SUPPOSE YOU CAN...
...DO ANY-THING TO...
...HELP?
ZORO (RUSTLE)
ZORO

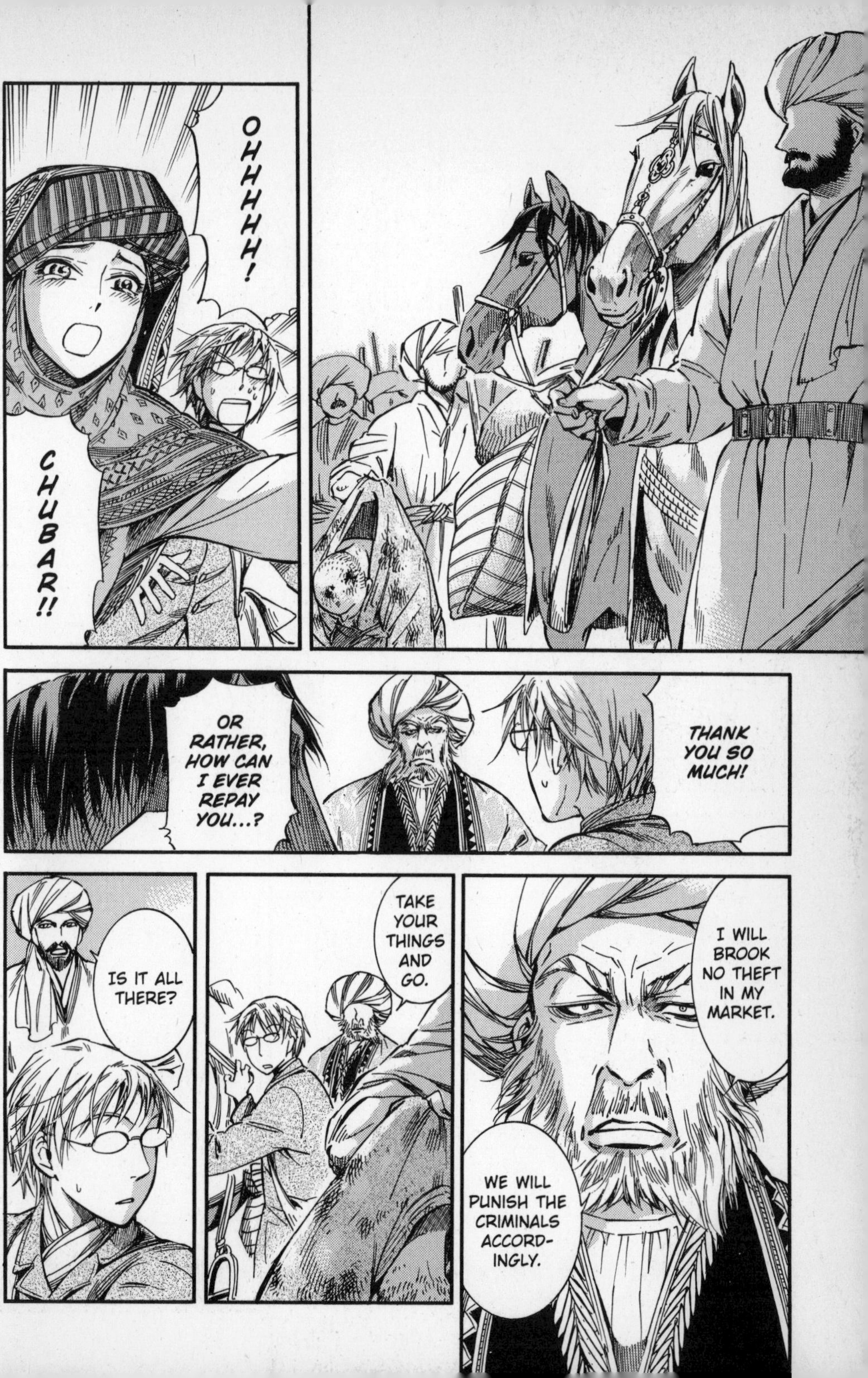
OHHHHHH!
CHUBAR!!
THANK YOU SO MUCH!
OR RATHER, HOW CAN I EVER REPAY YOU...?
I WILL BROOK NO THEFT IN MY MARKET.
WE WILL PUNISH THE CRIMINALS ACCORDINGLY.
TAKE YOUR THINGS AND GO.
IS IT ALL THERE?

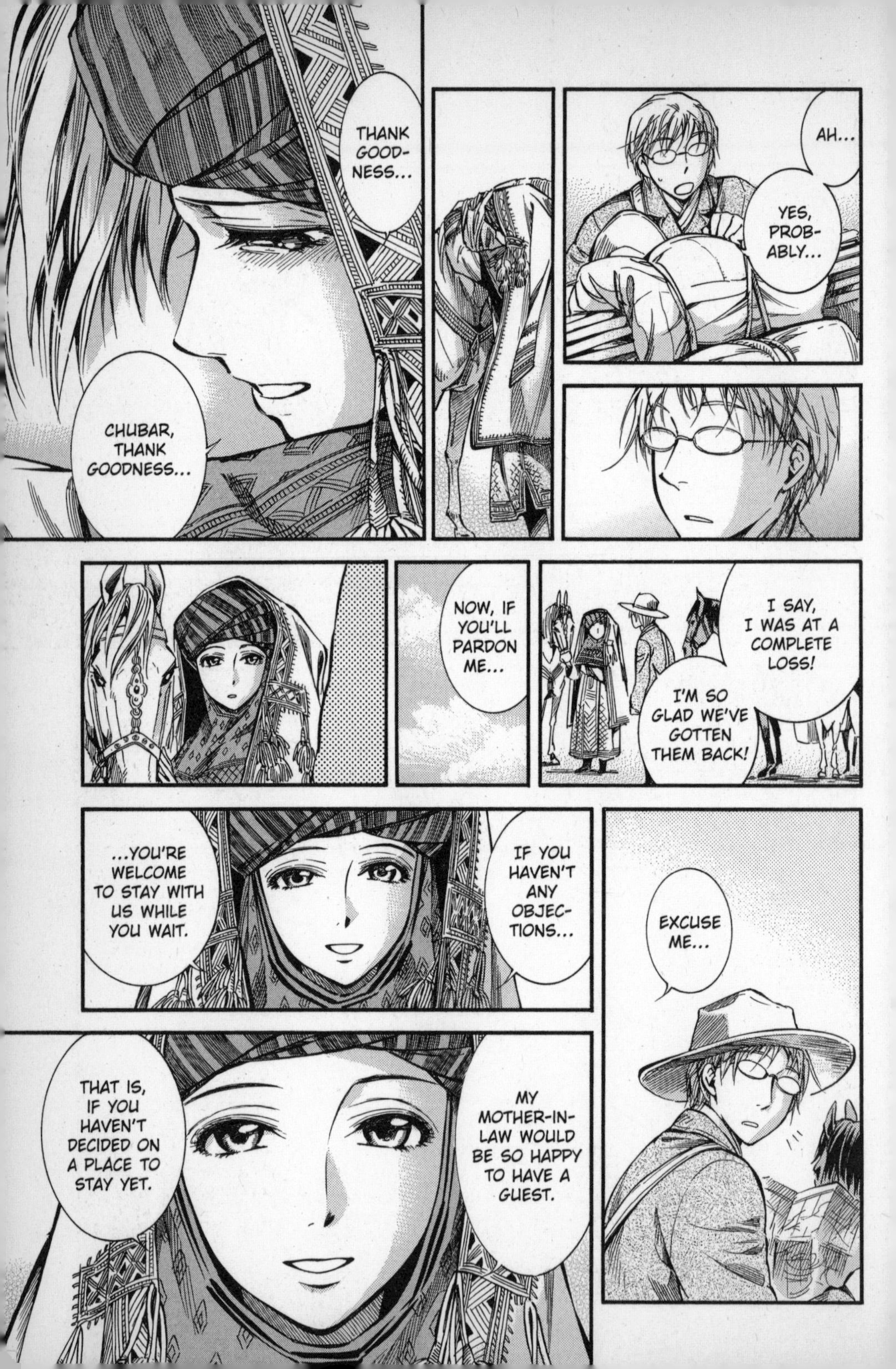
AH...
YES, PROBABLY...
THANK GOODNESS...
CHUBAR, THANK GOODNESS...
I SAY, I WAS AT A COMPLETE LOSS!
I'M SO GLAD WE'VE GOTTEN THEM BACK!
NOW, IF YOU'LL PARDON ME...
EXCUSE ME...
IF YOU HAVEN'T ANY OBJECTIONS...
...YOU'RE WELCOME TO STAY WITH US WHILE YOU WAIT.
MY MOTHER-IN-LAW WOULD BE SO HAPPY TO HAVE A GUEST.
THAT IS, IF YOU HAVEN'T DECIDED ON A PLACE TO STAY YET.

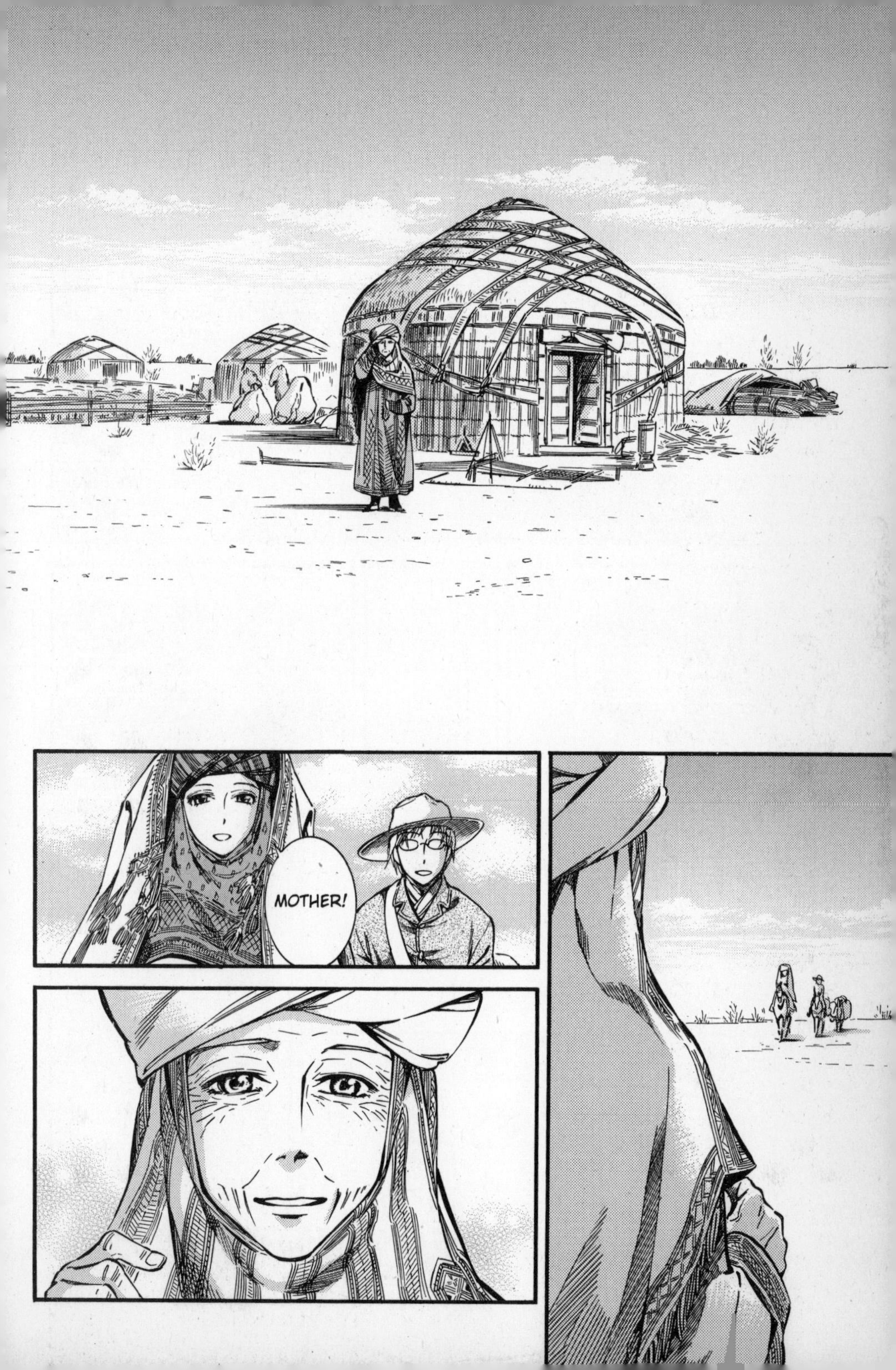
MOTHER!

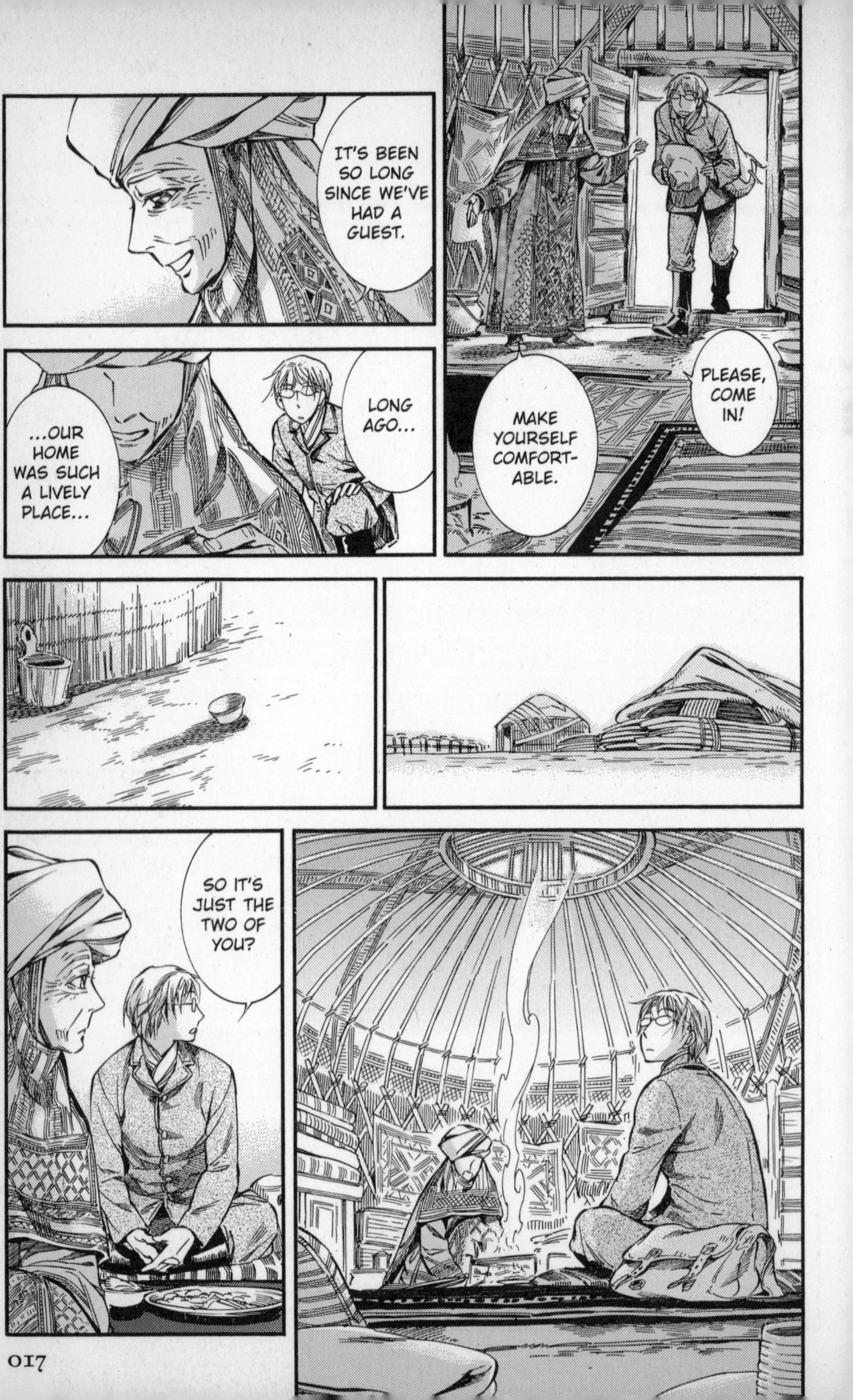
PLEASE, COME IN!
MAKE YOURSELF COMFORT-ABLE.
IT'S BEEN SO LONG SINCE WE'VE HAD A GUEST.
LONG AGO...
...OUR HOME WAS SUCH A LIVELY PLACE...
SO IT'S JUST THE TWO OF YOU?

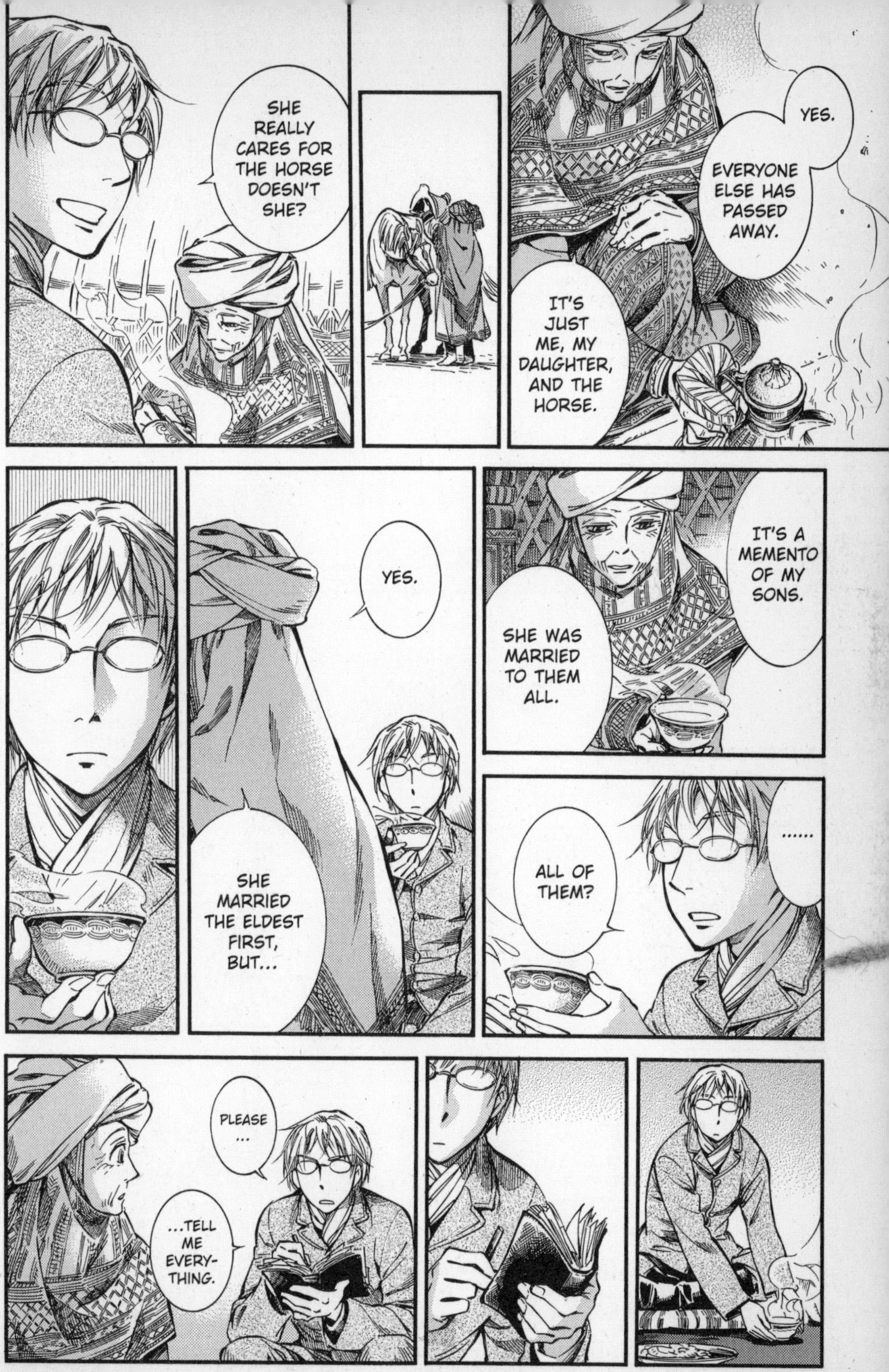
YES.
EVERYONE ELSE HAS PASSED AWAY.
IT'S JUST ME, MY DAUGHTER, AND THE HORSE.
SHE REALLY CARES FOR THE HORSE DOESN'T SHE?
IT'S A MEMENTO OF MY SONS.
SHE WAS MARRIED TO THEM ALL.
......
ALL OF THEM?
YES.
SHE MARRIED THE ELDEST FIRST, BUT...
PLEASE...
...TELL ME EVERY-THING.

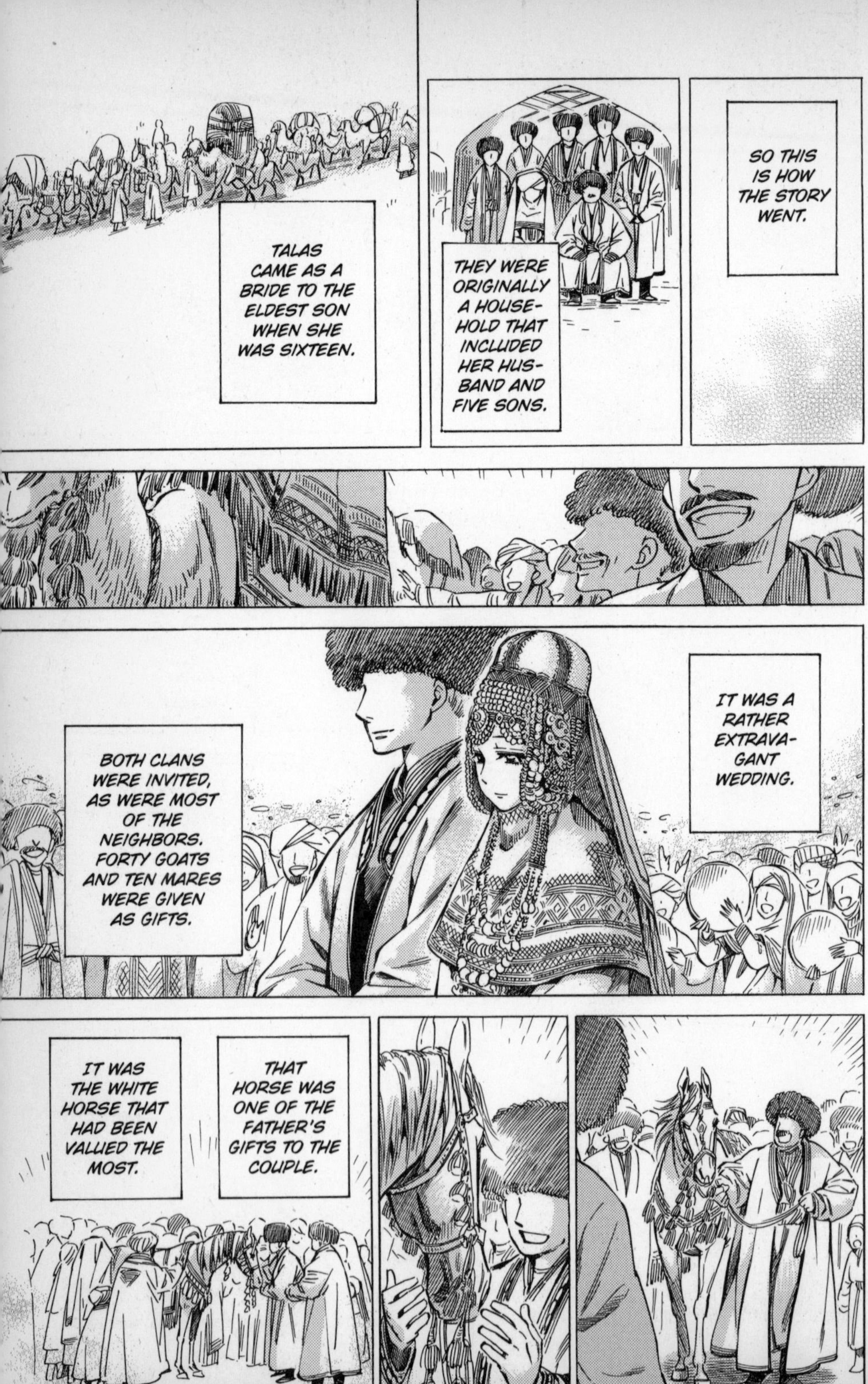
SO THIS IS HOW THE STORY WENT.
THEY WERE ORIGINALLY A HOUSEHOLD THAT INCLUDED HER HUSBAND AND FIVE SONS.
TALAS CAME AS A BRIDE TO THE ELDEST SON WHEN SHE WAS SIXTEEN.
IT WAS A RATHER EXTRAVAGANT WEDDING.
BOTH CLANS WERE INVITED, AS WERE MOST OF THE NEIGHBORS. FORTY GOATS AND TEN MARES WERE GIVEN AS GIFTS.
THAT HORSE WAS ONE OF THE FATHER'S GIFTS TO THE COUPLE.
IT WAS THE WHITE HORSE THAT HAD BEEN VALUED THE MOST.

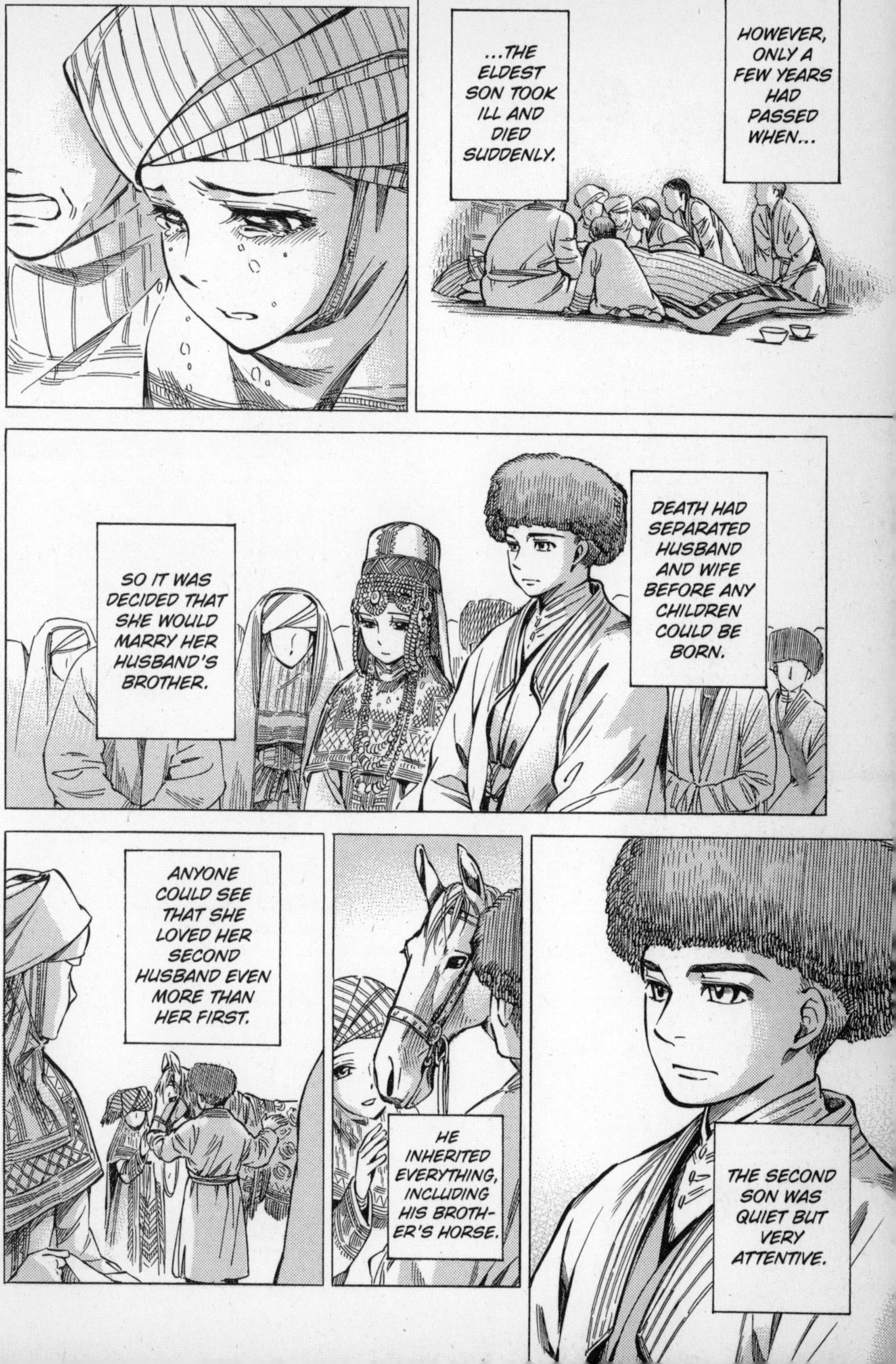
HOWEVER, ONLY A FEW YEARS HAD PASSED WHEN...
...THE ELDEST SON TOOK ILL AND DIED SUDDENLY.
DEATH HAD SEPARATED HUSBAND AND WIFE BEFORE ANY CHILDREN COULD BE BORN.
SO IT WAS DECIDED THAT SHE WOULD MARRY HER HUSBAND'S BROTHER.
THE SECOND SON WAS QUIET BUT VERY ATTENTIVE.
HE INHERITED EVERYTHING, INCLUDING HIS BROTH-ER'S HORSE.
ANYONE COULD SEE THAT SHE LOVED HER SECOND HUSBAND EVEN MORE THAN HER FIRST.

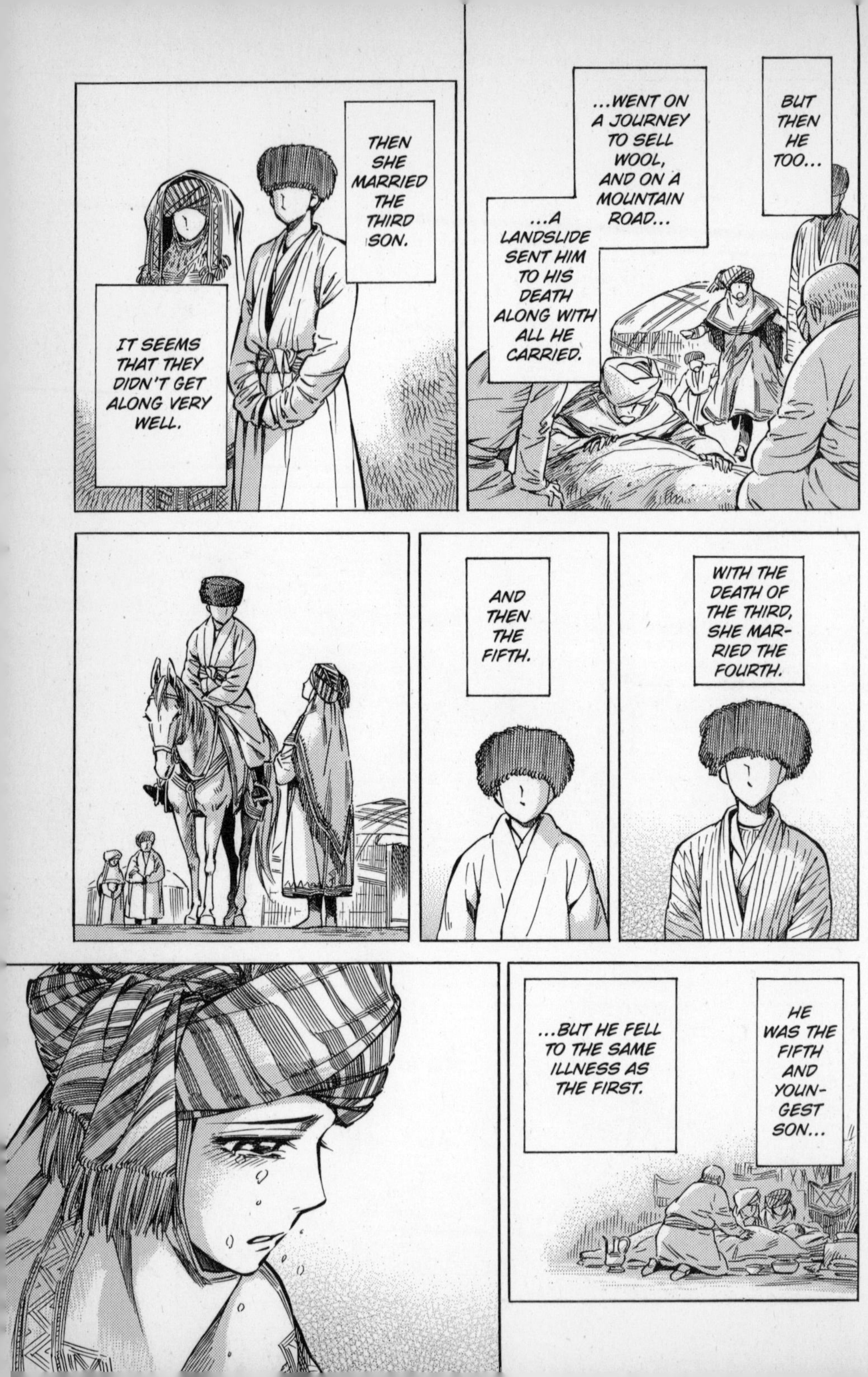
BUT THEN HE TOO...
...WENT ON A JOURNEY TO SELL WOOL, AND ON A MOUNTAIN ROAD...
...A LANDSLIDE SENT HIM TO HIS DEATH ALONG WITH ALL HE CARRIED.
THEN SHE MARRIED THE THIRD SON.
IT SEEMS THAT THEY DIDN'T GET ALONG VERY WELL.
WITH THE DEATH OF THE THIRD, SHE MARRIED THE FOURTH.
AND THEN THE FIFTH.
HE WAS THE FIFTH AND YOUNGEST SON...
...BUT HE FELL TO THE SAME ILLNESS AS THE FIRST.

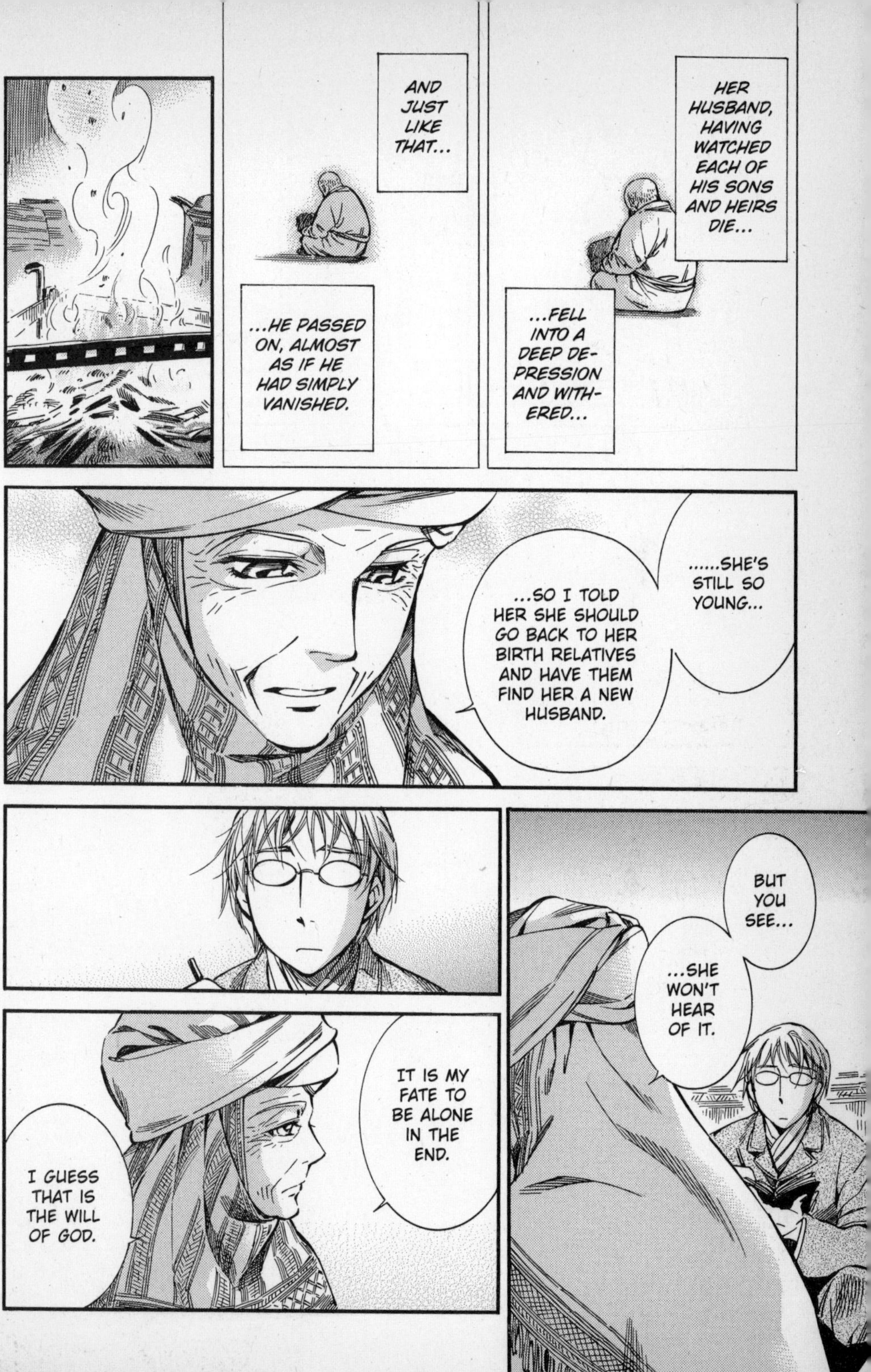
HER HUSBAND, HAVING WATCHED EACH OF HIS SONS AND HEIRS DIE...
...FELL INTO A DEEP DE-PRESSION AND WITH-ERED...
AND JUST LIKE THAT...
...HE PASSED ON, ALMOST AS IF HE HAD SIMPLY VANISHED.
......SHE'S STILL SO YOUNG...
...SO I TOLD HER SHE SHOULD GO BACK TO HER BIRTH RELATIVES AND HAVE THEM FIND HER A NEW HUSBAND.
BUT YOU SEE...
...SHE WON'T HEAR OF IT.
IT IS MY FATE TO BE ALONE IN THE END.
I GUESS THAT IS THE WILL OF GOD.

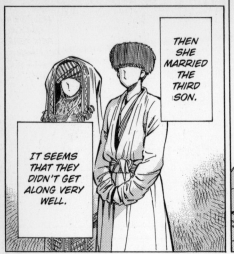

THEN SHE MARRIED THE THIRD SON.

IT SEEMS THAT THEY DIDN'T GET ALONG VERY WELL.

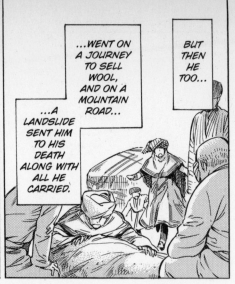

...WENT ON A JOURNEY TO SELL WOOL, AND ON A MOUNTAIN ROAD...

...A LANDSLIDE SENT HIM TO HIS DEATH ALONG WITH ALL HE CARRIED.

BUT THEN HE TOO...

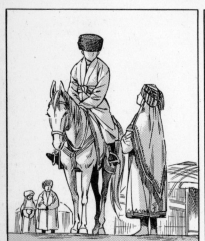

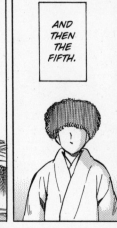

AND THEN THE FIFTH.

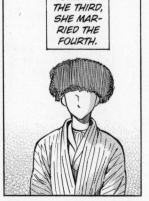

WITH THE DEATH OF THE THIRD, SHE MARRIED THE FOURTH.

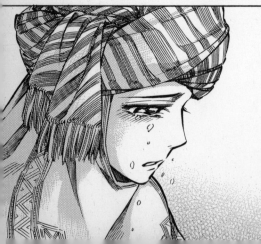

...BUT HE FELL TO THE SAME ILLNESS AS THE FIRST.

HE WAS THE FIFTH AND YOUNGEST SON...

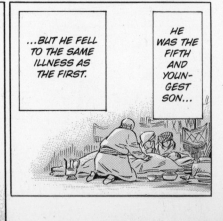

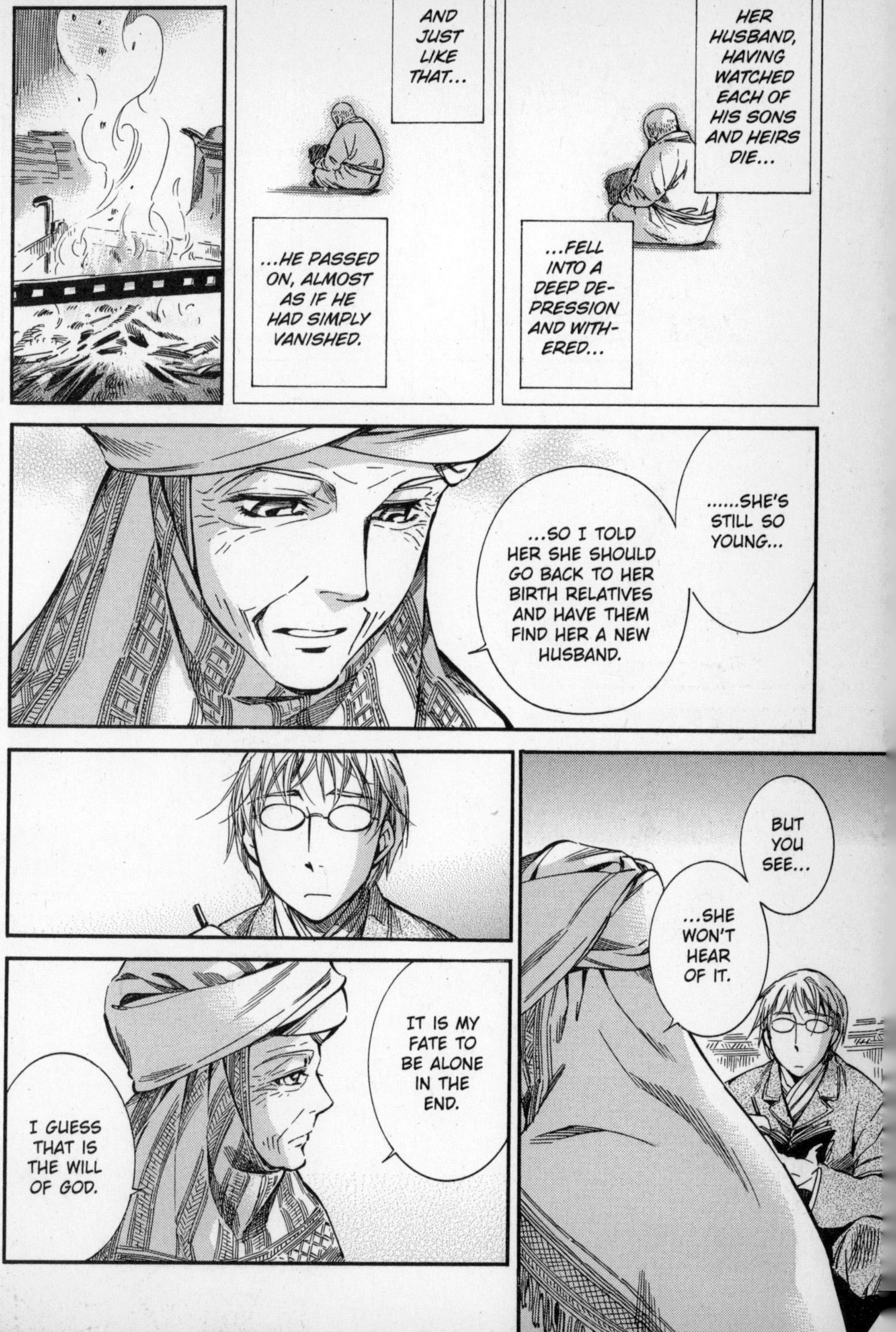
HER HUSBAND, HAVING WATCHED EACH OF HIS SONS AND HEIRS DIE...
...FELL INTO A DEEP DE-PRESSION AND WITH-ERED...
AND JUST LIKE THAT...
...HE PASSED ON, ALMOST AS IF HE HAD SIMPLY VANISHED.
......SHE'S STILL SO YOUNG...
...SO I TOLD HER SHE SHOULD GO BACK TO HER BIRTH RELATIVES AND HAVE THEM FIND HER A NEW HUSBAND.
BUT YOU SEE...
...SHE WON'T HEAR OF IT.
IT IS MY FATE TO BE ALONE IN THE END.
I GUESS THAT IS THE WILL OF GOD.

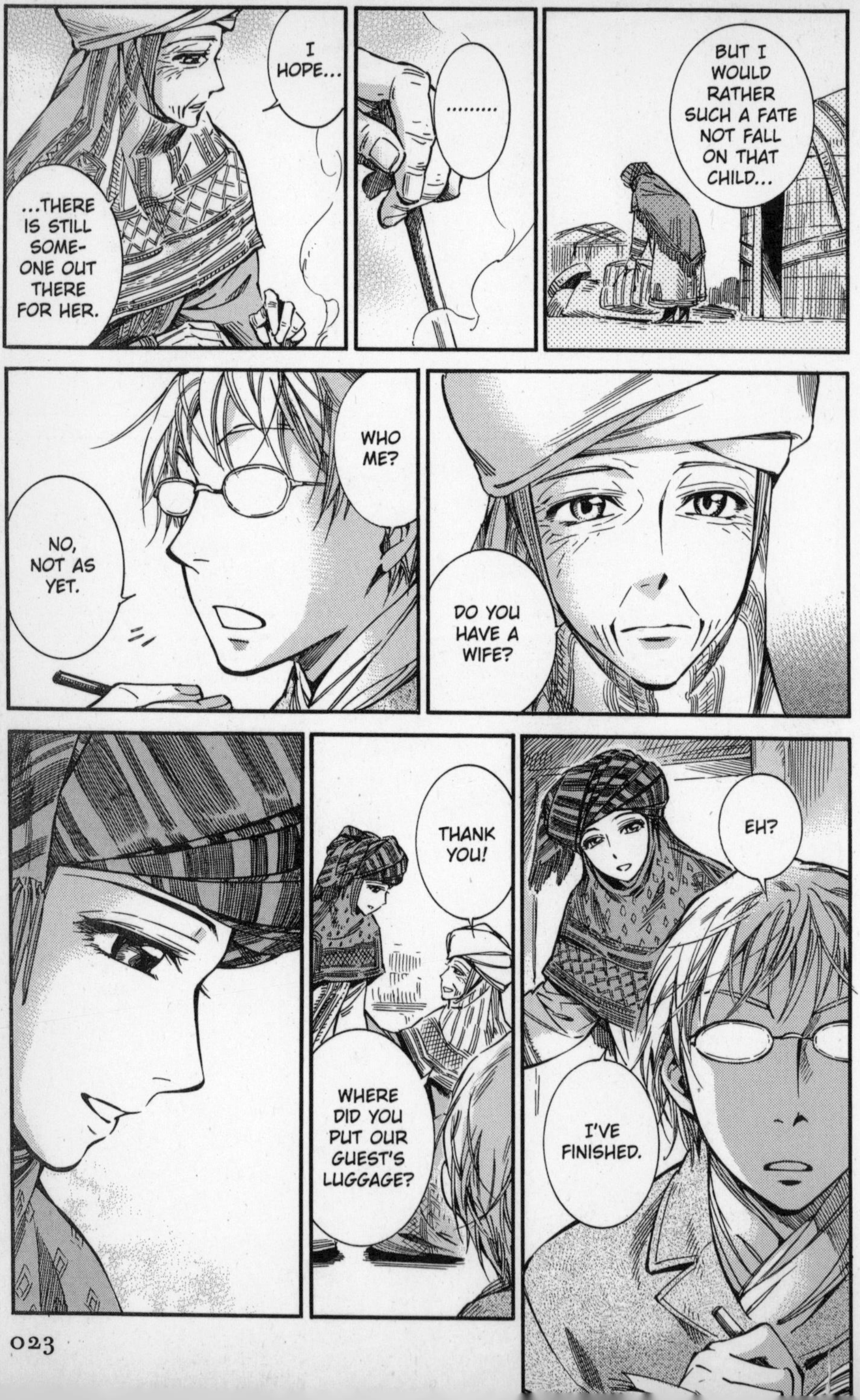
BUT I WOULD RATHER SUCH A FATE NOT FALL ON THAT CHILD...
....
I HOPE...
...THERE IS STILL SOME-ONE OUT THERE FOR HER.
DO YOU HAVE A WIFE?
WHO ME?
NO, NOT AS YET.
EH?
I'VE FINISHED.
THANK YOU!
WHERE DID YOU PUT OUR GUEST'S LUGGAGE?

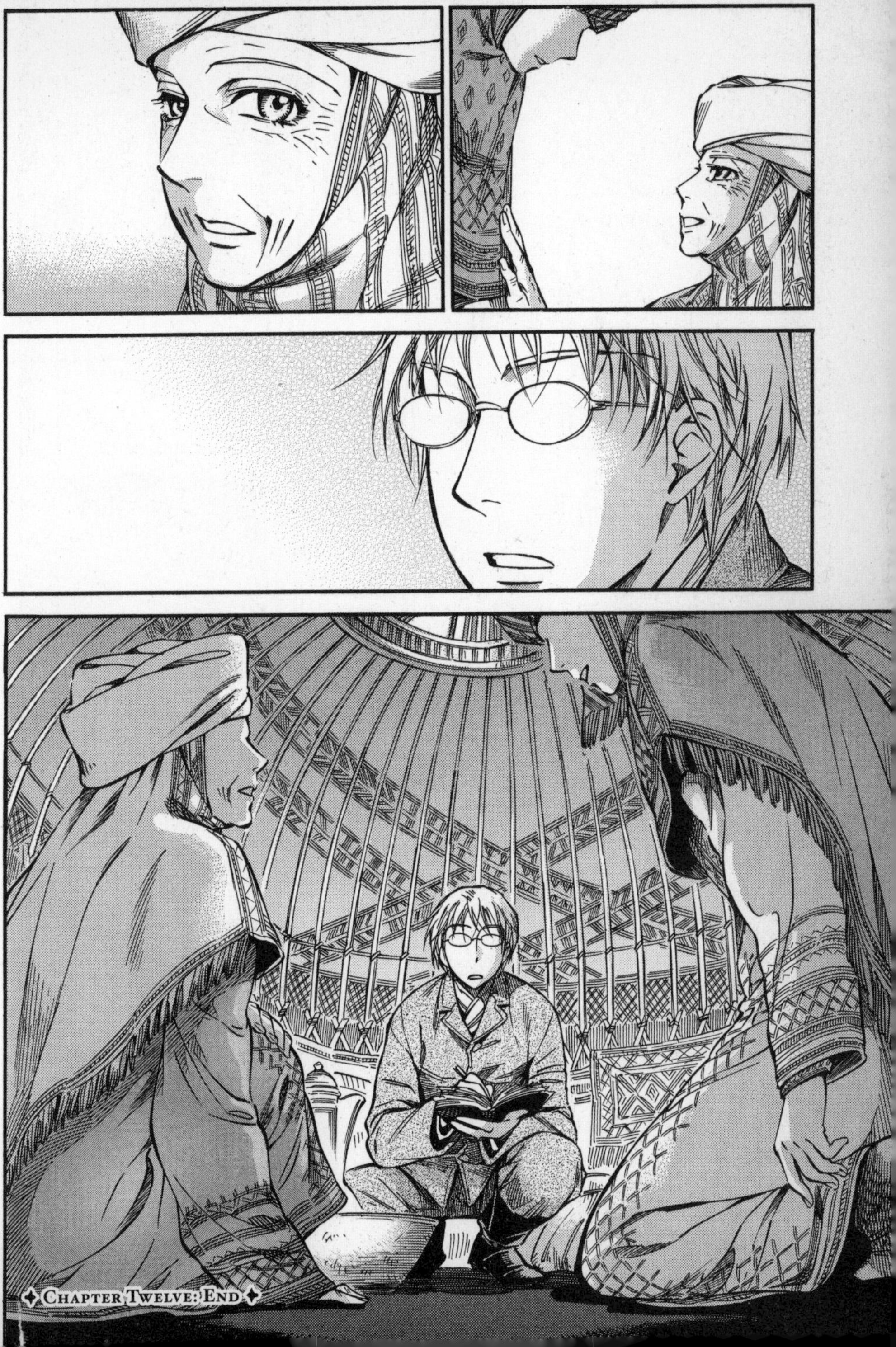
Chapter Twelve: End

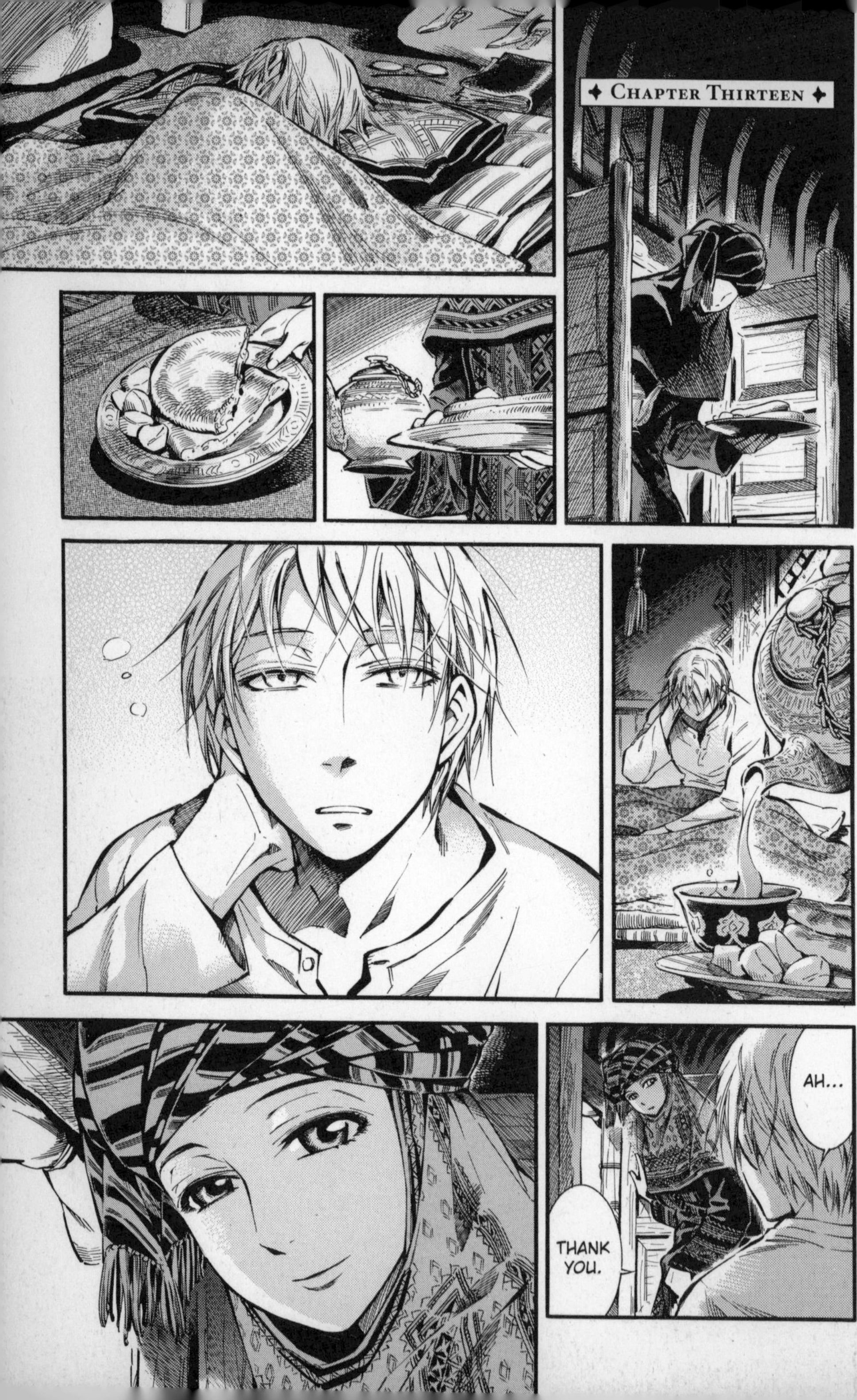
✦ Chapter Thirteen ✦
AH...
THANK YOU.

Chapter Thirteen
Entreaty

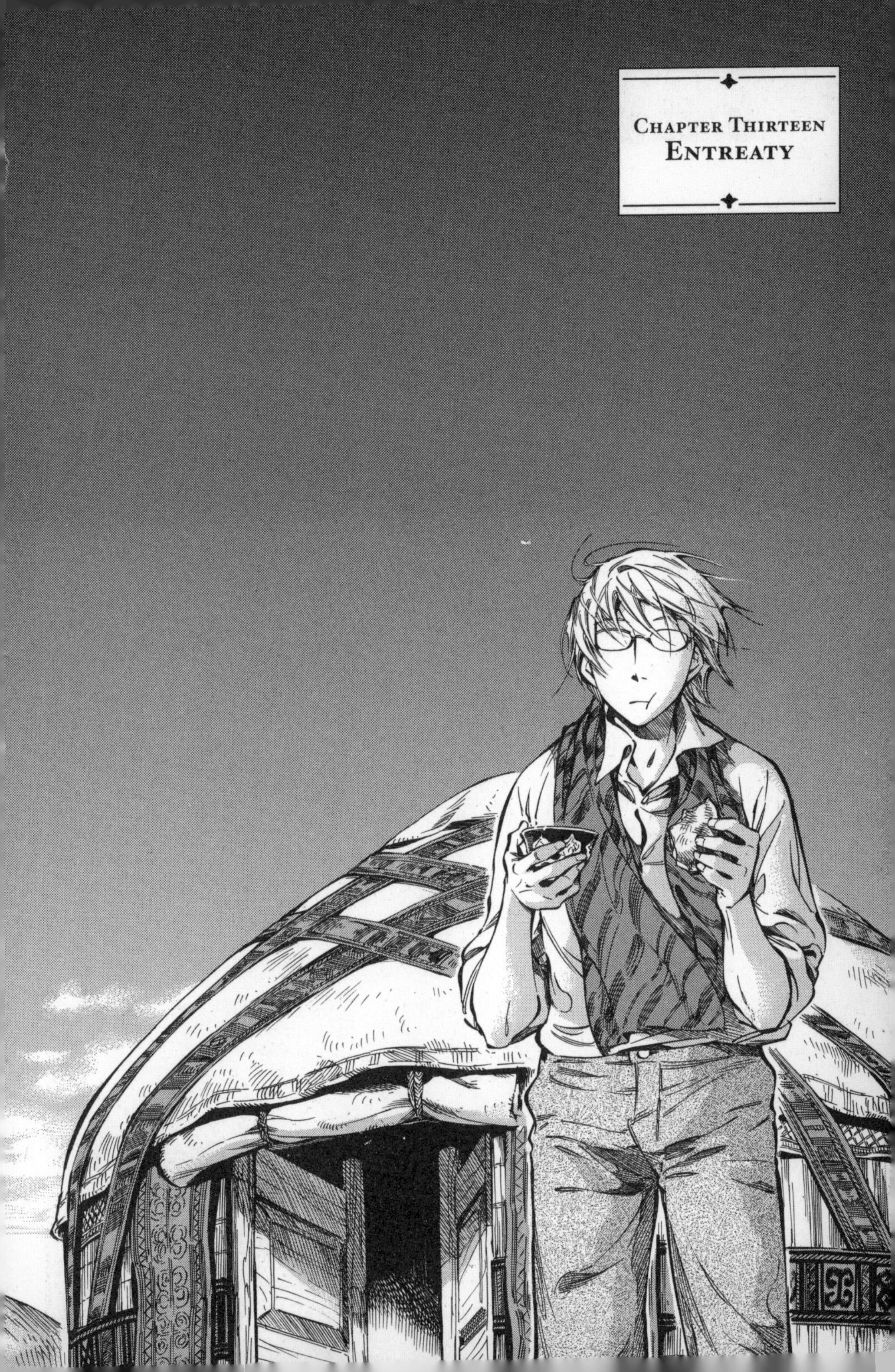

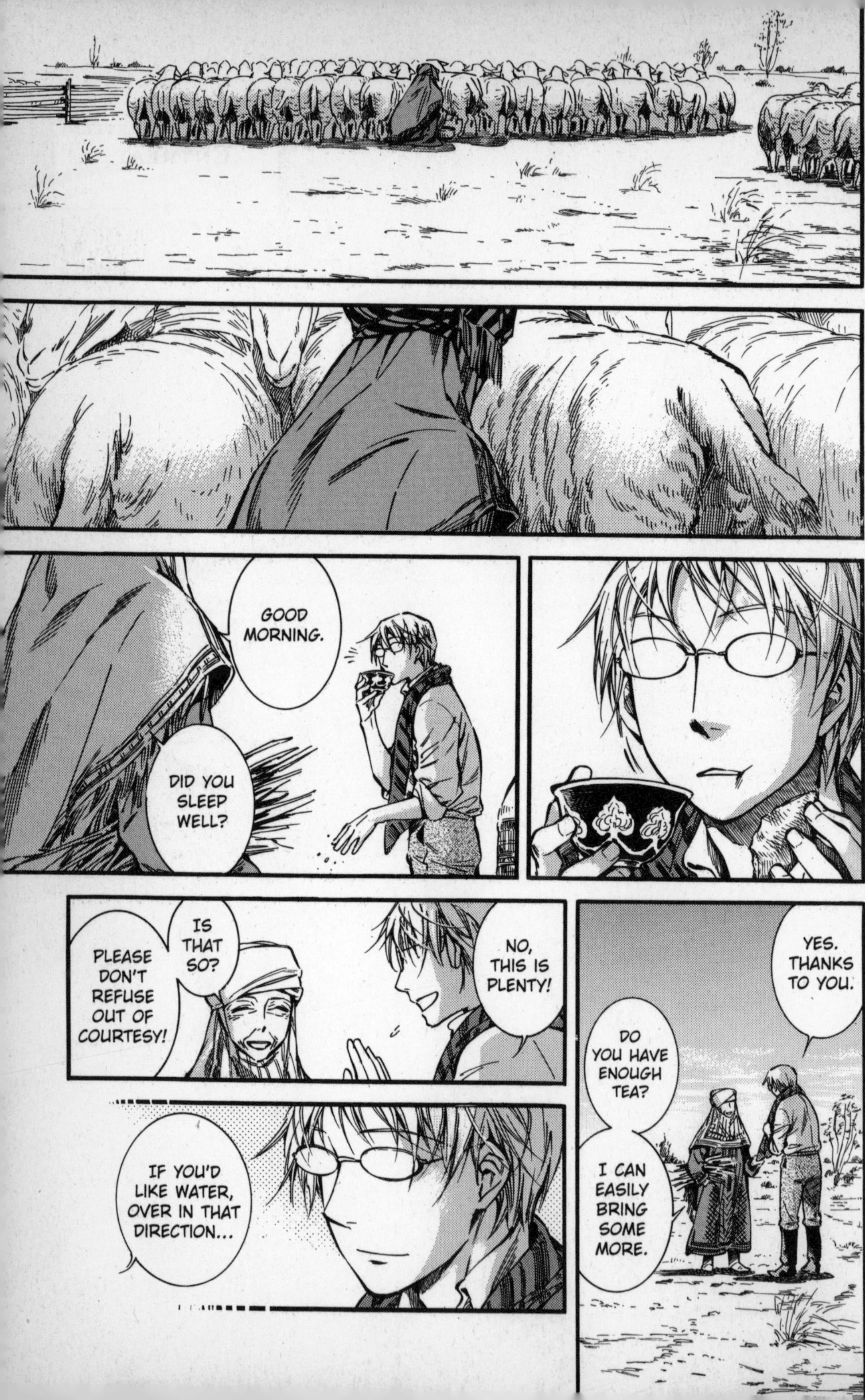
GOOD MORNING.
DID YOU SLEEP WELL?
YES. THANKS TO YOU.
DO YOU HAVE ENOUGH TEA?
I CAN EASILY BRING SOME MORE.
NO, THIS IS PLENTY!
IS THAT SO?
PLEASE DON'T REFUSE OUT OF COURTESY!
IF YOU'D LIKE WATER, OVER IN THAT DIRECTION...

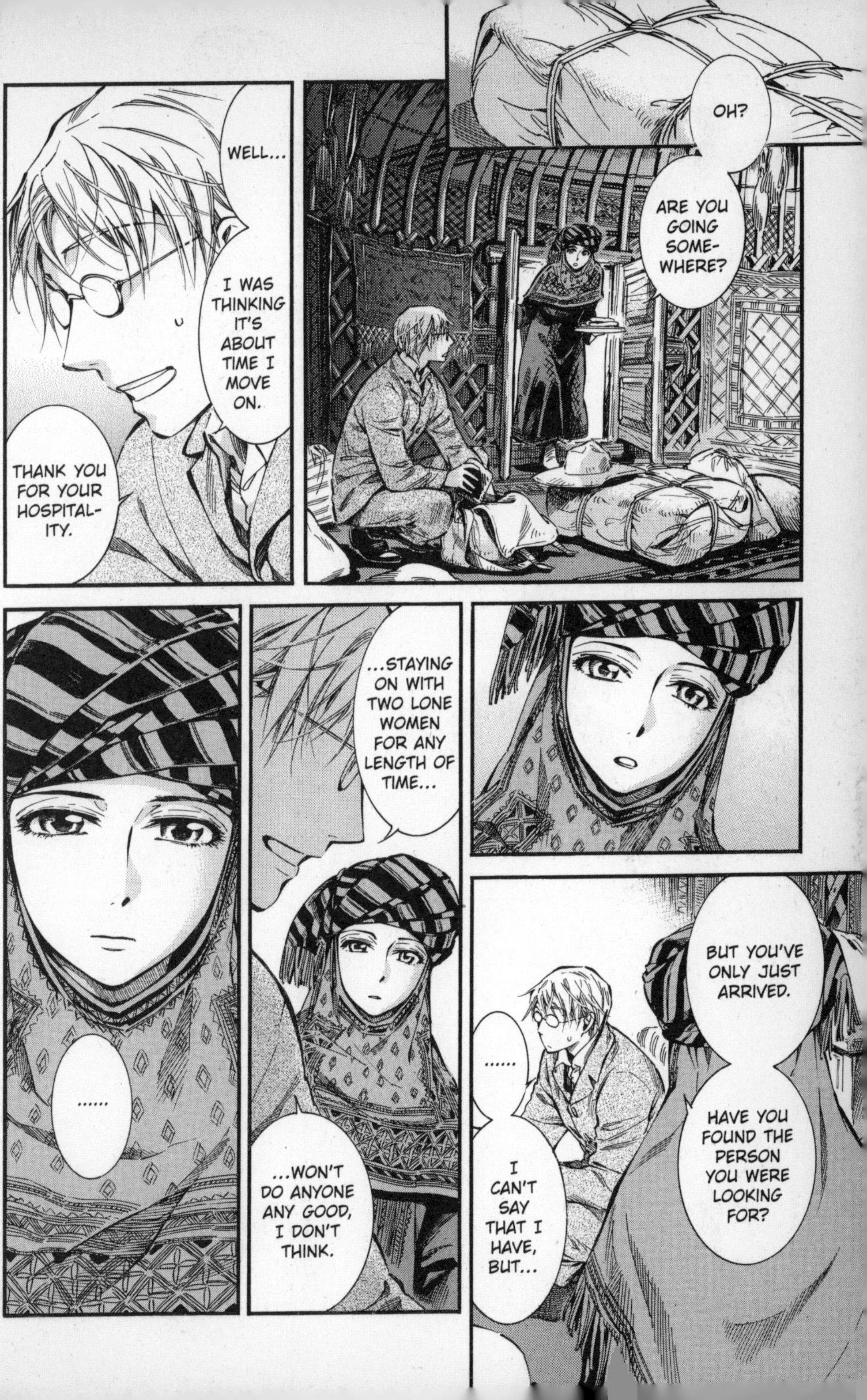
OH?
ARE YOU GOING SOME-WHERE?
WELL...
I WAS THINKING IT'S ABOUT TIME I MOVE ON.
THANK YOU FOR YOUR HOSPITAL-ITY.
BUT YOU'VE ONLY JUST ARRIVED.
HAVE YOU FOUND THE PERSON YOU WERE LOOKING FOR?
......
I CAN'T SAY THAT I HAVE, BUT...
...STAYING ON WITH TWO LONE WOMEN FOR ANY LENGTH OF TIME...
...WON'T DO ANYONE ANY GOOD, I DON'T THINK.
......

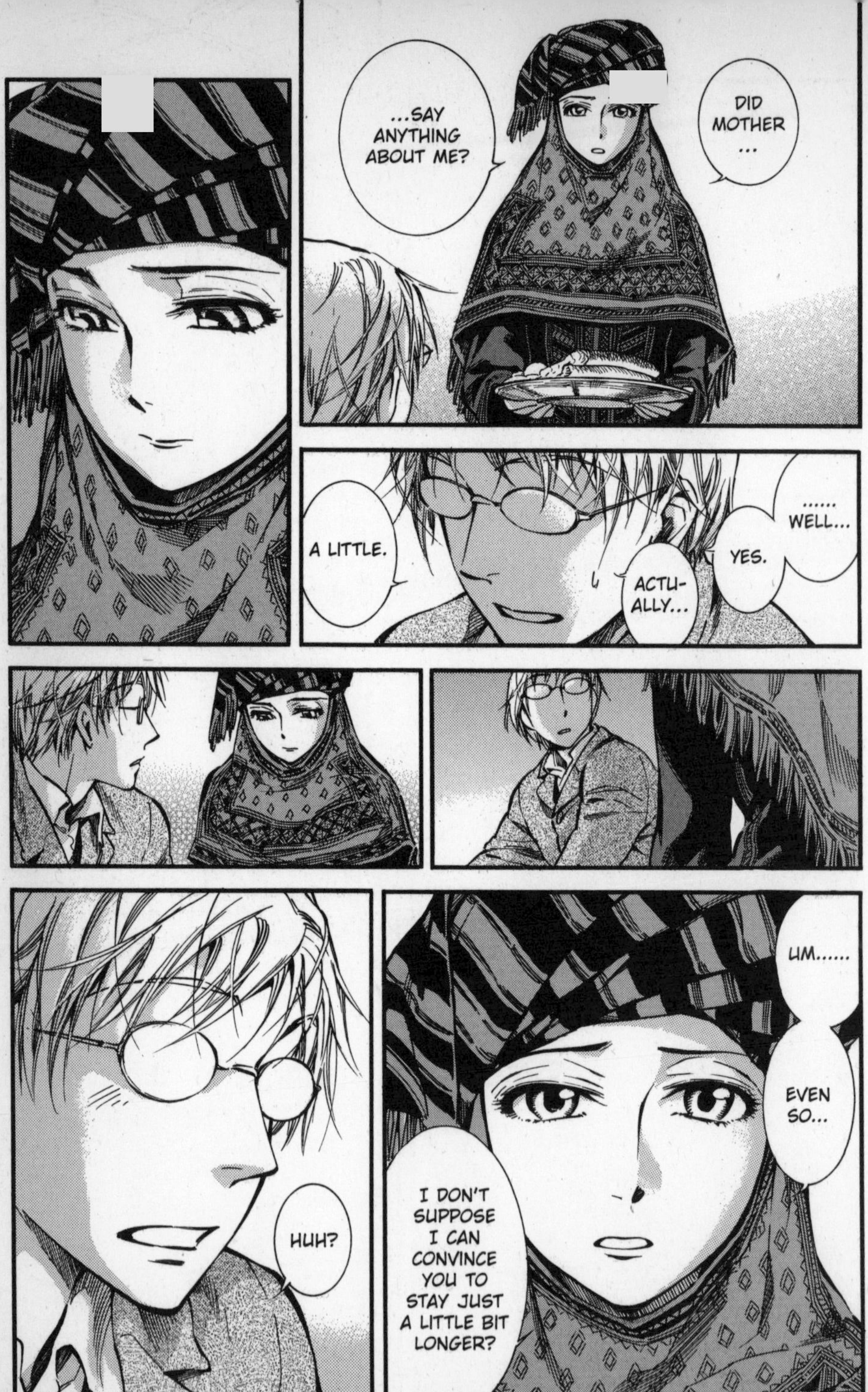
DID MOTHER ...
...SAY ANYTHING ABOUT ME?
...... WELL...
YES.
ACTU-ALLY...
A LITTLE.
UM......
EVEN SO...
I DON'T SUPPOSE I CAN CONVINCE YOU TO STAY JUST A LITTLE BIT LONGER?
HUH?

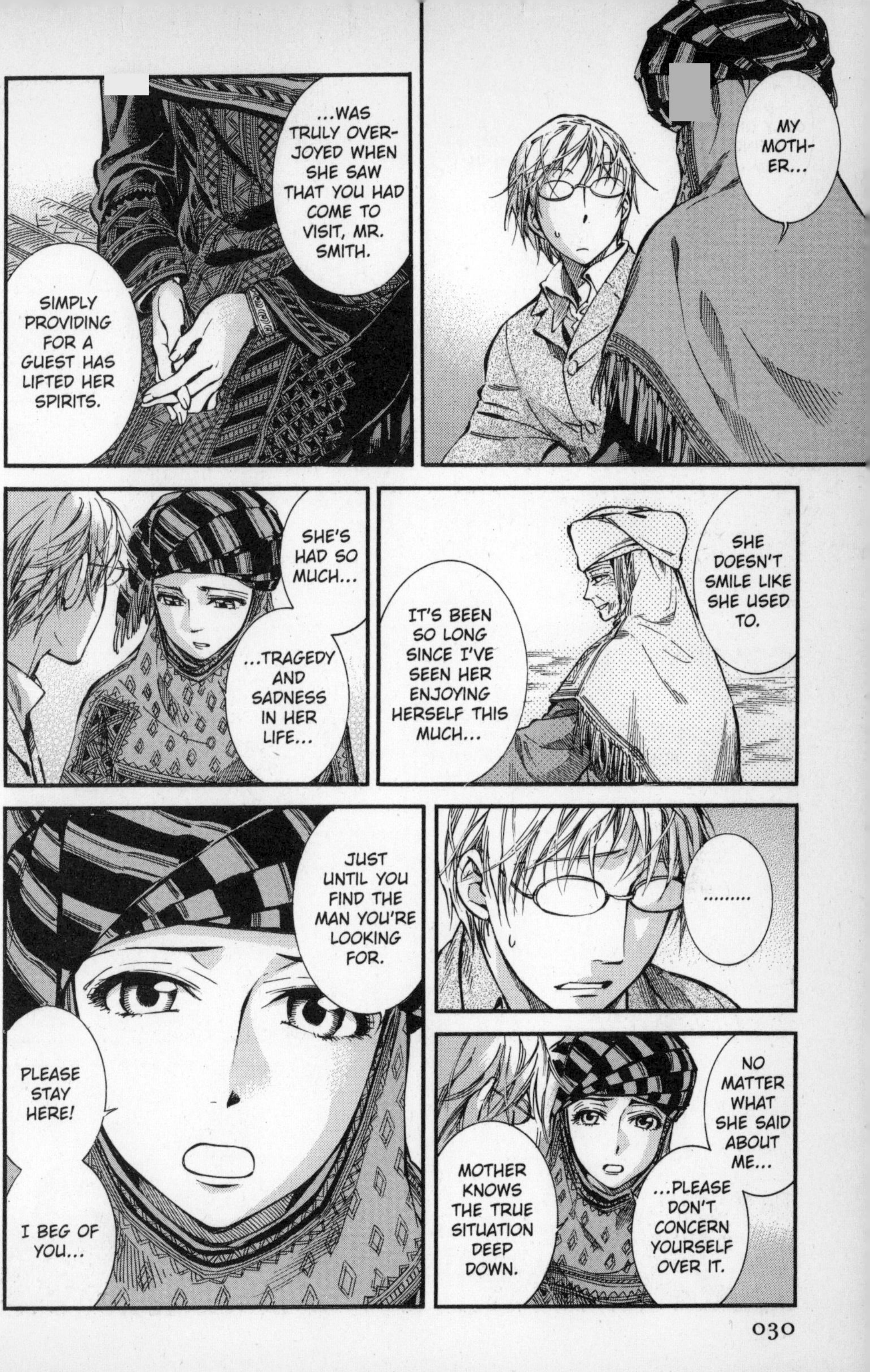
MY MOTHER...
...WAS TRULY OVERJOYED WHEN SHE SAW THAT YOU HAD COME TO VISIT, MR. SMITH.
SIMPLY PROVIDING FOR A GUEST HAS LIFTED HER SPIRITS.
SHE DOESN'T SMILE LIKE SHE USED TO.
IT'S BEEN SO LONG SINCE I'VE SEEN HER ENJOYING HERSELF THIS MUCH...
SHE'S HAD SO MUCH...
...TRAGEDY AND SADNESS IN HER LIFE...
....
NO MATTER WHAT SHE SAID ABOUT ME...
...PLEASE DON'T CONCERN YOURSELF OVER IT.
MOTHER KNOWS THE TRUE SITUATION DEEP DOWN.
JUST UNTIL YOU FIND THE MAN YOU'RE LOOKING FOR.
PLEASE STAY HERE!
I BEG OF YOU...

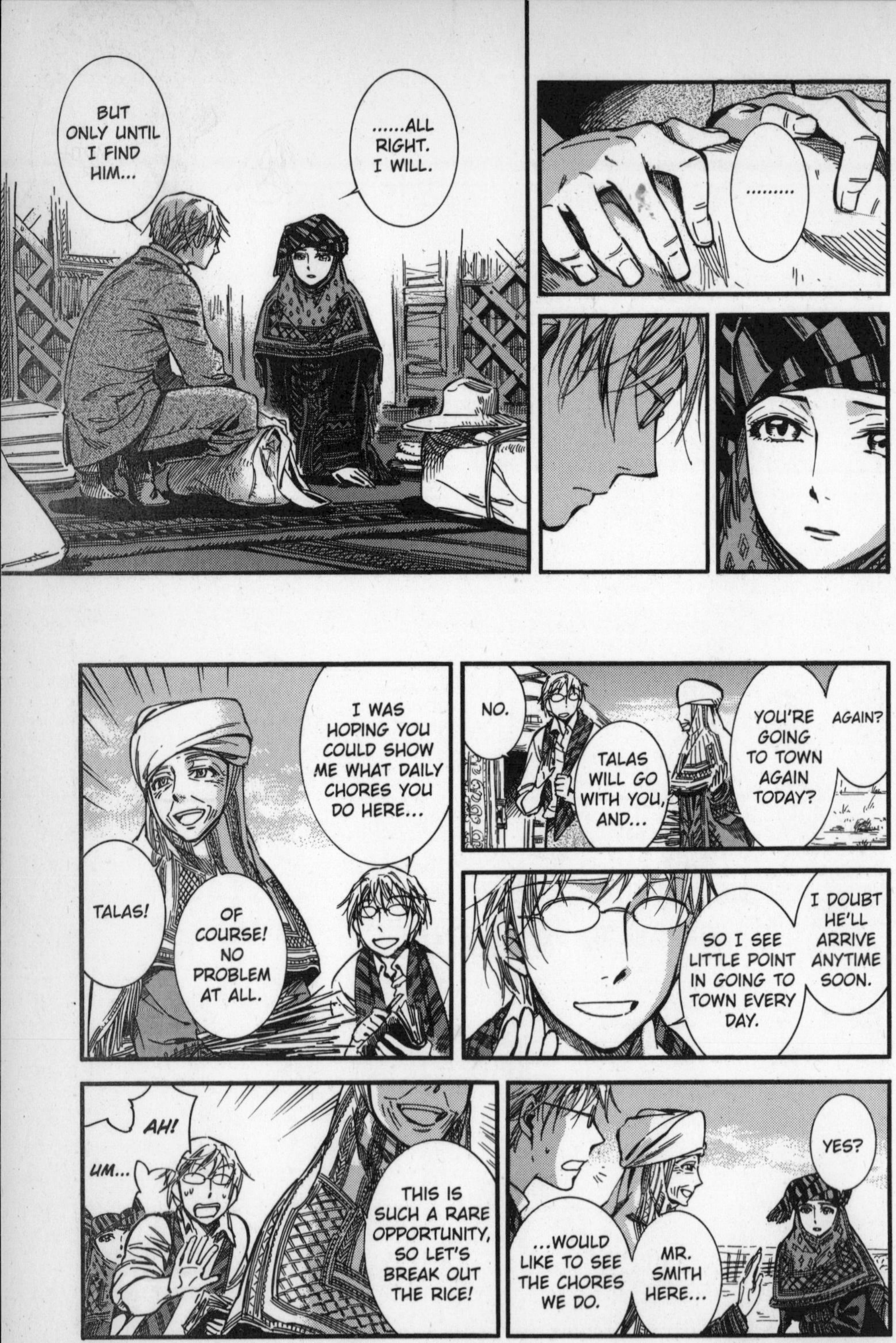
....
......ALL RIGHT. I WILL.
BUT ONLY UNTIL I FIND HIM...
YOU'RE GOING TO TOWN AGAIN TODAY?
AGAIN?
NO.
TALAS WILL GO WITH YOU, AND...
I DOUBT HE'LL ARRIVE ANYTIME SOON.
SO I SEE LITTLE POINT IN GOING TO TOWN EVERY DAY.
I WAS HOPING YOU COULD SHOW ME WHAT DAILY CHORES YOU DO HERE...
OF COURSE! NO PROBLEM AT ALL.
TALAS!
YES?
MR. SMITH HERE...
...WOULD LIKE TO SEE THE CHORES WE DO.
THIS IS SUCH A RARE OPPORTUNITY, SO LET'S BREAK OUT THE RICE!
AH!
UM...

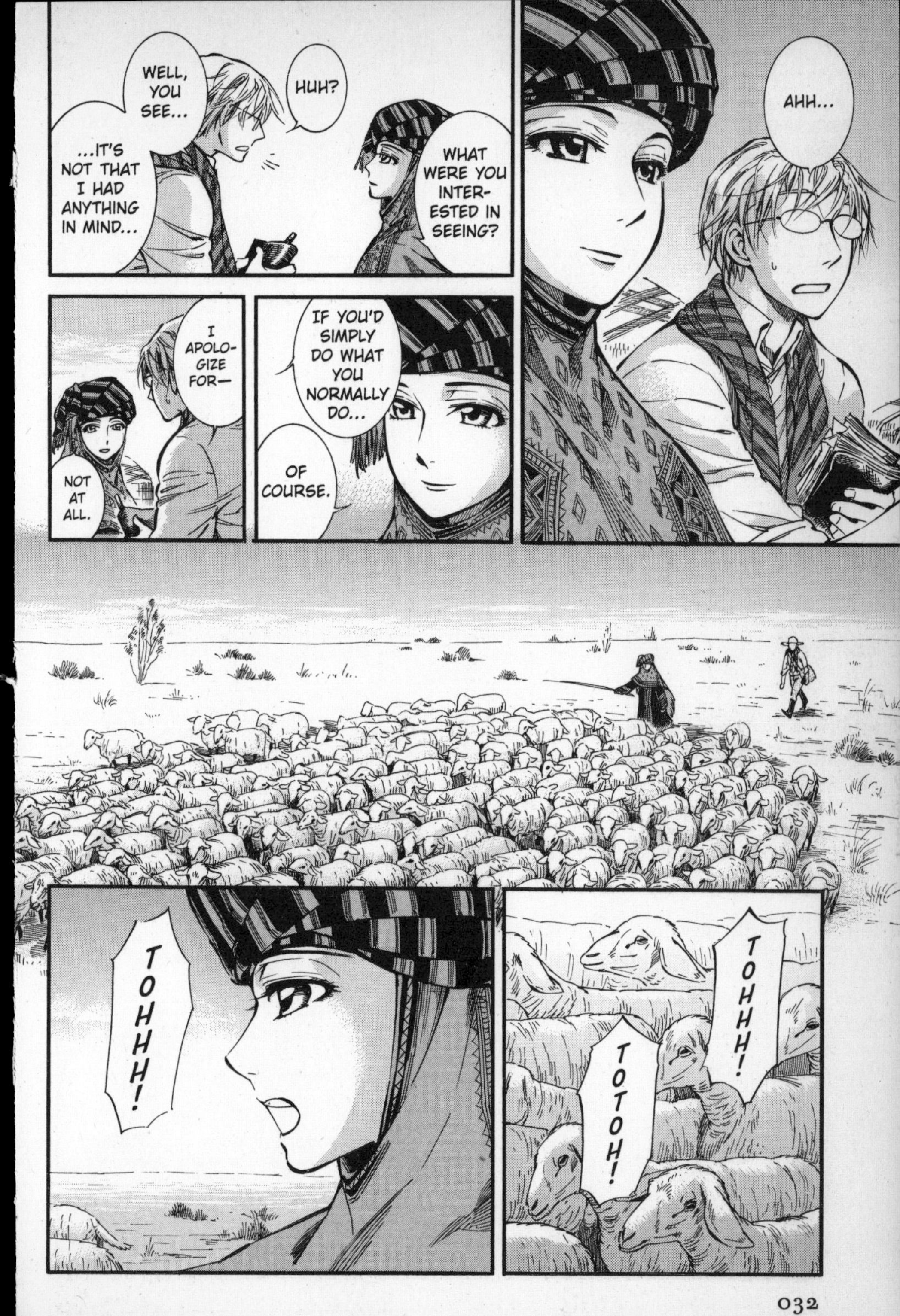
AHH...
WHAT WERE YOU INTERESTED IN SEEING?
HUH?
WELL, YOU SEE...
...IT'S NOT THAT I HAD ANYTHING IN MIND...
IF YOU'D SIMPLY DO WHAT YOU NORMALLY DO...
OF COURSE.
I APOLOGIZE FOR—
NOT AT ALL.
TOHHH!
TOTOH!
TOHHHH!

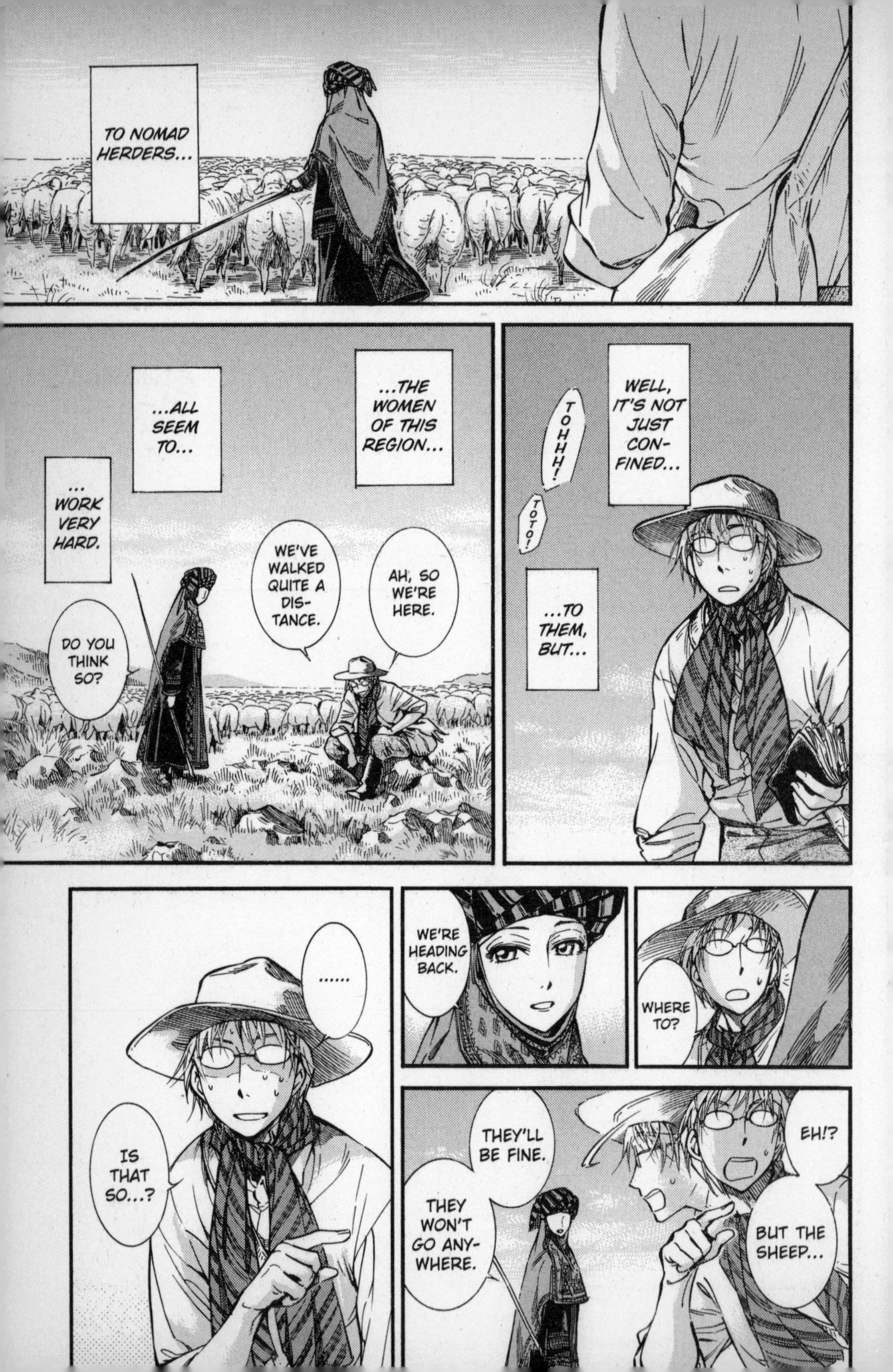
TO NOMAD HERDERS...
WELL, IT'S NOT JUST CONFINED...
TOHHH!
TOTO!
...TO THEM, BUT...
...THE WOMEN OF THIS REGION...
...ALL SEEM TO...
...WORK VERY HARD.
AH, SO WE'RE HERE.
WE'VE WALKED QUITE A DIS-TANCE.
DO YOU THINK SO?
WHERE TO?
WE'RE HEADING BACK.
EH!?
BUT THE SHEEP...
THEY'LL BE FINE.
THEY WON'T GO ANY-WHERE.
......
IS THAT SO...?

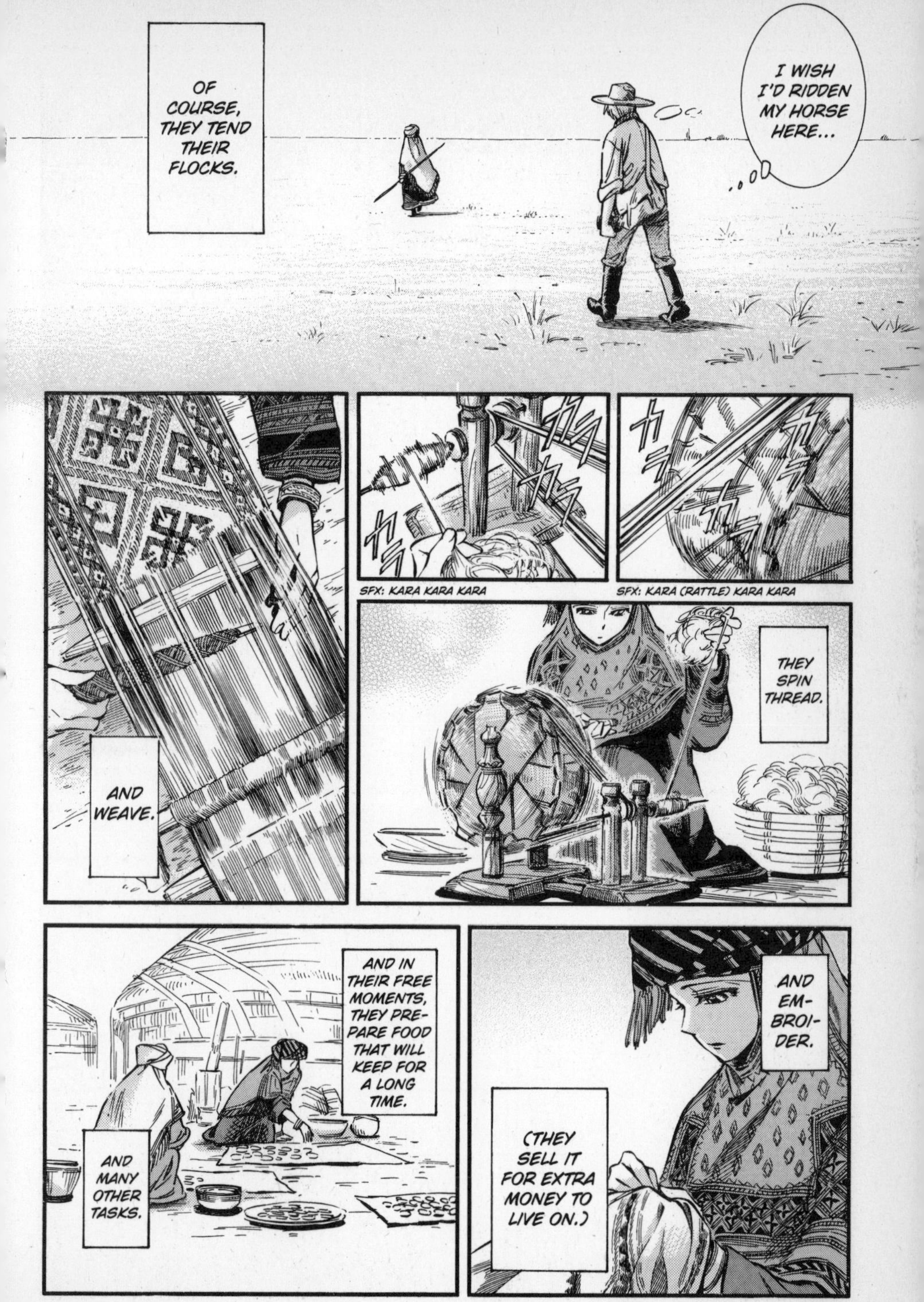
I WISH I'D RIDDEN MY HORSE HERE...
OF COURSE, THEY TEND THEIR FLOCKS.
SFX: KARA (RATTLE) KARA KARA
SFX: KARA KARA KARA
THEY SPIN THREAD.
AND WEAVE.
AND EM-BROI-DER.
(THEY SELL IT FOR EXTRA MONEY TO LIVE ON.)
AND IN THEIR FREE MOMENTS, THEY PRE-PARE FOOD THAT WILL KEEP FOR A LONG TIME.
AND MANY OTHER TASKS.

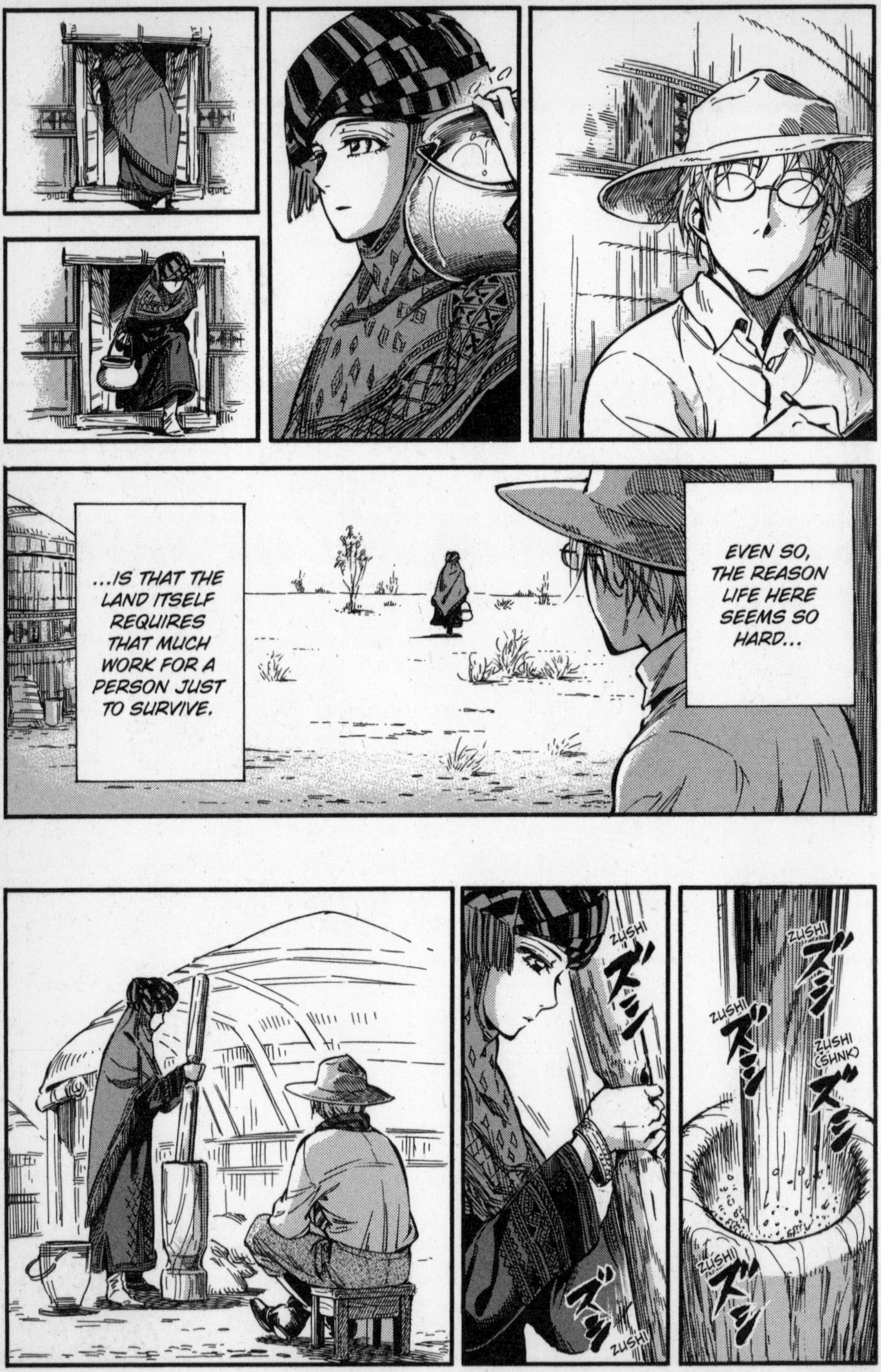
EVEN SO, THE REASON LIFE HERE SEEMS SO HARD...
...IS THAT THE LAND ITSELF REQUIRES THAT MUCH WORK FOR A PERSON JUST TO SURVIVE.
ZUSHI
ズシ
ZUSHI
ズシ
ZUSHI (SHNK)
ズシ
ZUSHI
ズシ
ZUSHI
ズシ
ZUSHI
ズシ

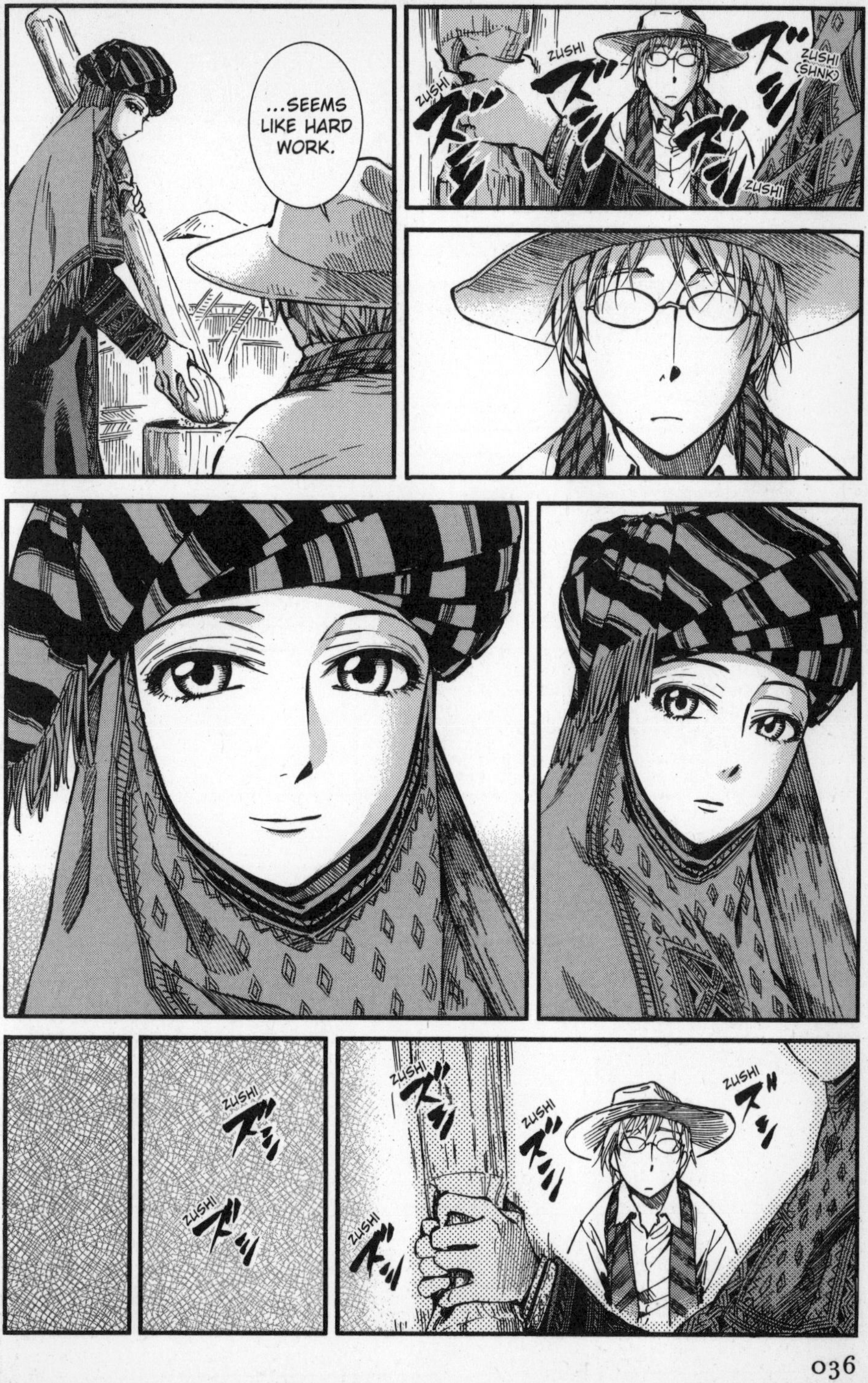
ZUSHI (SHNK)
ZUSHI
ZUSHI
ZUSHI
...SEEMS LIKE HARD WORK.
ZUSHI
ZUSHI
ZUSHI
ZUSHI
ZUSHI
ZUSHI

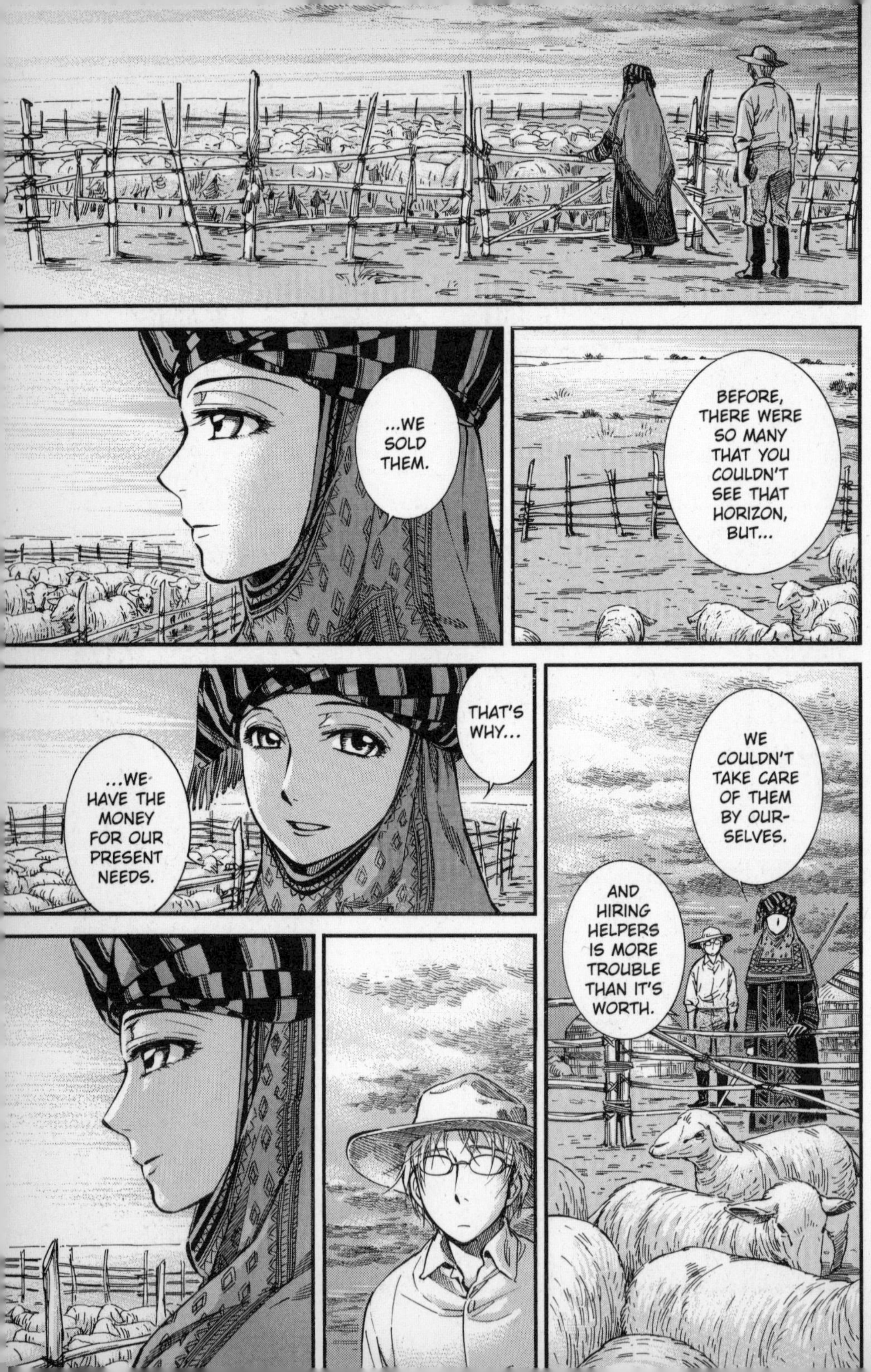
BEFORE, THERE WERE SO MANY THAT YOU COULDN'T SEE THAT HORIZON, BUT...
...WE SOLD THEM.
WE COULDN'T TAKE CARE OF THEM BY OUR-SELVES.
AND HIRING HELPERS IS MORE TROUBLE THAN IT'S WORTH.
THAT'S WHY...
...WE HAVE THE MONEY FOR OUR PRESENT NEEDS.

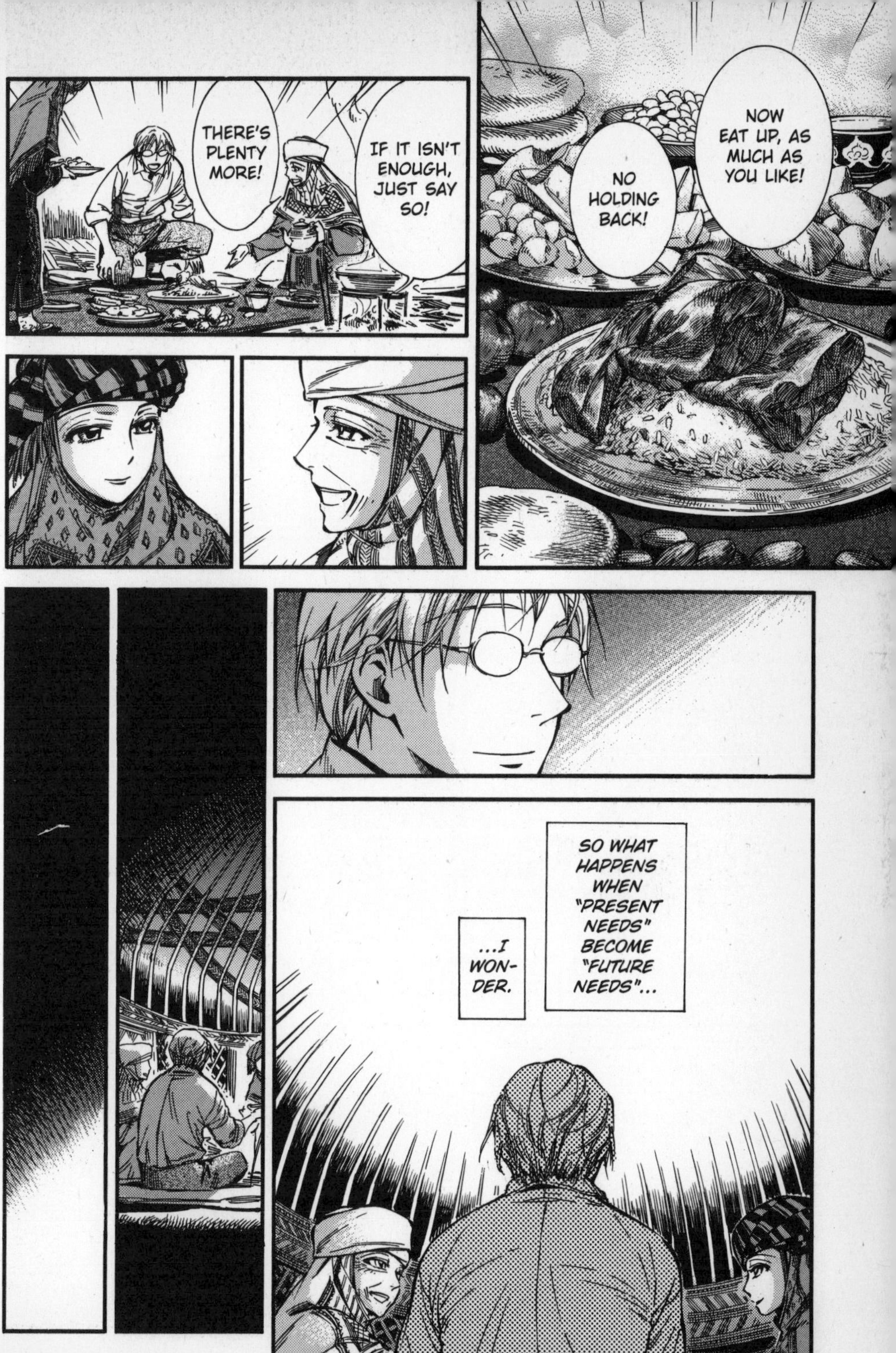
NOW EAT UP, AS MUCH AS YOU LIKE!
NO HOLDING BACK!
IF IT ISN'T ENOUGH, JUST SAY SO!
THERE'S PLENTY MORE!
SO WHAT HAPPENS WHEN "PRESENT NEEDS" BECOME "FUTURE NEEDS"...
...I WONDER.

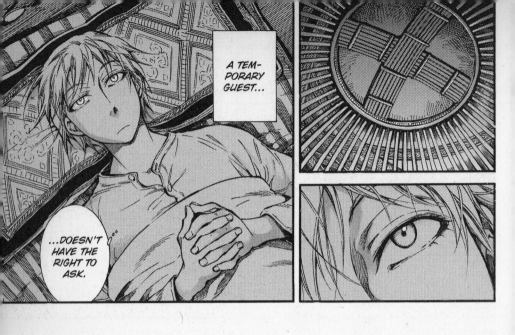

A TEM-PORARY GUEST...

...DOESN'T HAVE THE RIGHT TO ASK.

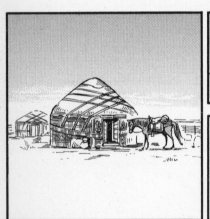

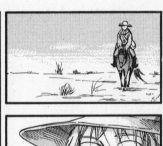

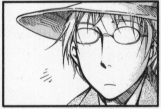

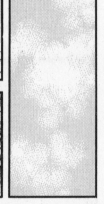

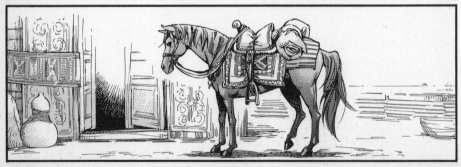

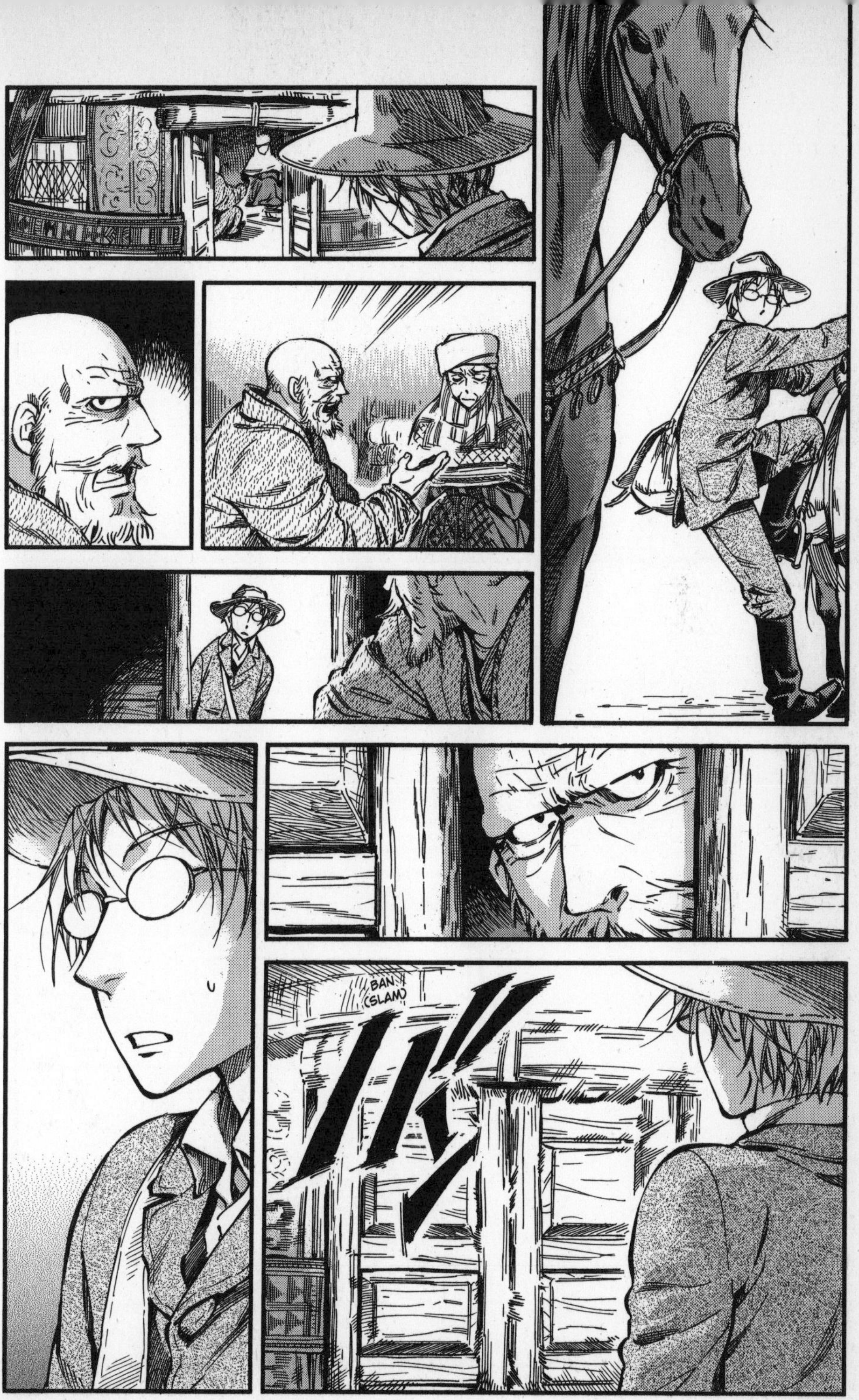
BAN
(SLAM)

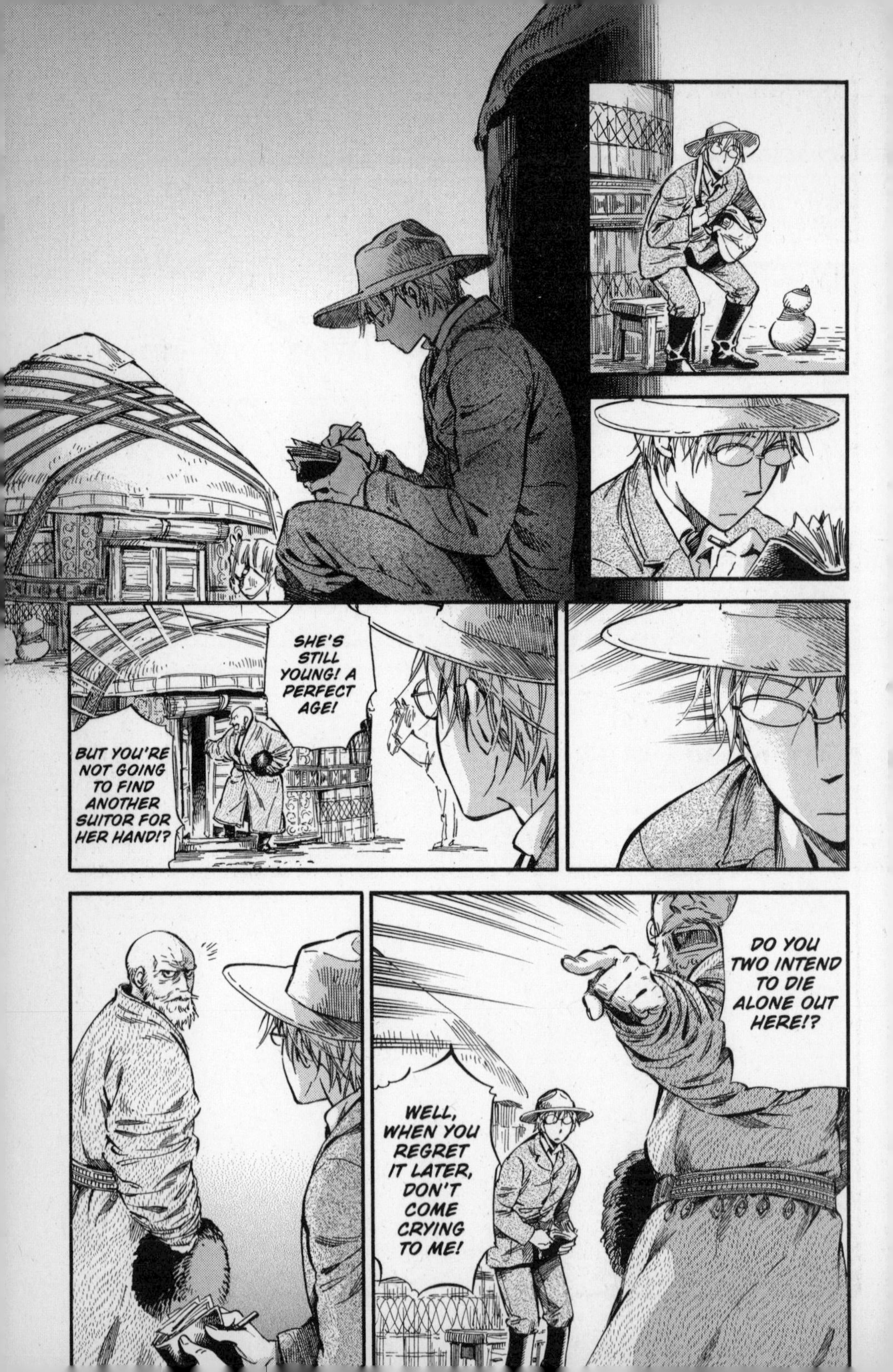
SHE'S STILL YOUNG! A PERFECT AGE!
BUT YOU'RE NOT GOING TO FIND ANOTHER SUITOR FOR HER HAND!?
DO YOU TWO INTEND TO DIE ALONE OUT HERE!?
WELL, WHEN YOU REGRET IT LATER, DON'T COME CRYING TO ME!

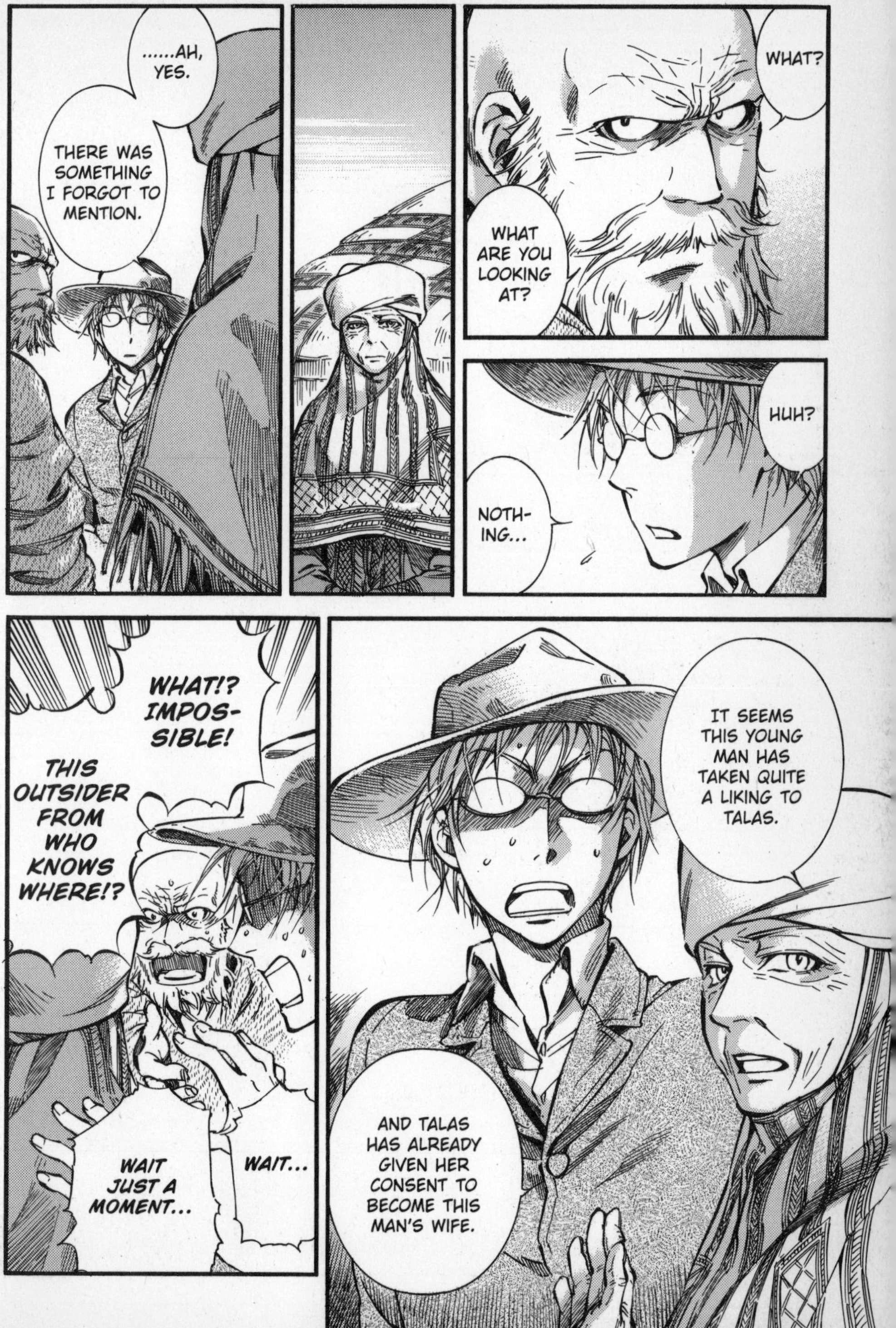
WHAT?
WHAT ARE YOU LOOKING AT?
HUH?
NOTH-ING...
......AH, YES.
THERE WAS SOMETHING I FORGOT TO MENTION.
IT SEEMS THIS YOUNG MAN HAS TAKEN QUITE A LIKING TO TALAS.
AND TALAS HAS ALREADY GIVEN HER CONSENT TO BECOME THIS MAN'S WIFE.
WHAT!? IMPOS-SIBLE!
THIS OUTSIDER FROM WHO KNOWS WHERE!?
WAIT...
WAIT JUST A MOMENT...

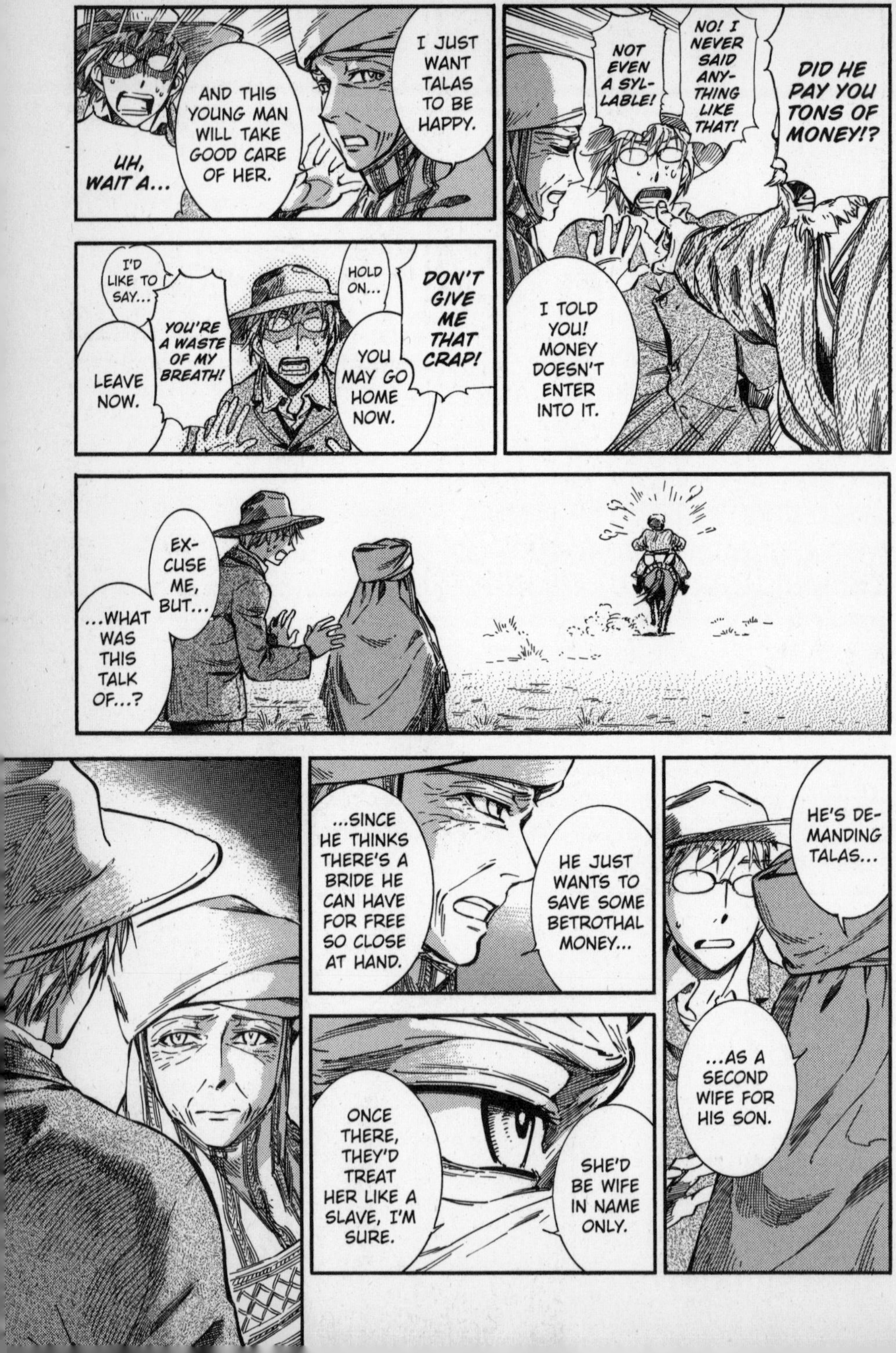
DID HE PAY YOU TONS OF MONEY!?
NO! I NEVER SAID ANYTHING LIKE THAT!
NOT EVEN A SYLLABLE!
I TOLD YOU! MONEY DOESN'T ENTER INTO IT.
I JUST WANT TALAS TO BE HAPPY.
AND THIS YOUNG MAN WILL TAKE GOOD CARE OF HER.
UH, WAIT A...
DON'T GIVE ME THAT CRAP!
HOLD ON...
YOU MAY GO HOME NOW.
I'D LIKE TO SAY...
YOU'RE A WASTE OF MY BREATH!
LEAVE NOW.
EX-CUSE ME, BUT...
...WHAT WAS THIS TALK OF...?
HE'S DE-MANDING TALAS...
...AS A SECOND WIFE FOR HIS SON.
HE JUST WANTS TO SAVE SOME BETROTHAL MONEY...
...SINCE HE THINKS THERE'S A BRIDE HE CAN HAVE FOR FREE SO CLOSE AT HAND.
SHE'D BE WIFE IN NAME ONLY.
ONCE THERE, THEY'D TREAT HER LIKE A SLAVE, I'M SURE.

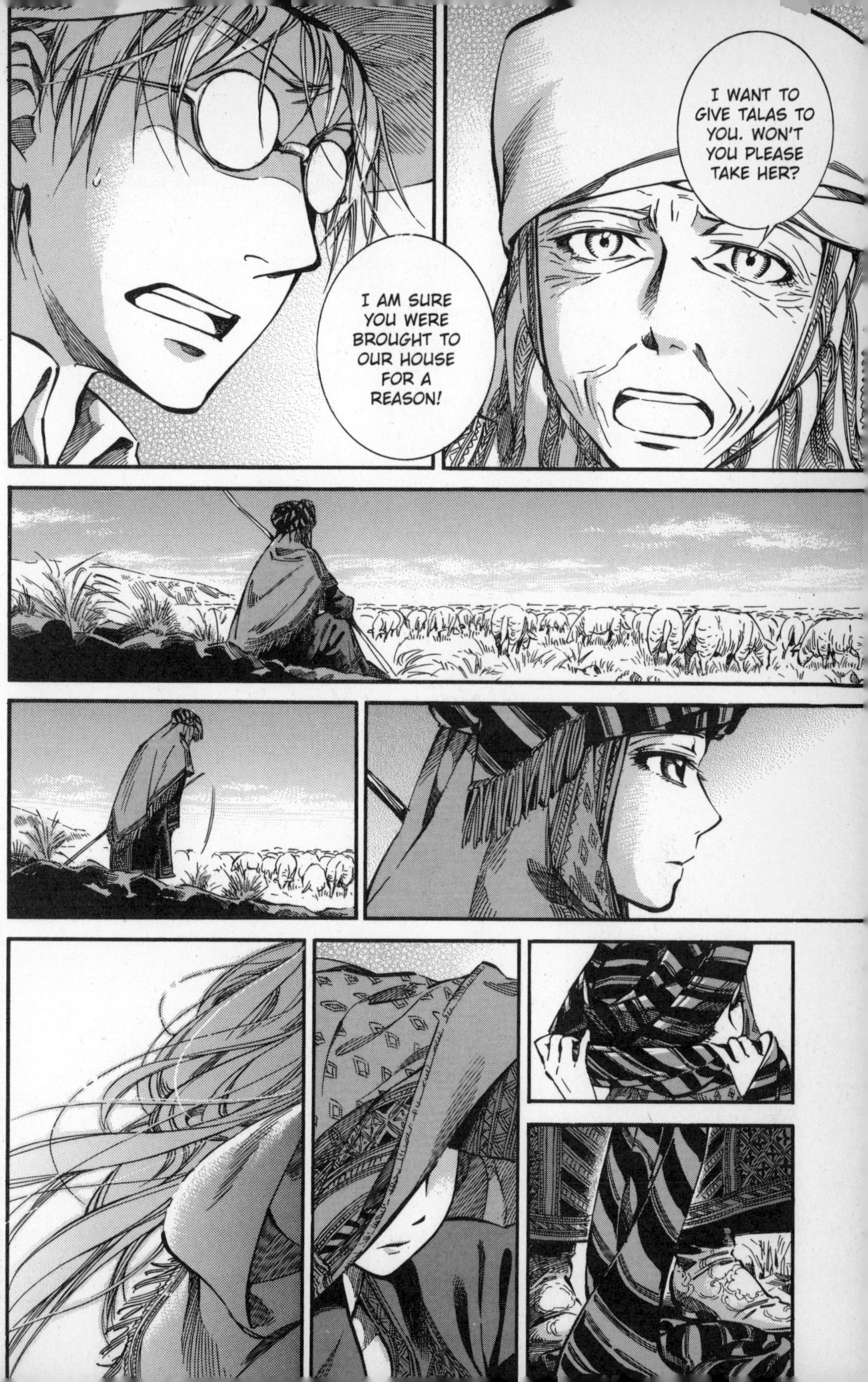
I WANT TO GIVE TALAS TO YOU. WON'T YOU PLEASE TAKE HER?
I AM SURE YOU WERE BROUGHT TO OUR HOUSE FOR A REASON!

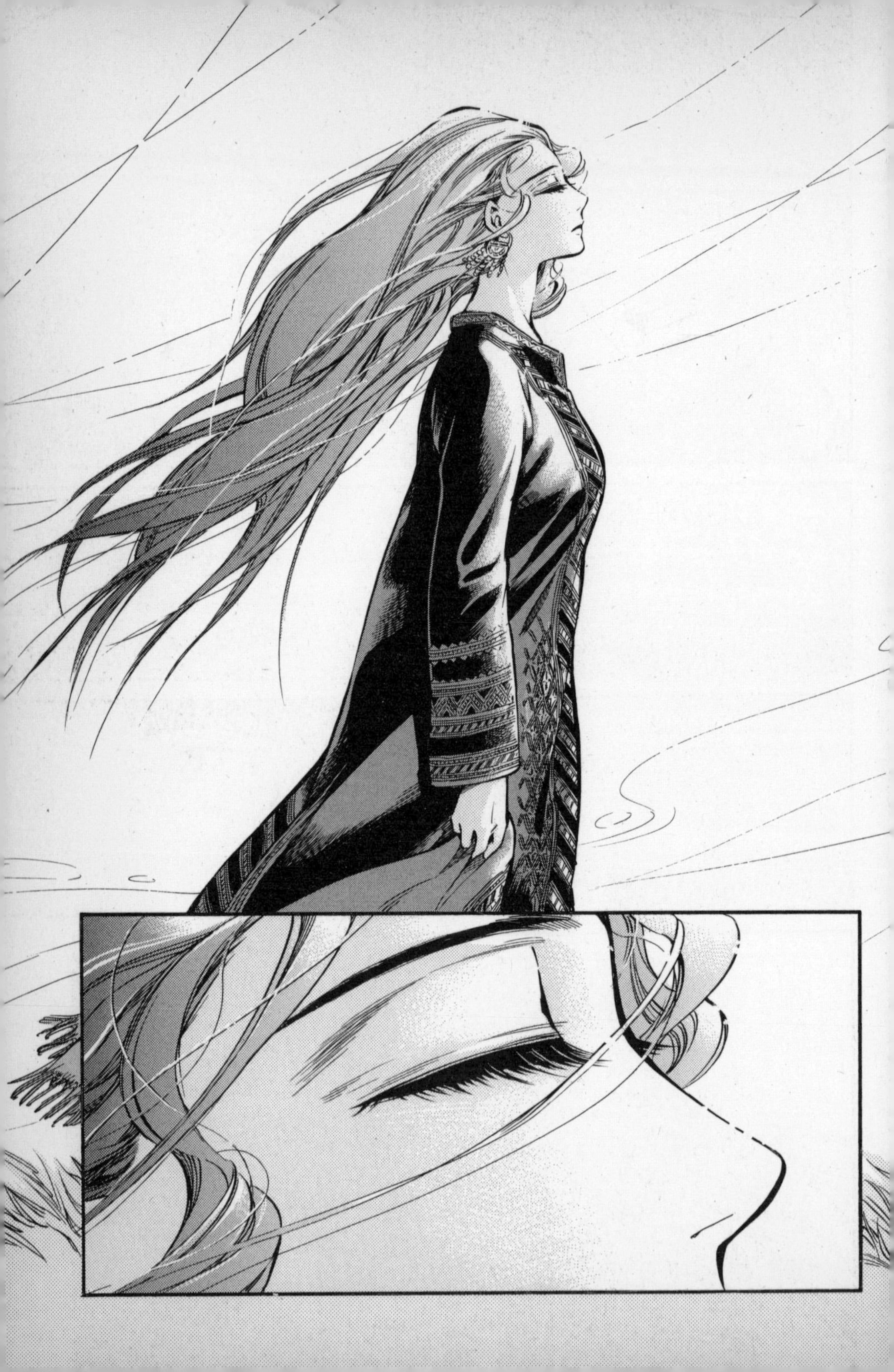

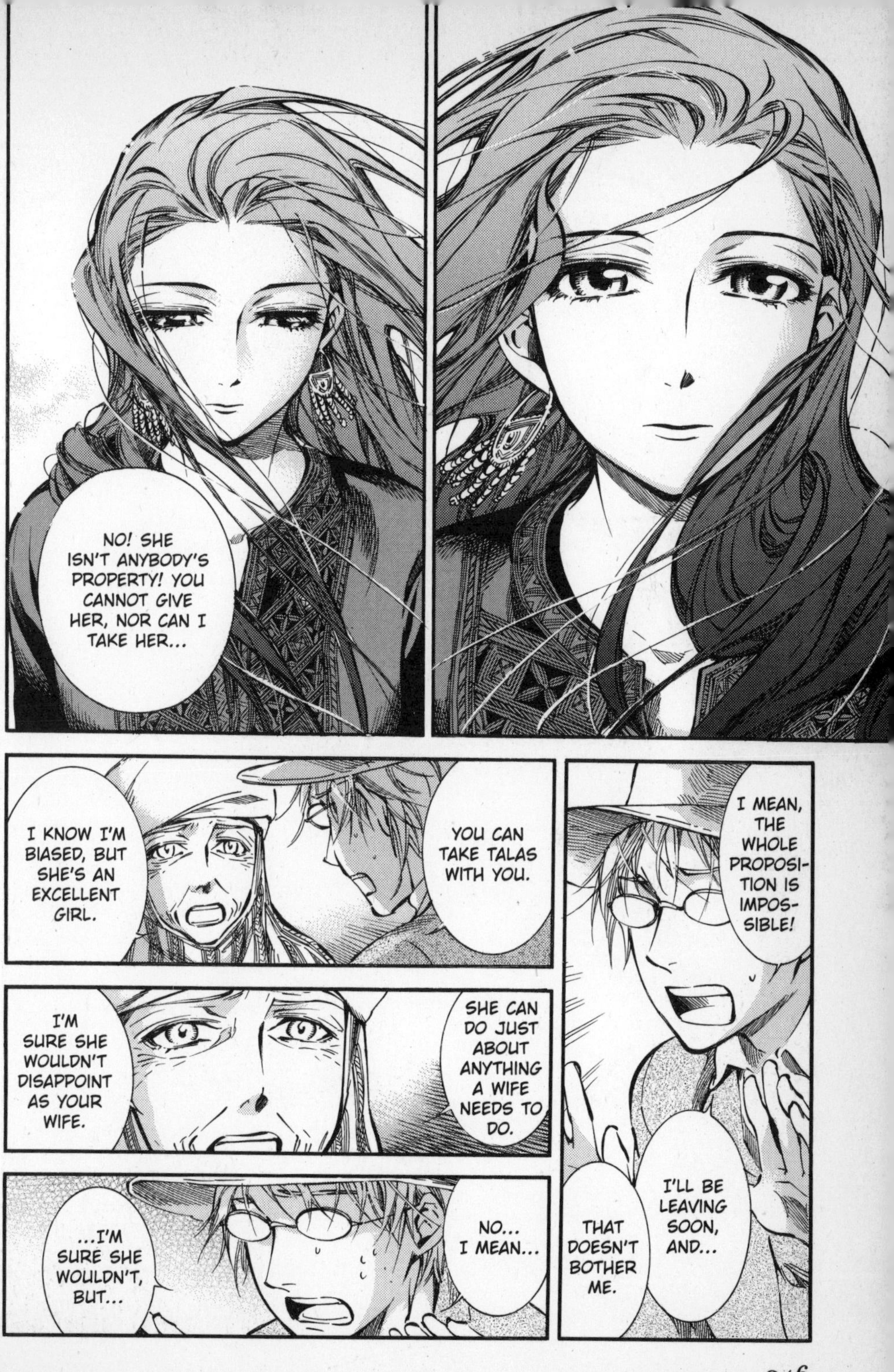
NO! SHE ISN'T ANYBODY'S PROPERTY! YOU CANNOT GIVE HER, NOR CAN I TAKE HER...
I MEAN, THE WHOLE PROPOSITION IS IMPOSSIBLE!
I'LL BE LEAVING SOON, AND...
THAT DOESN'T BOTHER ME.
YOU CAN TAKE TALAS WITH YOU.
I KNOW I'M BIASED, BUT SHE'S AN EXCELLENT GIRL.
SHE CAN DO JUST ABOUT ANYTHING A WIFE NEEDS TO DO.
I'M SURE SHE WOULDN'T DISAPPOINT AS YOUR WIFE.
NO... I MEAN...
...I'M SURE SHE WOULDN'T, BUT...

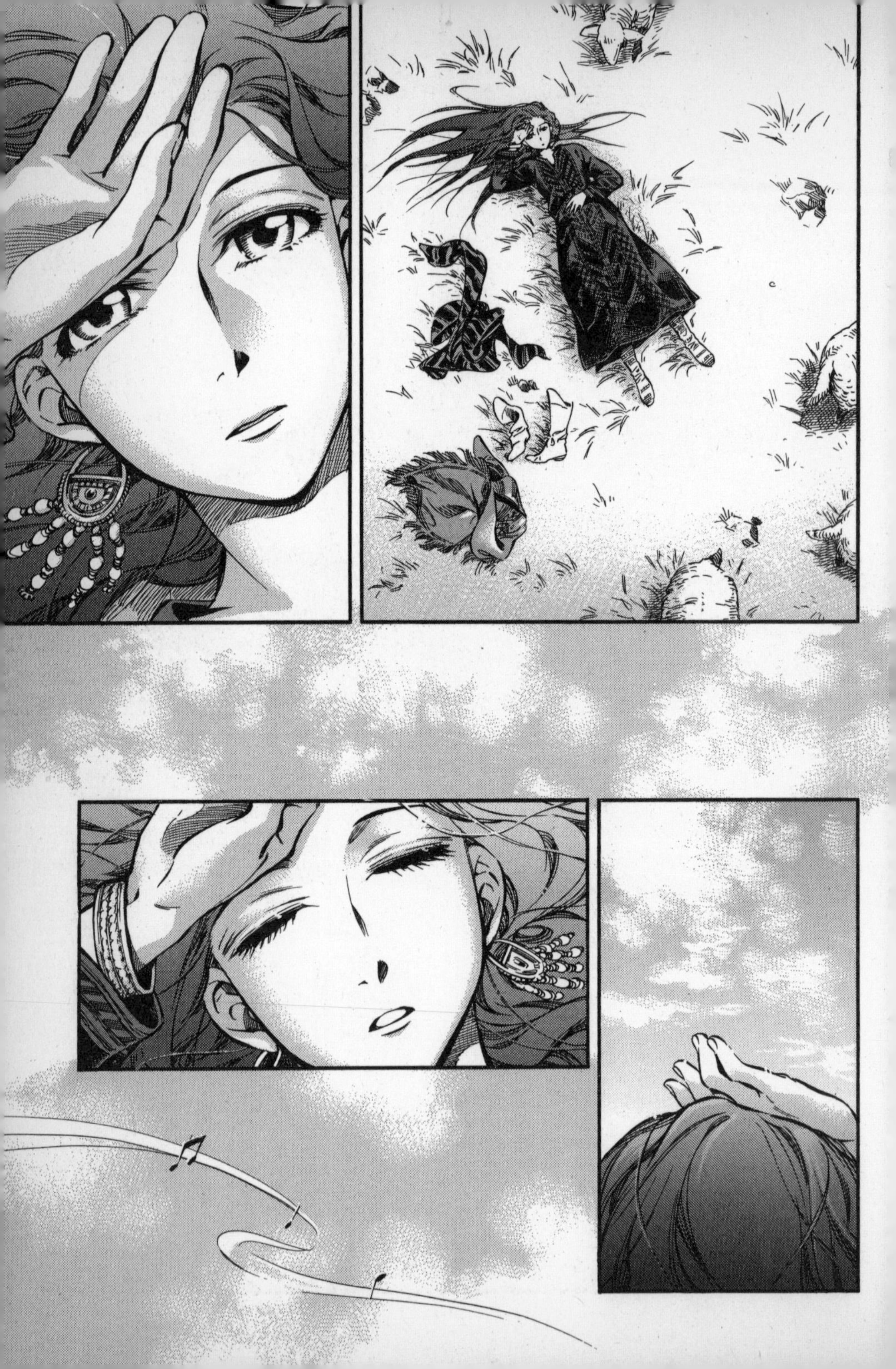

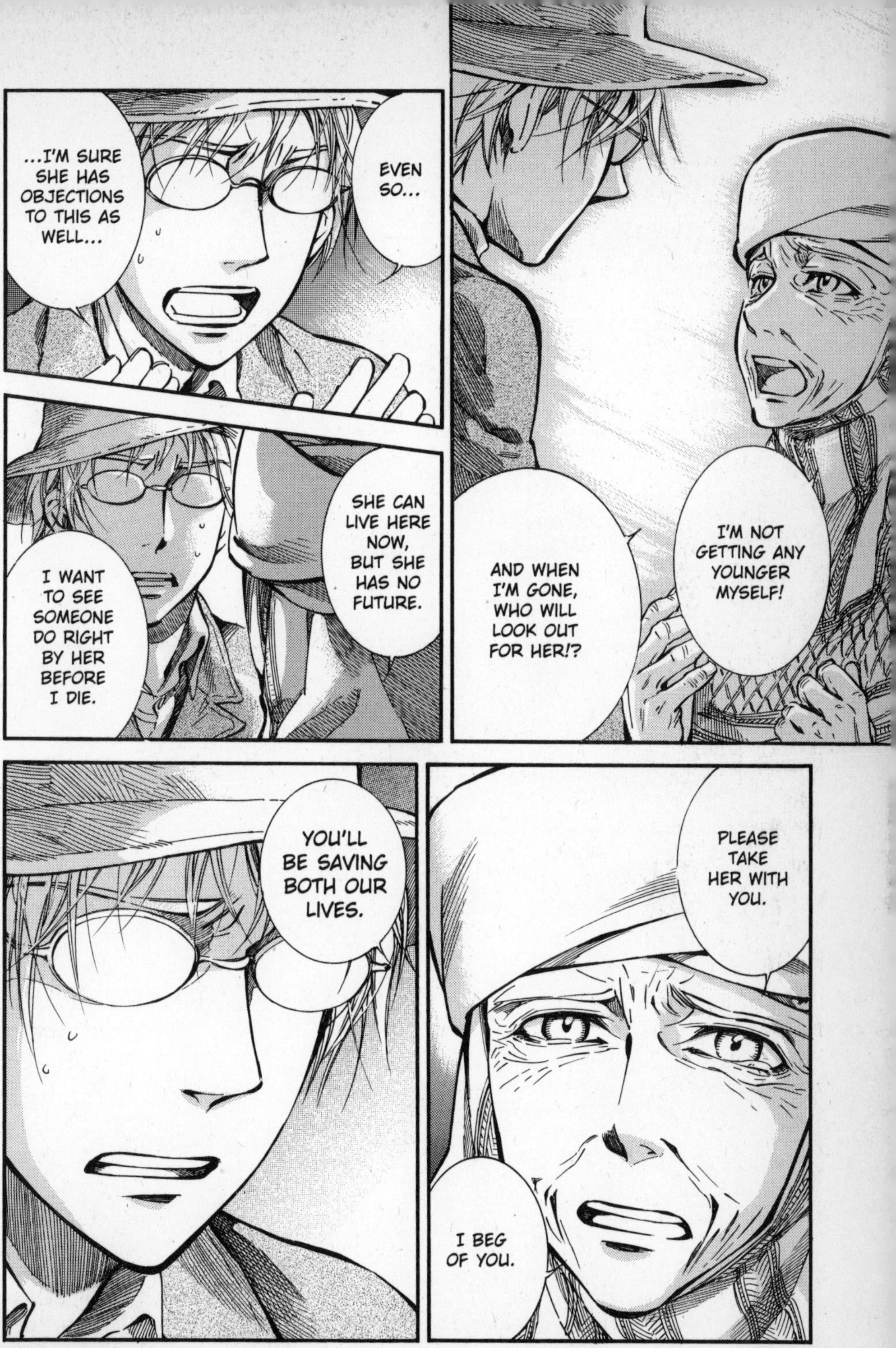
I'M NOT GETTING ANY YOUNGER MYSELF!
AND WHEN I'M GONE, WHO WILL LOOK OUT FOR HER!?
EVEN SO...
...I'M SURE SHE HAS OBJECTIONS TO THIS AS WELL...
SHE CAN LIVE HERE NOW, BUT SHE HAS NO FUTURE.
I WANT TO SEE SOMEONE DO RIGHT BY HER BEFORE I DIE.
PLEASE TAKE HER WITH YOU.
I BEG OF YOU.
YOU'LL BE SAVING BOTH OUR LIVES.

✦ Chapter Thirteen: End ✦

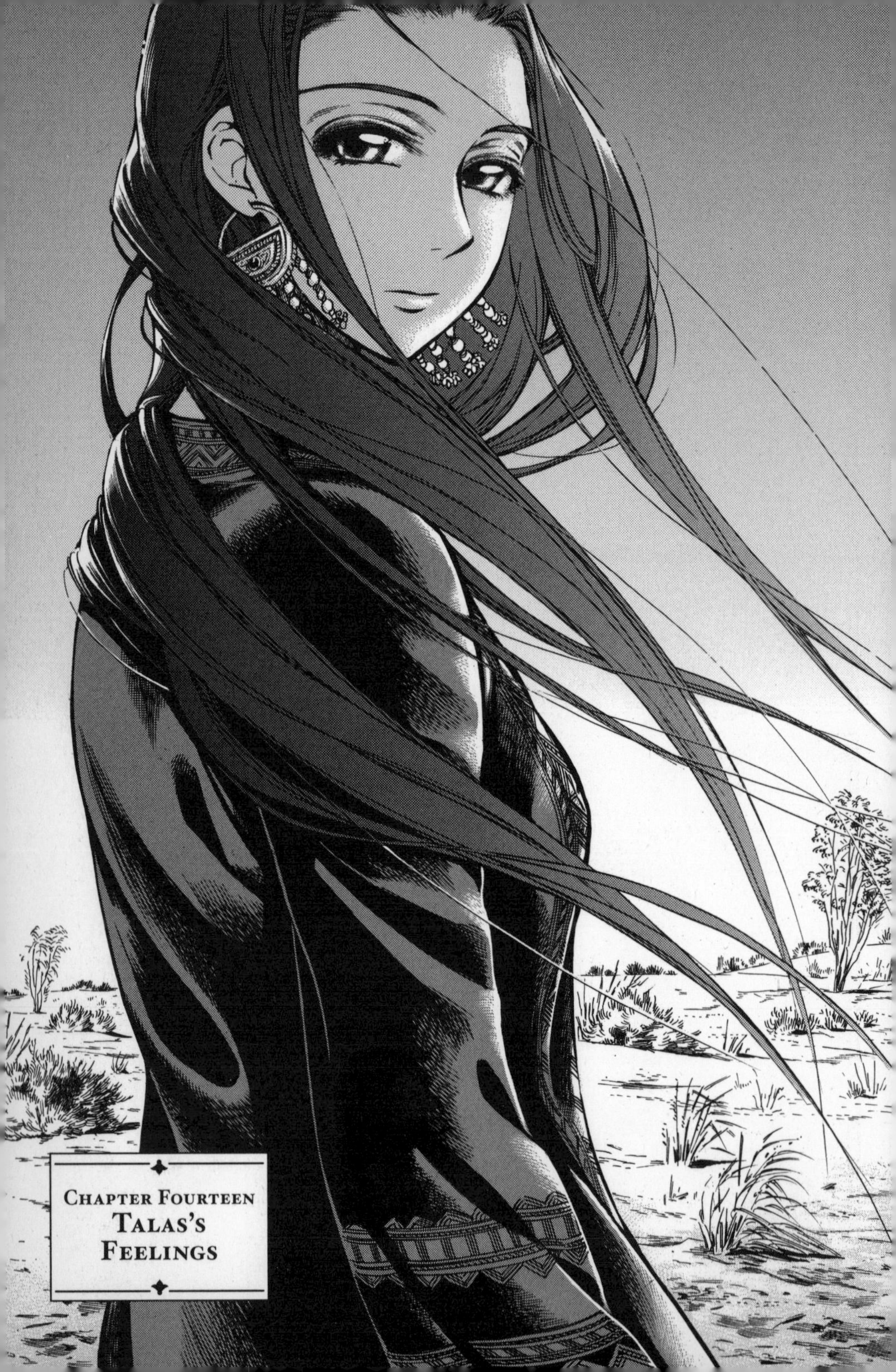
CHAPTER FOURTEEN
TALAS'S
FEELINGS

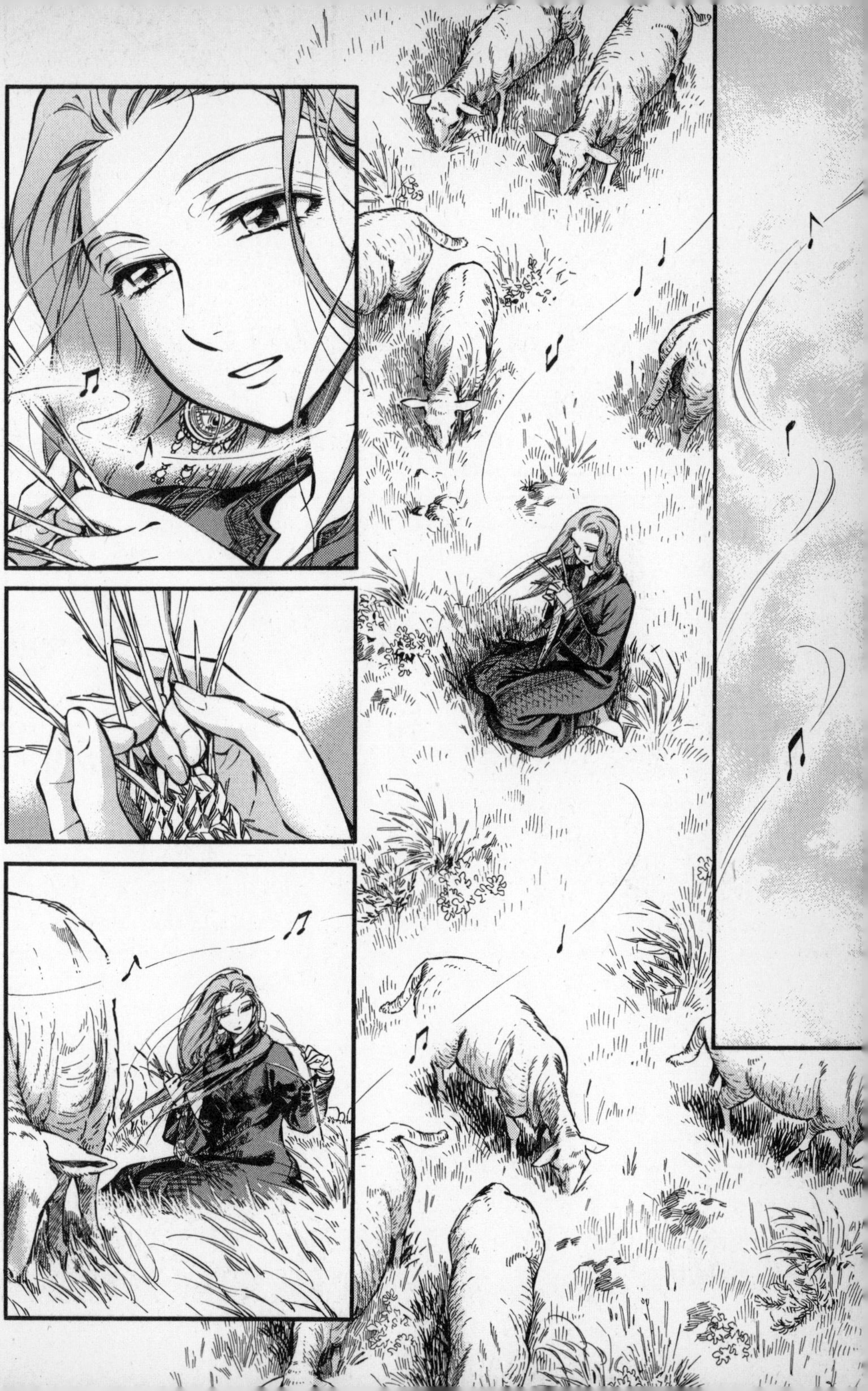

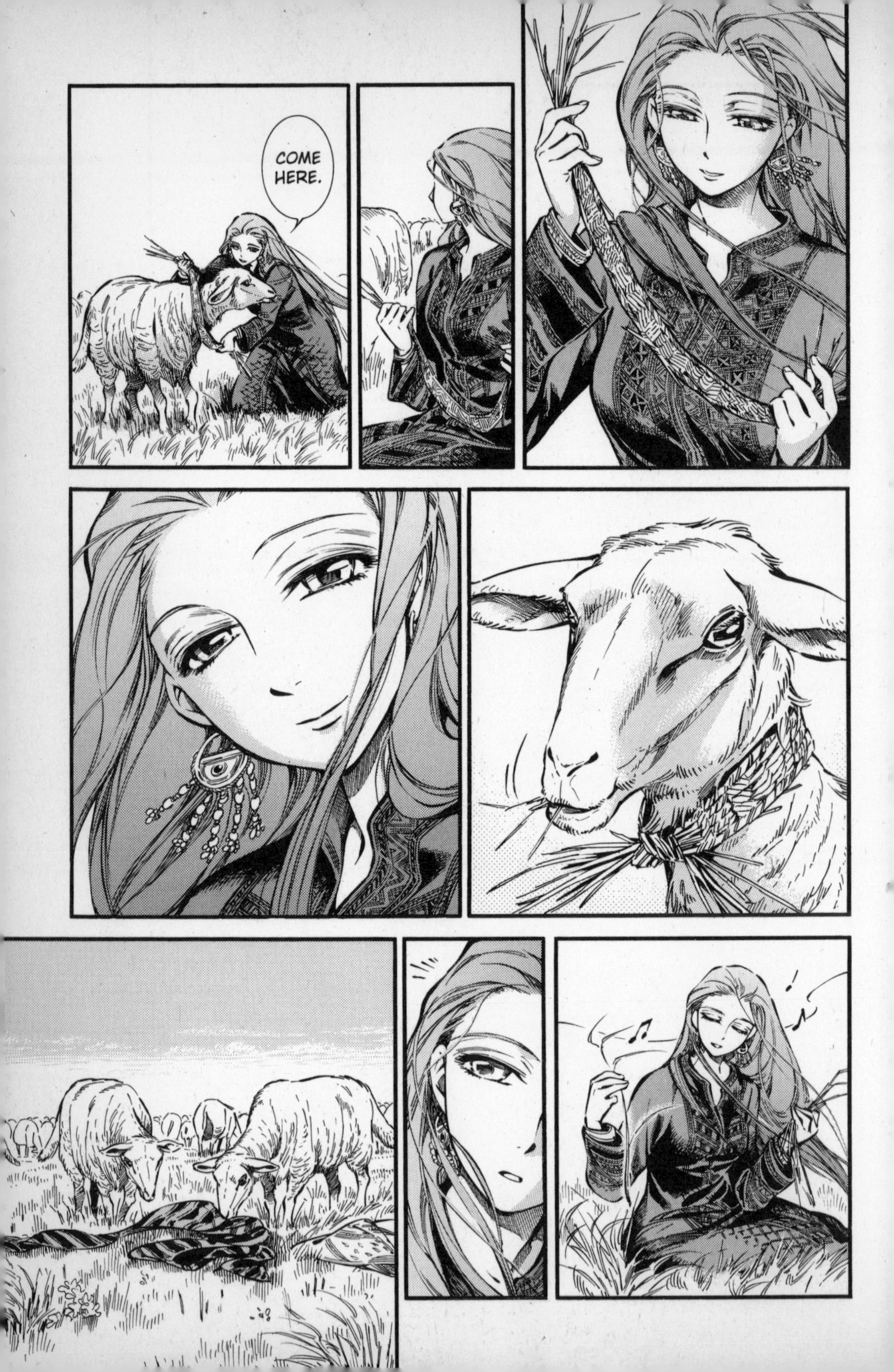
COME HERE.

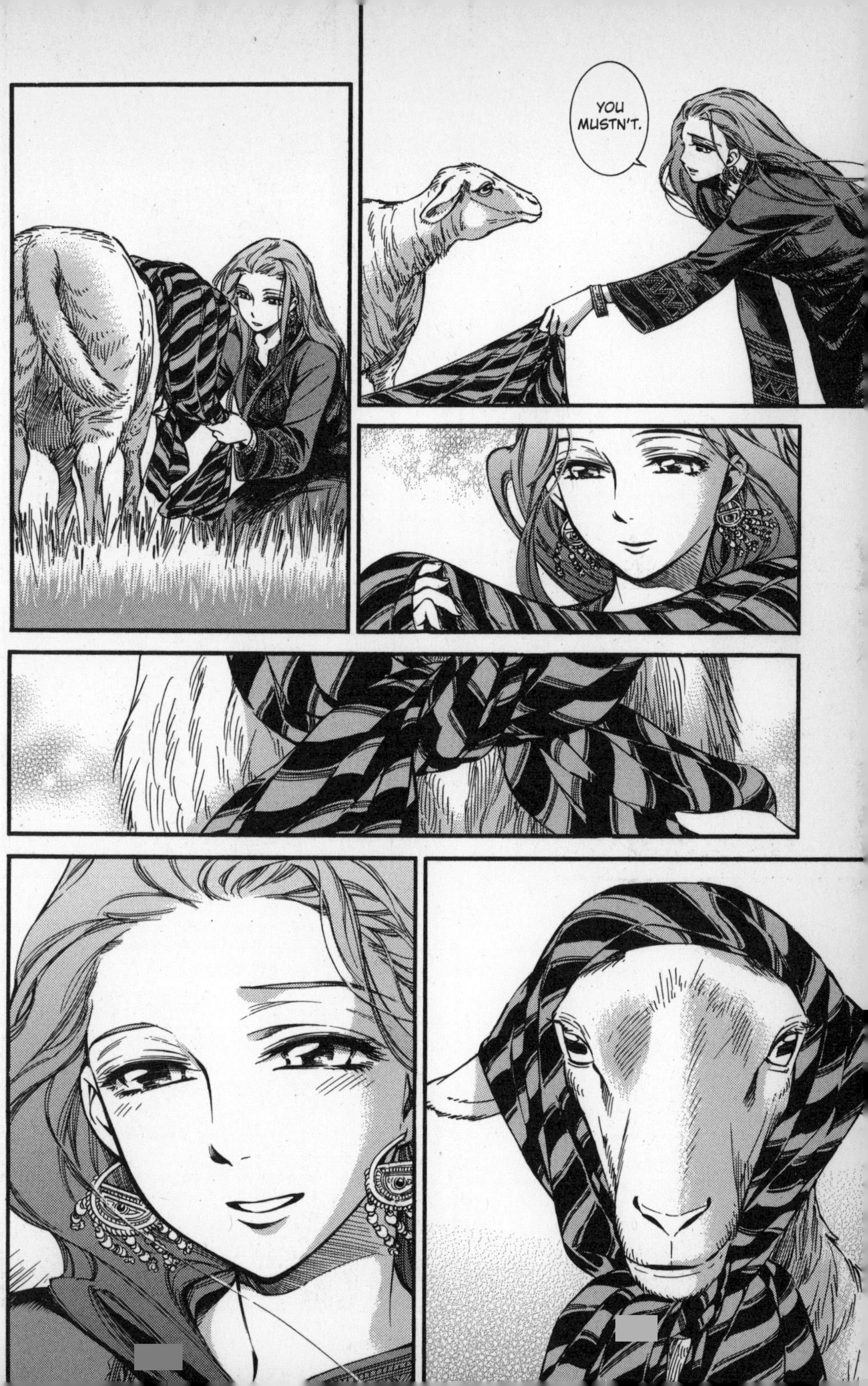
YOU MUSTN'T.

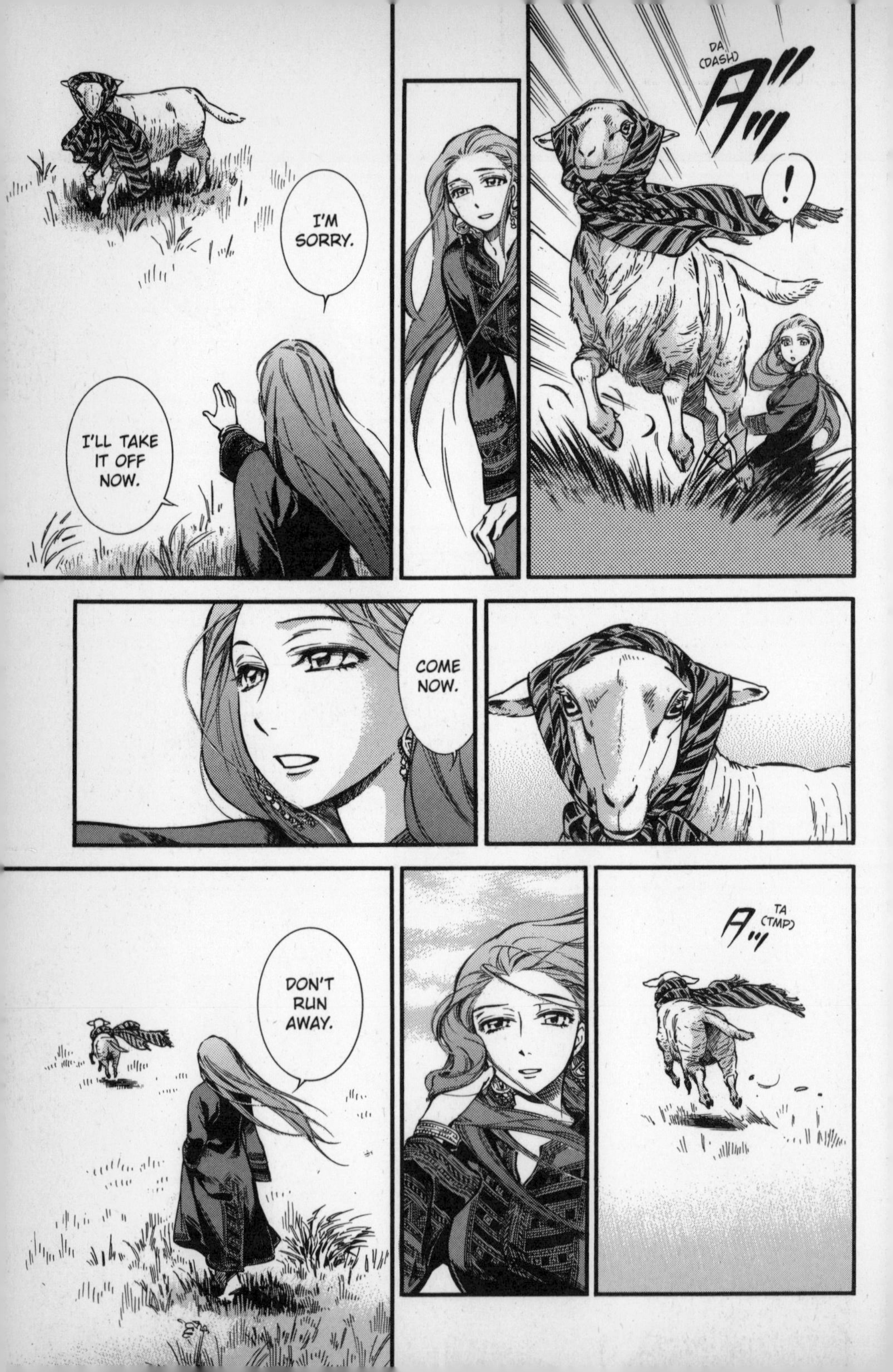
DA (DASH)
ダッ
!
I'M SORRY.
I'LL TAKE IT OFF NOW.
COME NOW.
TA (TMP)
タッ
DON'T RUN AWAY.

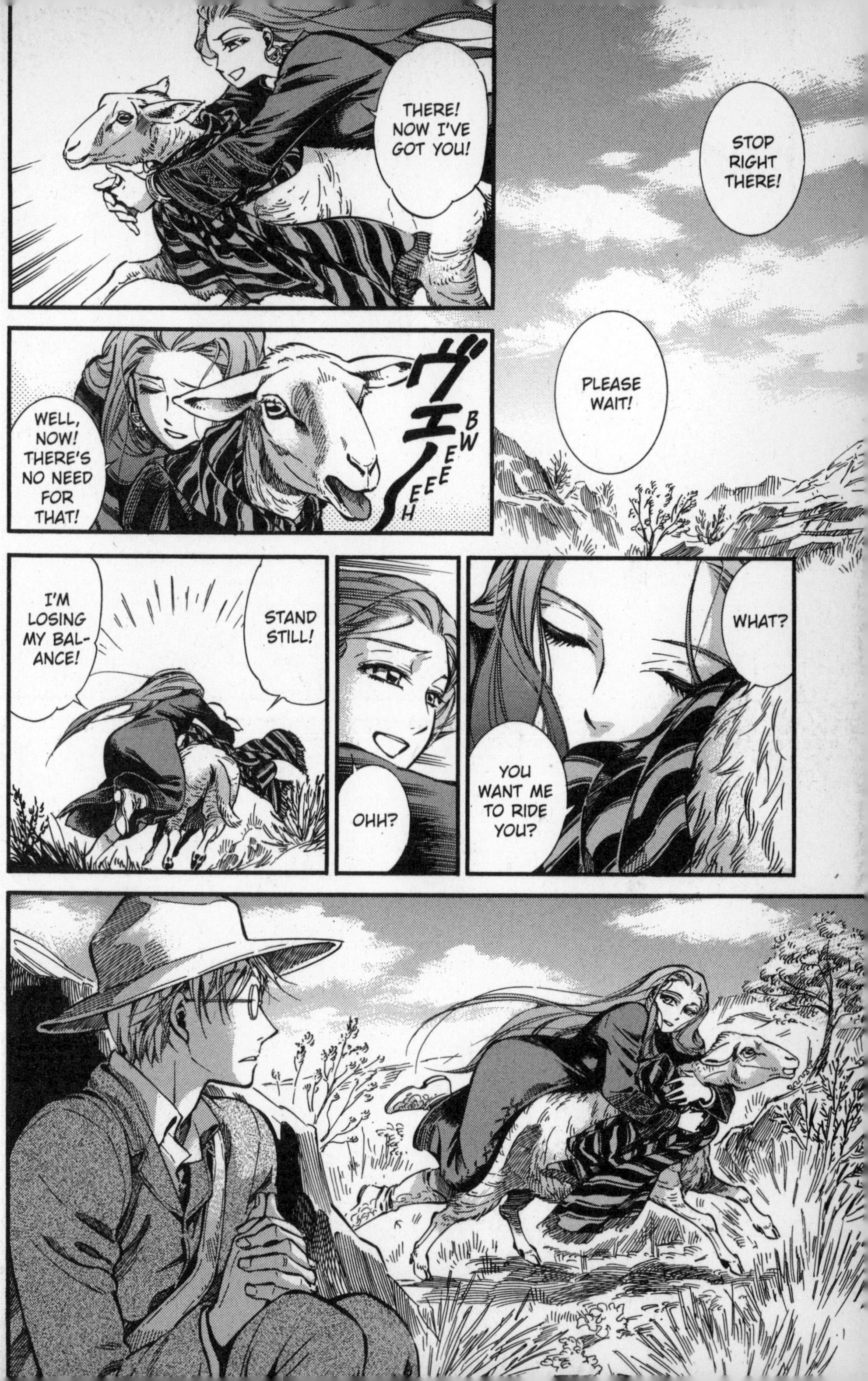

STOP RIGHT THERE!
PLEASE WAIT!
THERE! NOW I'VE GOT YOU!
ヴェー
BWEEEEH
WELL, NOW! THERE'S NO NEED FOR THAT!
WHAT?
YOU WANT ME TO RIDE YOU?
OHH?
STAND STILL!
I'M LOSING MY BAL-ANCE!

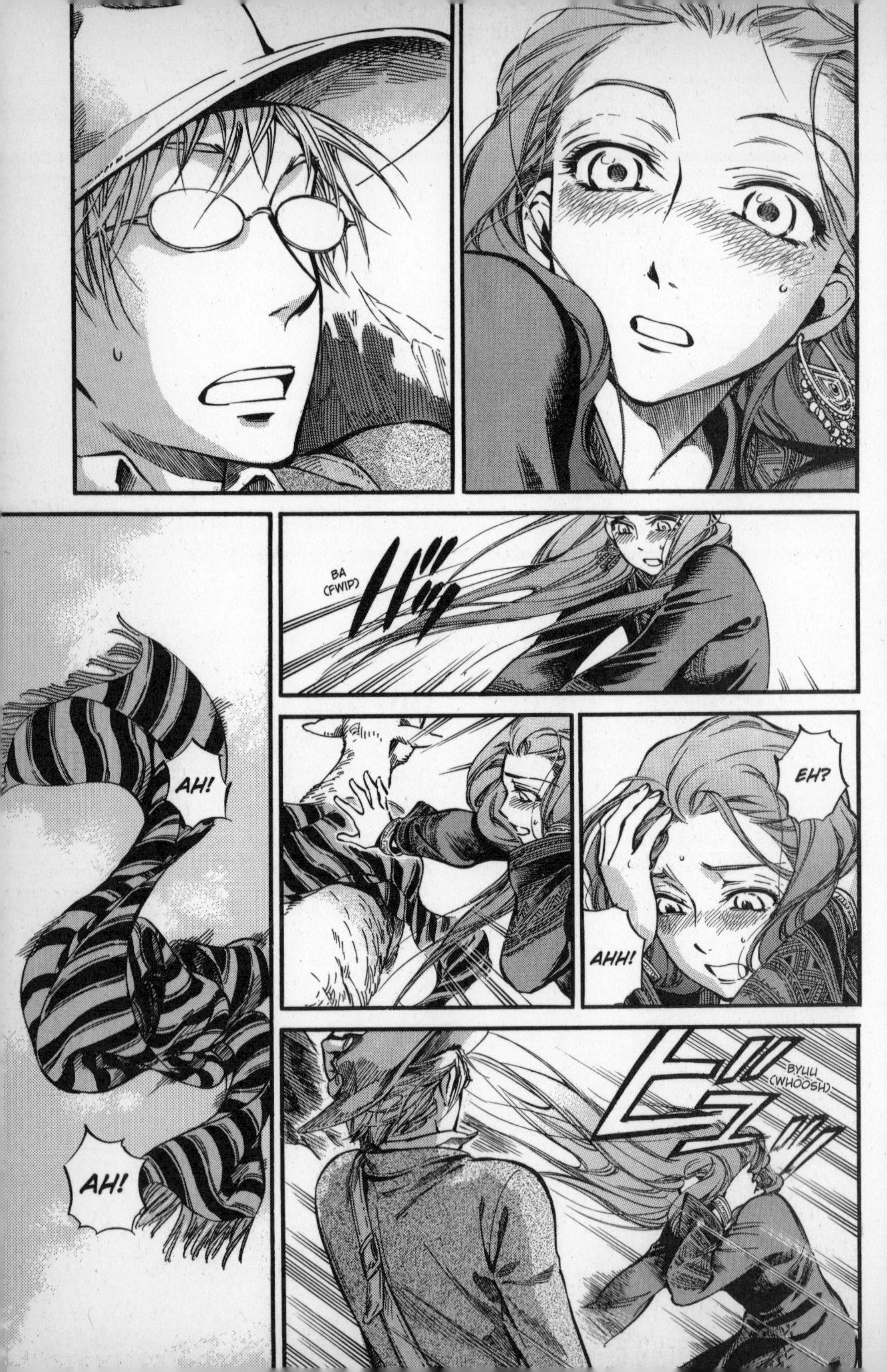
BA (FWIP)
EH?
AHH!
BYUU (WHOOSH)
AH!
AH!

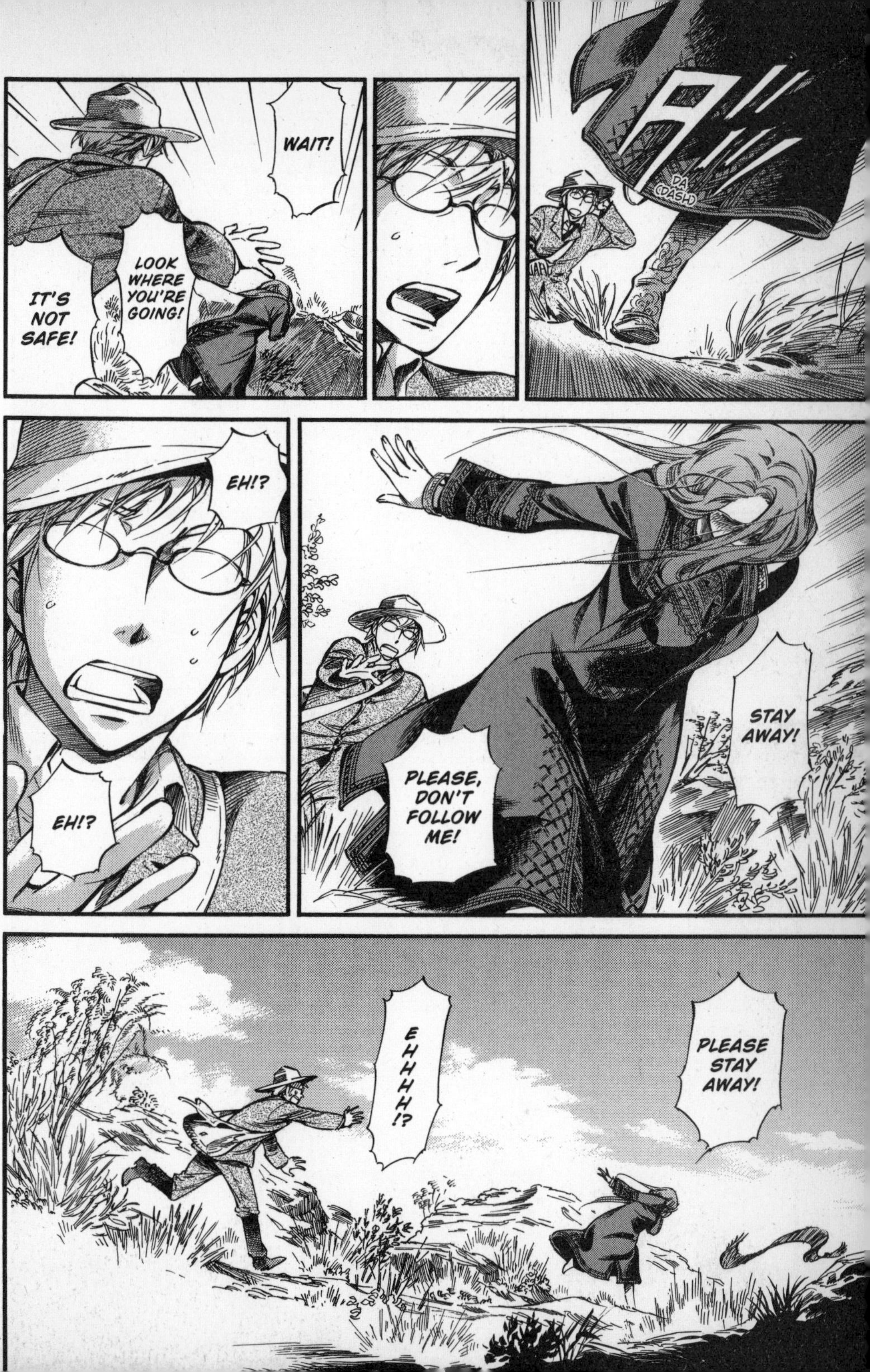
DA (DASH)
WAIT!
LOOK WHERE YOU'RE GOING!
IT'S NOT SAFE!
STAY AWAY!
PLEASE, DON'T FOLLOW ME!
EH!?
EH!?
PLEASE STAY AWAY!
EHHHH!?

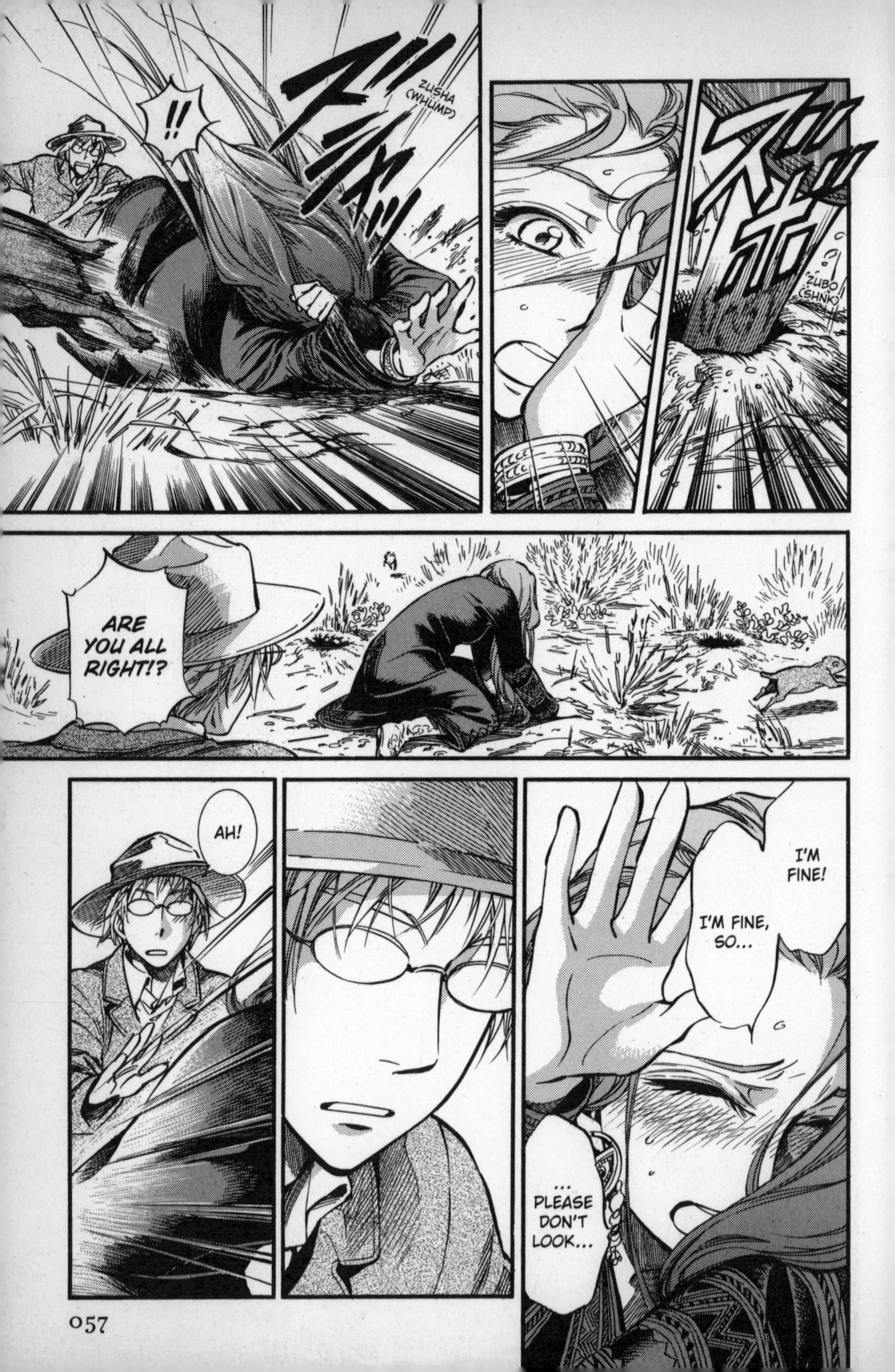
ZUBO (SHNK)
ZUSHA (WHUMP)
!!
ARE YOU ALL RIGHT!?
I'M FINE!
I'M FINE, SO...
... PLEASE DON'T LOOK...
AH!

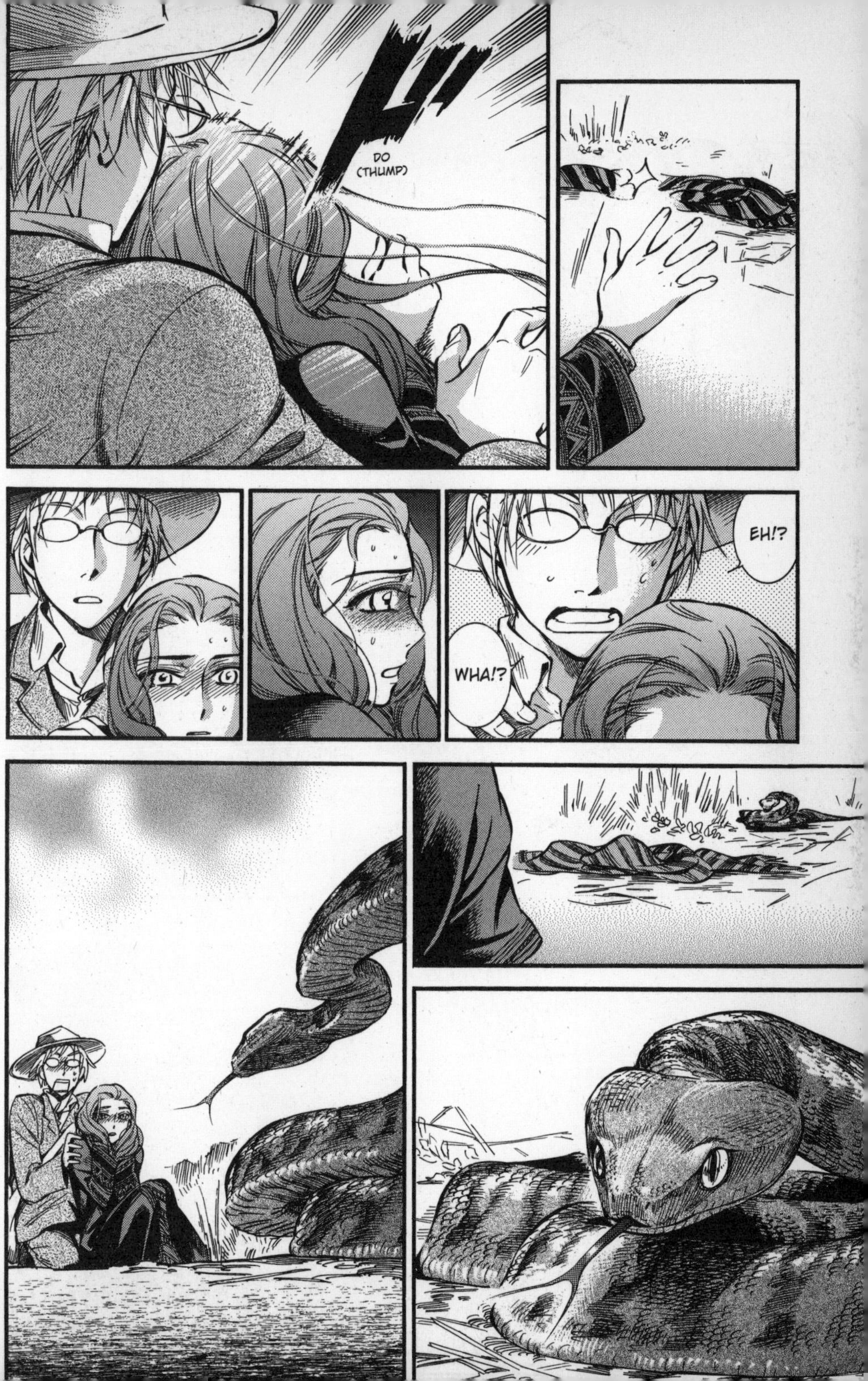
DO
(THUMP)
EH!?
WHA!?

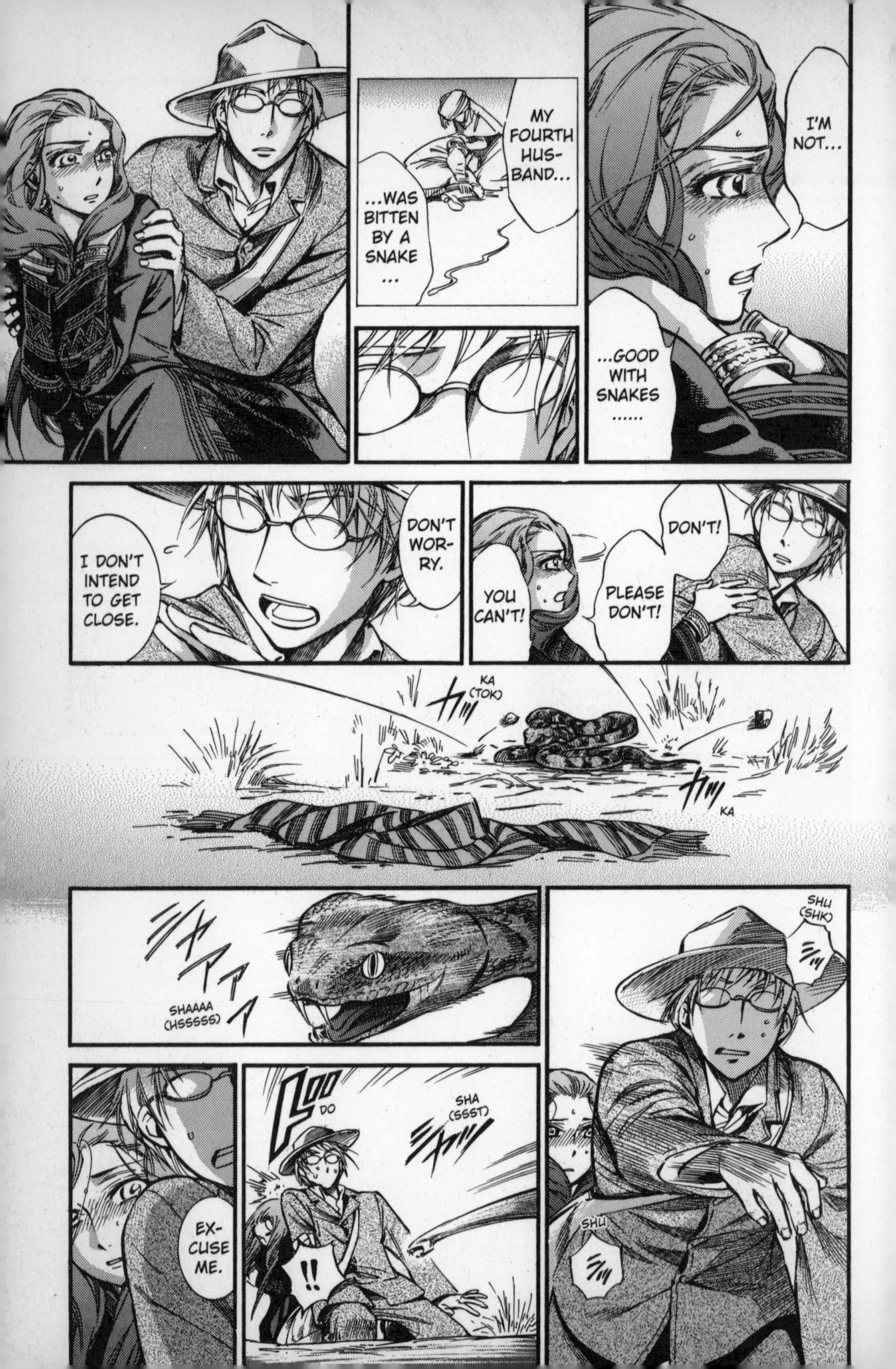
I'M NOT...
...GOOD WITH SNAKES ......
MY FOURTH HUS-BAND...
...WAS BITTEN BY A SNAKE ...
DON'T!
PLEASE DON'T!
YOU CAN'T!
DON'T WOR-RY.
I DON'T INTEND TO GET CLOSE.
KA (TOK)
KA
SHU (SHK)
SHU
SHAAAA (HSSSSS)
DO
SHA (SSST)
!!
EX-CUSE ME.

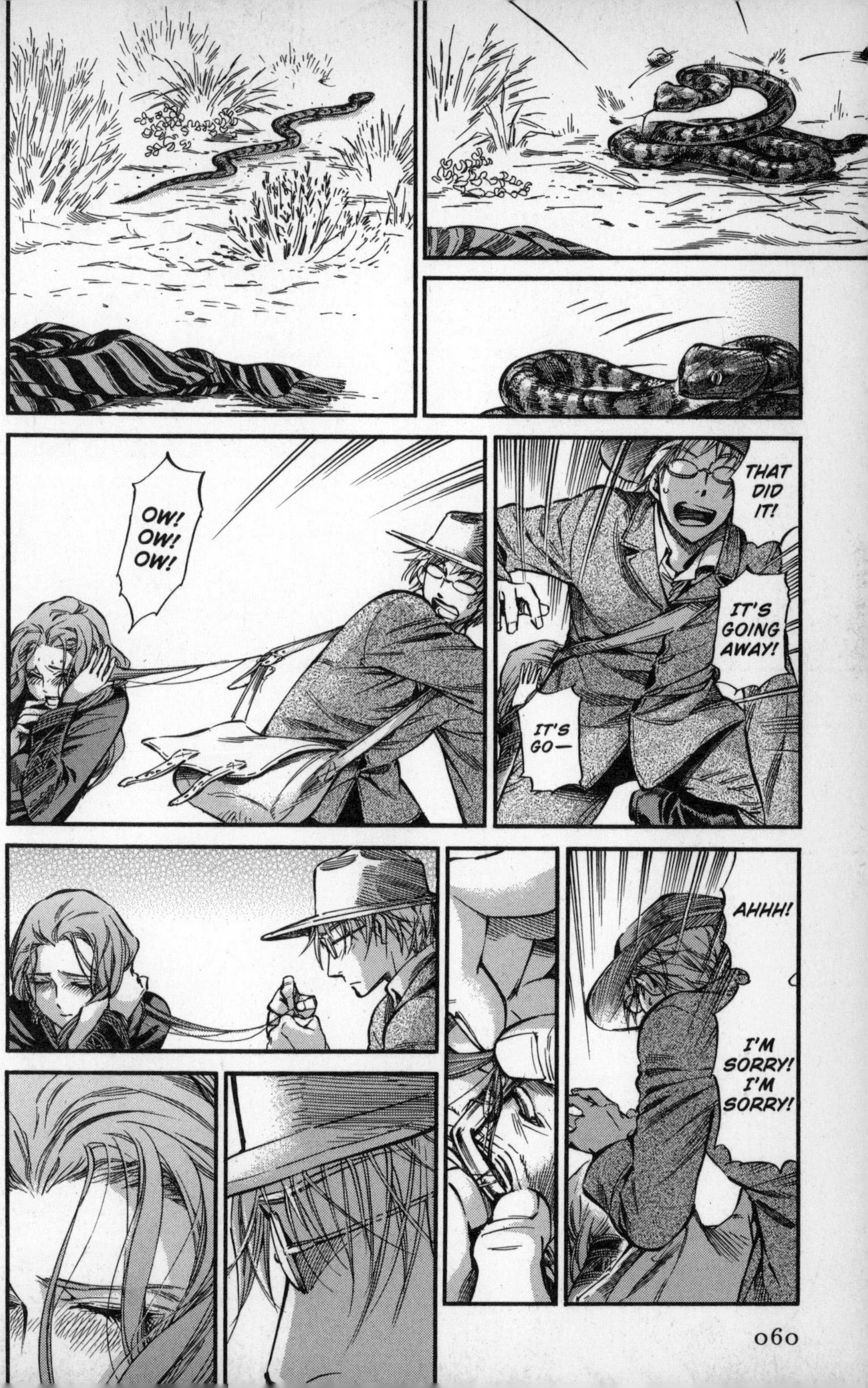
THAT DID IT!
IT'S GOING AWAY!
IT'S GO—
OW! OW! OW!
AHHH!
I'M SORRY! I'M SORRY!

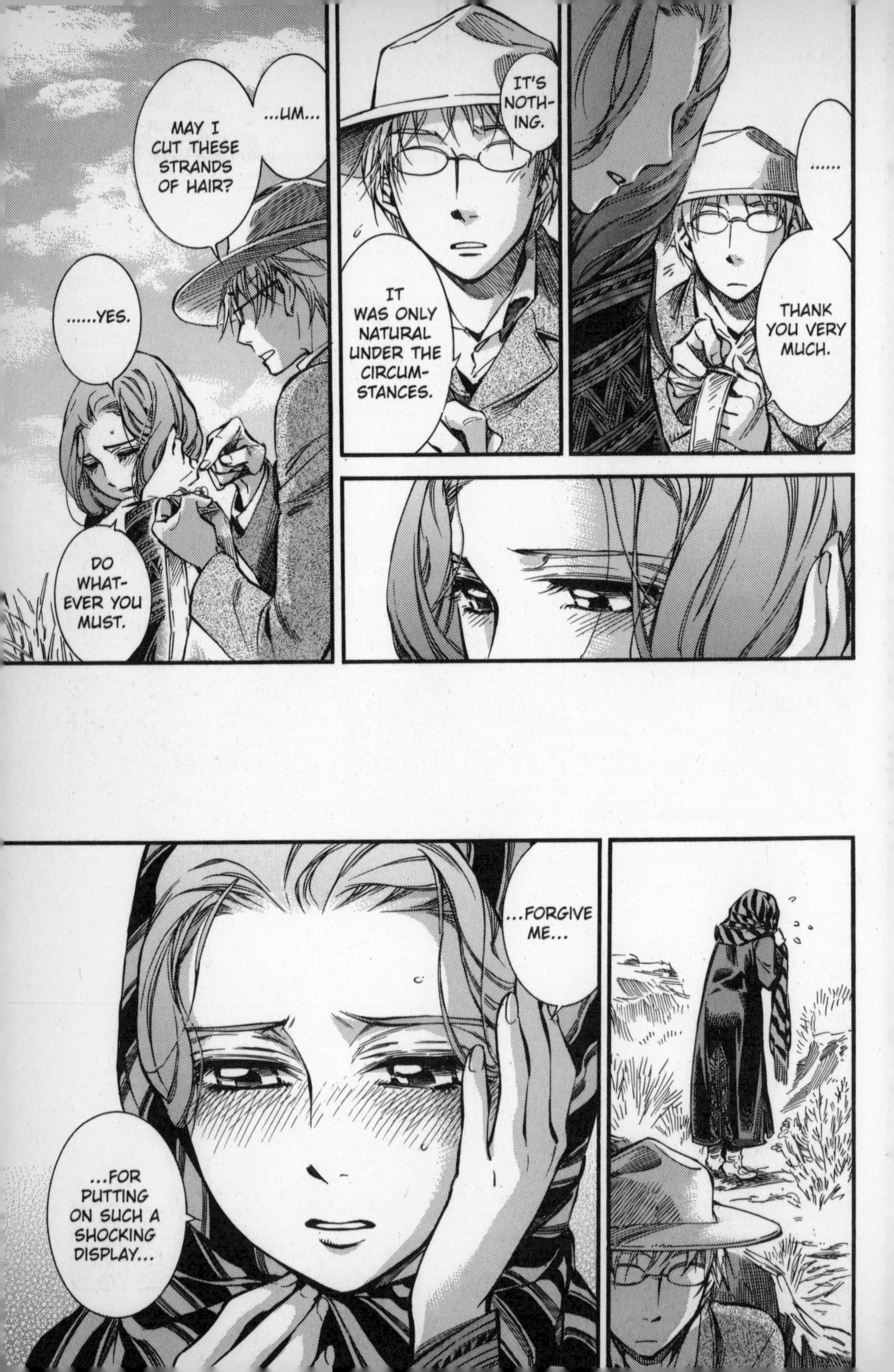
......
THANK YOU VERY MUCH.
IT'S NOTHING.
IT WAS ONLY NATURAL UNDER THE CIRCUMSTANCES.
...UM...
MAY I CUT THESE STRANDS OF HAIR?
......YES.
DO WHATEVER YOU MUST.
...FORGIVE ME...
...FOR PUTTING ON SUCH A SHOCKING DISPLAY...

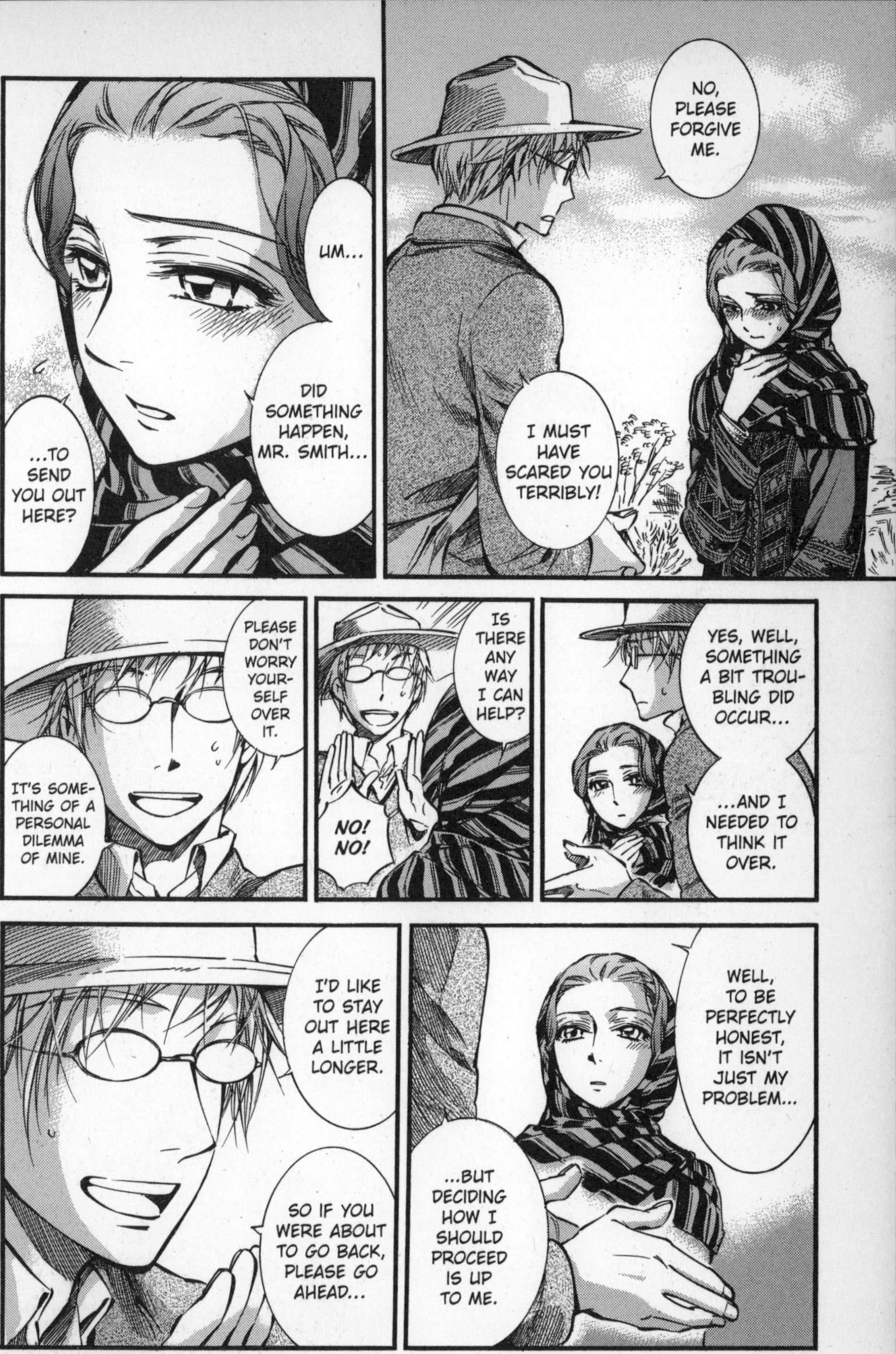
NO, PLEASE FORGIVE ME.
I MUST HAVE SCARED YOU TERRIBLY!
UM...
DID SOMETHING HAPPEN, MR. SMITH...
...TO SEND YOU OUT HERE?
YES, WELL, SOMETHING A BIT TROUBLING DID OCCUR...
...AND I NEEDED TO THINK IT OVER.
IS THERE ANY WAY I CAN HELP?
NO! NO!
PLEASE DON'T WORRY YOURSELF OVER IT.
IT'S SOMETHING OF A PERSONAL DILEMMA OF MINE.
WELL, TO BE PERFECTLY HONEST, IT ISN'T JUST MY PROBLEM...
...BUT DECIDING HOW I SHOULD PROCEED IS UP TO ME.
I'D LIKE TO STAY OUT HERE A LITTLE LONGER.
SO IF YOU WERE ABOUT TO GO BACK, PLEASE GO AHEAD...

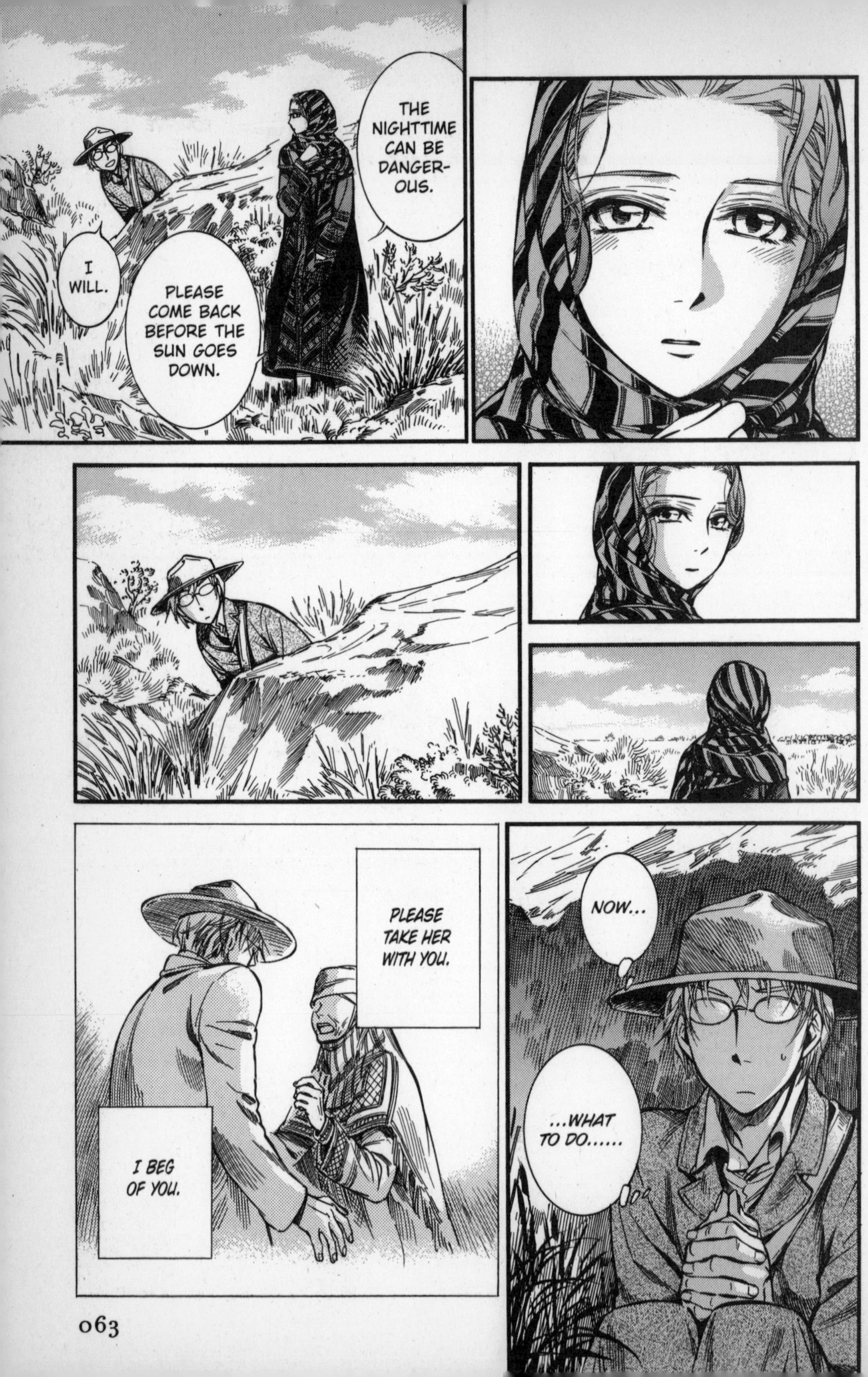
THE NIGHTTIME CAN BE DANGER-OUS.
PLEASE COME BACK BEFORE THE SUN GOES DOWN.
I WILL.
NOW...
...WHAT TO DO......
PLEASE TAKE HER WITH YOU.
I BEG OF YOU.

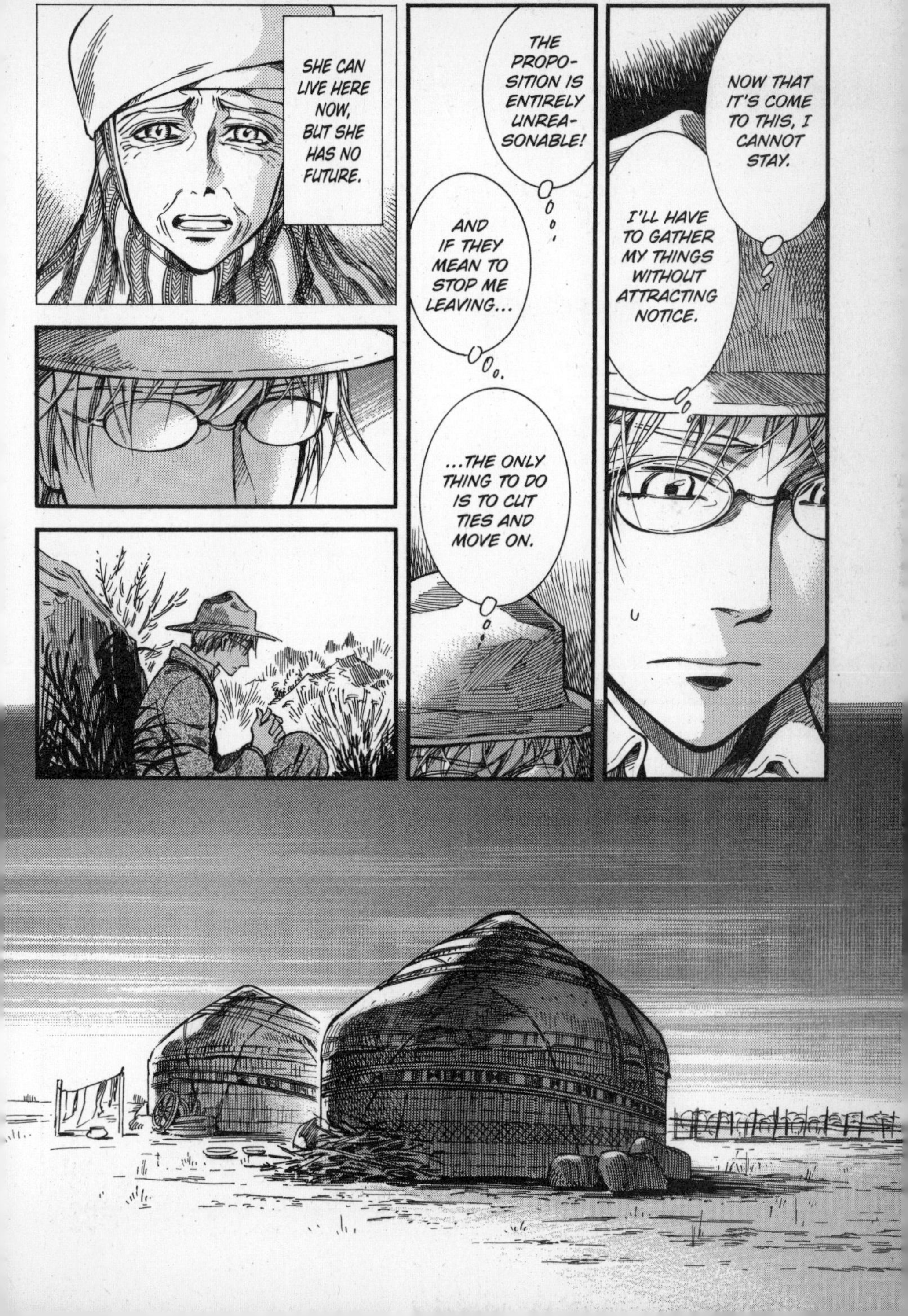
NOW THAT IT'S COME TO THIS, I CANNOT STAY.
I'LL HAVE TO GATHER MY THINGS WITHOUT ATTRACTING NOTICE.
THE PROPO-SITION IS ENTIRELY UNREA-SONABLE!
AND IF THEY MEAN TO STOP ME LEAVING...
...THE ONLY THING TO DO IS TO CUT TIES AND MOVE ON.
SHE CAN LIVE HERE NOW, BUT SHE HAS NO FUTURE.

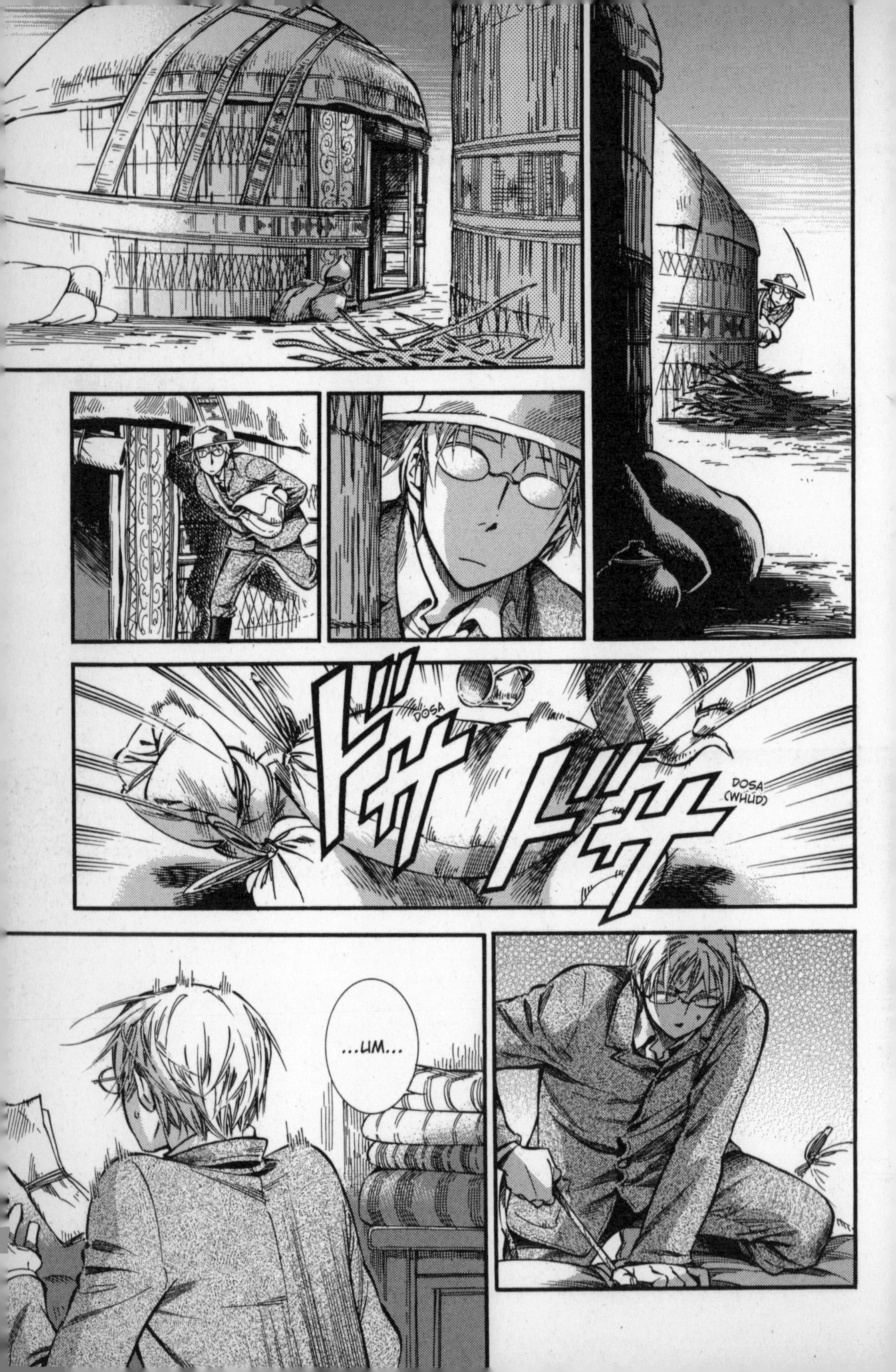
DOSA
DOSA (WHUD)
...UM...

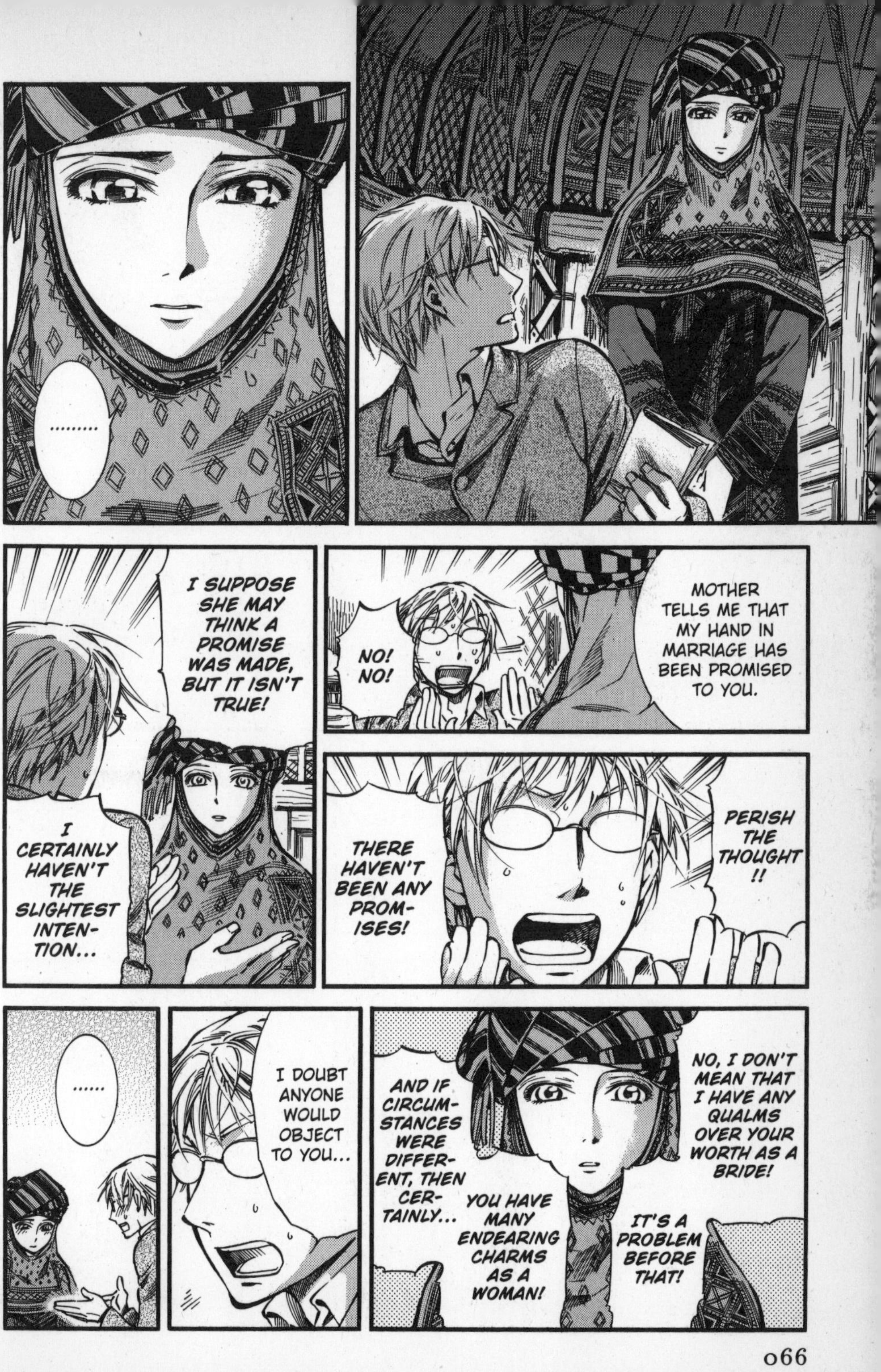
....
MOTHER TELLS ME THAT MY HAND IN MARRIAGE HAS BEEN PROMISED TO YOU.
NO! NO!
PERISH THE THOUGHT!!
THERE HAVEN'T BEEN ANY PROM-ISES!
I SUPPOSE SHE MAY THINK A PROMISE WAS MADE, BUT IT ISN'T TRUE!
I CERTAINLY HAVEN'T THE SLIGHTEST INTEN-TION...
NO, I DON'T MEAN THAT I HAVE ANY QUALMS OVER YOUR WORTH AS A BRIDE!
AND IF CIRCUM-STANCES WERE DIFFER-ENT, THEN CER-TAINLY...
IT'S A PROBLEM BEFORE THAT!
YOU HAVE MANY ENDEARING CHARMS AS A WOMAN!
I DOUBT ANYONE WOULD OBJECT TO YOU...
......

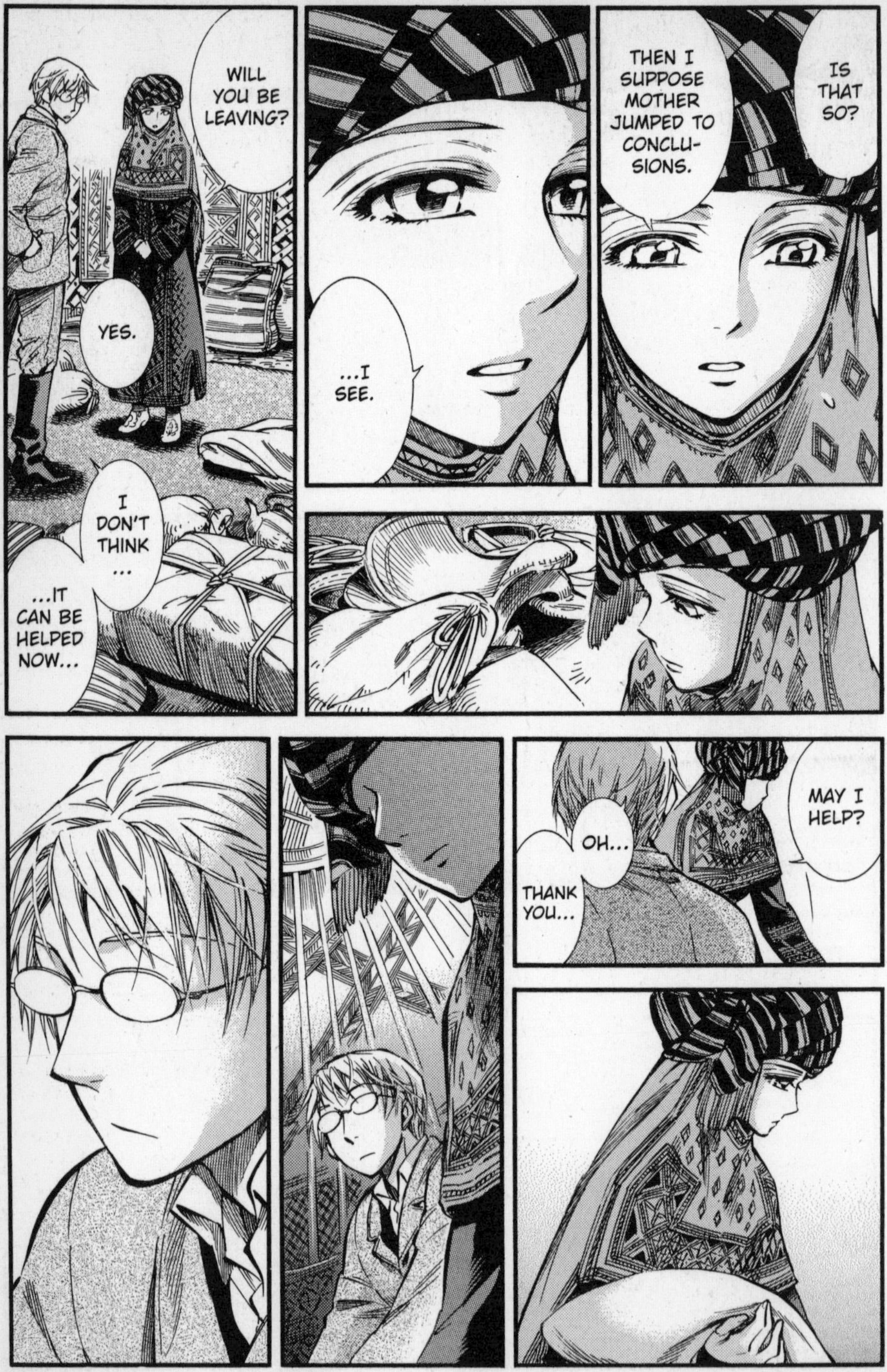
IS THAT SO?
THEN I SUPPOSE MOTHER JUMPED TO CONCLUSIONS.
...I SEE.
WILL YOU BE LEAVING?
YES.
I DON'T THINK...
...IT CAN BE HELPED NOW...
MAY I HELP?
OH...
THANK YOU...

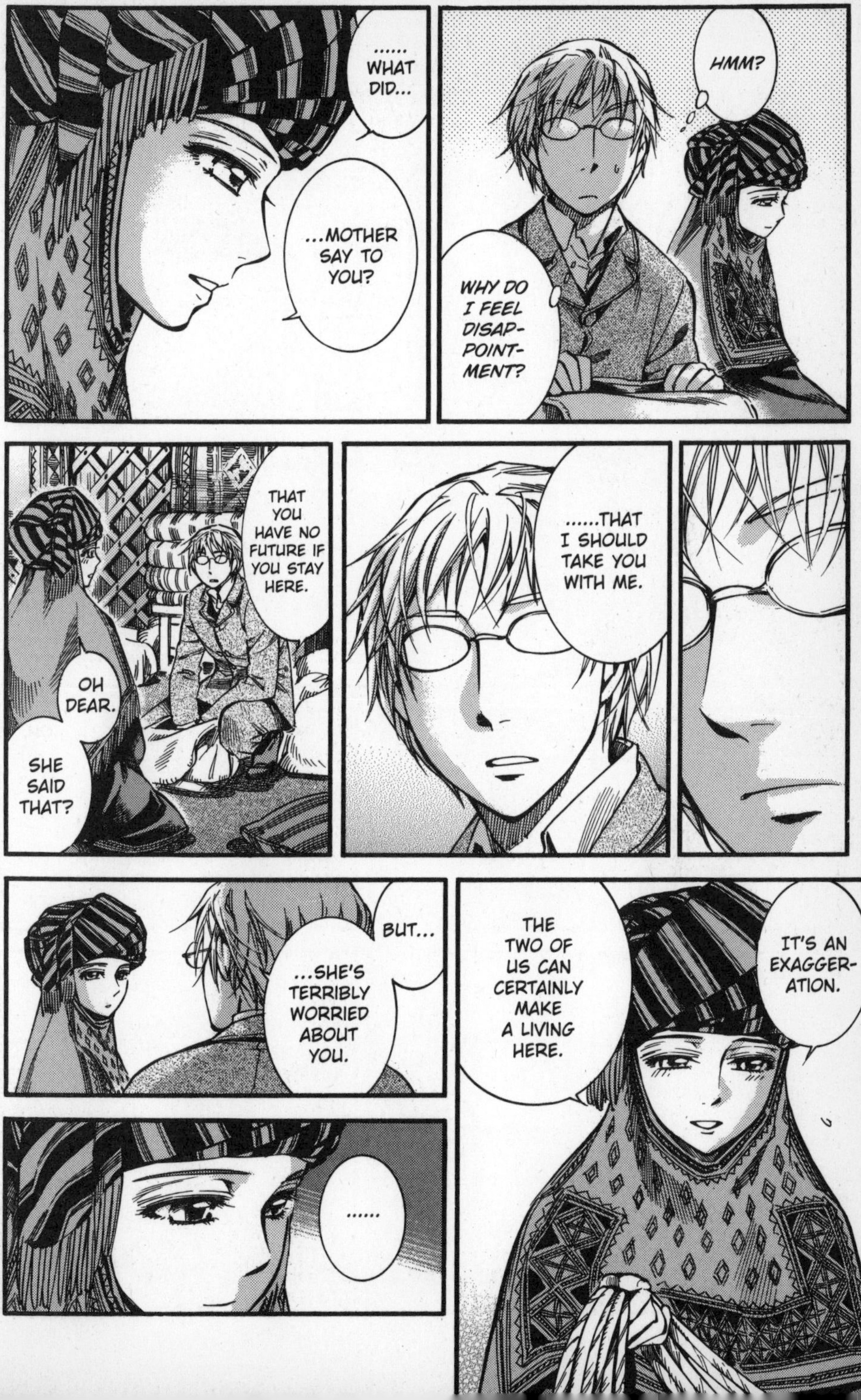
HMM?
WHY DO I FEEL DISAP-POINT-MENT?
......WHAT DID...
...MOTHER SAY TO YOU?
......THAT I SHOULD TAKE YOU WITH ME.
THAT YOU HAVE NO FUTURE IF YOU STAY HERE.
OH DEAR.
SHE SAID THAT?
IT'S AN EXAGGER-ATION.
THE TWO OF US CAN CERTAINLY MAKE A LIVING HERE.
BUT...
...SHE'S TERRIBLY WORRIED ABOUT YOU.
......

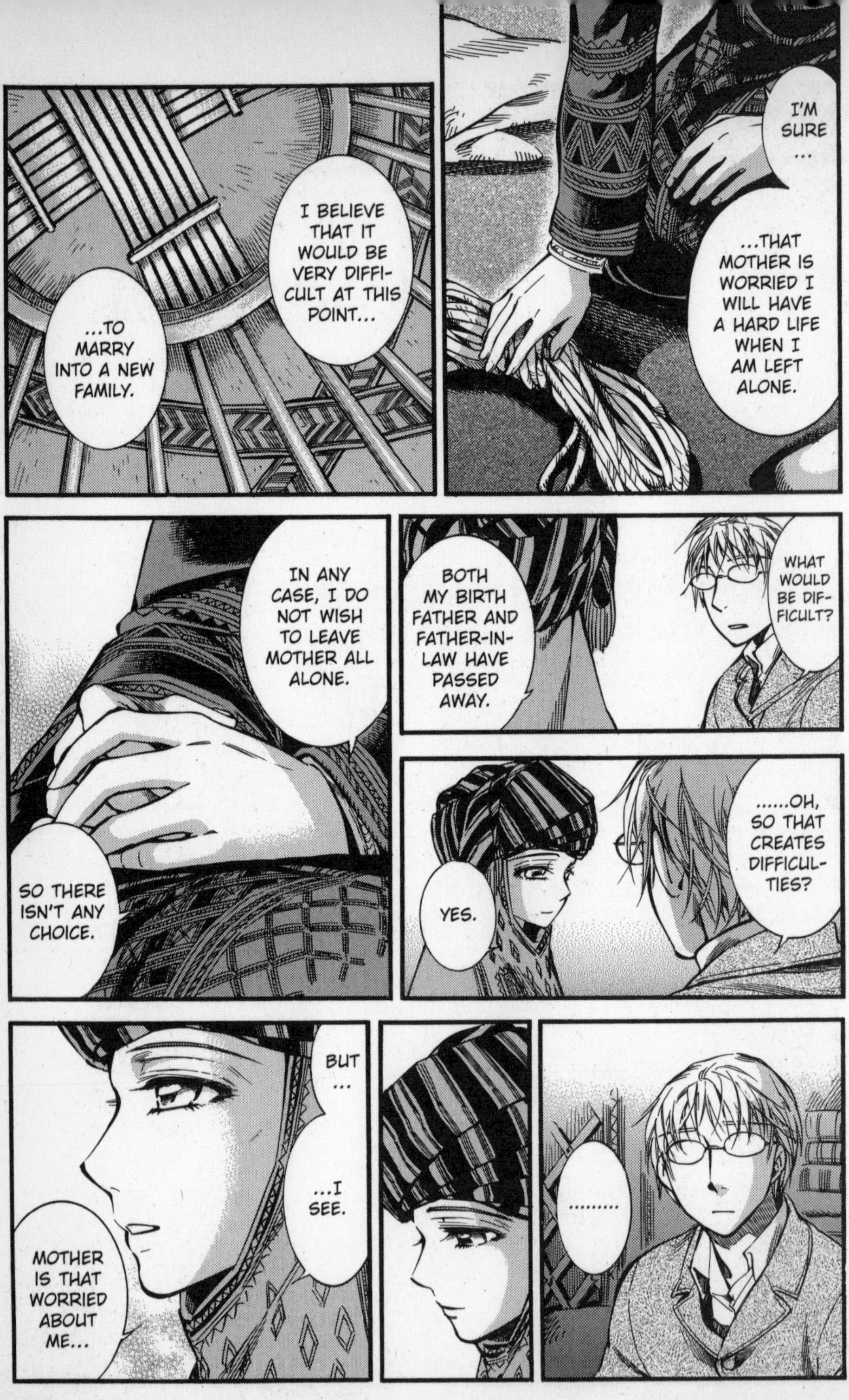
I'M SURE...
...THAT MOTHER IS WORRIED I WILL HAVE A HARD LIFE WHEN I AM LEFT ALONE.
I BELIEVE THAT IT WOULD BE VERY DIFFICULT AT THIS POINT...
...TO MARRY INTO A NEW FAMILY.
WHAT WOULD BE DIFFICULT?
BOTH MY BIRTH FATHER AND FATHER-IN-LAW HAVE PASSED AWAY.
......OH, SO THAT CREATES DIFFICULTIES?
YES.
IN ANY CASE, I DO NOT WISH TO LEAVE MOTHER ALL ALONE.
SO THERE ISN'T ANY CHOICE.
....
...I SEE.
BUT...
MOTHER IS THAT WORRIED ABOUT ME...

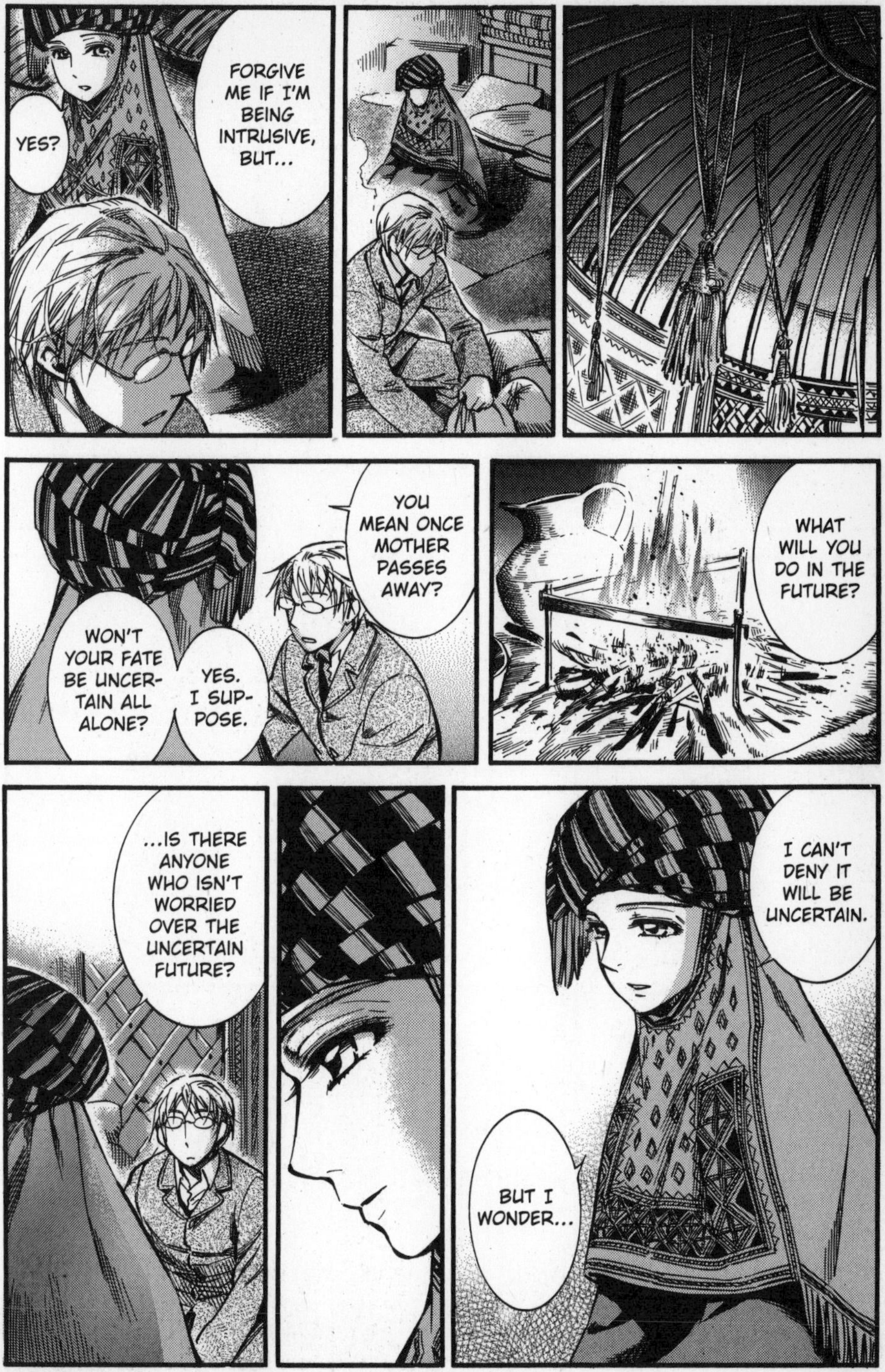
FORGIVE ME IF I'M BEING INTRUSIVE, BUT...
YES?
WHAT WILL YOU DO IN THE FUTURE?
YOU MEAN ONCE MOTHER PASSES AWAY?
YES. I SUPPOSE.
WON'T YOUR FATE BE UNCERTAIN ALL ALONE?
I CAN'T DENY IT WILL BE UNCERTAIN.
BUT I WONDER...
...IS THERE ANYONE WHO ISN'T WORRIED OVER THE UNCERTAIN FUTURE?

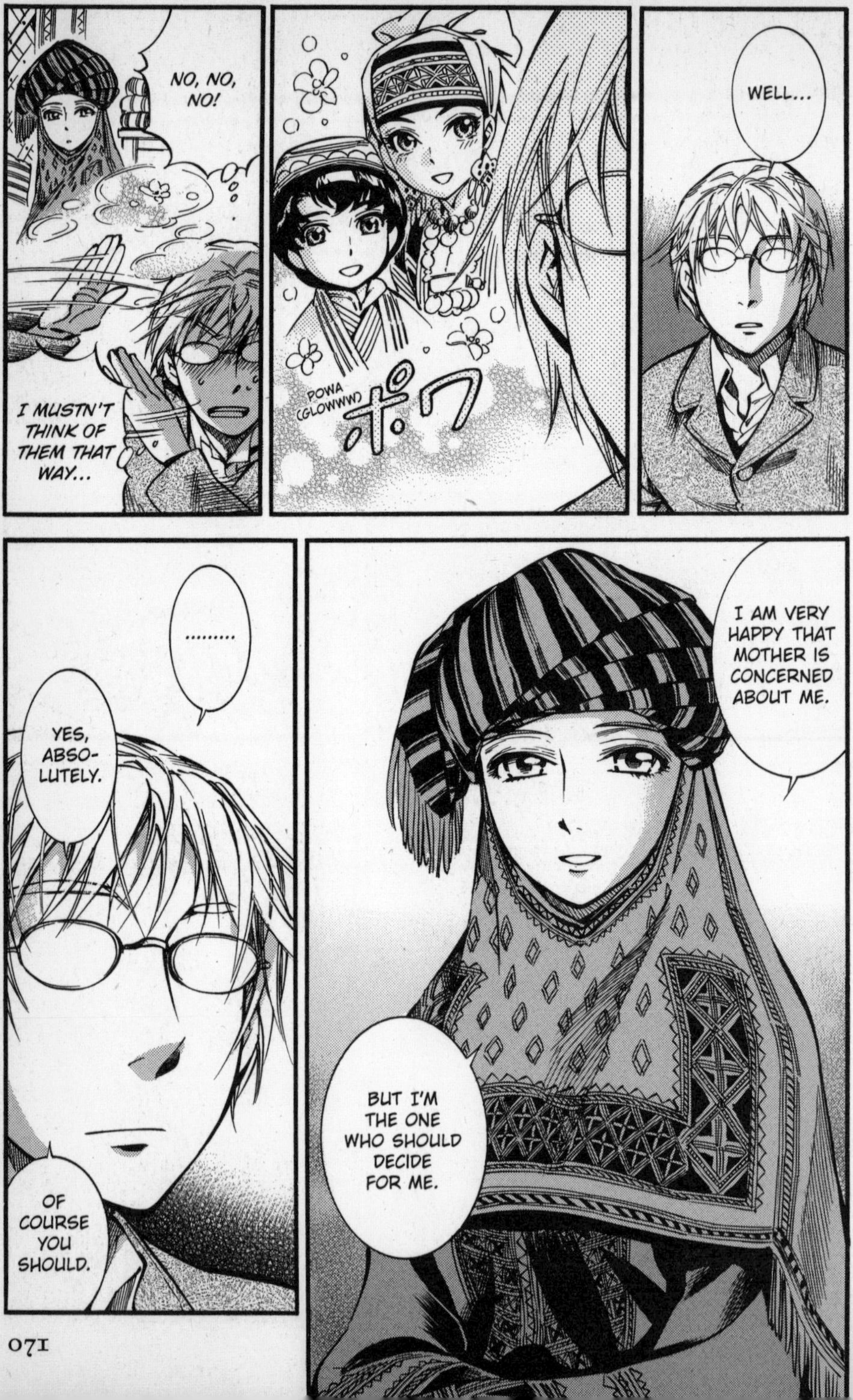
WELL...
POWA (GLOWWW)
ポワ
NO, NO, NO!
I MUSTN'T THINK OF THEM THAT WAY...
I AM VERY HAPPY THAT MOTHER IS CONCERNED ABOUT ME.
BUT I'M THE ONE WHO SHOULD DECIDE FOR ME.
....
YES, ABSOLUTELY.
OF COURSE YOU SHOULD.

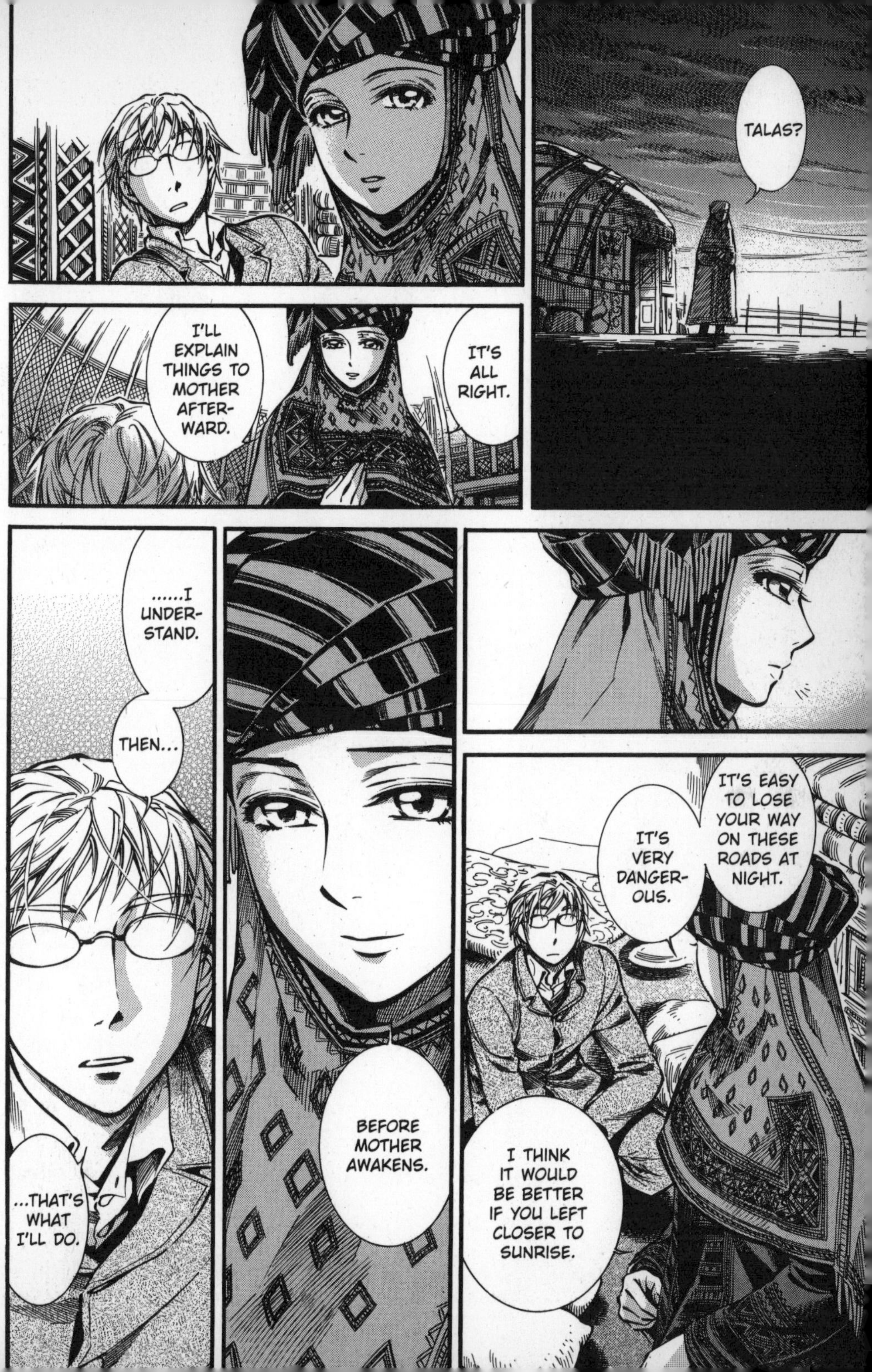
TALAS?
IT'S ALL RIGHT.
I'LL EXPLAIN THINGS TO MOTHER AFTER-WARD.
IT'S EASY TO LOSE YOUR WAY ON THESE ROADS AT NIGHT.
IT'S VERY DANGER-OUS.
I THINK IT WOULD BE BETTER IF YOU LEFT CLOSER TO SUNRISE.
BEFORE MOTHER AWAKENS.
......I UNDER-STAND.
THEN...
...THAT'S WHAT I'LL DO.

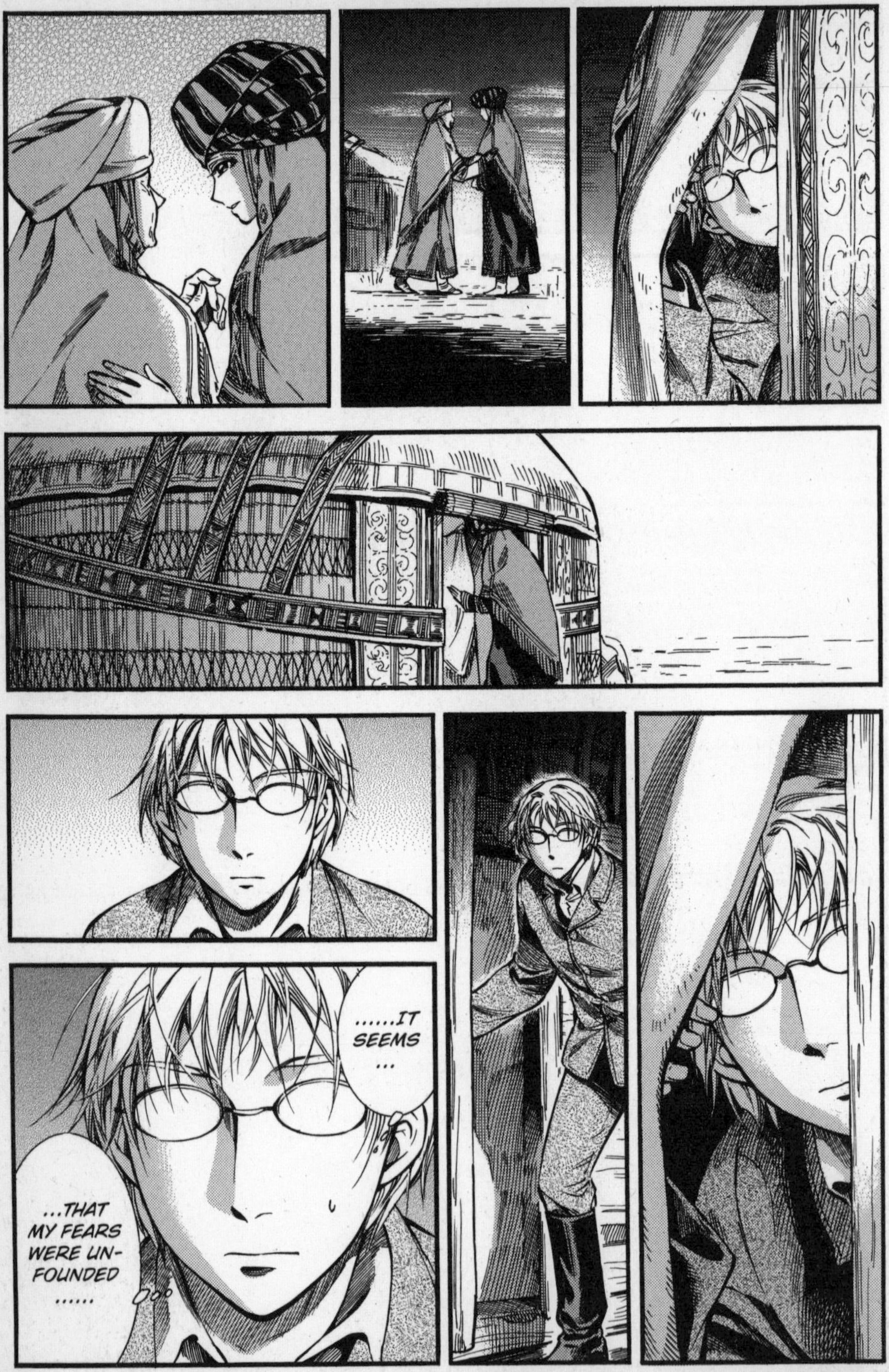
......IT SEEMS ...
...THAT MY FEARS WERE UN-FOUNDED ......

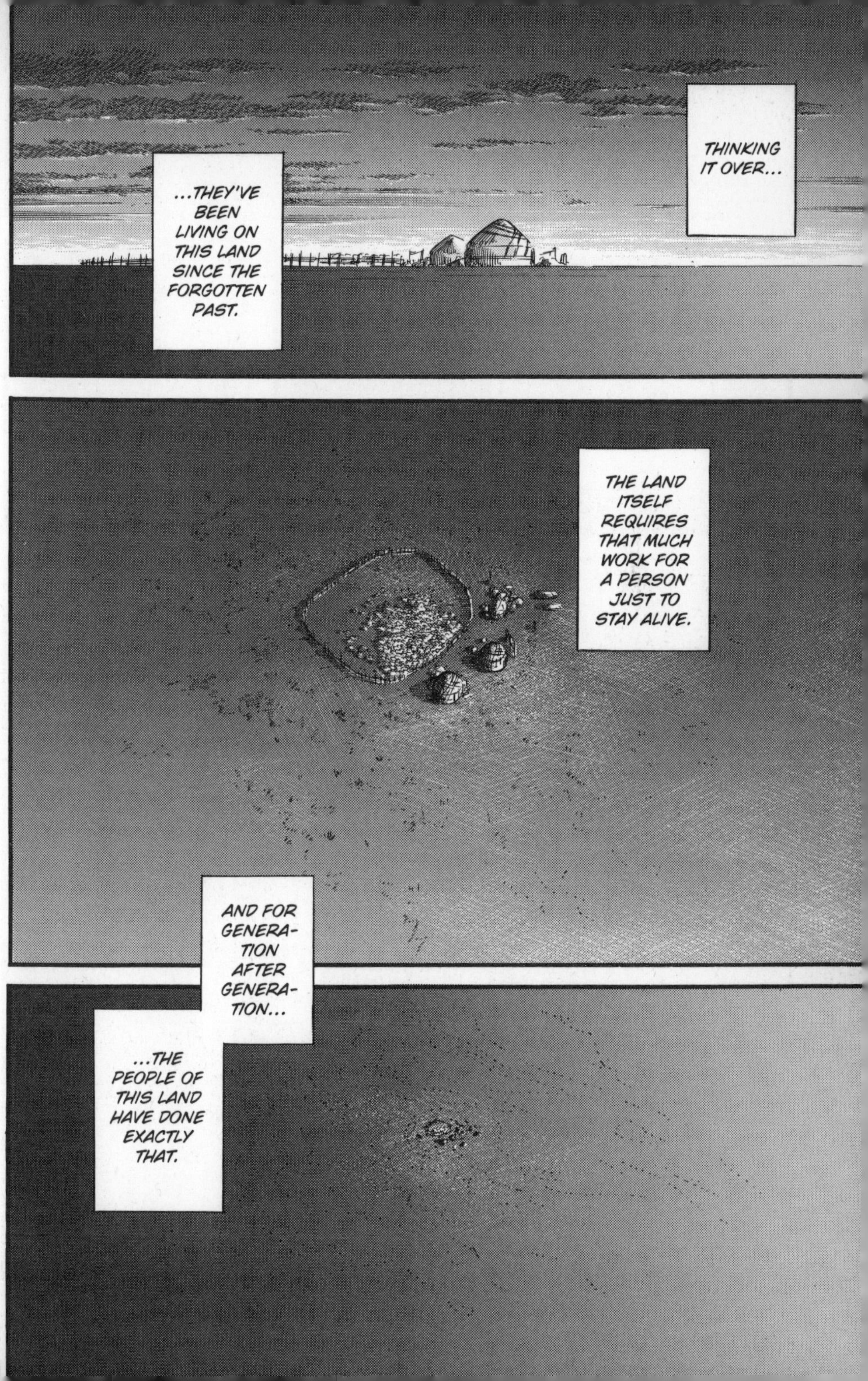
THINKING IT OVER...
...THEY'VE BEEN LIVING ON THIS LAND SINCE THE FORGOTTEN PAST.
THE LAND ITSELF REQUIRES THAT MUCH WORK FOR A PERSON JUST TO STAY ALIVE.
AND FOR GENERATION AFTER GENERATION...
...THE PEOPLE OF THIS LAND HAVE DONE EXACTLY THAT.

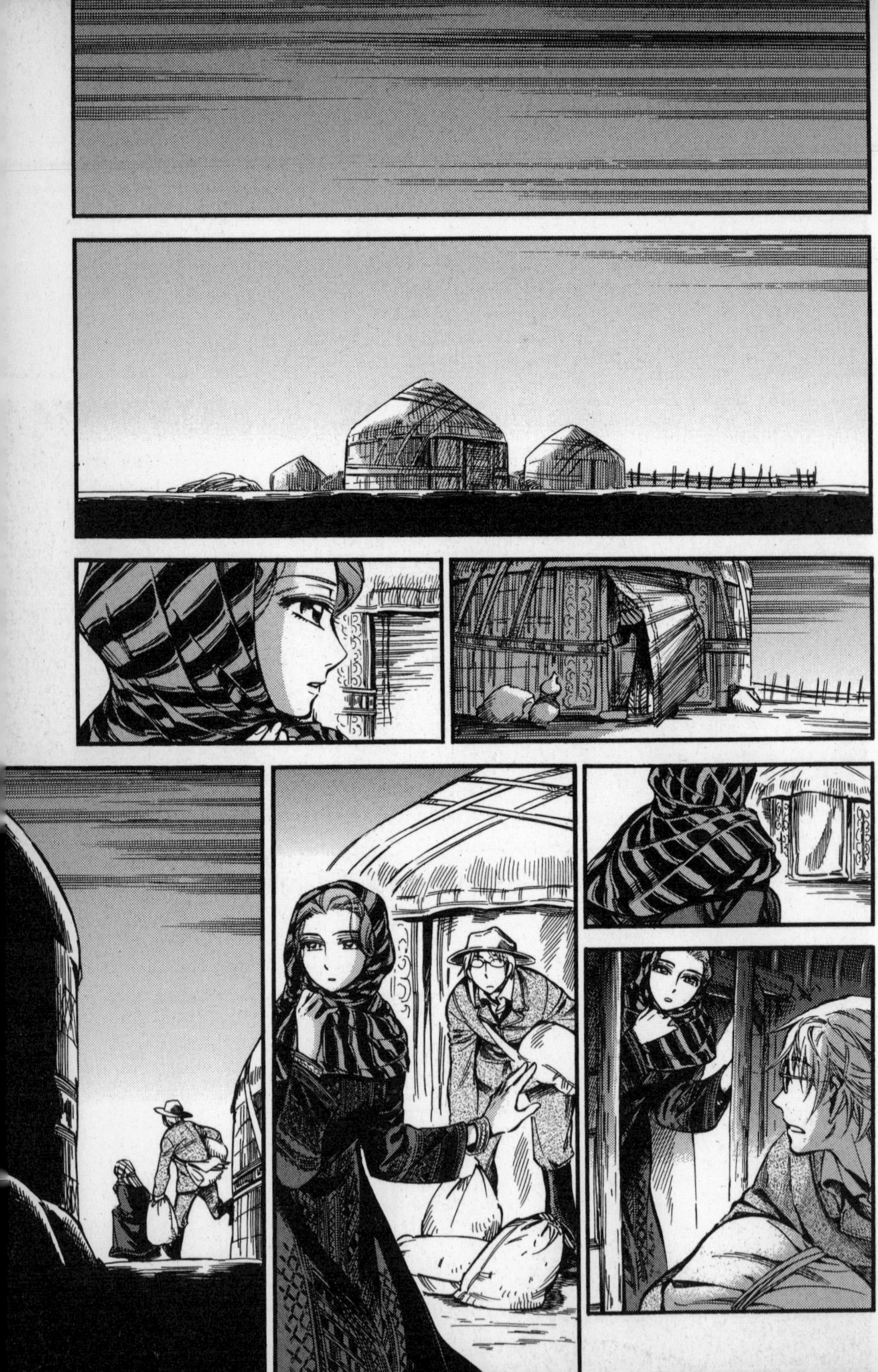

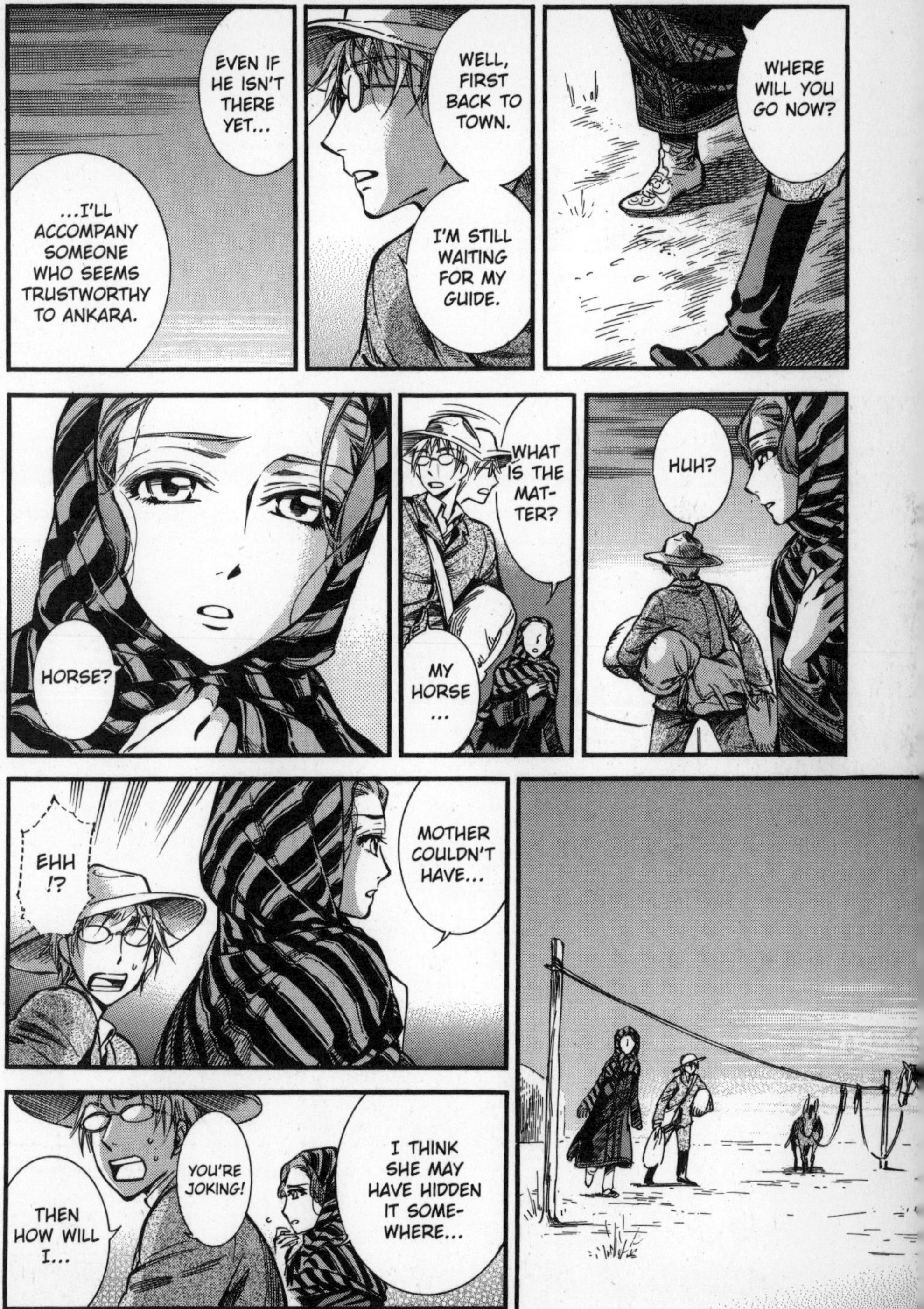
WHERE WILL YOU GO NOW?
WELL, FIRST BACK TO TOWN.
I'M STILL WAITING FOR MY GUIDE.
EVEN IF HE ISN'T THERE YET...
...I'LL ACCOMPANY SOMEONE WHO SEEMS TRUSTWORTHY TO ANKARA.
HUH?
WHAT IS THE MAT-TER?
MY HORSE...
HORSE?
MOTHER COULDN'T HAVE...
EHH!?
I THINK SHE MAY HAVE HIDDEN IT SOME-WHERE...
YOU'RE JOKING!
THEN HOW WILL I...

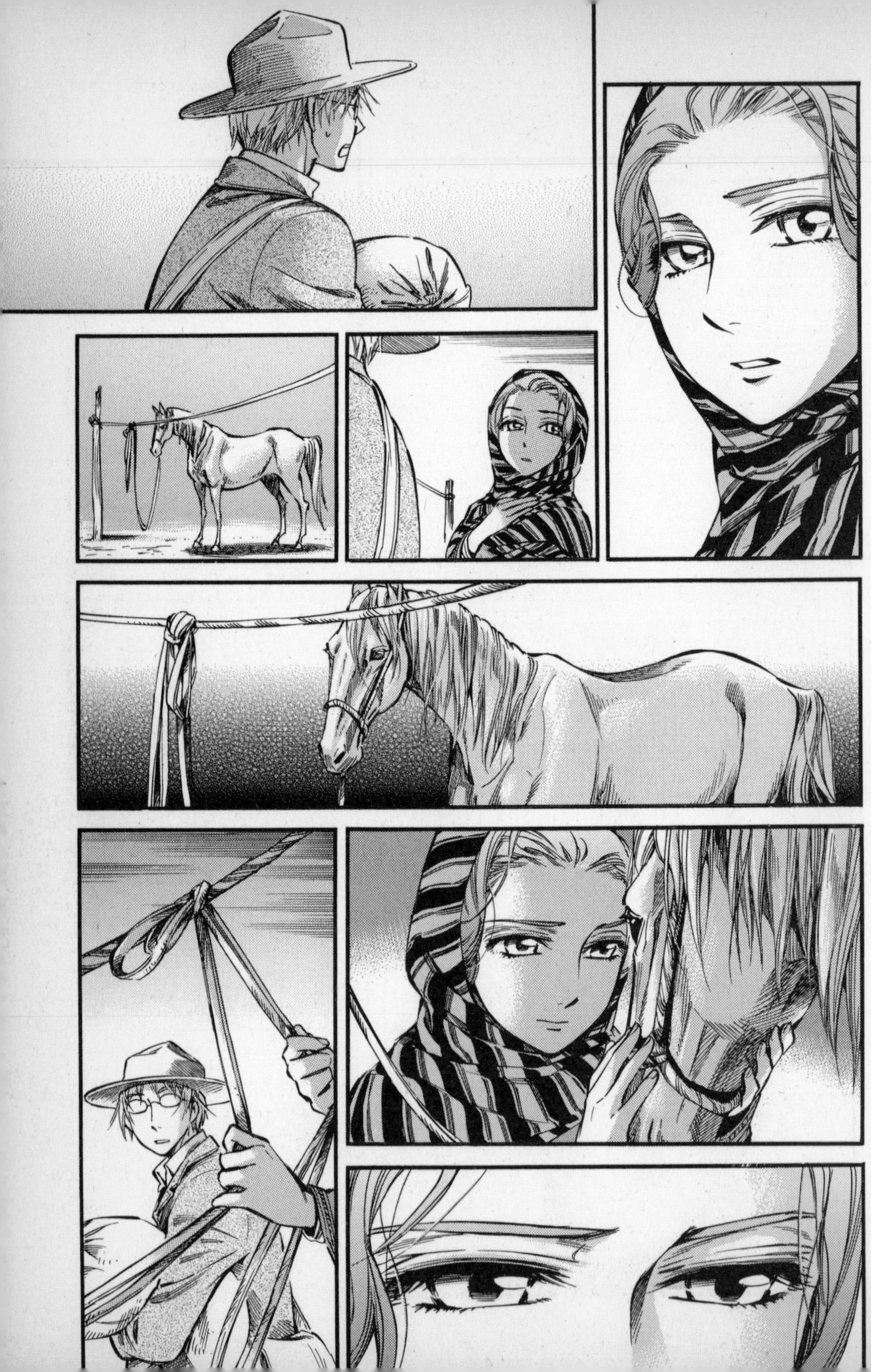

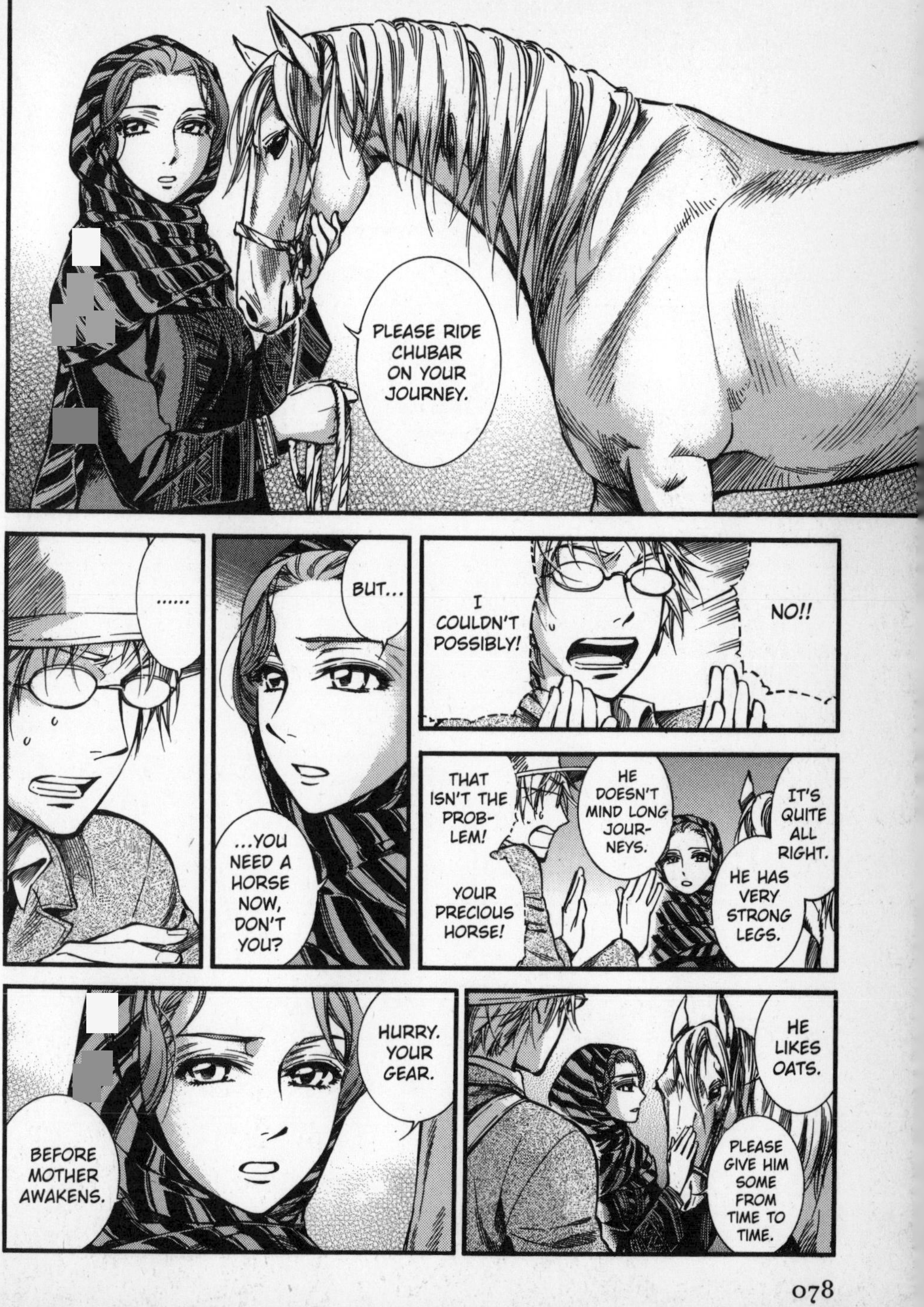
PLEASE RIDE CHUBAR ON YOUR JOURNEY.
NO!!
I COULDN'T POSSIBLY!
IT'S QUITE ALL RIGHT.
HE HAS VERY STRONG LEGS.
HE DOESN'T MIND LONG JOUR-NEYS.
THAT ISN'T THE PROB-LEM!
YOUR PRECIOUS HORSE!
BUT...
...YOU NEED A HORSE NOW, DON'T YOU?
......
HE LIKES OATS.
PLEASE GIVE HIM SOME FROM TIME TO TIME.
HURRY. YOUR GEAR.
BEFORE MOTHER AWAKENS.

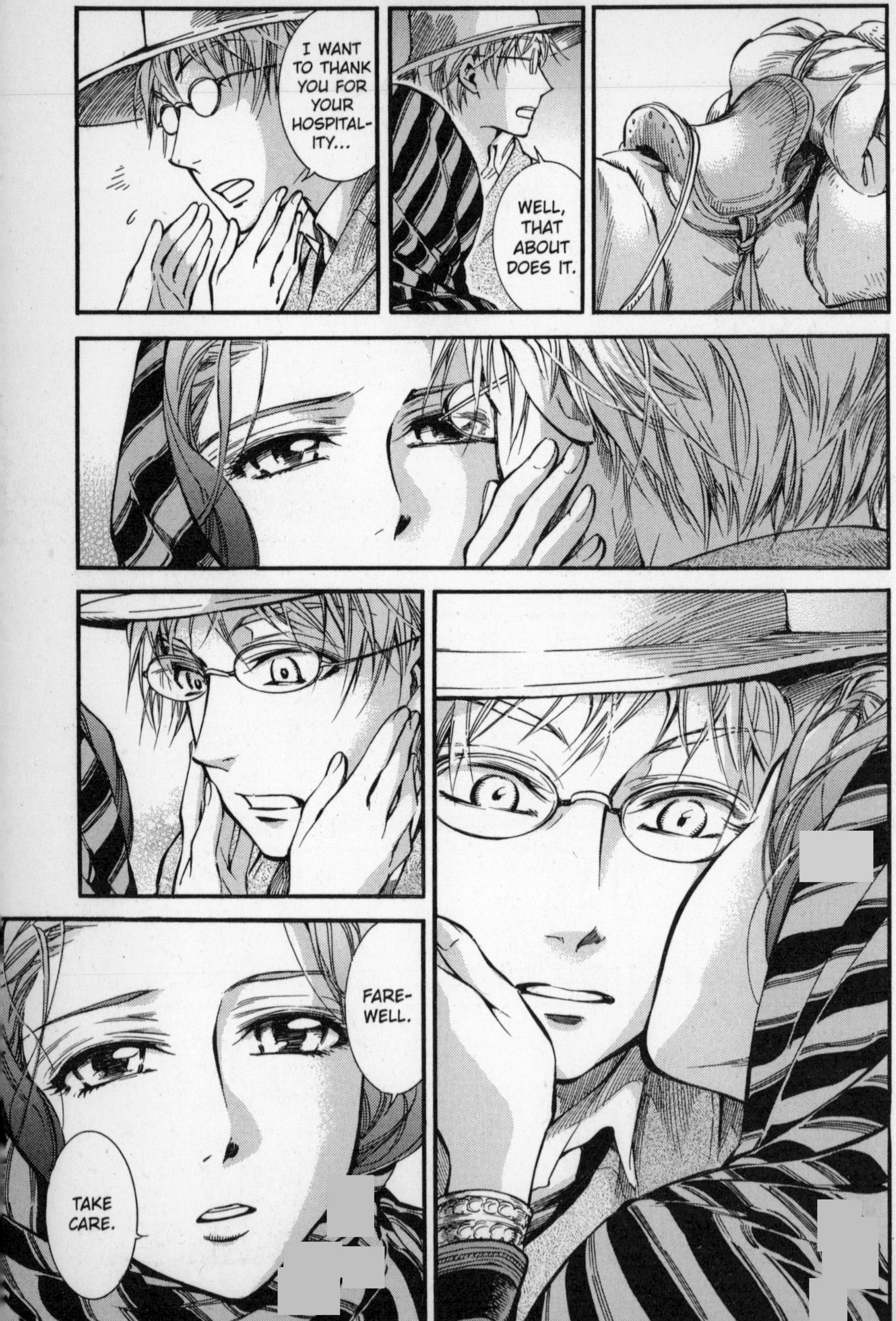
WELL, THAT ABOUT DOES IT.
I WANT TO THANK YOU FOR YOUR HOSPITALITY...
FARE-WELL.
TAKE CARE.

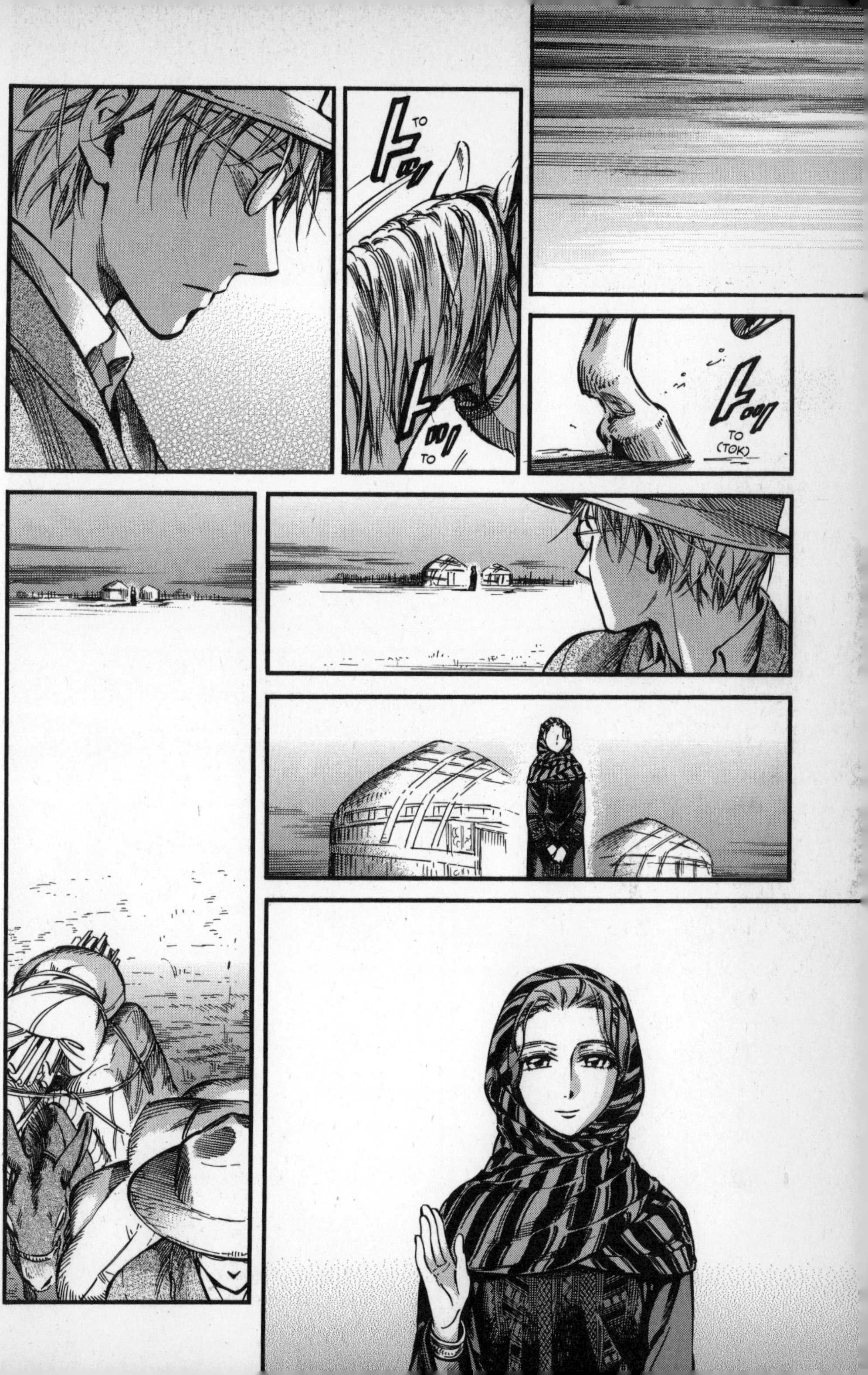
TO
(TOK)
TO
TO

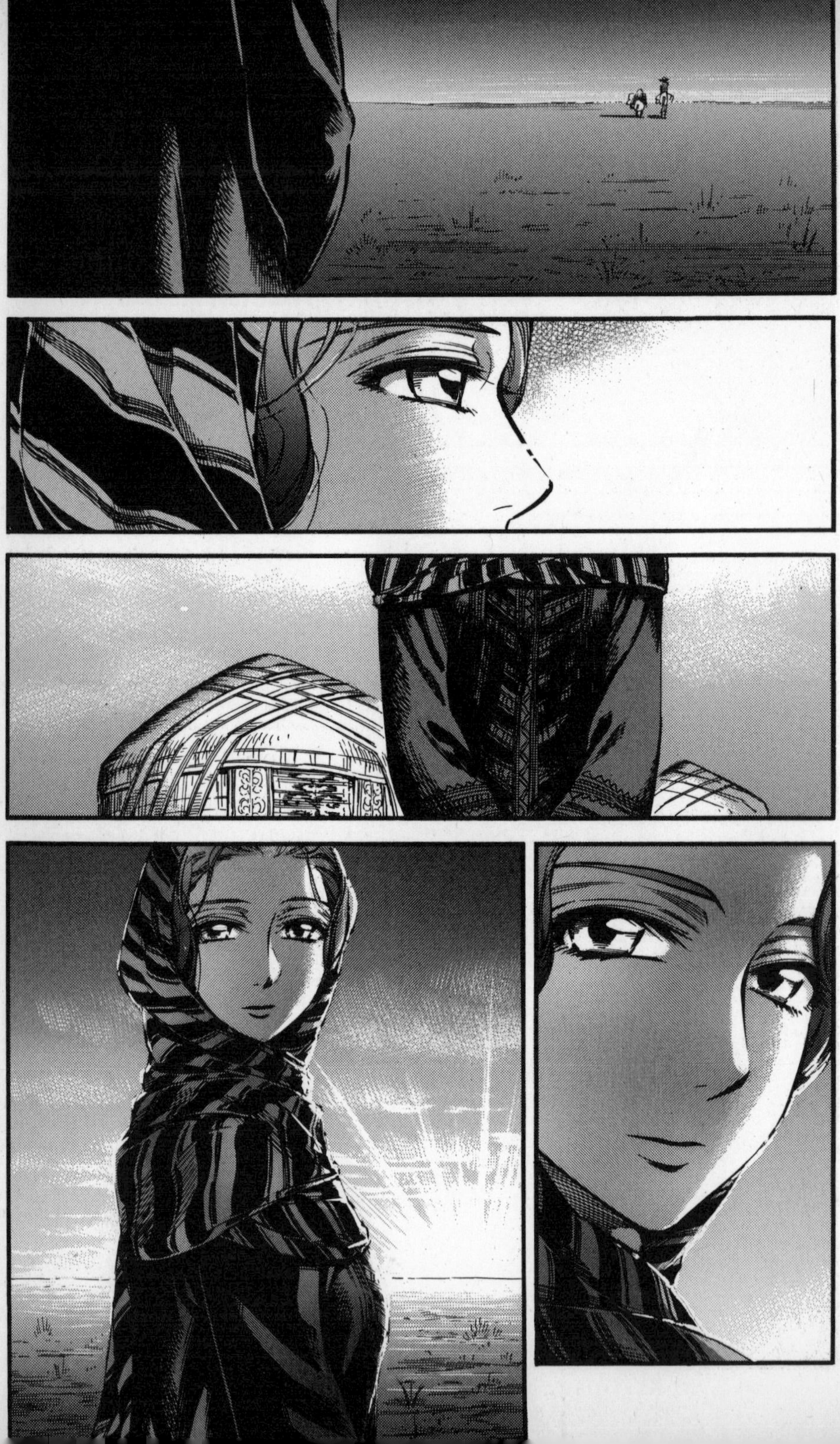

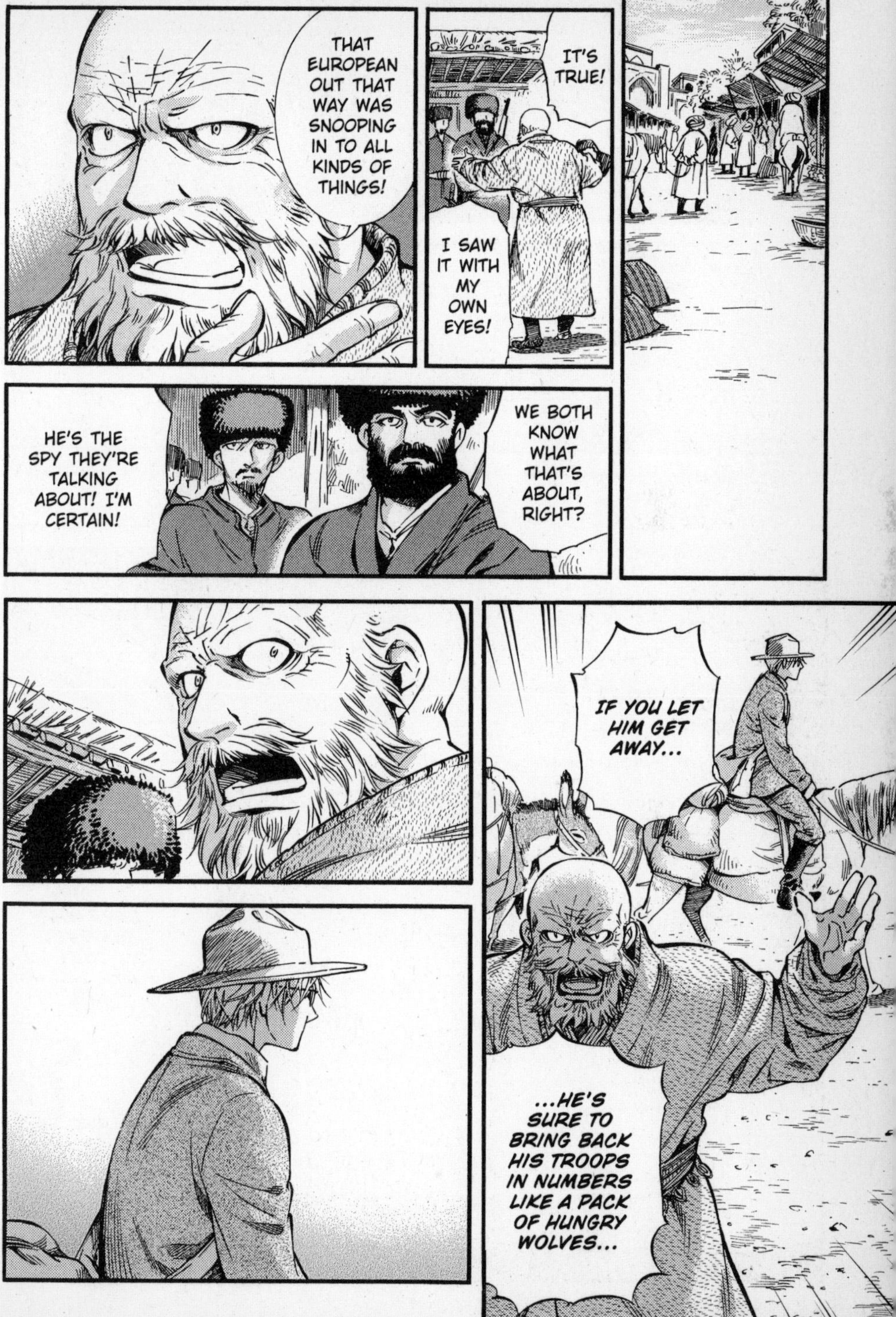
IT'S TRUE!
I SAW IT WITH MY OWN EYES!
THAT EUROPEAN OUT THAT WAY WAS SNOOPING IN TO ALL KINDS OF THINGS!
WE BOTH KNOW WHAT THAT'S ABOUT, RIGHT?
HE'S THE SPY THEY'RE TALKING ABOUT! I'M CERTAIN!
IF YOU LET HIM GET AWAY...
...HE'S SURE TO BRING BACK HIS TROOPS IN NUMBERS LIKE A PACK OF HUNGRY WOLVES...

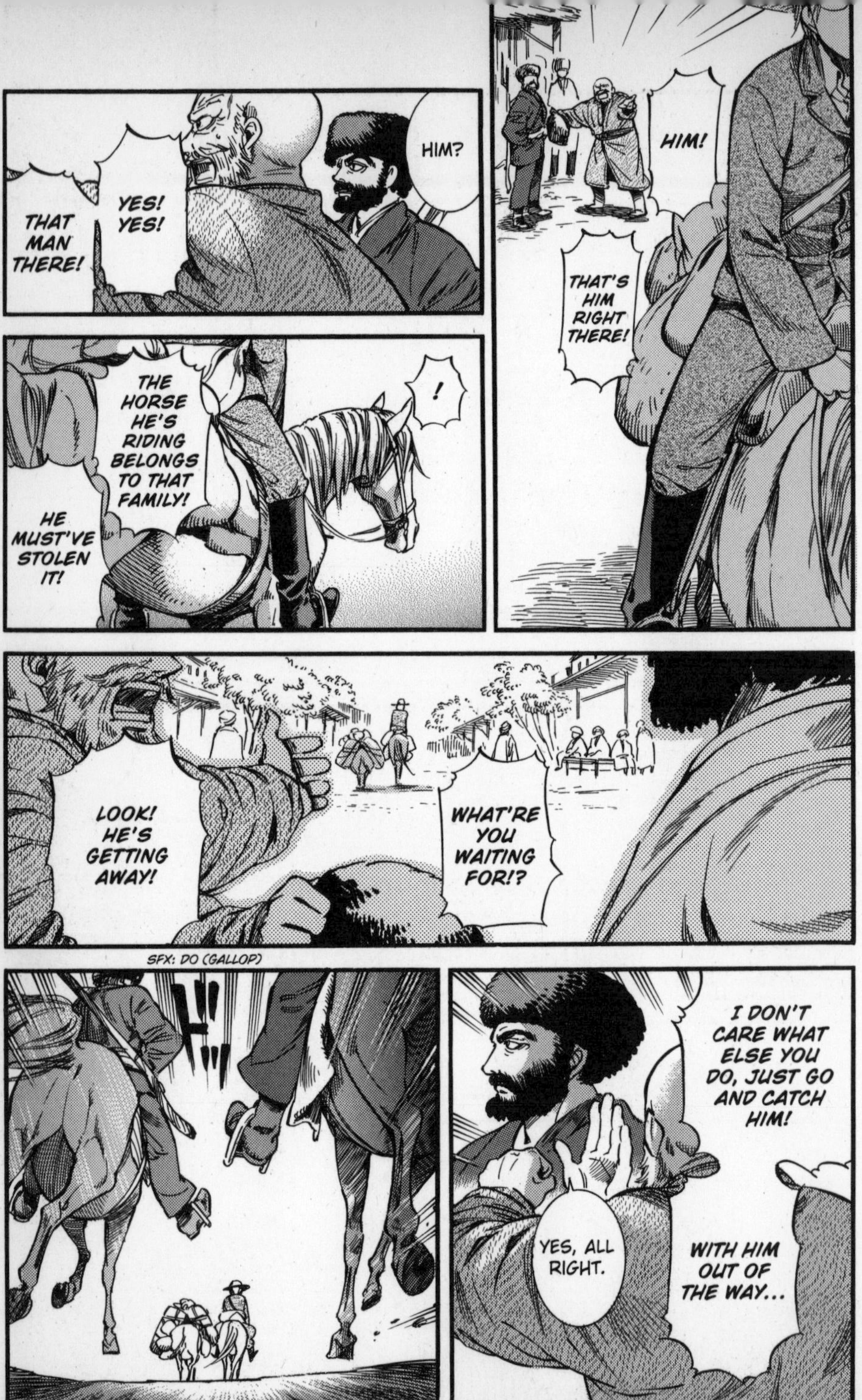
HIM!
THAT'S HIM RIGHT THERE!
HIM?
YES! YES!
THAT MAN THERE!
!
THE HORSE HE'S RIDING BELONGS TO THAT FAMILY!
HE MUST'VE STOLEN IT!
WHAT'RE YOU WAITING FOR!?
LOOK! HE'S GETTING AWAY!
I DON'T CARE WHAT ELSE YOU DO, JUST GO AND CATCH HIM!
YES, ALL RIGHT.
WITH HIM OUT OF THE WAY...
SFX: DO (GALLOP)

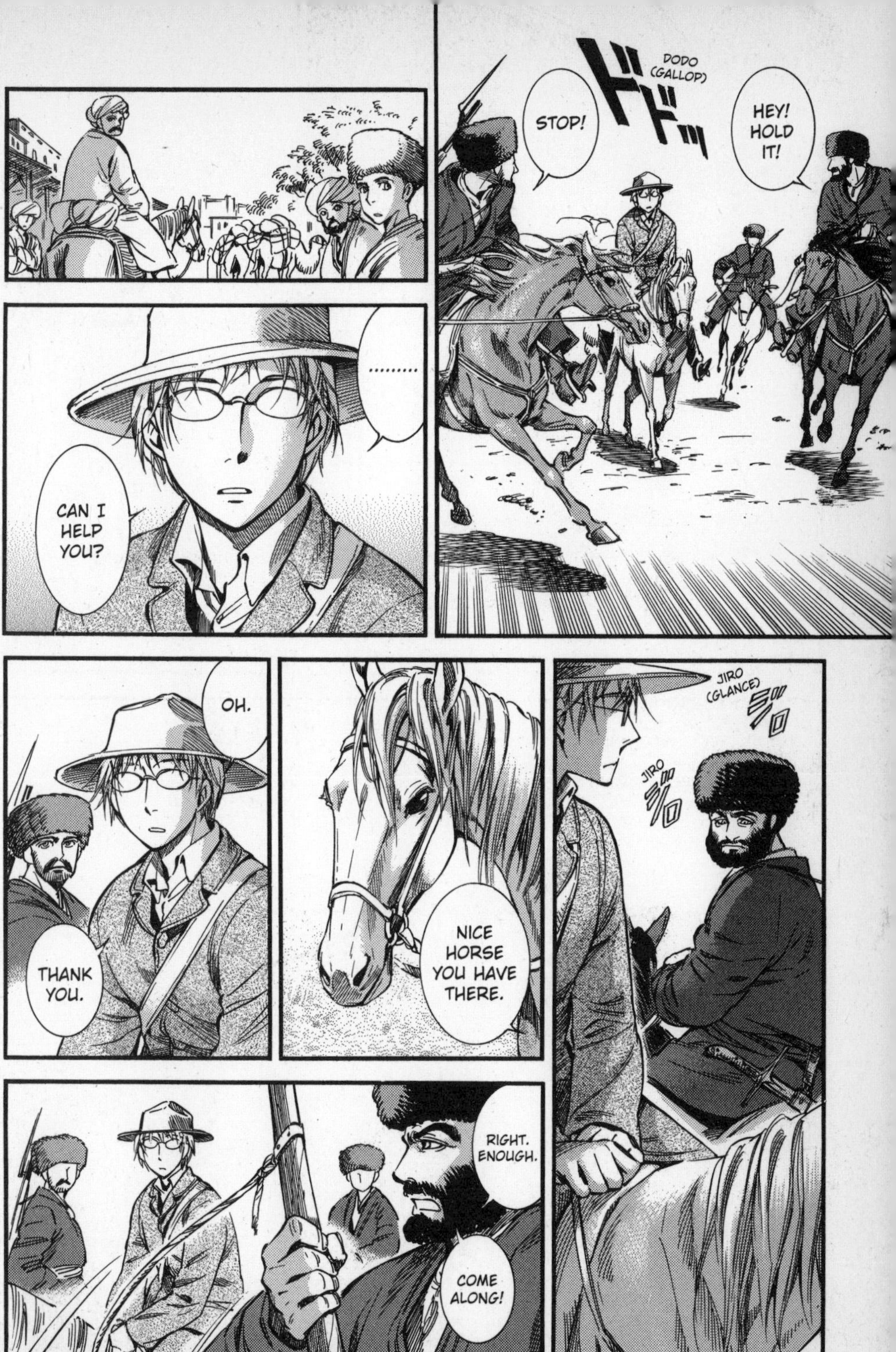
DODO (GALLOP)
HEY! HOLD IT!
STOP!
....
CAN I HELP YOU?
JIRO (GLANCE)
JIRO
NICE HORSE YOU HAVE THERE.
OH.
THANK YOU.
RIGHT. ENOUGH.
COME ALONG!

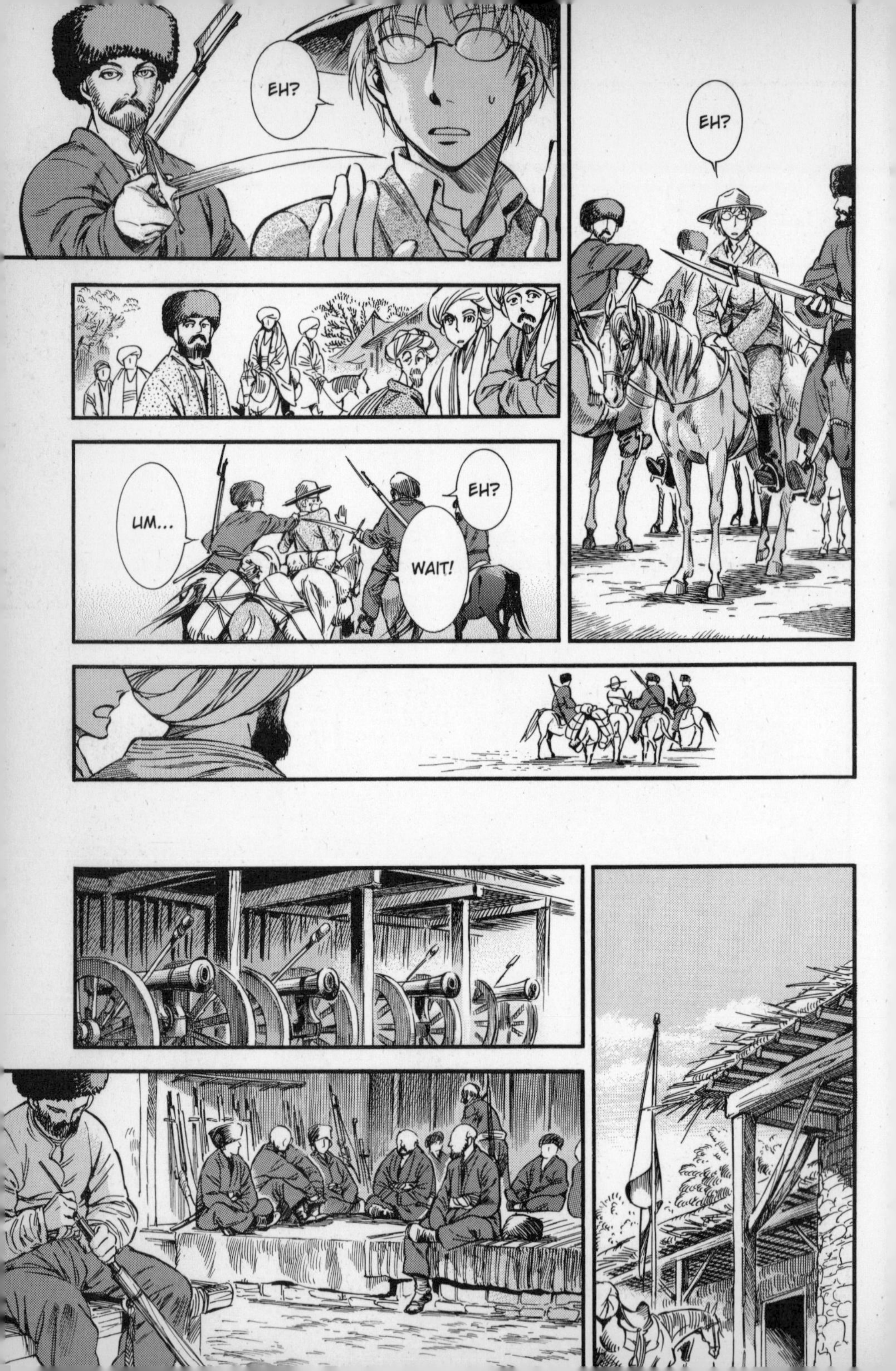
EH?
EH?
EH?
WAIT!
UM...

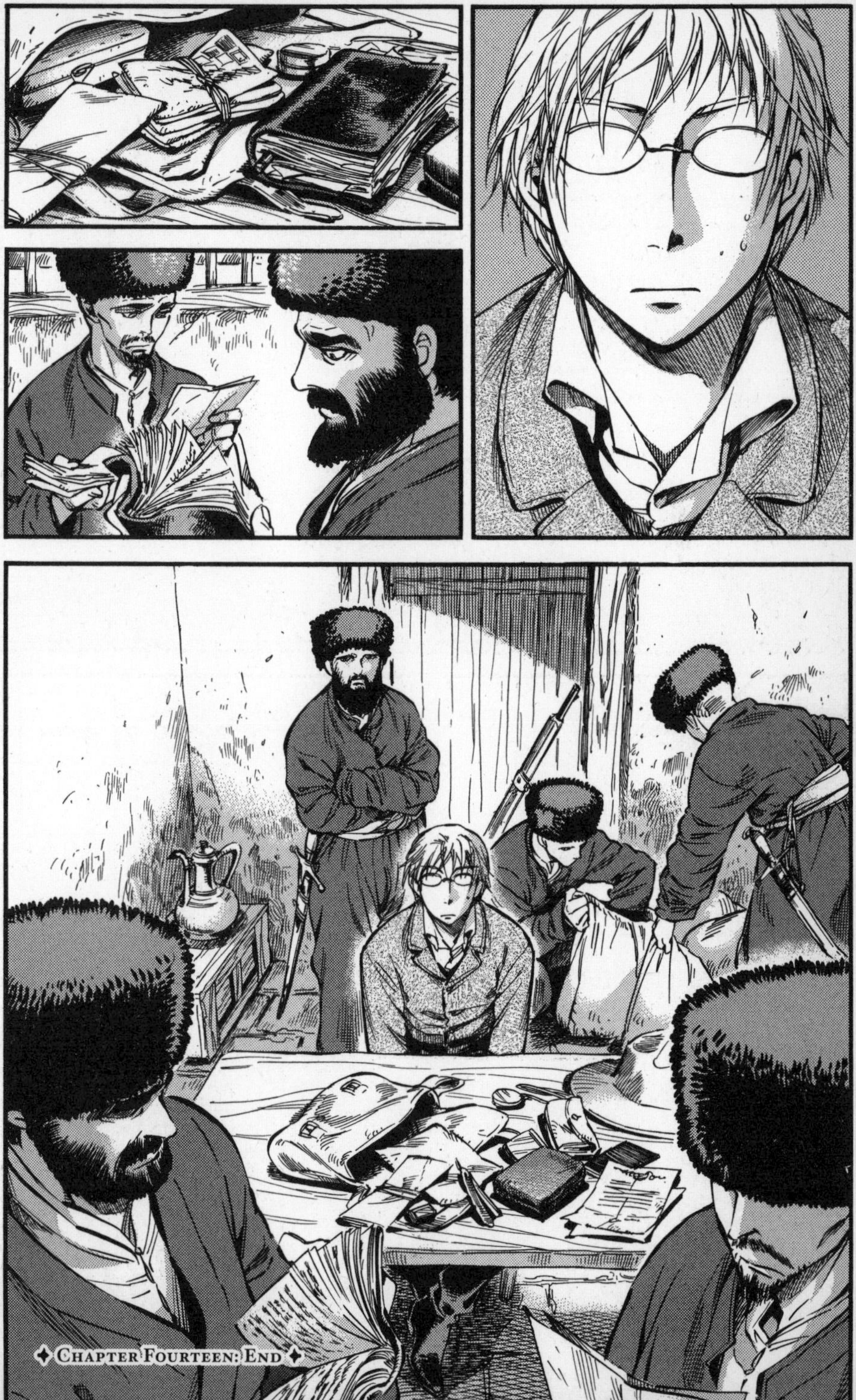
CHAPTER FOURTEEN: END

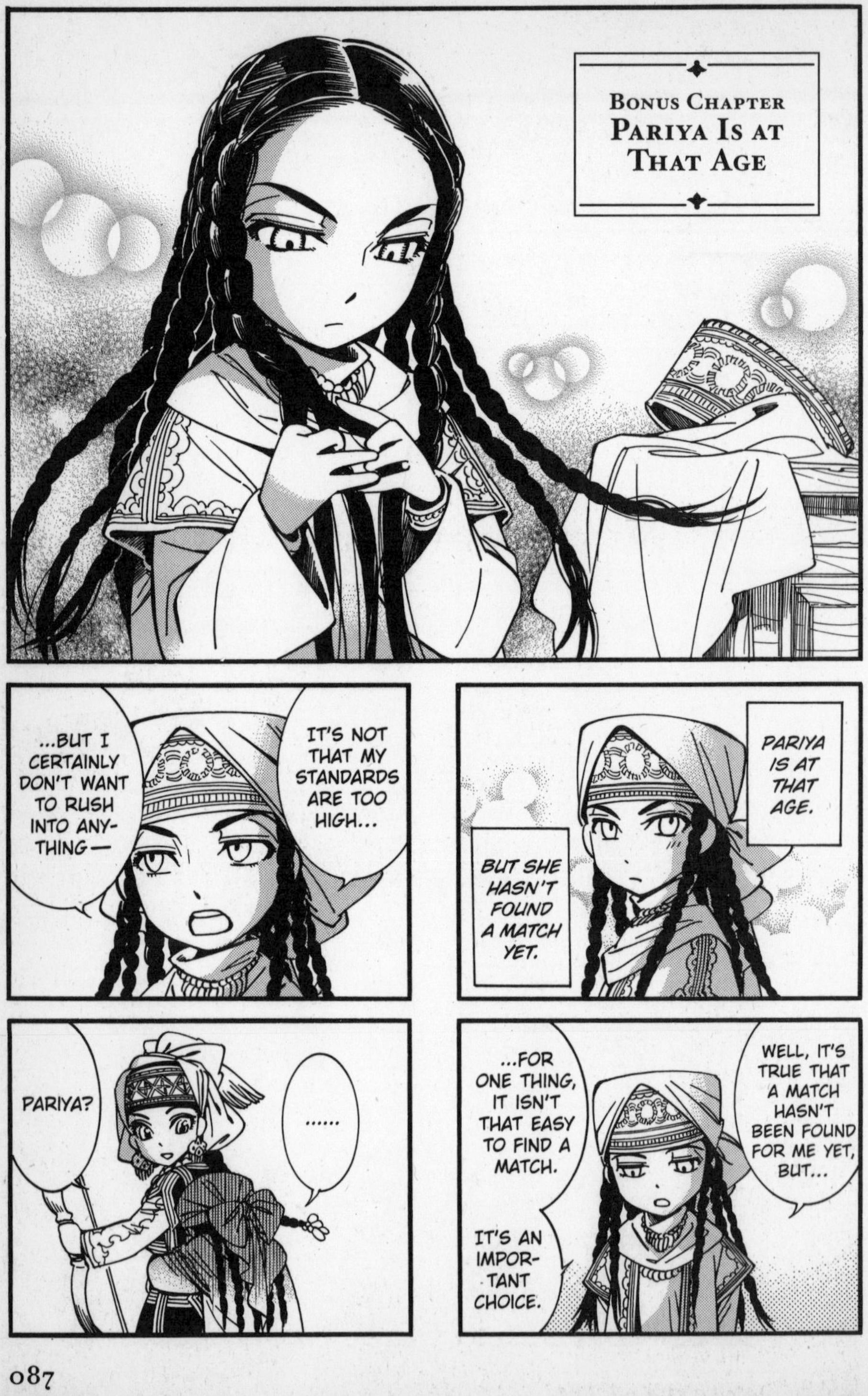
Bonus Chapter
Pariya Is at That Age
PARIYA IS AT THAT AGE.
BUT SHE HASN'T FOUND A MATCH YET.
IT'S NOT THAT MY STANDARDS ARE TOO HIGH...
...BUT I CERTAINLY DON'T WANT TO RUSH INTO ANYTHING—
WELL, IT'S TRUE THAT A MATCH HASN'T BEEN FOUND FOR ME YET, BUT...
...FOR ONE THING, IT ISN'T THAT EASY TO FIND A MATCH.
IT'S AN IMPORTANT CHOICE.
......
PARIYA?

MY FATHER...

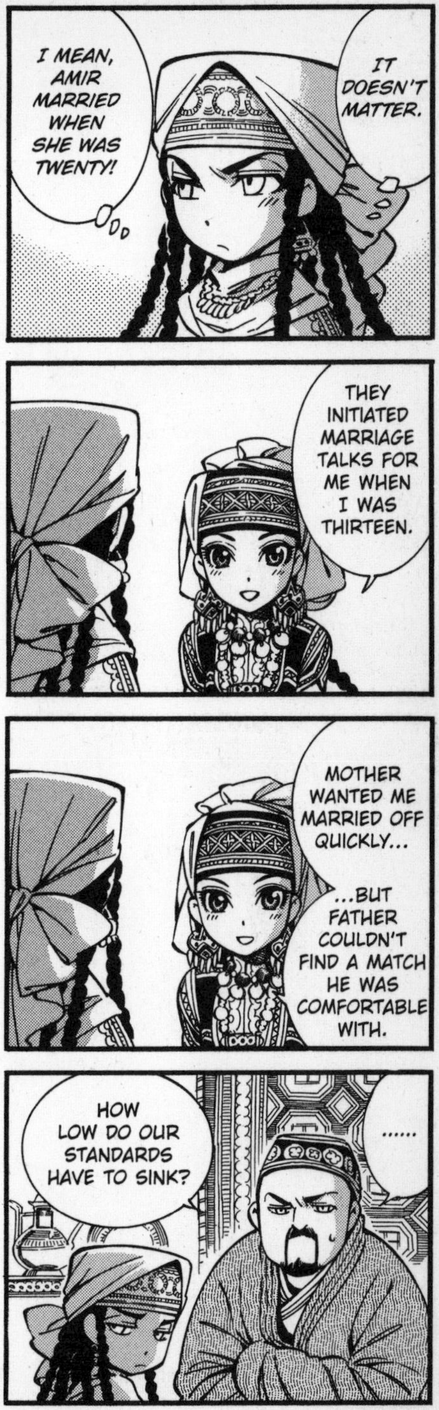
IT DOESN'T MATTER.
I MEAN, AMIR MARRIED WHEN SHE WAS TWENTY!
THEY INITIATED MARRIAGE TALKS FOR ME WHEN I WAS THIRTEEN.
MOTHER WANTED ME MARRIED OFF QUICKLY...
...BUT FATHER COULDN'T FIND A MATCH HE WAS COMFORTABLE WITH.
......
HOW LOW DO OUR STANDARDS HAVE TO SINK?

MODERATION

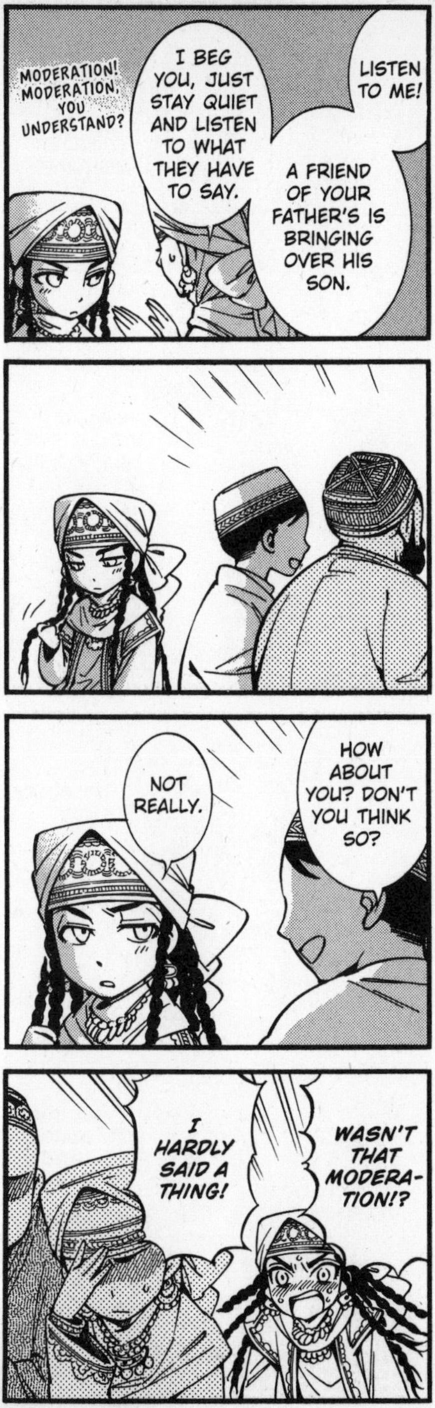
LISTEN TO ME!
A FRIEND OF YOUR FATHER'S IS BRINGING OVER HIS SON.
I BEG YOU, JUST STAY QUIET AND LISTEN TO WHAT THEY HAVE TO SAY.
MODERATION! MODERATION, YOU UNDERSTAND?
HOW ABOUT YOU? DON'T YOU THINK SO?
NOT REALLY.
WASN'T THAT MODERATION!?
I HARDLY SAID A THING!

UNEXPECTEDLY...

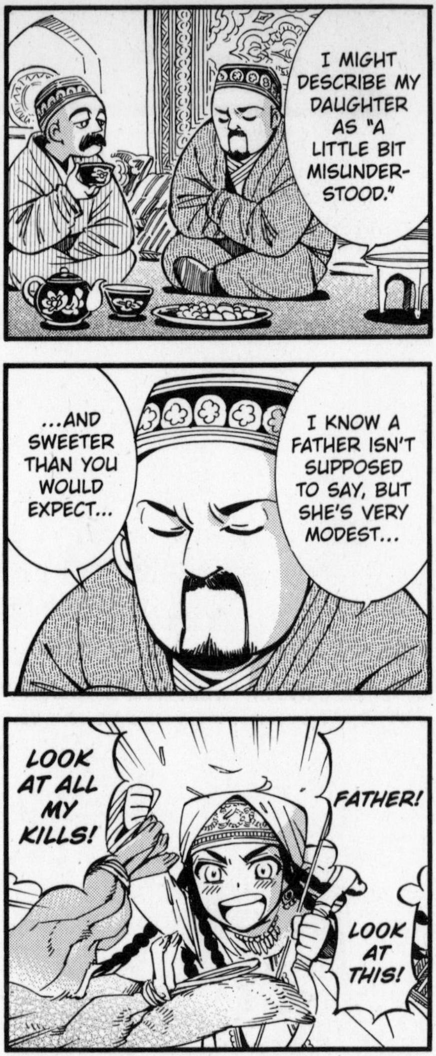
I MIGHT DESCRIBE MY DAUGHTER AS "A LITTLE BIT MISUNDER-STOOD."
I KNOW A FATHER ISN'T SUPPOSED TO SAY, BUT SHE'S VERY MODEST...
...AND SWEETER THAN YOU WOULD EXPECT...
FATHER!
LOOK AT THIS!
LOOK AT ALL MY KILLS!
I BROUGHT DOWN THIS ONE...
...AND AMIR GOT THOSE!
PARIYA!

EMBROIDERY

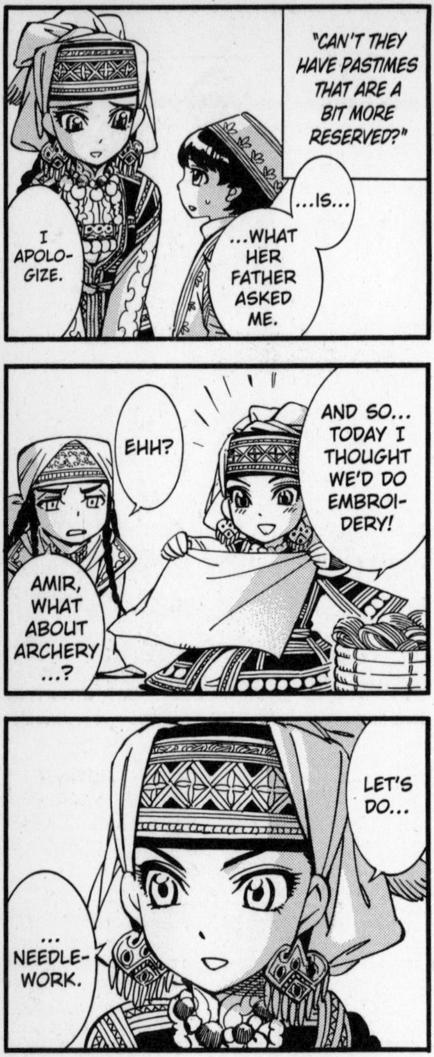
"CAN'T THEY HAVE PASTIMES THAT ARE A BIT MORE RESERVED?"
...IS...
...WHAT HER FATHER ASKED ME.
I APOLO-GIZE.
AND SO... TODAY I THOUGHT WE'D DO EMBROI-DERY!
EHH?
AMIR, WHAT ABOUT ARCHERY ...?
LET'S DO...
... NEEDLE-WORK.
IT'S THE FIRST TIME SHE'S SEEN THIS SIDE OF AMIR, EH?

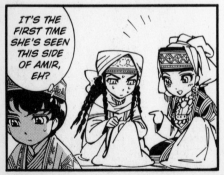

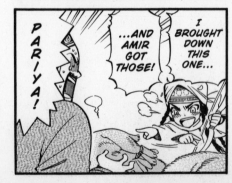

STRONG POINT

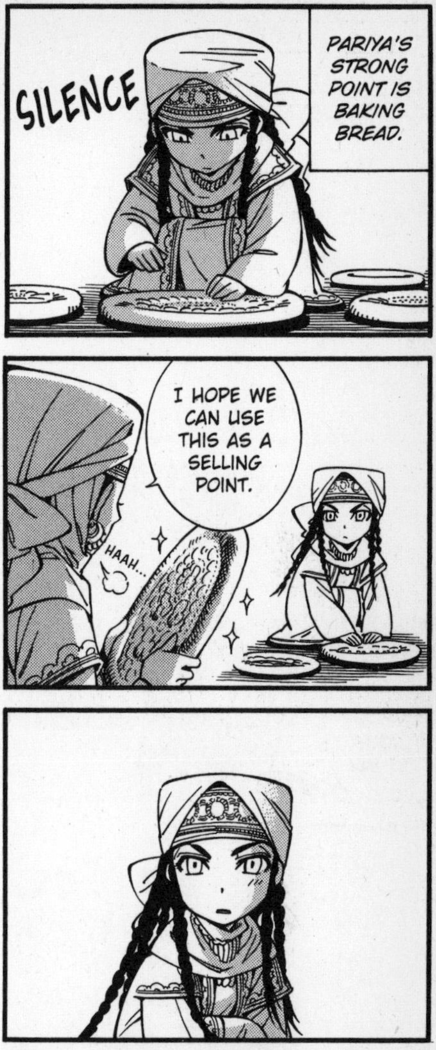
PARIYA'S STRONG POINT IS BAKING BREAD.
SILENCE
I HOPE WE CAN USE THIS AS A SELLING POINT.
HAAH...
I CAN OPEN UP A BREAD STAND!
DON'T GIVE UP.
IN FINDING YOU A MATCH.

THE THING ABOUT MEN

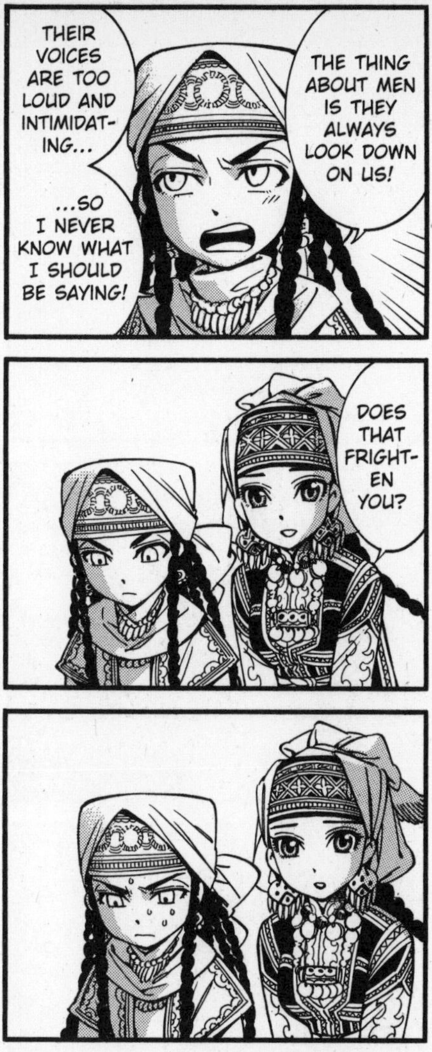
THE THING ABOUT MEN IS THEY ALWAYS LOOK DOWN ON US!
THEIR VOICES ARE TOO LOUD AND INTIMIDAT-ING...
...SO I NEVER KNOW WHAT I SHOULD BE SAYING!
DOES THAT FRIGHT-EN YOU?

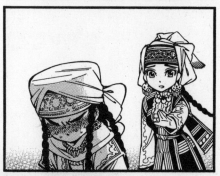

✦ Bonus Chapter: End ✦

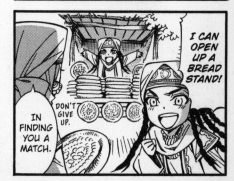

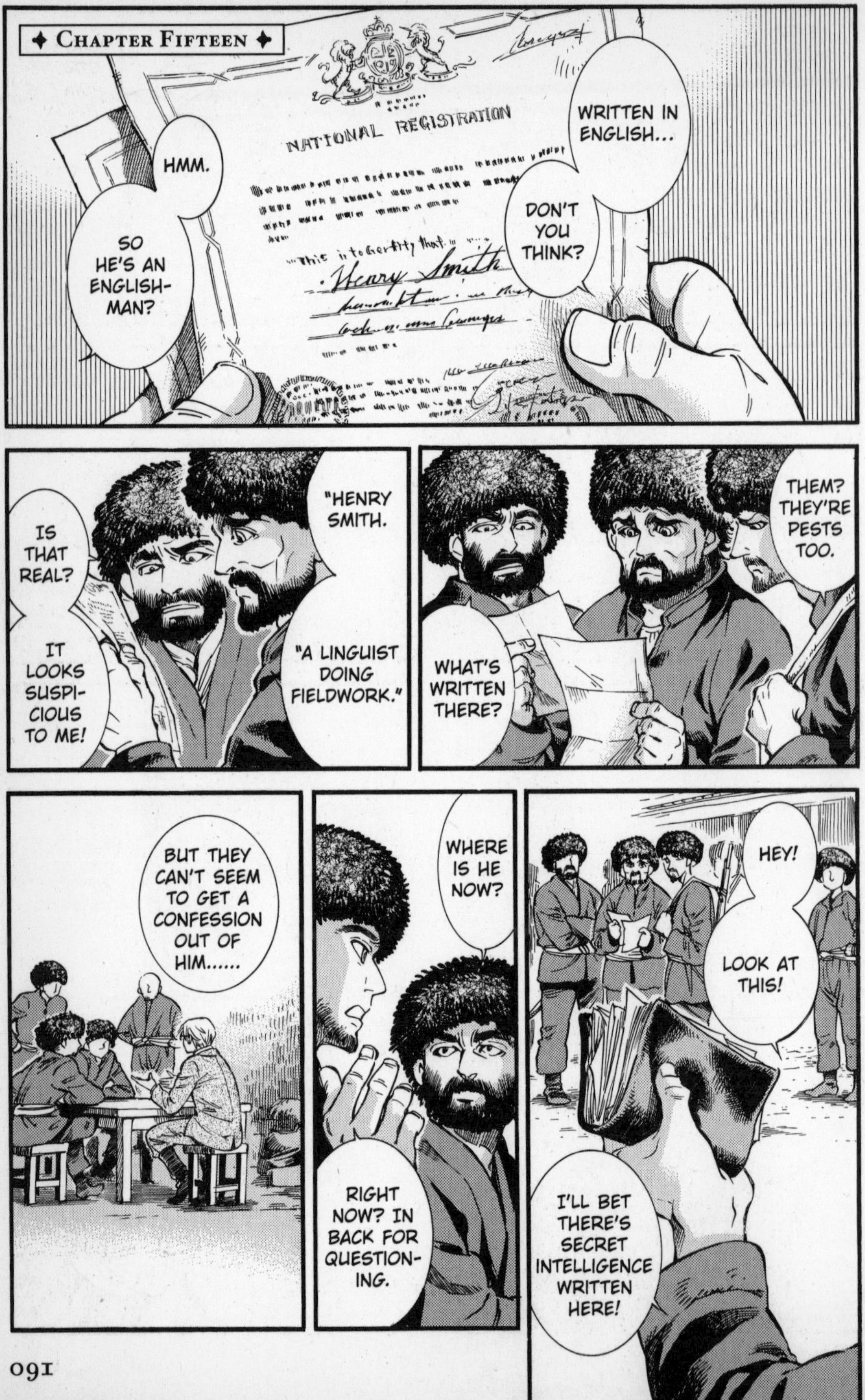

✦ CHAPTER FIFTEEN ✦
NATIONAL REGISTRATION
Henry Smith
WRITTEN IN ENGLISH...
DON'T YOU THINK?
HMM.
SO HE'S AN ENGLISHMAN?
THEM? THEY'RE PESTS TOO.
WHAT'S WRITTEN THERE?
"HENRY SMITH.
"A LINGUIST DOING FIELDWORK."
IS THAT REAL?
IT LOOKS SUSPICIOUS TO ME!
HEY!
LOOK AT THIS!
I'LL BET THERE'S SECRET INTELLIGENCE WRITTEN HERE!
WHERE IS HE NOW?
RIGHT NOW? IN BACK FOR QUESTIONING.
BUT THEY CAN'T SEEM TO GET A CONFESSION OUT OF HIM......

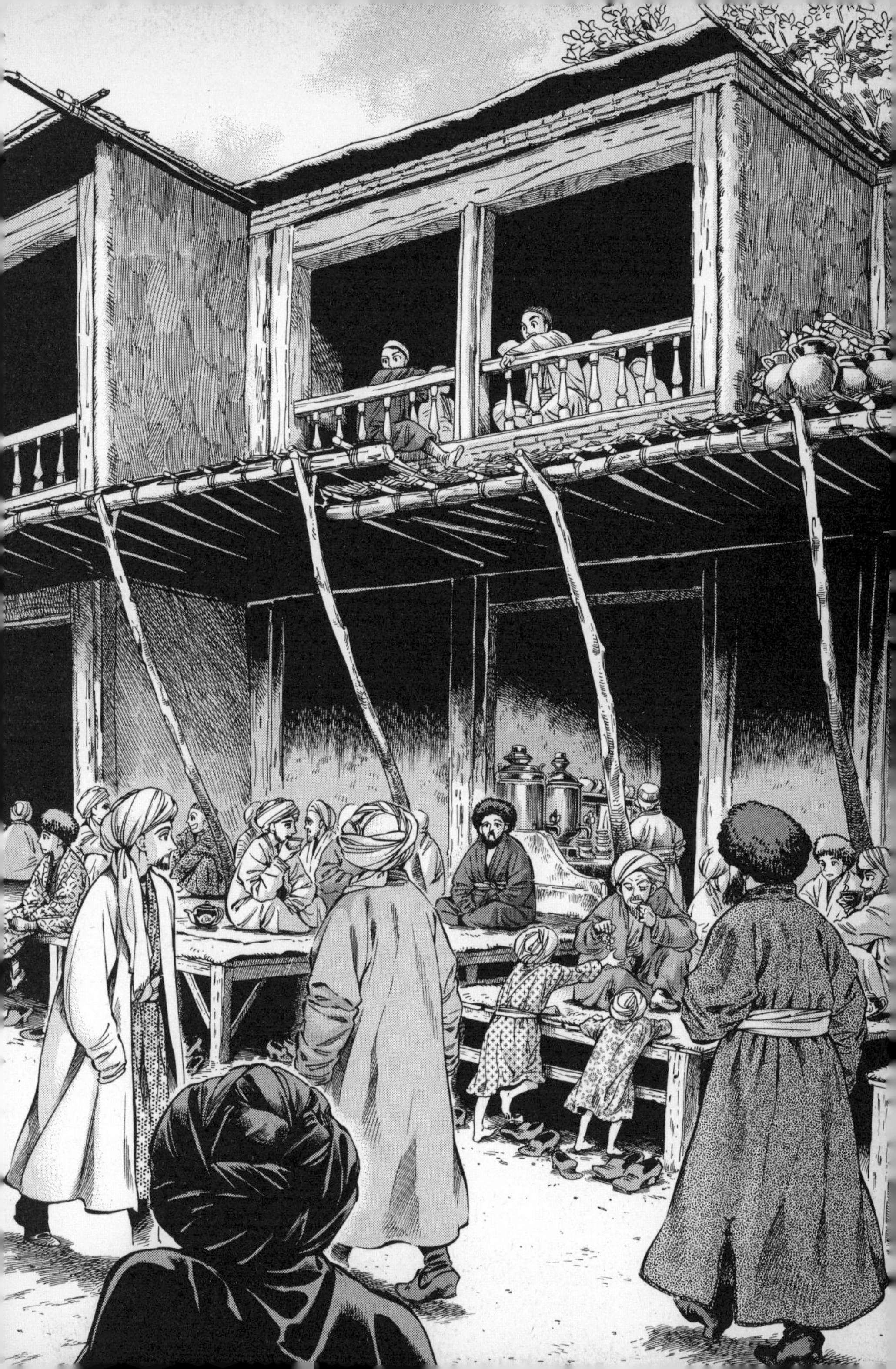

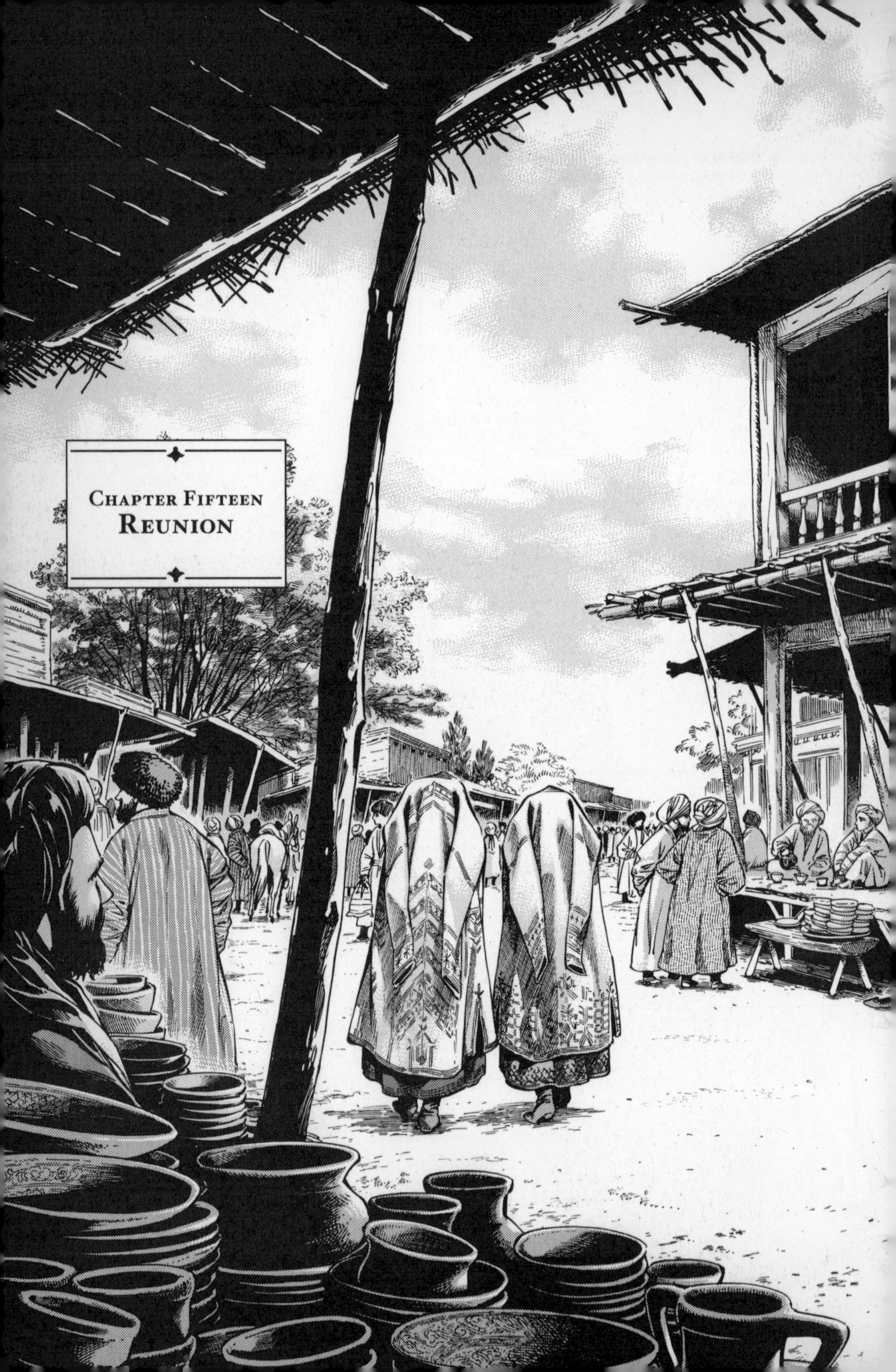

Chapter Fifteen
Reunion

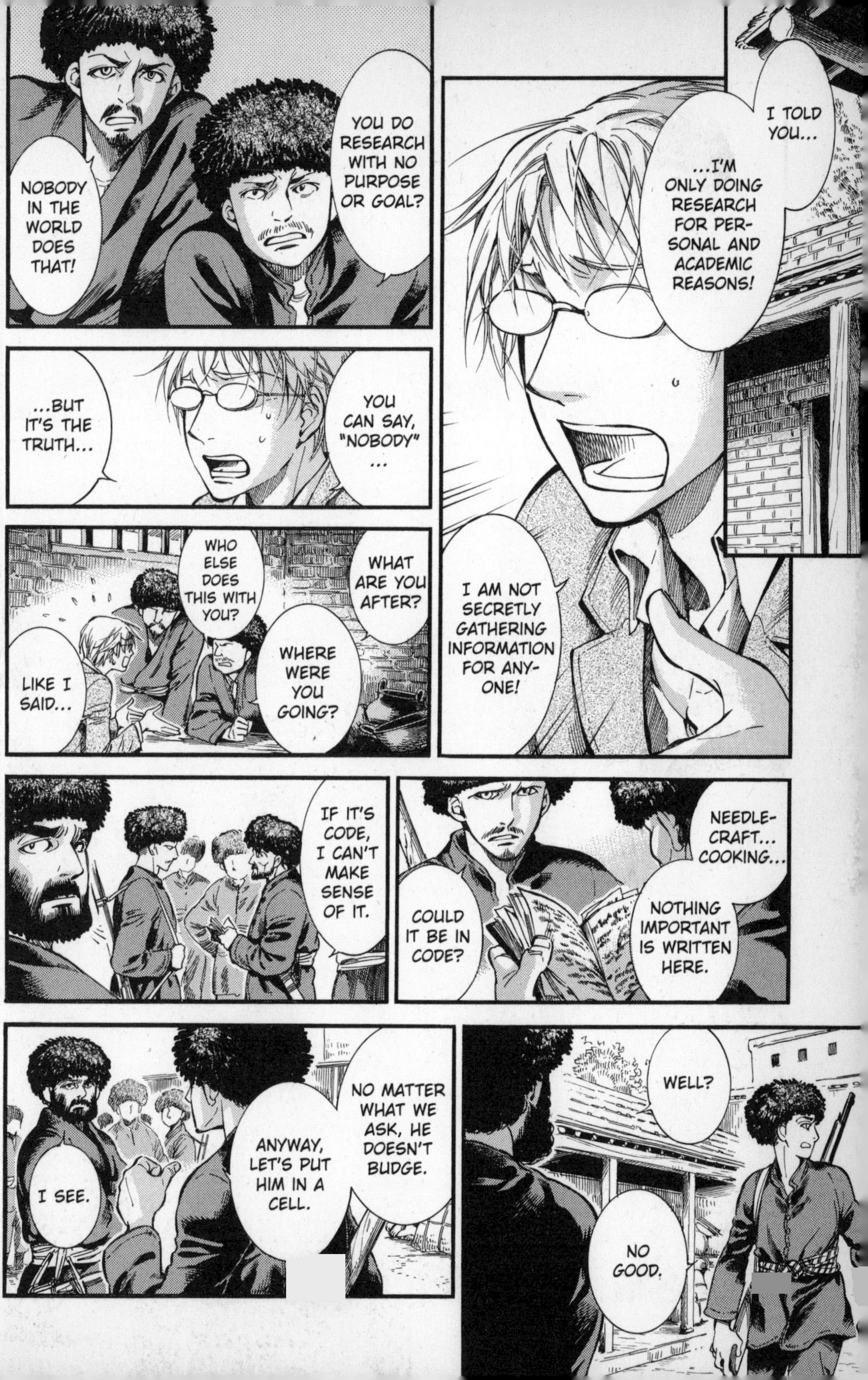
I TOLD YOU...
...I'M ONLY DOING RESEARCH FOR PER-SONAL AND ACADEMIC REASONS!
I AM NOT SECRETLY GATHERING INFORMATION FOR ANY-ONE!
YOU DO RESEARCH WITH NO PURPOSE OR GOAL?
NOBODY IN THE WORLD DOES THAT!
YOU CAN SAY, "NOBODY" ...
...BUT IT'S THE TRUTH...
WHAT ARE YOU AFTER?
WHO ELSE DOES THIS WITH YOU?
WHERE WERE YOU GOING?
LIKE I SAID...
NEEDLE-CRAFT... COOKING...
NOTHING IMPORTANT IS WRITTEN HERE.
COULD IT BE IN CODE?
IF IT'S CODE, I CAN'T MAKE SENSE OF IT.
WELL?
NO GOOD.
NO MATTER WHAT WE ASK, HE DOESN'T BUDGE.
ANYWAY, LET'S PUT HIM IN A CELL.
I SEE.

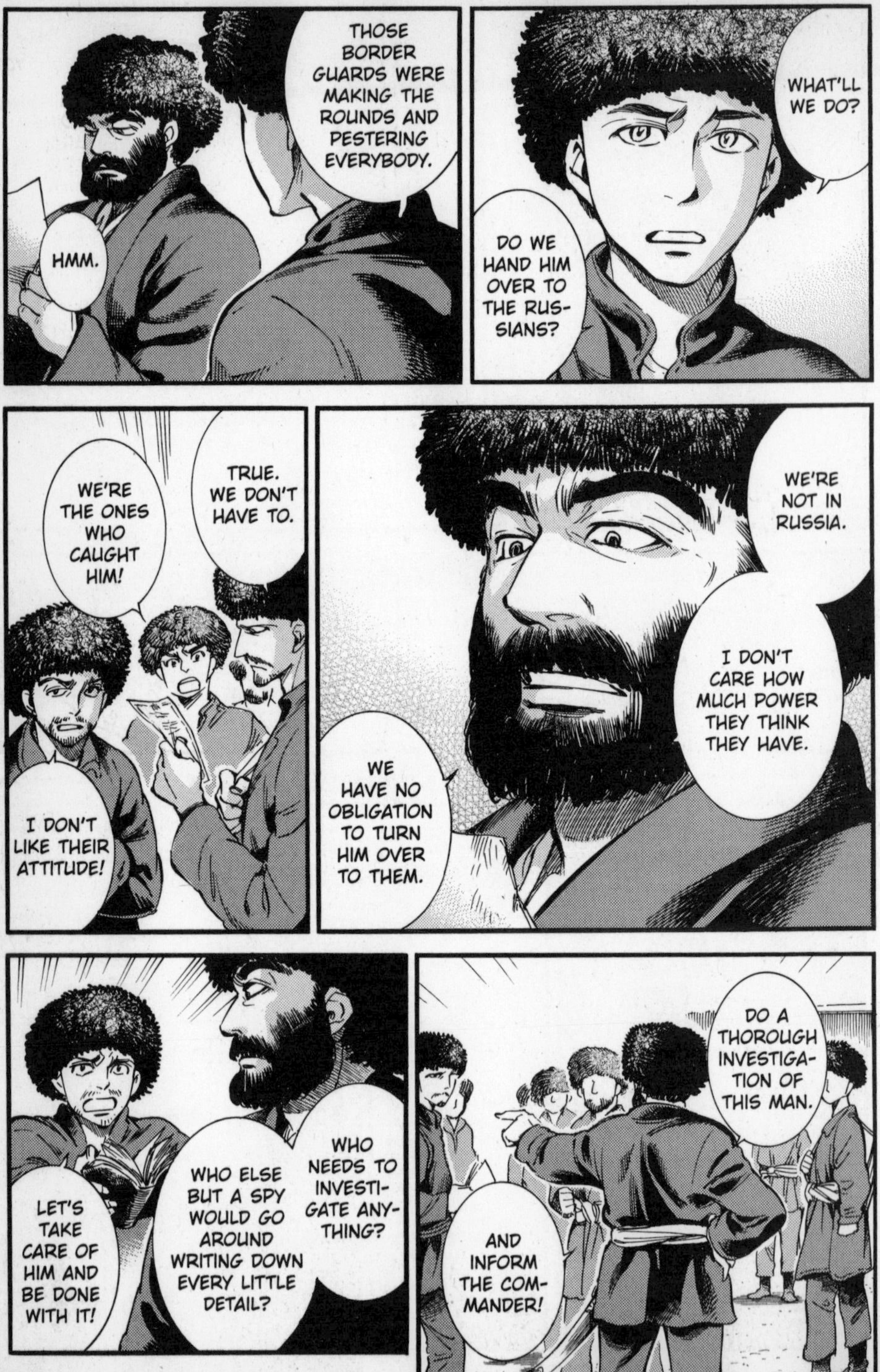
WHAT'LL WE DO?
DO WE HAND HIM OVER TO THE RUSSIANS?
THOSE BORDER GUARDS WERE MAKING THE ROUNDS AND PESTERING EVERYBODY.
HMM.
WE'RE NOT IN RUSSIA.
I DON'T CARE HOW MUCH POWER THEY THINK THEY HAVE.
WE HAVE NO OBLIGATION TO TURN HIM OVER TO THEM.
TRUE. WE DON'T HAVE TO.
WE'RE THE ONES WHO CAUGHT HIM!
I DON'T LIKE THEIR ATTITUDE!
DO A THOROUGH INVESTIGATION OF THIS MAN.
AND INFORM THE COMMANDER!
WHO NEEDS TO INVESTIGATE ANYTHING?
WHO ELSE BUT A SPY WOULD GO AROUND WRITING DOWN EVERY LITTLE DETAIL?
LET'S TAKE CARE OF HIM AND BE DONE WITH IT!

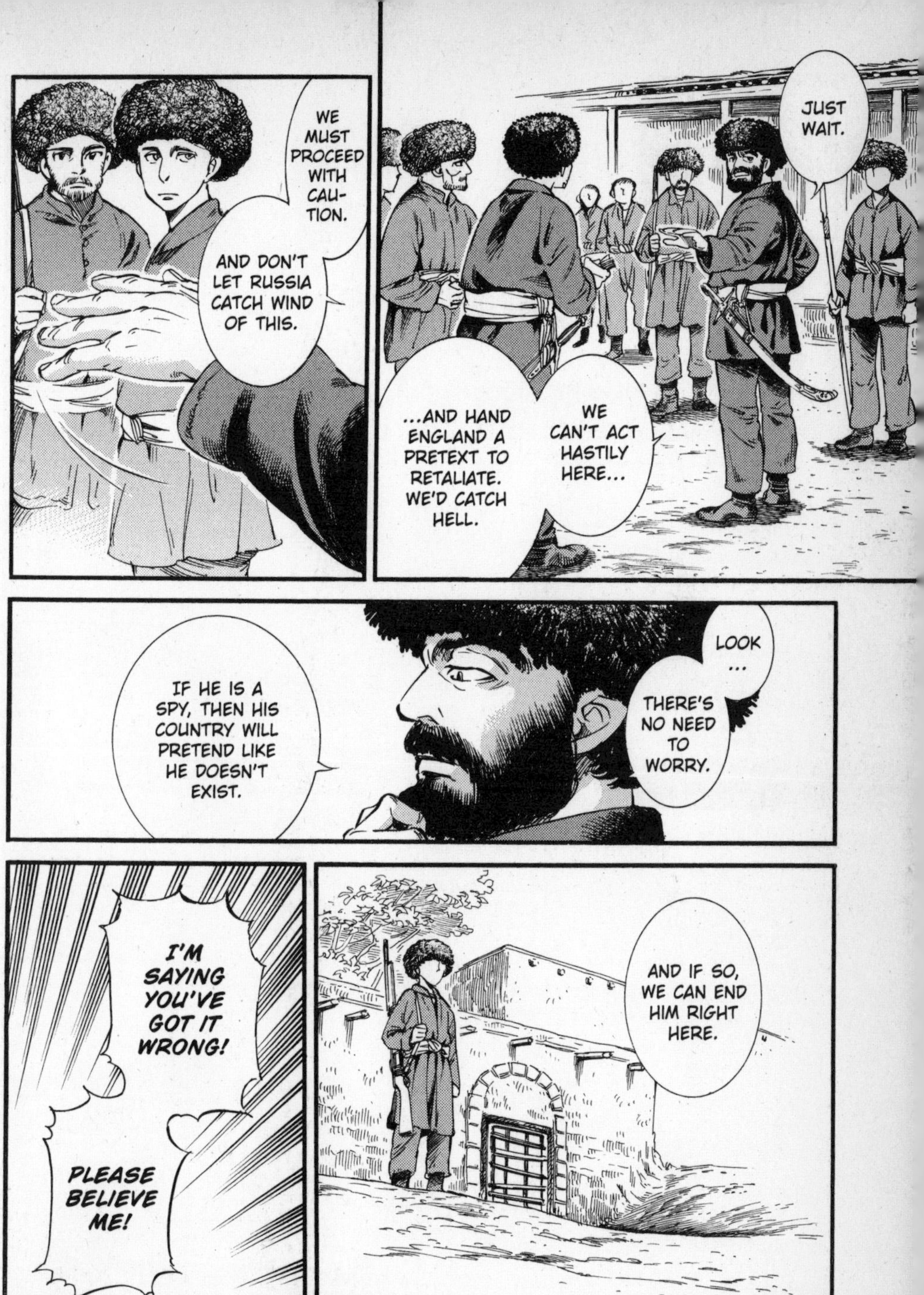
JUST WAIT.
WE CAN'T ACT HASTILY HERE...
...AND HAND ENGLAND A PRETEXT TO RETALIATE. WE'D CATCH HELL.
WE MUST PROCEED WITH CAU-TION.
AND DON'T LET RUSSIA CATCH WIND OF THIS.
LOOK...
THERE'S NO NEED TO WORRY.
IF HE IS A SPY, THEN HIS COUNTRY WILL PRETEND LIKE HE DOESN'T EXIST.
AND IF SO, WE CAN END HIM RIGHT HERE.
I'M SAYING YOU'VE GOT IT WRONG!
PLEASE BELIEVE ME!

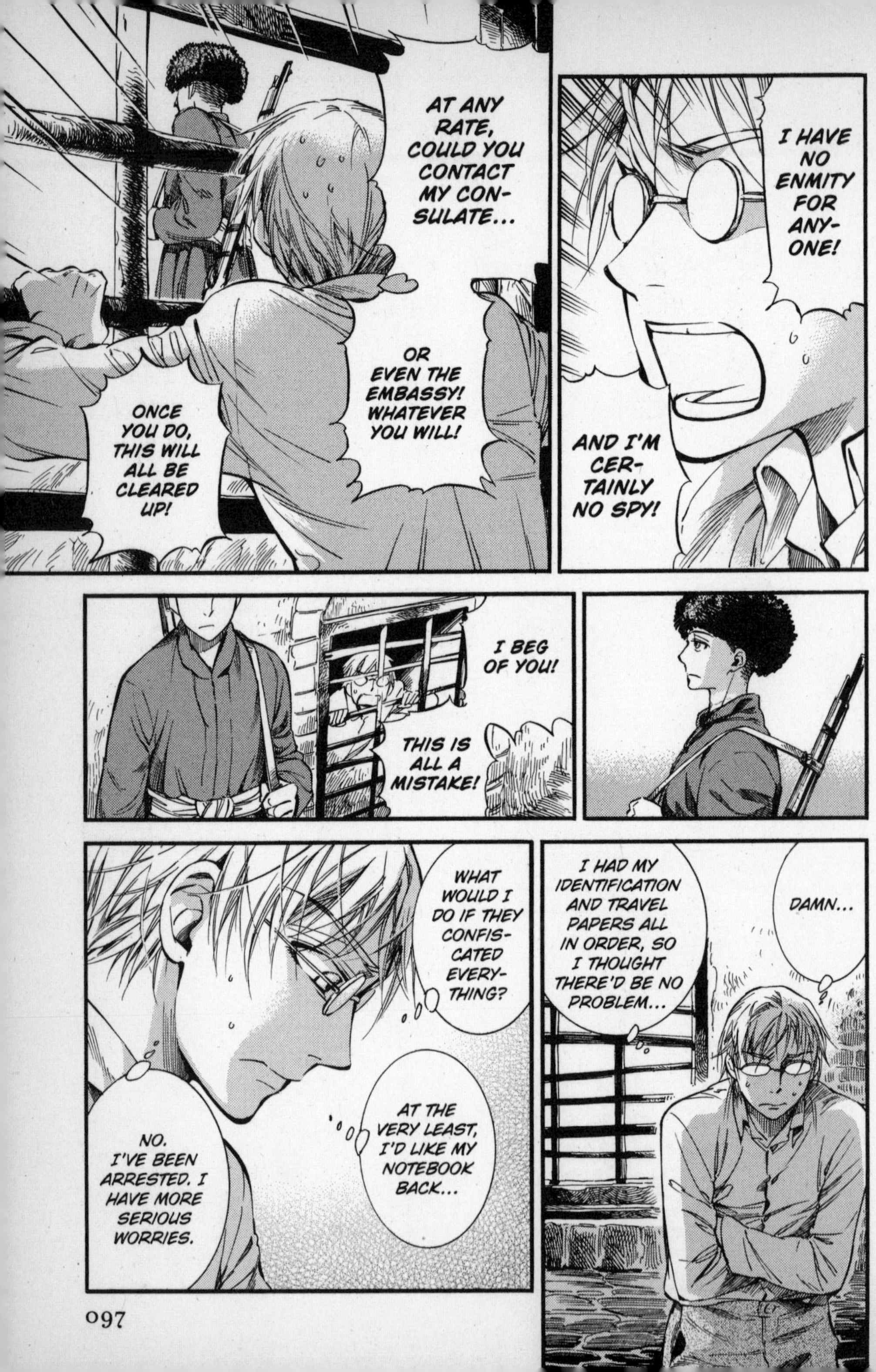
I HAVE NO ENMITY FOR ANYONE!
AND I'M CERTAINLY NO SPY!
AT ANY RATE, COULD YOU CONTACT MY CONSULATE...
OR EVEN THE EMBASSY! WHATEVER YOU WILL!
ONCE YOU DO, THIS WILL ALL BE CLEARED UP!
I BEG OF YOU!
THIS IS ALL A MISTAKE!
DAMN...
I HAD MY IDENTIFICATION AND TRAVEL PAPERS ALL IN ORDER, SO I THOUGHT THERE'D BE NO PROBLEM...
WHAT WOULD I DO IF THEY CONFISCATED EVERYTHING?
AT THE VERY LEAST, I'D LIKE MY NOTEBOOK BACK...
NO. I'VE BEEN ARRESTED. I HAVE MORE SERIOUS WORRIES.

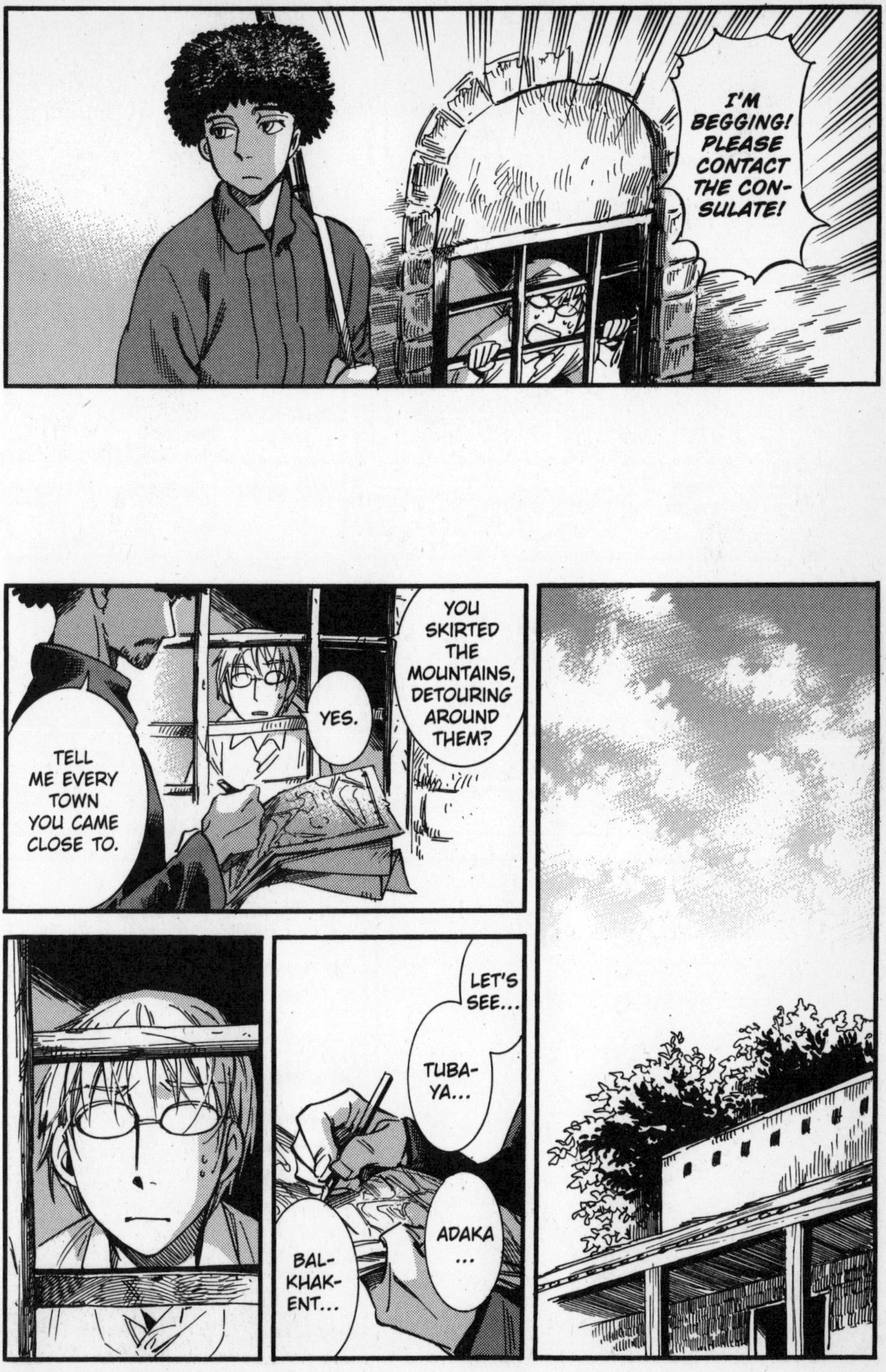
I'M BEGGING! PLEASE CONTACT THE CON-SULATE!
YOU SKIRTED THE MOUNTAINS, DETOURING AROUND THEM?
YES.
TELL ME EVERY TOWN YOU CAME CLOSE TO.
LET'S SEE...
TUBA-YA...
ADAKA ...
BAL-KHAK-ENT...

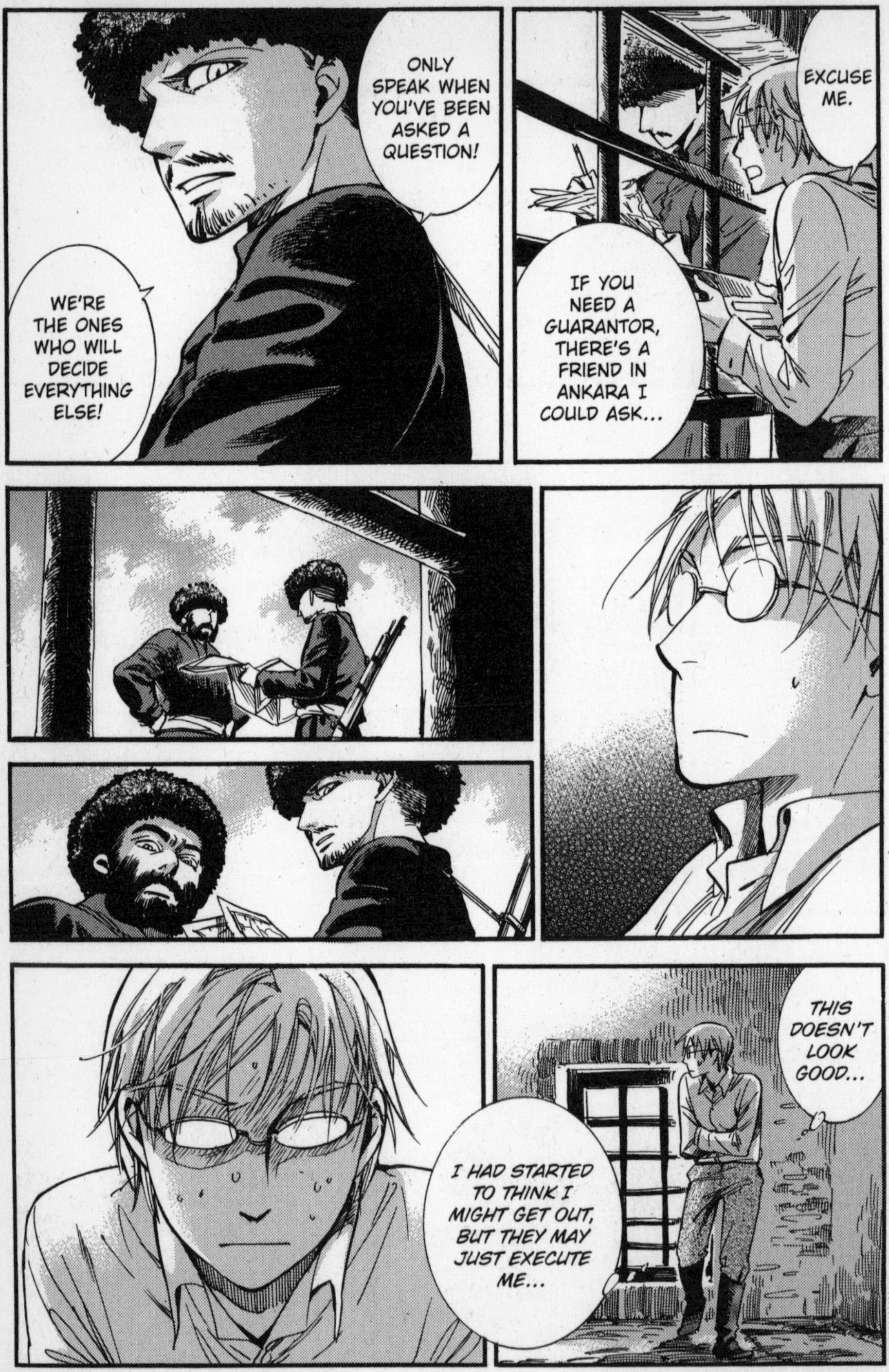
EXCUSE ME.
IF YOU NEED A GUARANTOR, THERE'S A FRIEND IN ANKARA I COULD ASK...
ONLY SPEAK WHEN YOU'VE BEEN ASKED A QUESTION!
WE'RE THE ONES WHO WILL DECIDE EVERYTHING ELSE!
THIS DOESN'T LOOK GOOD...
I HAD STARTED TO THINK I MIGHT GET OUT, BUT THEY MAY JUST EXECUTE ME...

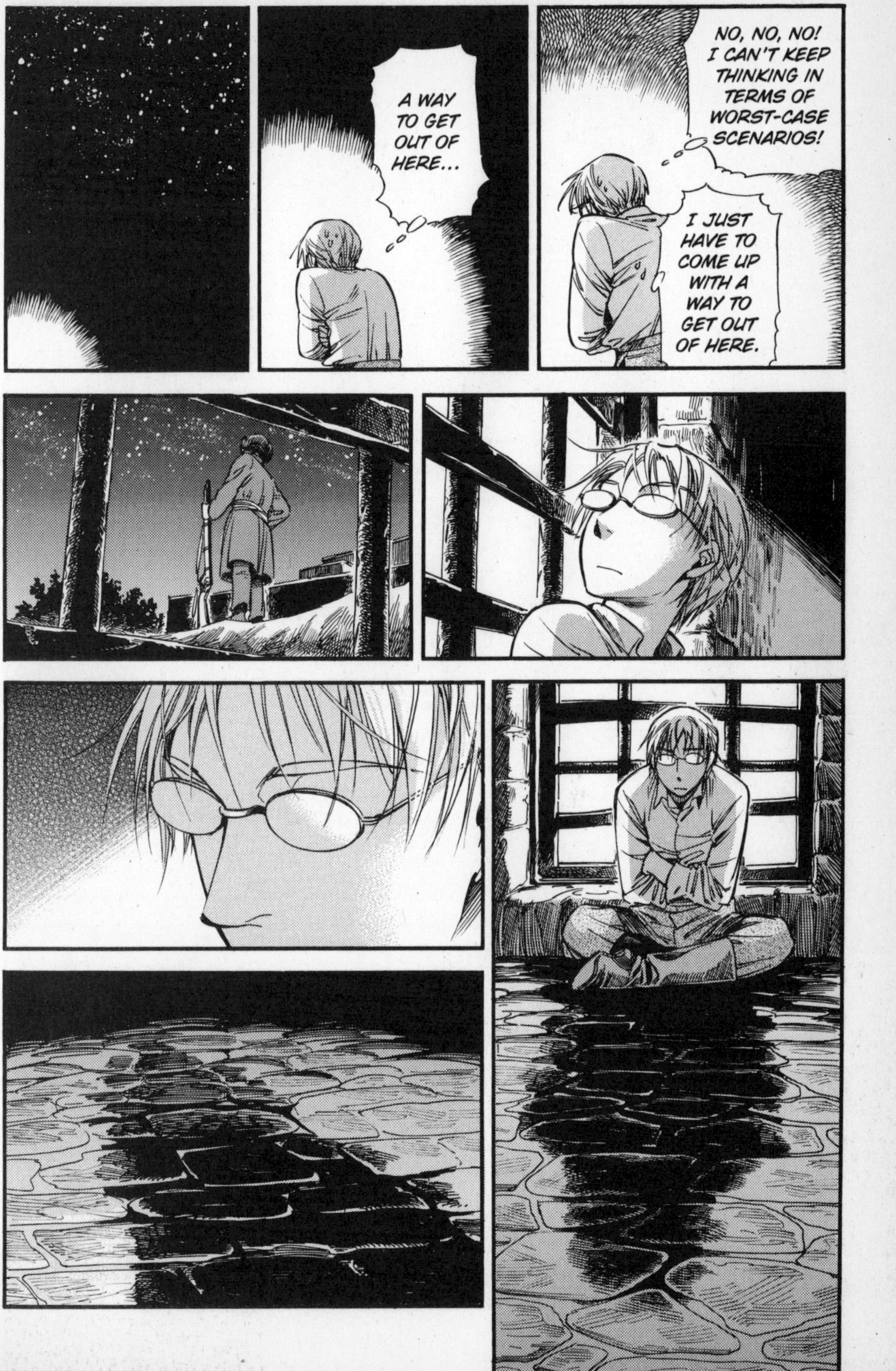
NO, NO, NO! I CAN'T KEEP THINKING IN TERMS OF WORST-CASE SCENARIOS!
I JUST HAVE TO COME UP WITH A WAY TO GET OUT OF HERE.
A WAY TO GET OUT OF HERE...

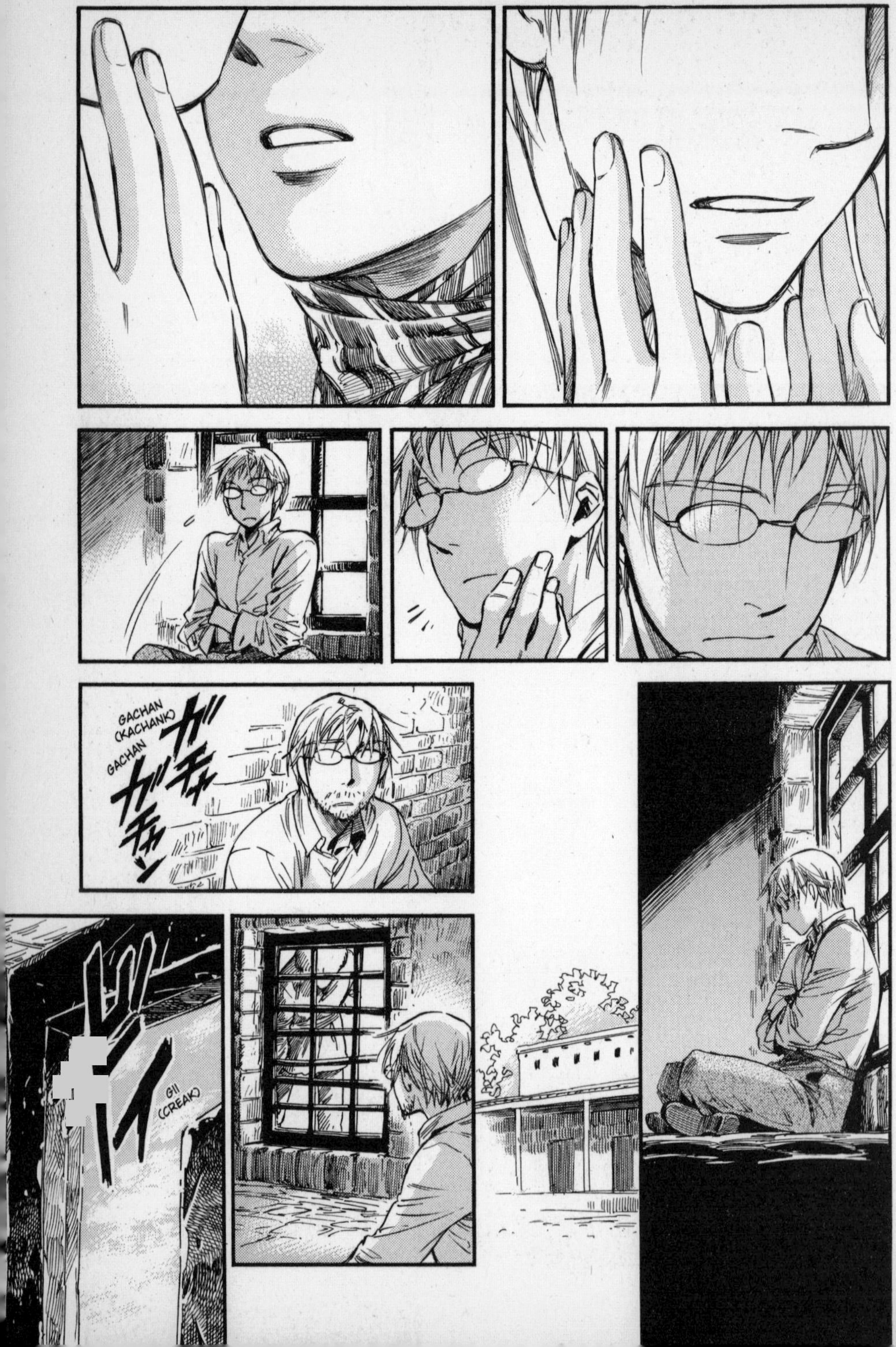
ガチャ
GACHAN (KACHANK)
ガチャン
GACHAN
GII (CREAK)

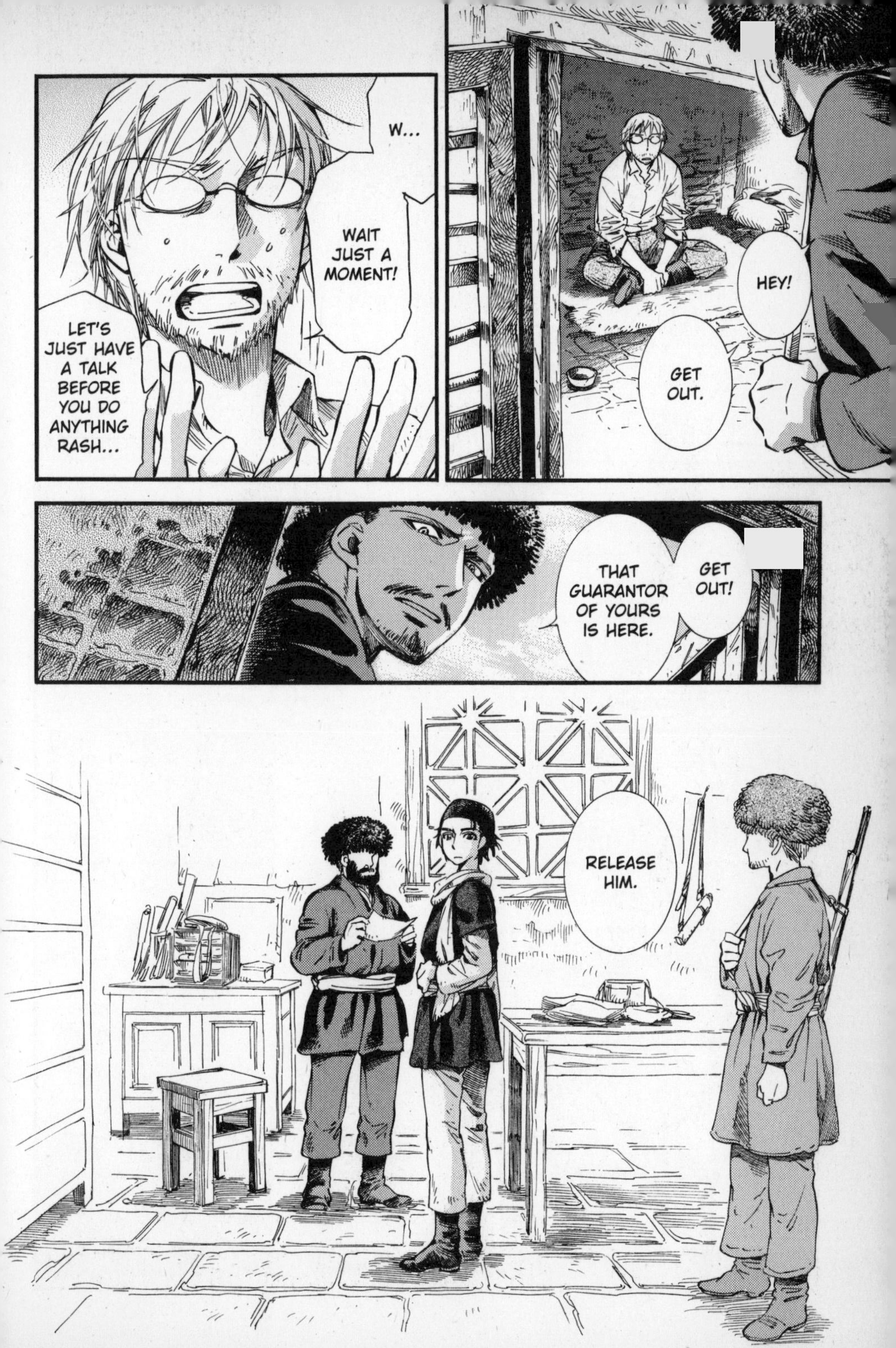
HEY!
GET OUT.
W...
WAIT JUST A MOMENT!
LET'S JUST HAVE A TALK BEFORE YOU DO ANYTHING RASH...
GET OUT!
THAT GUARANTOR OF YOURS IS HERE.
RELEASE HIM.

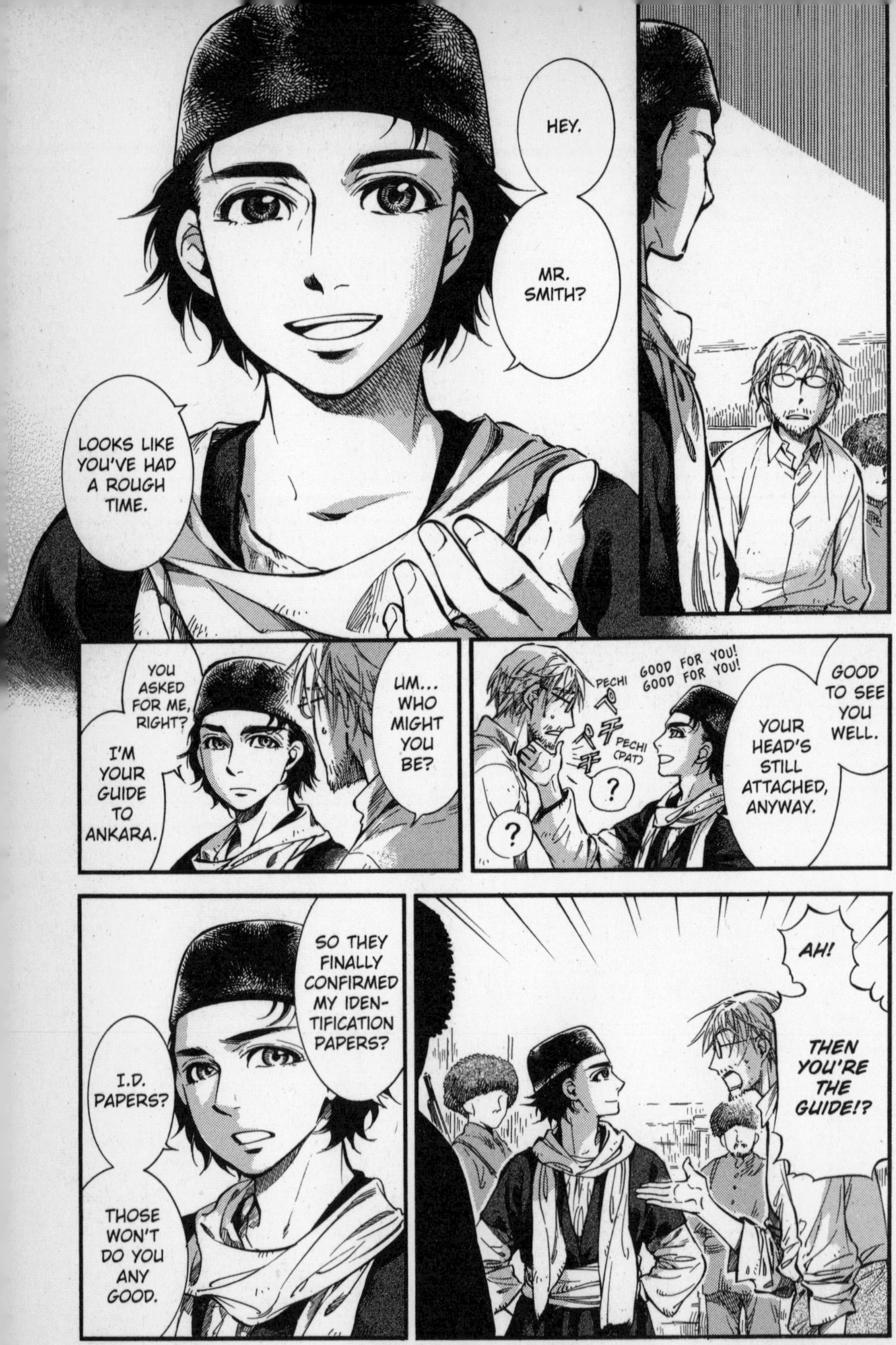
HEY.
MR. SMITH?
LOOKS LIKE YOU'VE HAD A ROUGH TIME.
GOOD TO SEE YOU WELL.
YOUR HEAD'S STILL ATTACHED, ANYWAY.
GOOD FOR YOU! GOOD FOR YOU!
PECHI
PECHI (PAT)
?
?
UM... WHO MIGHT YOU BE?
YOU ASKED FOR ME, RIGHT?
I'M YOUR GUIDE TO ANKARA.
AH!
THEN YOU'RE THE GUIDE!?
SO THEY FINALLY CONFIRMED MY IDENTIFICATION PAPERS?
I.D. PAPERS?
THOSE WON'T DO YOU ANY GOOD.

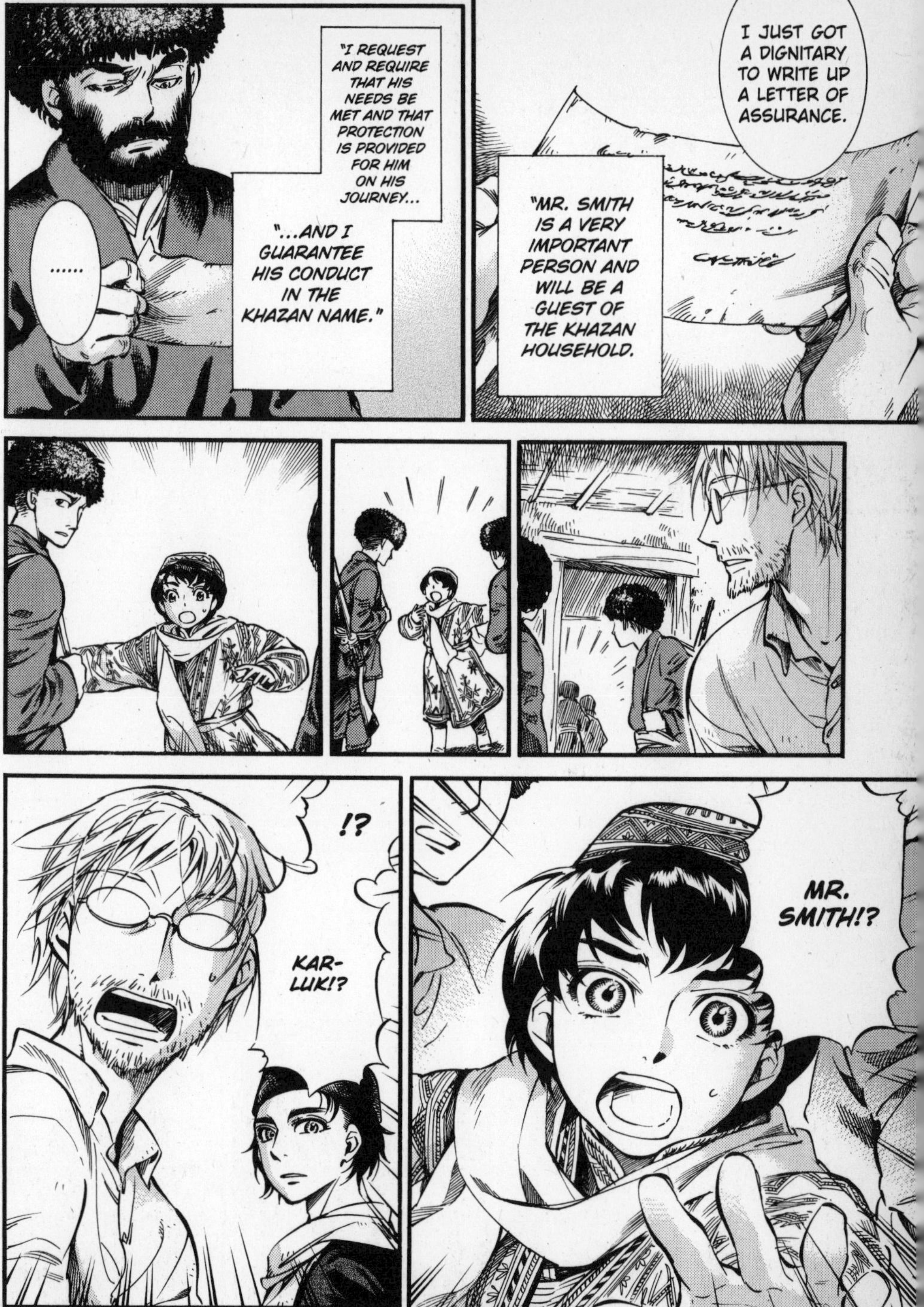
I JUST GOT A DIGNITARY TO WRITE UP A LETTER OF ASSURANCE.
"MR. SMITH IS A VERY IMPORTANT PERSON AND WILL BE A GUEST OF THE KHAZAN HOUSEHOLD.
"I REQUEST AND REQUIRE THAT HIS NEEDS BE MET AND THAT PROTECTION IS PROVIDED FOR HIM ON HIS JOURNEY...
"...AND I GUARANTEE HIS CONDUCT IN THE KHAZAN NAME."
......
MR. SMITH!?
!?
KAR-LUK!?

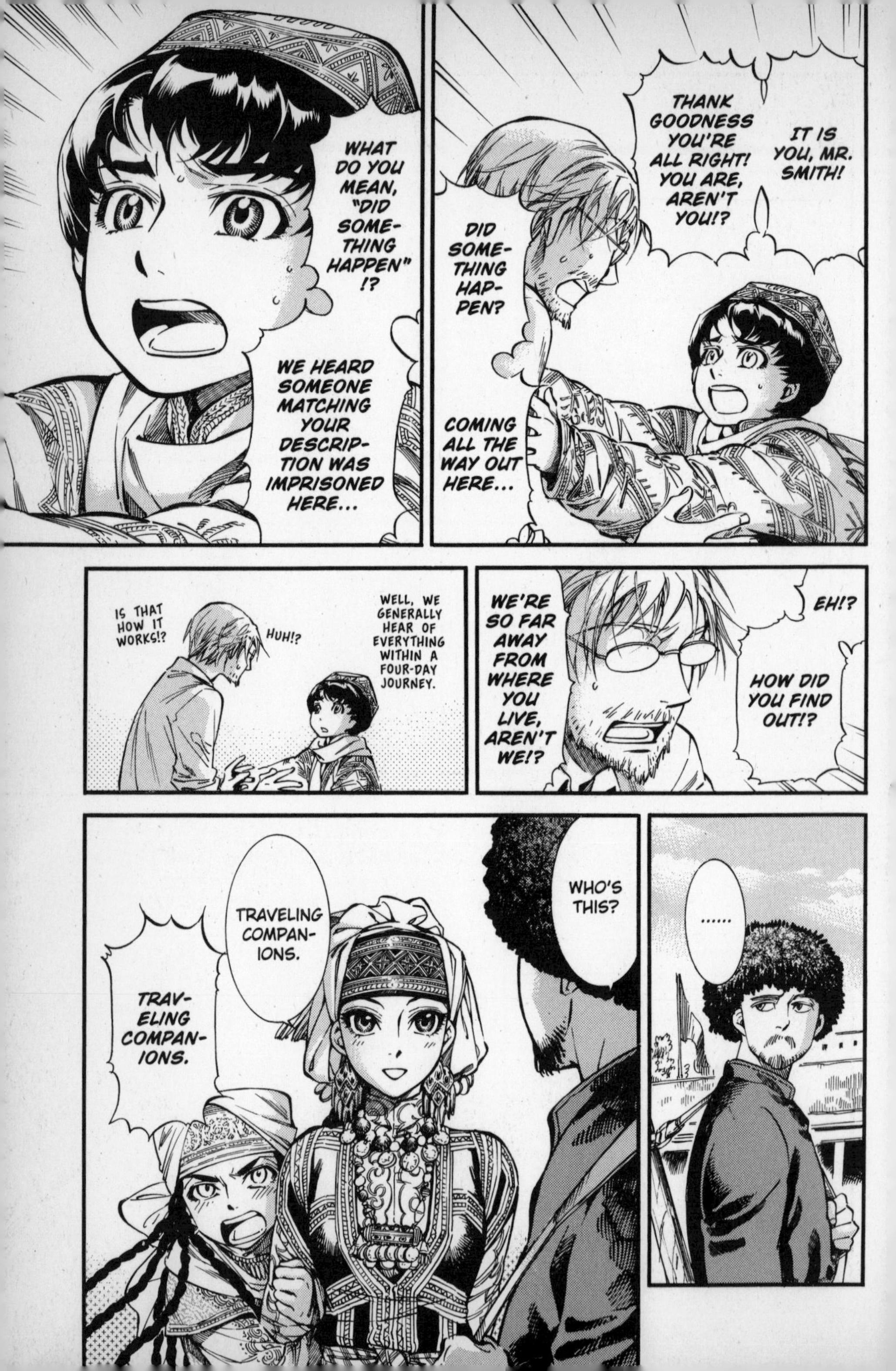
IT IS YOU, MR. SMITH!
THANK GOODNESS YOU'RE ALL RIGHT! YOU ARE, AREN'T YOU!?
DID SOMETHING HAPPEN?
COMING ALL THE WAY OUT HERE...
WHAT DO YOU MEAN, "DID SOMETHING HAPPEN"!?
WE HEARD SOMEONE MATCHING YOUR DESCRIPTION WAS IMPRISONED HERE...
EH!?
HOW DID YOU FIND OUT!?
WE'RE SO FAR AWAY FROM WHERE YOU LIVE, AREN'T WE!?
WELL, WE GENERALLY HEAR OF EVERYTHING WITHIN A FOUR-DAY JOURNEY.
HUH!?
IS THAT HOW IT WORKS!?
......
WHO'S THIS?
TRAVELING COMPANIONS.
TRAVELING COMPANIONS.

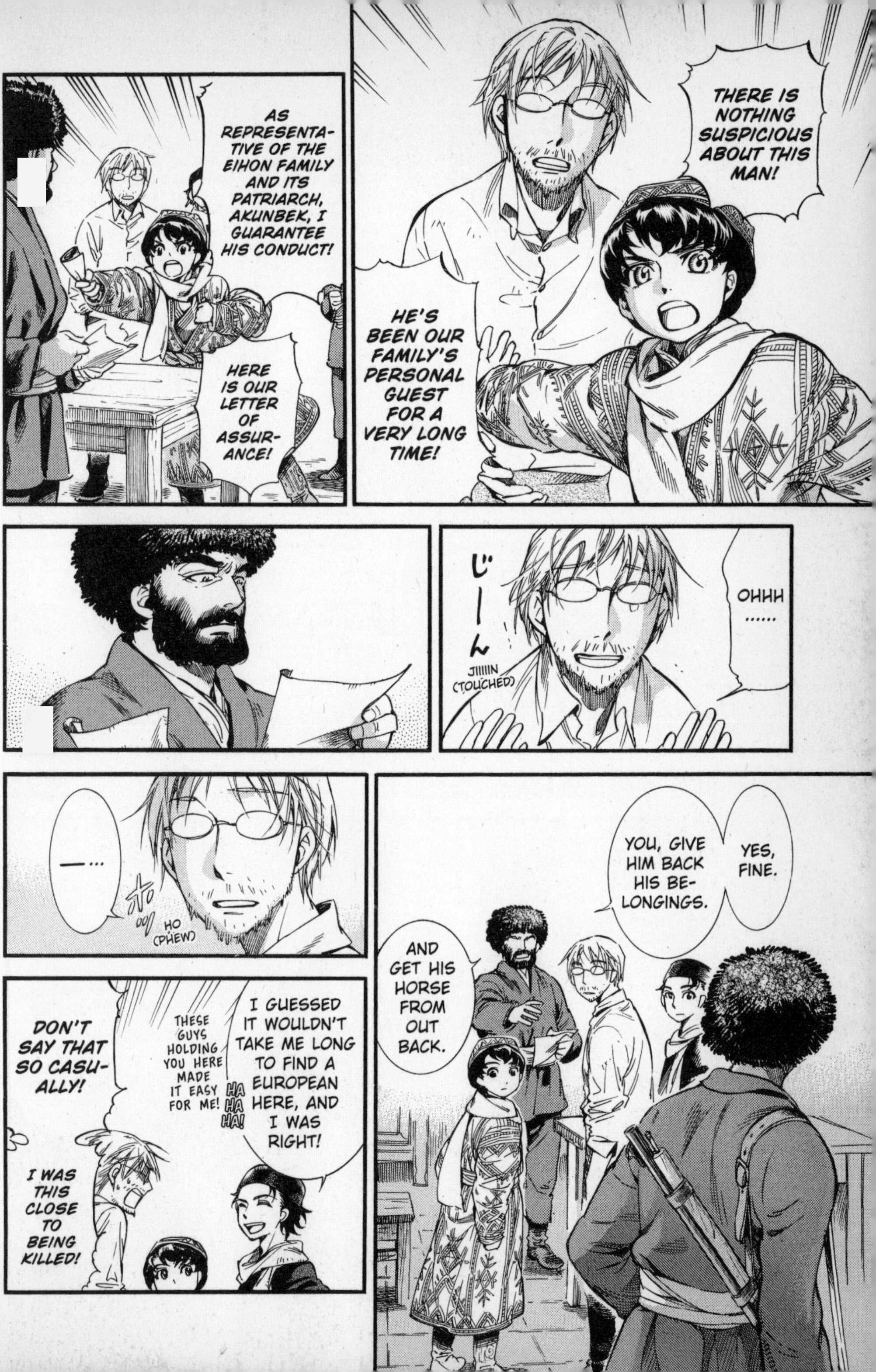
THERE IS NOTHING SUSPICIOUS ABOUT THIS MAN!
HE'S BEEN OUR FAMILY'S PERSONAL GUEST FOR A VERY LONG TIME!
AS REPRESENTATIVE OF THE EIHON FAMILY AND ITS PATRIARCH, AKUNBEK, I GUARANTEE HIS CONDUCT!
HERE IS OUR LETTER OF ASSURANCE!
OHHH ......
じーん
JIIIIN (TOUCHED)
YES, FINE.
YOU, GIVE HIM BACK HIS BELONGINGS.
AND GET HIS HORSE FROM OUT BACK.
—...
HO (PHEW)
I GUESSED IT WOULDN'T TAKE ME LONG TO FIND A EUROPEAN HERE, AND I WAS RIGHT!
HA HA HA!
THESE GUYS HOLDING YOU HERE MADE IT EASY FOR ME!
DON'T SAY THAT SO CASUALLY!
I WAS THIS CLOSE TO BEING KILLED!

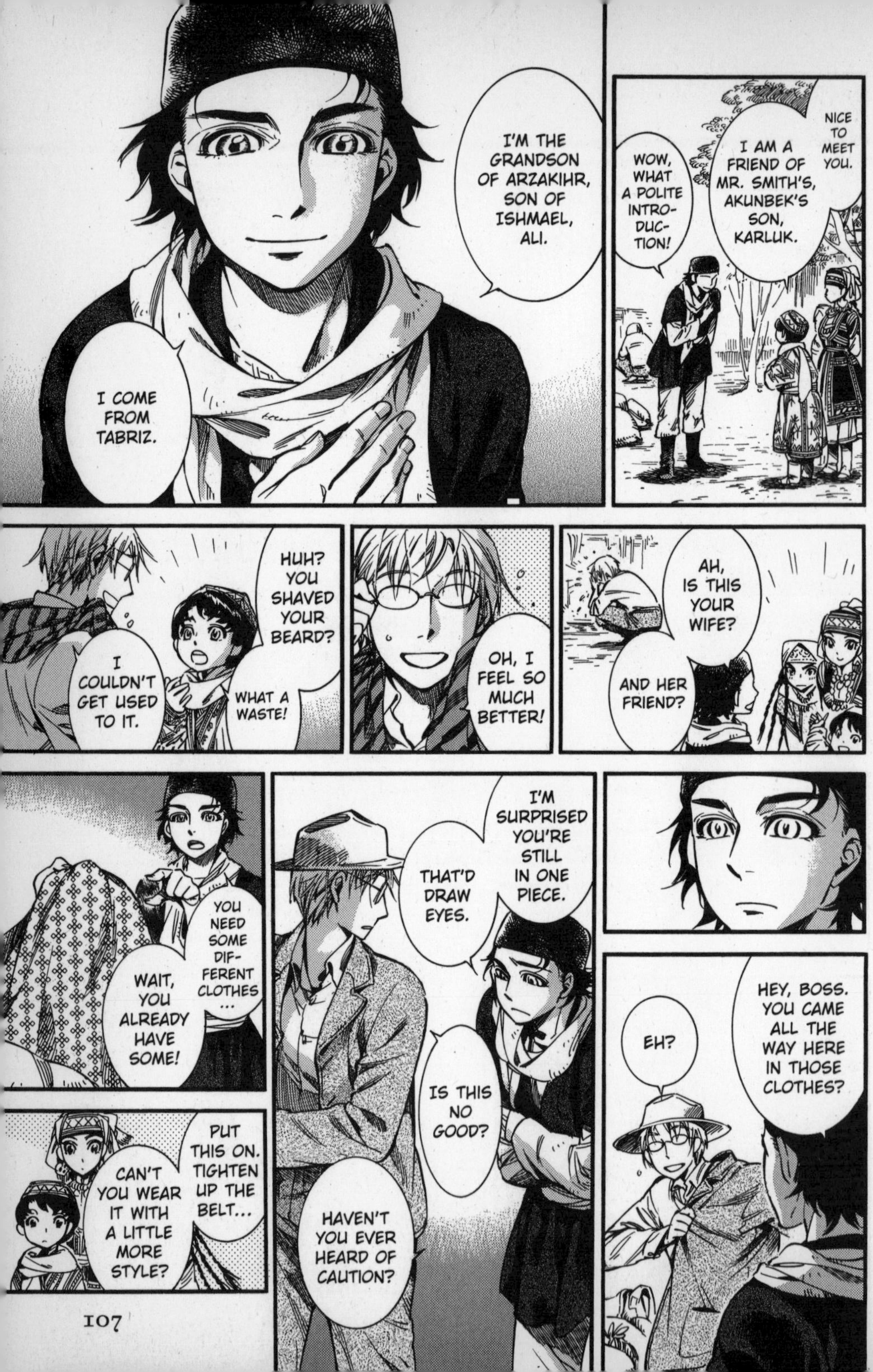

NICE TO MEET YOU.
I AM A FRIEND OF MR. SMITH'S, AKUNBEK'S SON, KARLUK.
WOW, WHAT A POLITE INTRO-DUCTION!
I'M THE GRANDSON OF ARZAKIHR, SON OF ISHMAEL, ALI.
I COME FROM TABRIZ.
AH, IS THIS YOUR WIFE?
AND HER FRIEND?
OH, I FEEL SO MUCH BETTER!
HUH? YOU SHAVED YOUR BEARD?
WHAT A WASTE!
I COULDN'T GET USED TO IT.
HEY, BOSS. YOU CAME ALL THE WAY HERE IN THOSE CLOTHES?
EH?
I'M SURPRISED YOU'RE STILL IN ONE PIECE.
THAT'D DRAW EYES.
IS THIS NO GOOD?
HAVEN'T YOU EVER HEARD OF CAUTION?
YOU NEED SOME DIF-FERENT CLOTHES...
WAIT, YOU ALREADY HAVE SOME!
PUT THIS ON. TIGHTEN UP THE BELT...
CAN'T YOU WEAR IT WITH A LITTLE MORE STYLE?

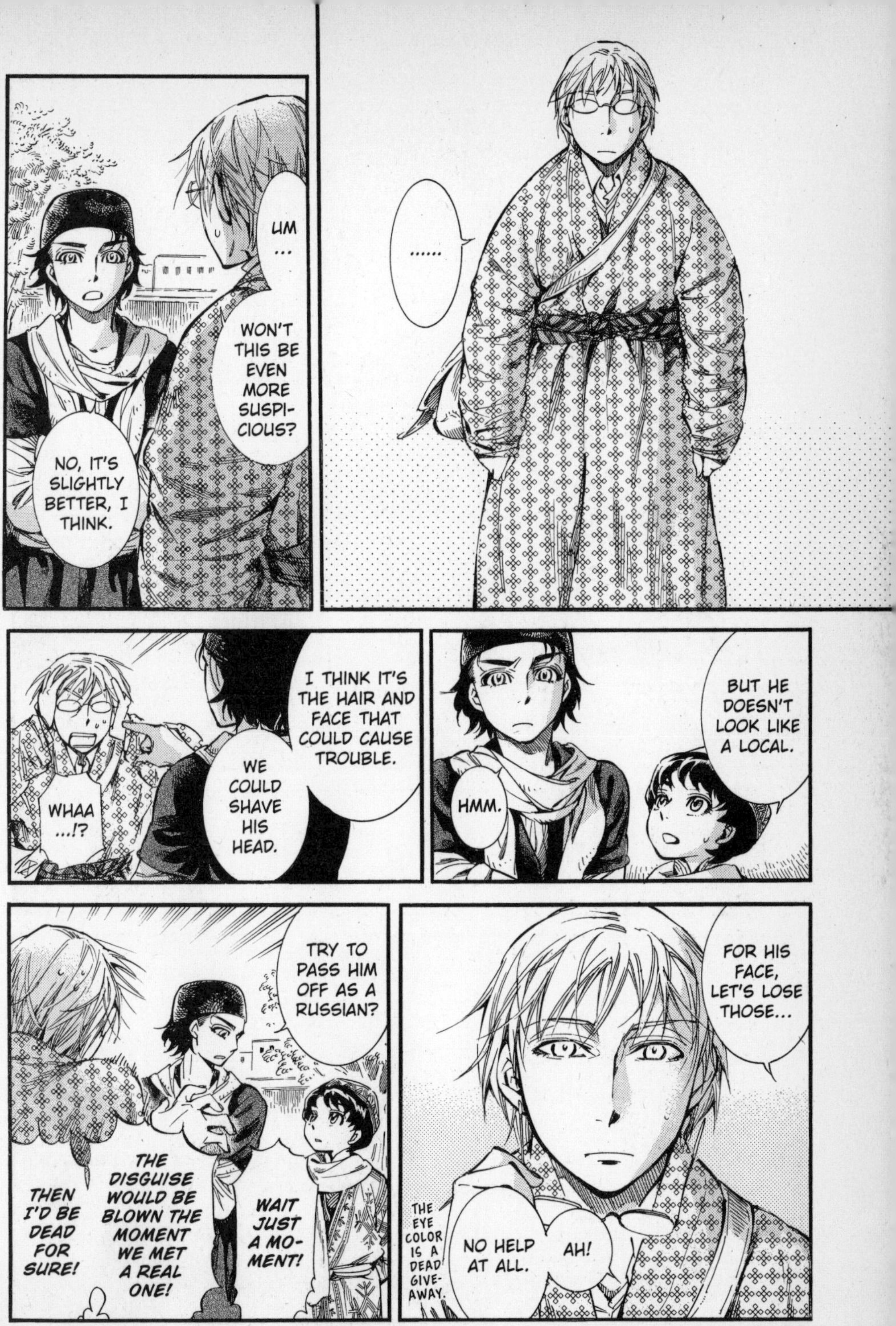
......
UM ...
WON'T THIS BE EVEN MORE SUSPICIOUS?
NO, IT'S SLIGHTLY BETTER, I THINK.
BUT HE DOESN'T LOOK LIKE A LOCAL.
HMM.
I THINK IT'S THE HAIR AND FACE THAT COULD CAUSE TROUBLE.
WE COULD SHAVE HIS HEAD.
WHAA ...!?
FOR HIS FACE, LET'S LOSE THOSE...
AH!
NO HELP AT ALL.
THE EYE COLOR IS A DEAD GIVE-AWAY.
TRY TO PASS HIM OFF AS A RUSSIAN?
WAIT JUST A MO-MENT!
THE DISGUISE WOULD BE BLOWN THE MOMENT WE MET A REAL ONE!
THEN I'D BE DEAD FOR SURE!

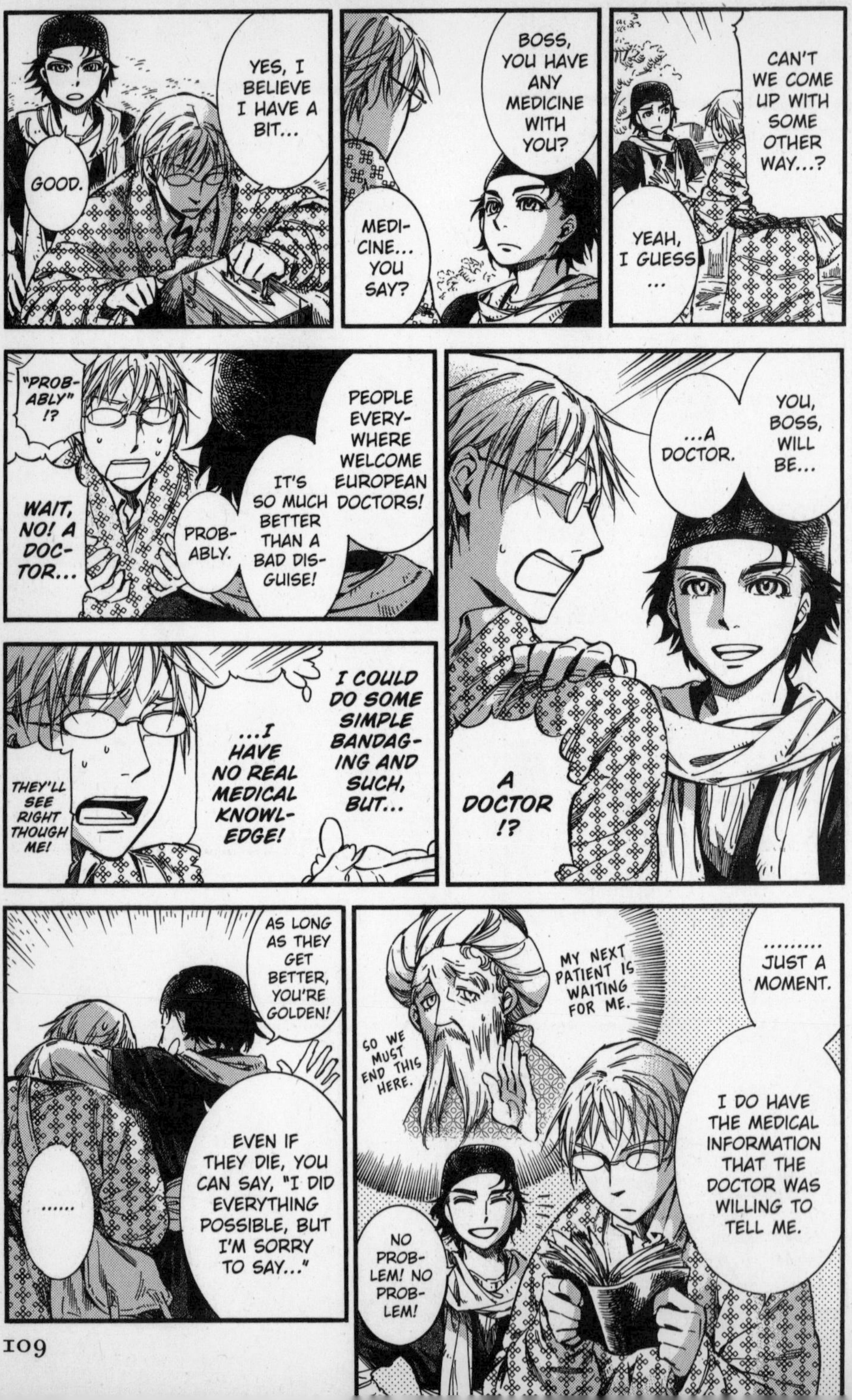
CAN'T WE COME UP WITH SOME OTHER WAY...?
YEAH, I GUESS ...
BOSS, YOU HAVE ANY MEDICINE WITH YOU?
MEDI-CINE... YOU SAY?
YES, I BELIEVE I HAVE A BIT...
GOOD.
YOU, BOSS, WILL BE...
...A DOCTOR.
A DOCTOR !?
PEOPLE EVERY-WHERE WELCOME EUROPEAN DOCTORS!
IT'S SO MUCH BETTER THAN A BAD DIS-GUISE!
PROB-ABLY.
"PROB-ABLY" !?
WAIT, NO! A DOC-TOR...
I COULD DO SOME SIMPLE BANDAG-ING AND SUCH, BUT...
...I HAVE NO REAL MEDICAL KNOWL-EDGE!
THEY'LL SEE RIGHT THOUGH ME!
.... JUST A MOMENT.
MY NEXT PATIENT IS WAITING FOR ME.
SO WE MUST END THIS HERE.
I DO HAVE THE MEDICAL INFORMATION THAT THE DOCTOR WAS WILLING TO TELL ME.
NO PROB-LEM! NO PROB-LEM!
AS LONG AS THEY GET BETTER, YOU'RE GOLDEN!
EVEN IF THEY DIE, YOU CAN SAY, "I DID EVERYTHING POSSIBLE, BUT I'M SORRY TO SAY..."
......

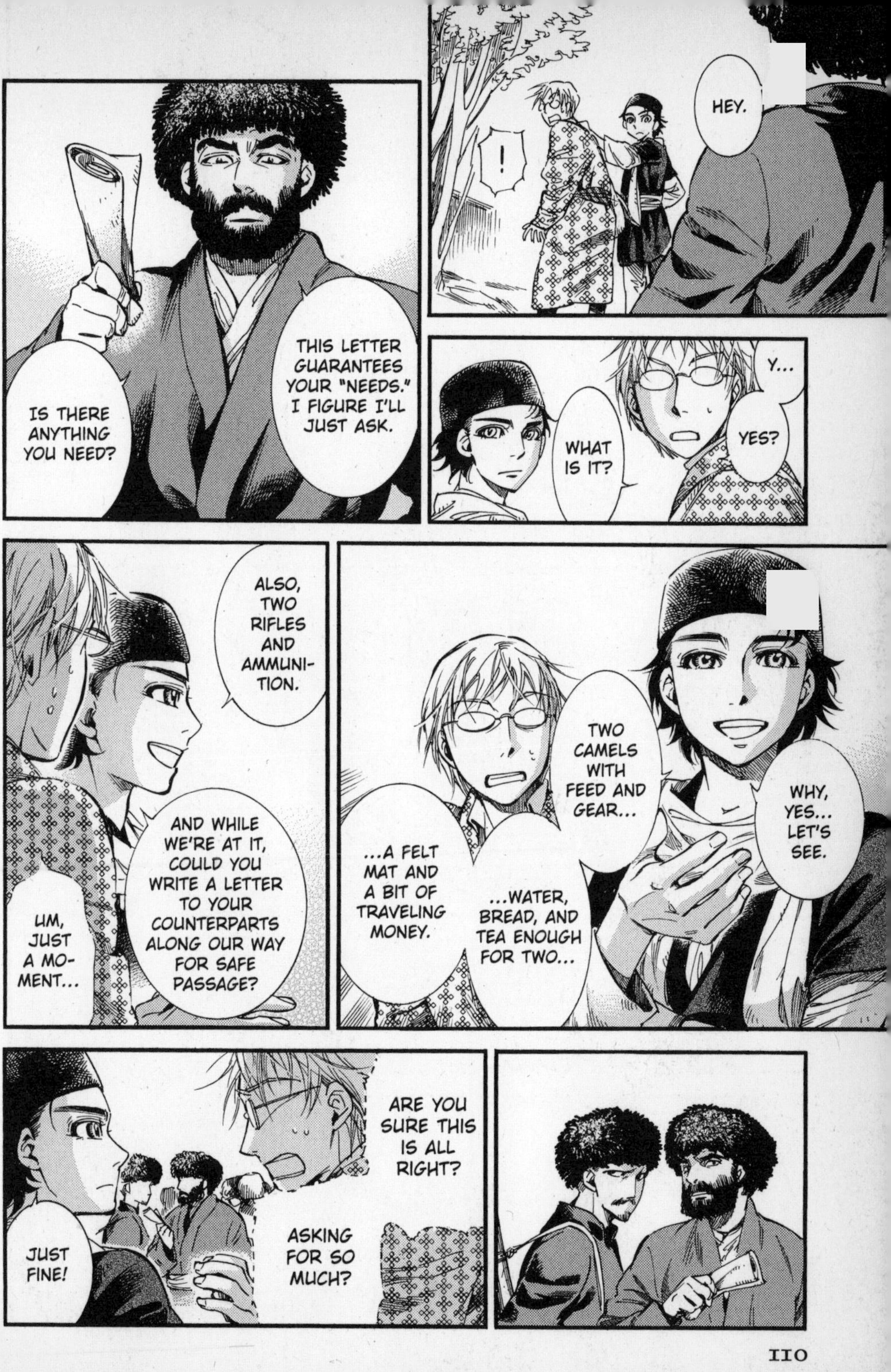
HEY.
!
Y...
YES?
WHAT IS IT?
THIS LETTER GUARANTEES YOUR "NEEDS." I FIGURE I'LL JUST ASK.
IS THERE ANYTHING YOU NEED?
WHY, YES... LET'S SEE.
TWO CAMELS WITH FEED AND GEAR...
...WATER, BREAD, AND TEA ENOUGH FOR TWO...
...A FELT MAT AND A BIT OF TRAVELING MONEY.
ALSO, TWO RIFLES AND AMMUNITION.
AND WHILE WE'RE AT IT, COULD YOU WRITE A LETTER TO YOUR COUNTERPARTS ALONG OUR WAY FOR SAFE PASSAGE?
UM, JUST A MOMENT...
ARE YOU SURE THIS IS ALL RIGHT?
ASKING FOR SO MUCH?
JUST FINE!

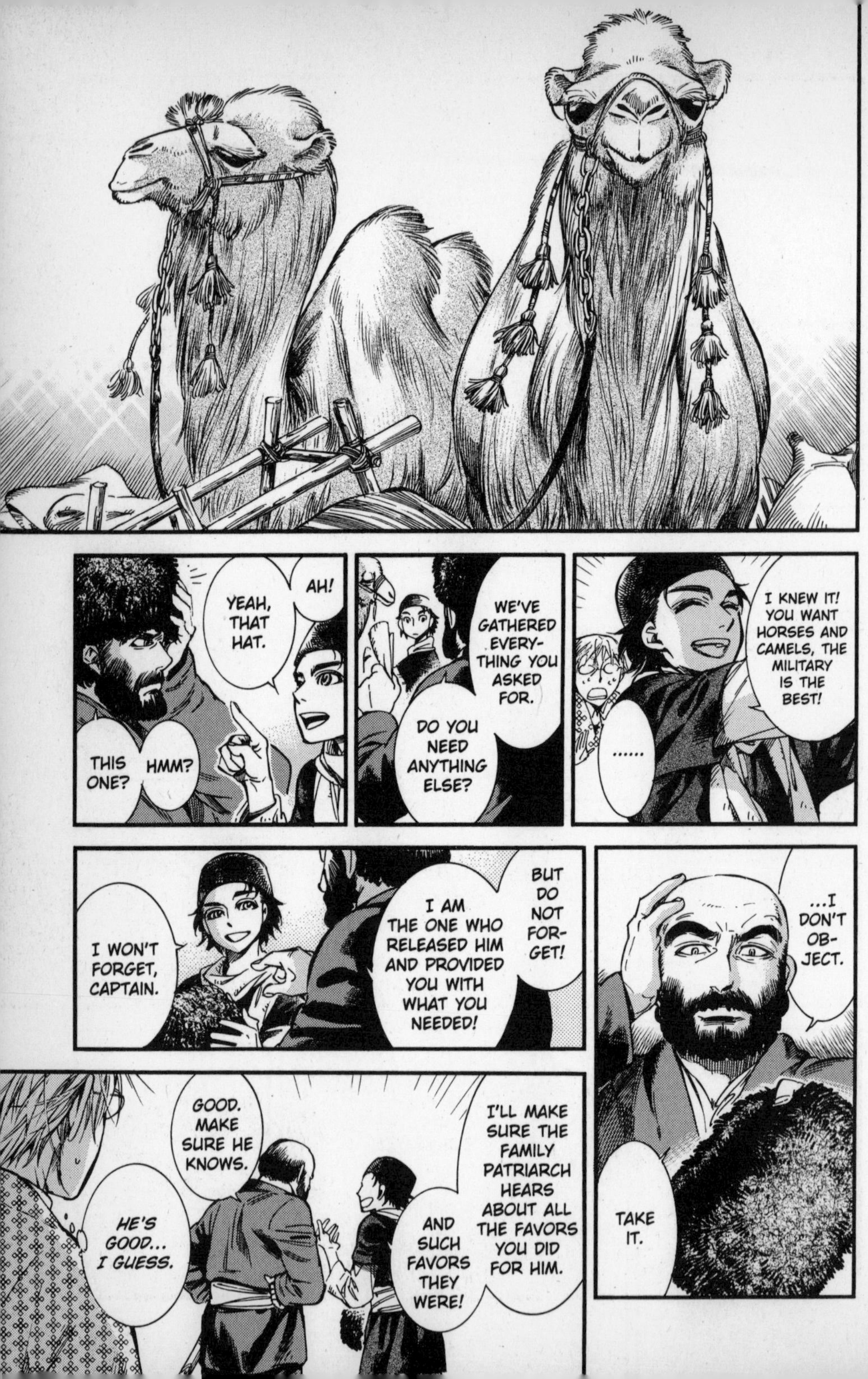
I KNEW IT! YOU WANT HORSES AND CAMELS, THE MILITARY IS THE BEST!
......
WE'VE GATHERED EVERY-THING YOU ASKED FOR.
DO YOU NEED ANYTHING ELSE?
AH!
YEAH, THAT HAT.
HMM?
THIS ONE?
...I DON'T OB-JECT.
TAKE IT.
BUT DO NOT FOR-GET!
I AM THE ONE WHO RELEASED HIM AND PROVIDED YOU WITH WHAT YOU NEEDED!
I WON'T FORGET, CAPTAIN.
I'LL MAKE SURE THE FAMILY PATRIARCH HEARS ABOUT ALL THE FAVORS YOU DID FOR HIM.
AND SUCH FAVORS THEY WERE!
GOOD. MAKE SURE HE KNOWS.
HE'S GOOD... I GUESS.

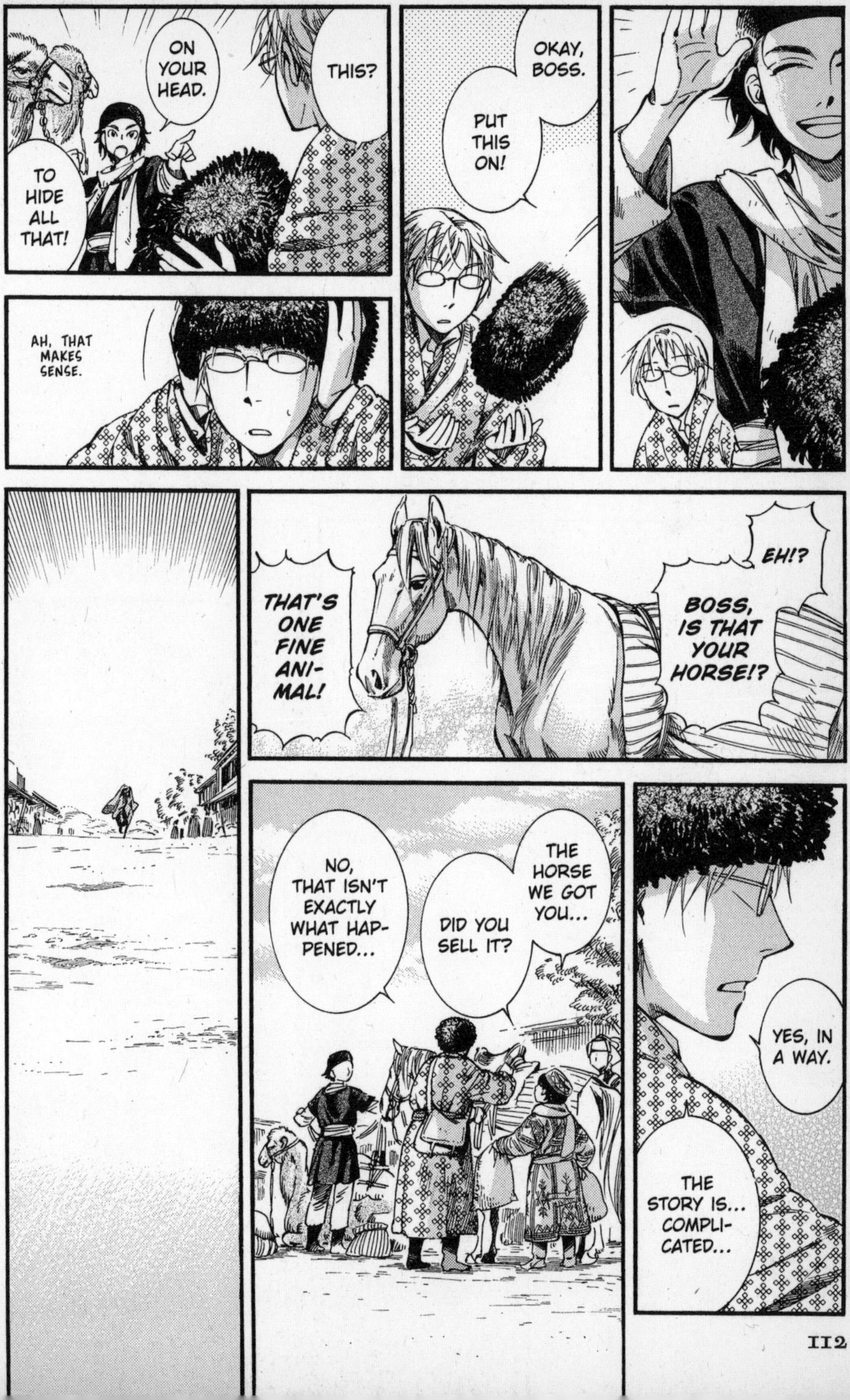
OKAY, BOSS.
PUT THIS ON!
THIS?
ON YOUR HEAD.
TO HIDE ALL THAT!
AH, THAT MAKES SENSE.
EH!?
BOSS, IS THAT YOUR HORSE!?
THAT'S ONE FINE ANI-MAL!
YES, IN A WAY.
THE STORY IS... COMPLI-CATED...
THE HORSE WE GOT YOU...
DID YOU SELL IT?
NO, THAT ISN'T EXACTLY WHAT HAP-PENED...

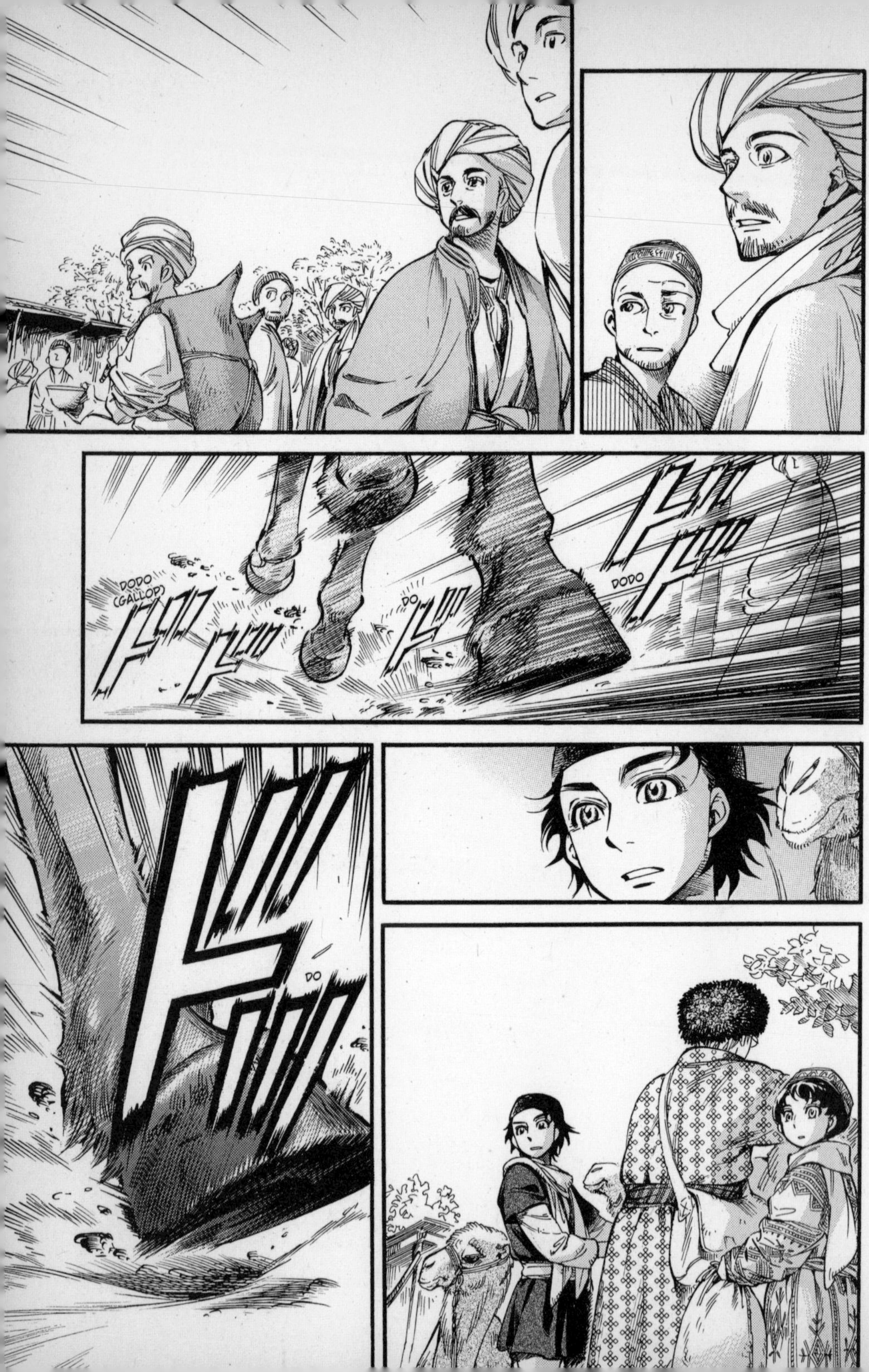
DODO
DO
DODO (GALLOP)
DO

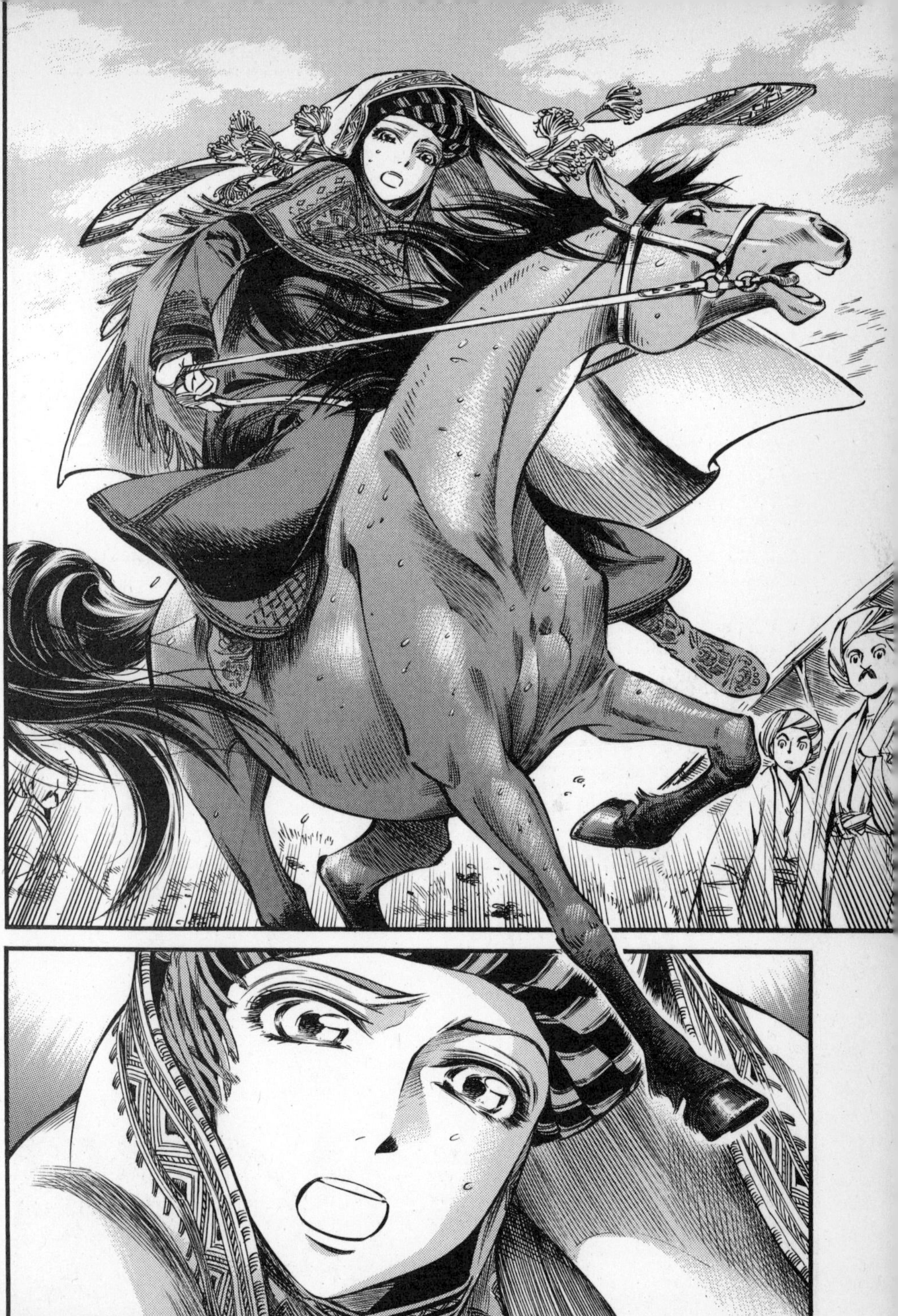

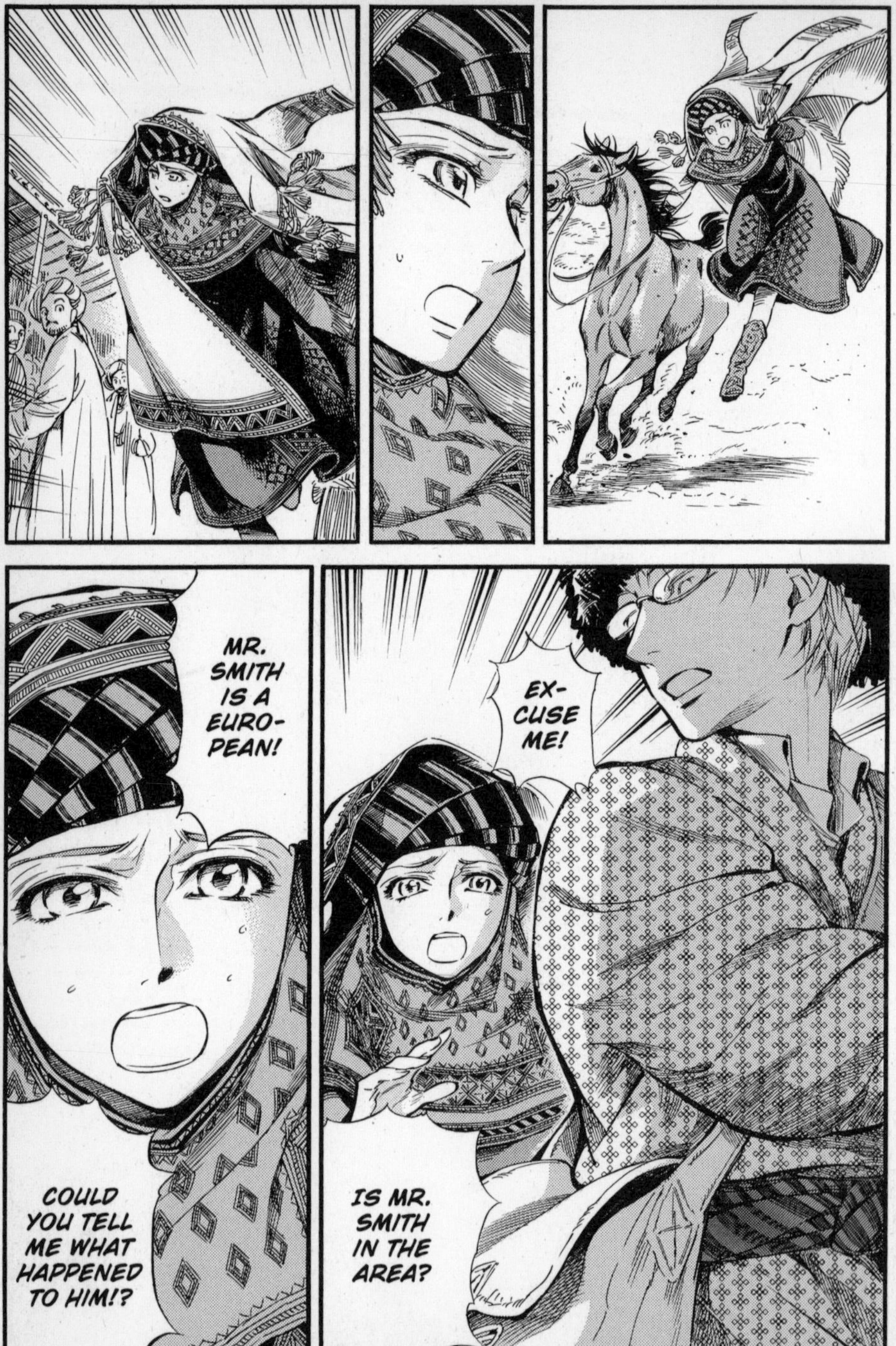
EX-CUSE ME!
IS MR. SMITH IN THE AREA?
MR. SMITH IS A EURO-PEAN!
COULD YOU TELL ME WHAT HAPPENED TO HIM!?

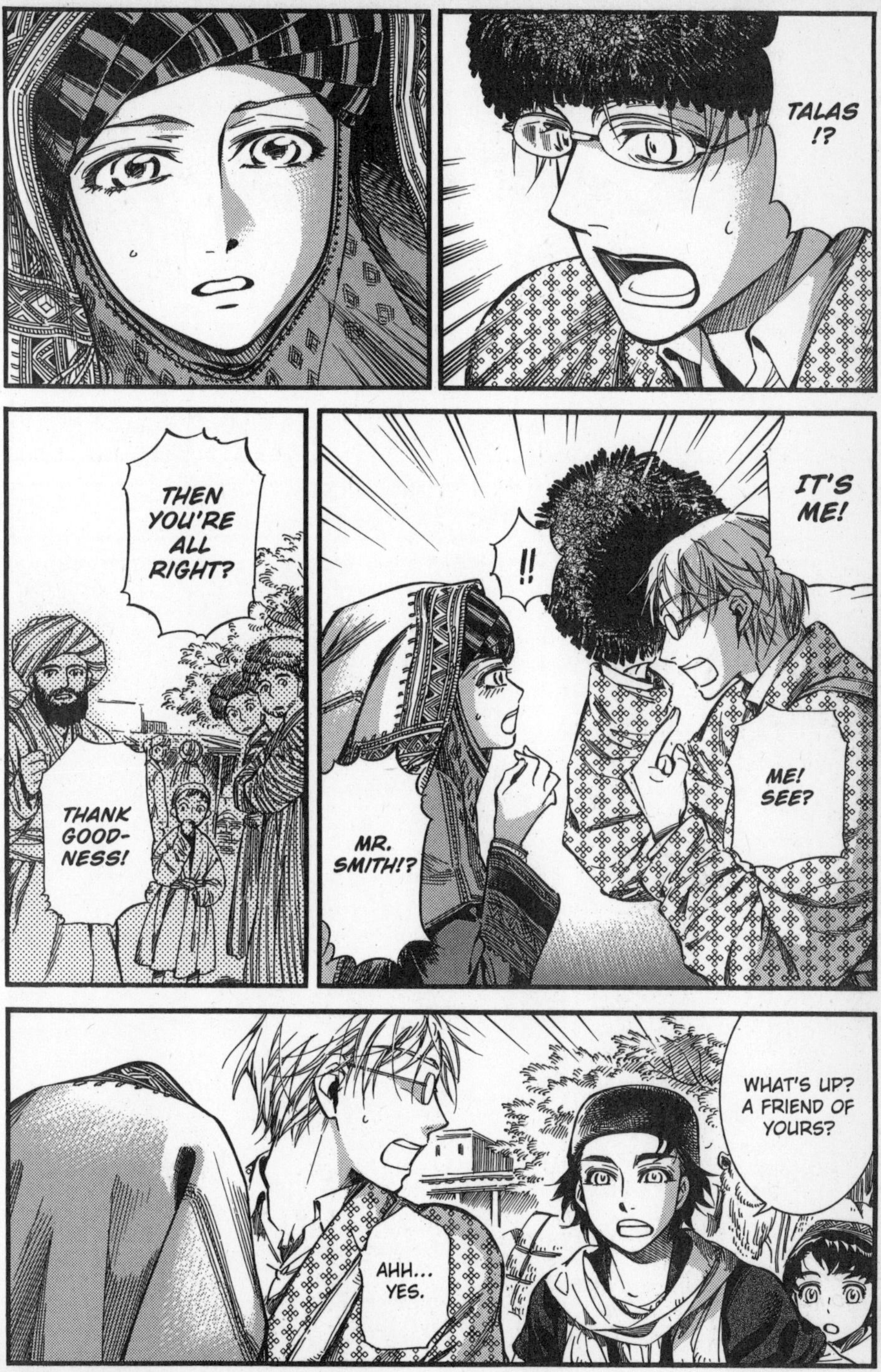
TALAS !?
IT'S ME!
!!
ME! SEE?
MR. SMITH!?
THEN YOU'RE ALL RIGHT?
THANK GOOD-NESS!
WHAT'S UP? A FRIEND OF YOURS?
AHH... YES.

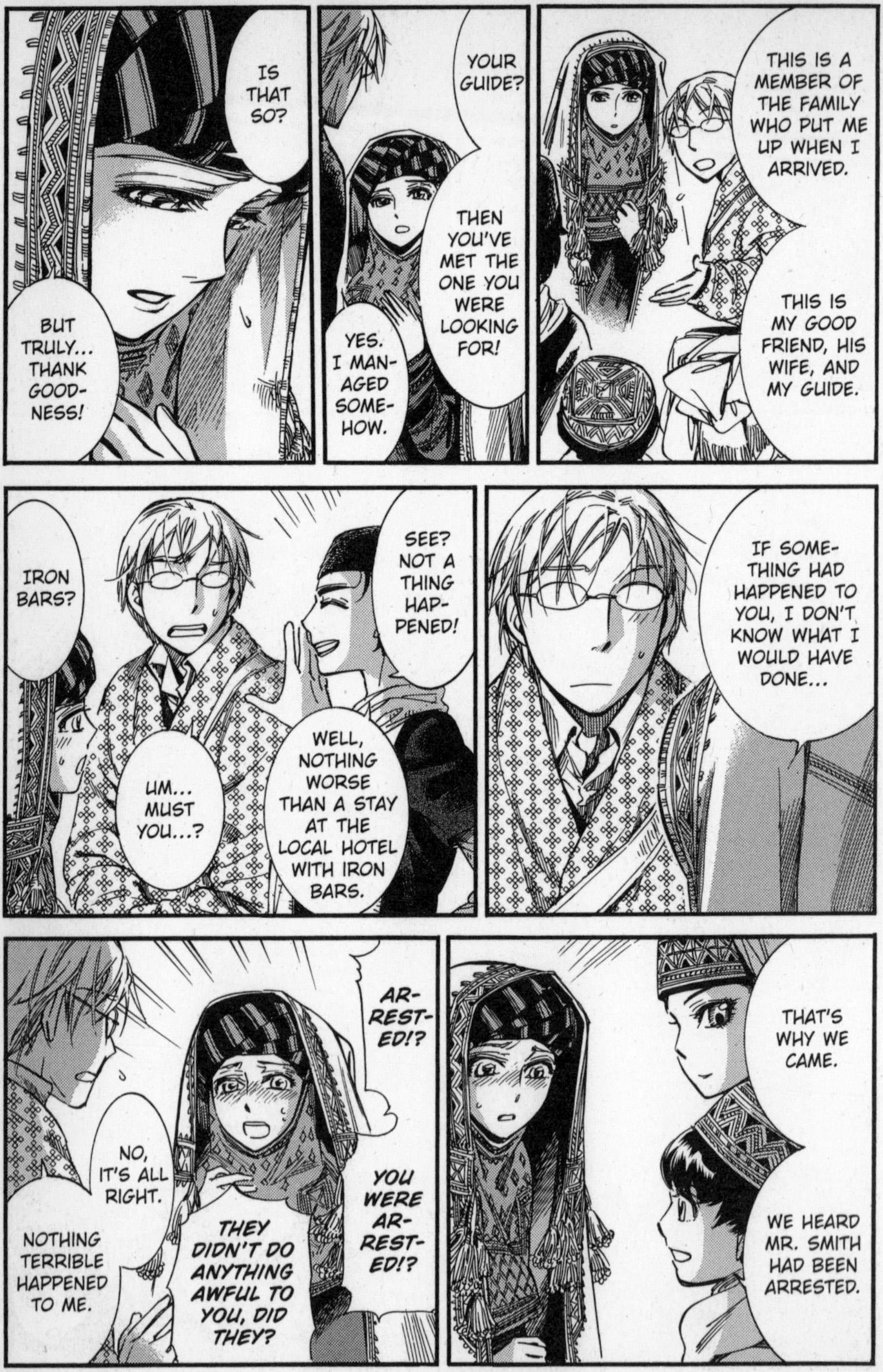
THIS IS A MEMBER OF THE FAMILY WHO PUT ME UP WHEN I ARRIVED.
THIS IS MY GOOD FRIEND, HIS WIFE, AND MY GUIDE.
YOUR GUIDE?
THEN YOU'VE MET THE ONE YOU WERE LOOKING FOR!
YES. I MANAGED SOMEHOW.
IS THAT SO?
BUT TRULY... THANK GOODNESS!
IF SOMETHING HAD HAPPENED TO YOU, I DON'T KNOW WHAT I WOULD HAVE DONE...
SEE? NOT A THING HAPPENED!
WELL, NOTHING WORSE THAN A STAY AT THE LOCAL HOTEL WITH IRON BARS.
IRON BARS?
UM... MUST YOU...?
WE HEARD MR. SMITH HAD BEEN ARRESTED.
THAT'S WHY WE CAME.
ARRESTED!?
YOU WERE ARRESTED!?
THEY DIDN'T DO ANYTHING AWFUL TO YOU, DID THEY?
NO, IT'S ALL RIGHT.
NOTHING TERRIBLE HAPPENED TO ME.

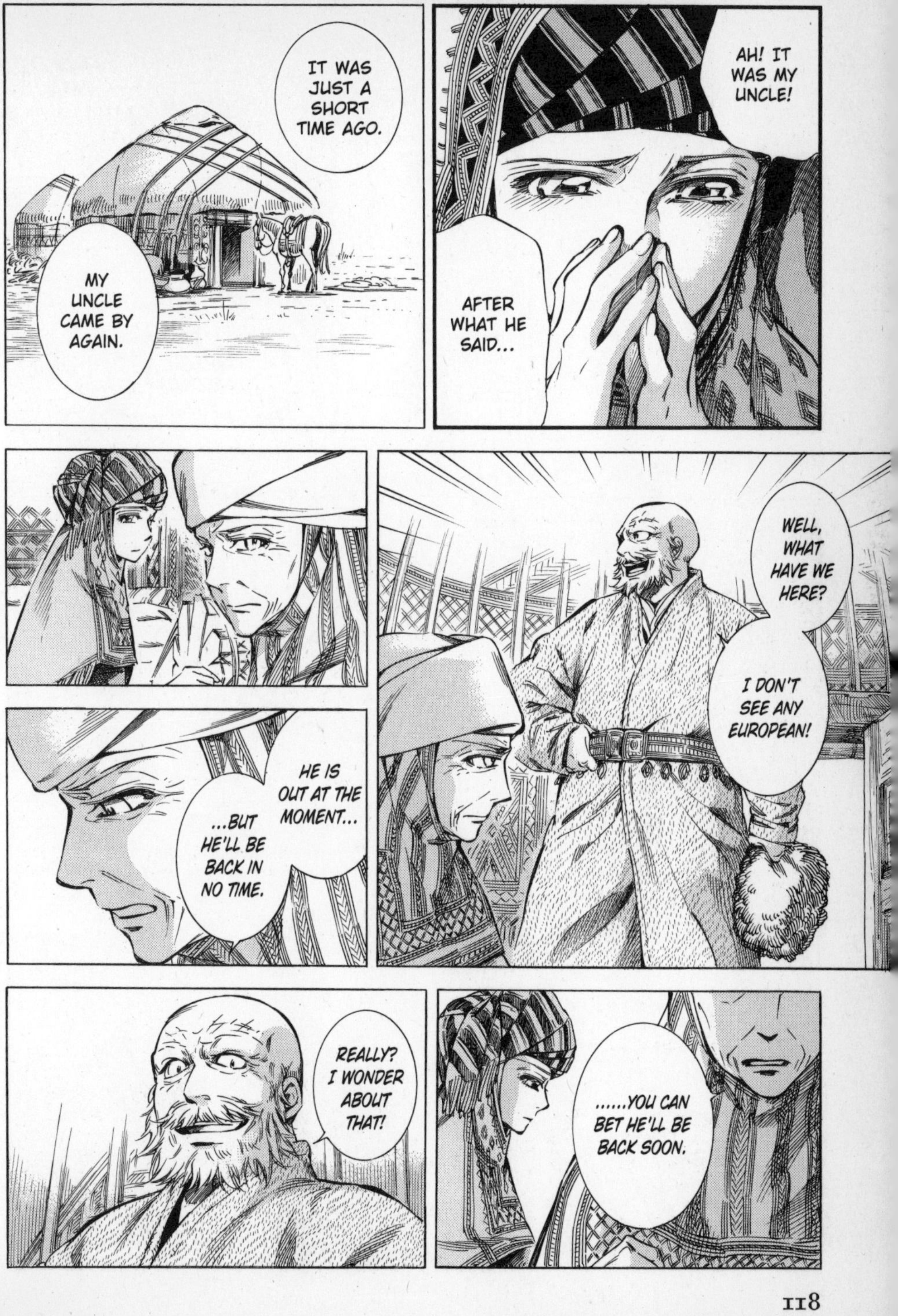
AH! IT WAS MY UNCLE!
AFTER WHAT HE SAID...
IT WAS JUST A SHORT TIME AGO.
MY UNCLE CAME BY AGAIN.
WELL, WHAT HAVE WE HERE?
I DON'T SEE ANY EUROPEAN!
HE IS OUT AT THE MOMENT...
...BUT HE'LL BE BACK IN NO TIME.
......YOU CAN BET HE'LL BE BACK SOON.
REALLY? I WONDER ABOUT THAT!

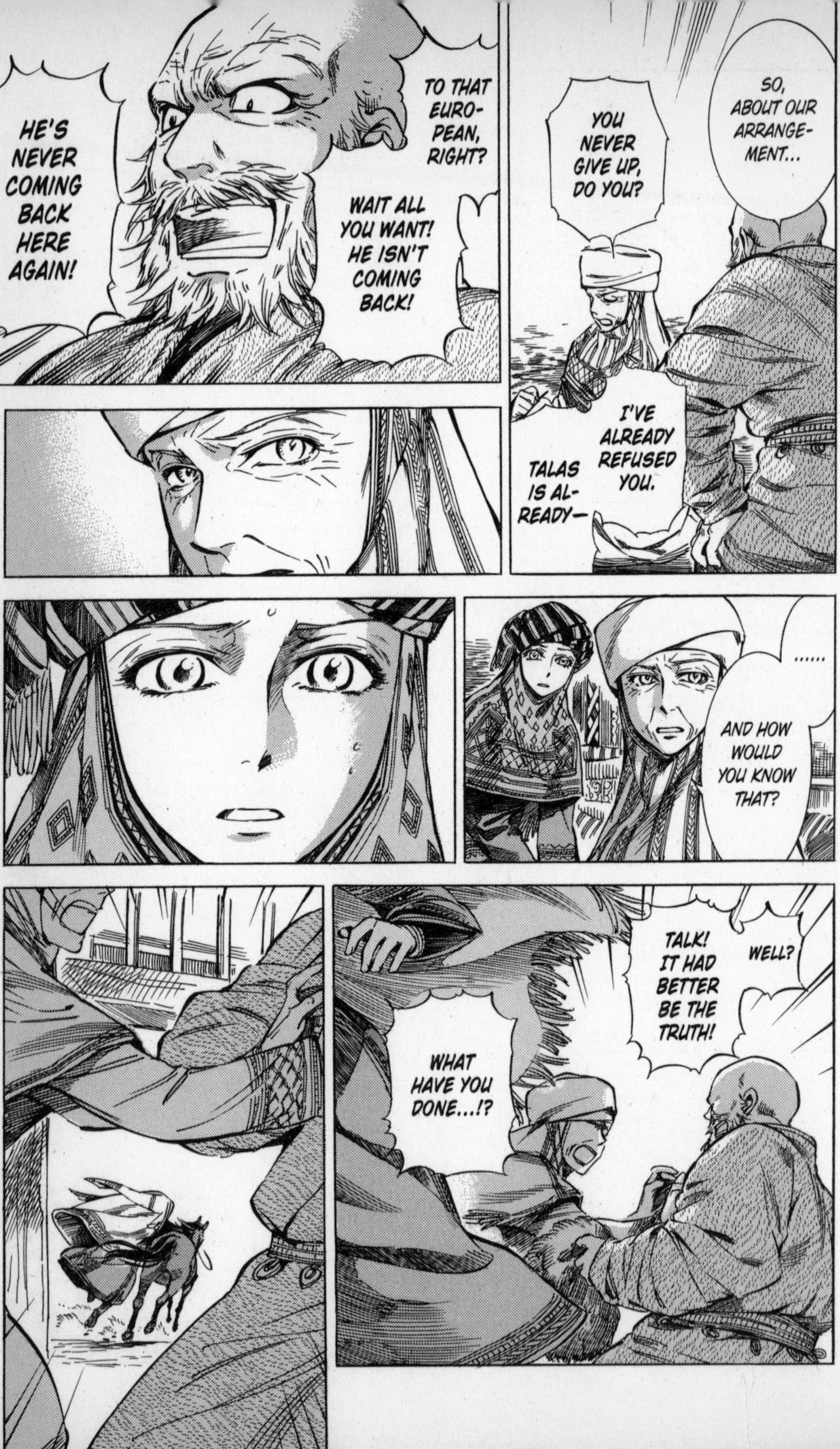
SO, ABOUT OUR ARRANGE-MENT...
YOU NEVER GIVE UP, DO YOU?
I'VE ALREADY REFUSED YOU.
TALAS IS AL-READY—
TO THAT EURO-PEAN, RIGHT?
HE'S NEVER COMING BACK HERE AGAIN!
WAIT ALL YOU WANT! HE ISN'T COMING BACK!
......
AND HOW WOULD YOU KNOW THAT?
WELL?
TALK! IT HAD BETTER BE THE TRUTH!
WHAT HAVE YOU DONE...!?

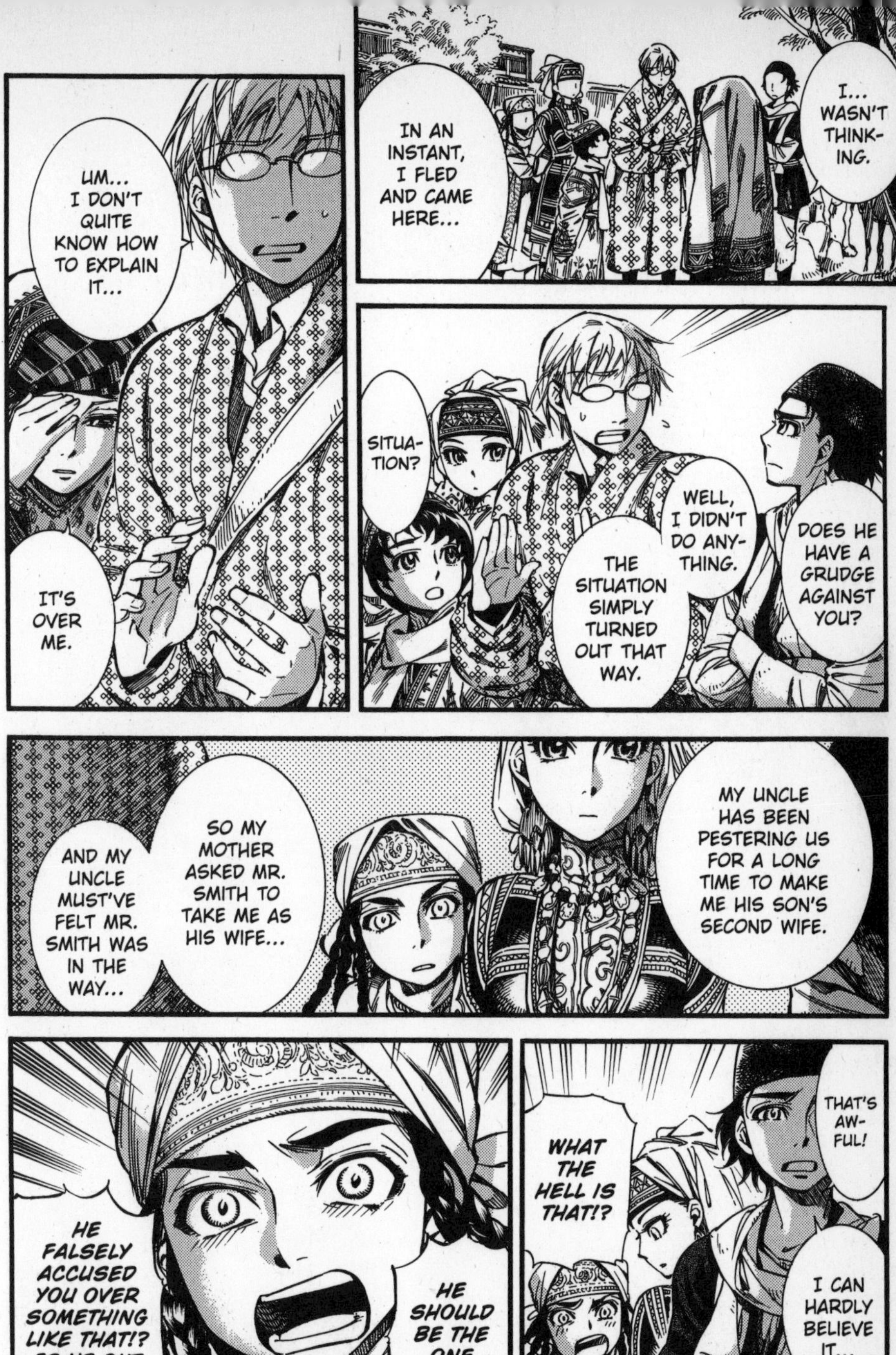
I... WASN'T THINKING.
IN AN INSTANT, I FLED AND CAME HERE...
DOES HE HAVE A GRUDGE AGAINST YOU?
WELL, I DIDN'T DO ANYTHING.
THE SITUATION SIMPLY TURNED OUT THAT WAY.
SITUATION?
UM... I DON'T QUITE KNOW HOW TO EXPLAIN IT...
IT'S OVER ME.
MY UNCLE HAS BEEN PESTERING US FOR A LONG TIME TO MAKE ME HIS SON'S SECOND WIFE.
SO MY MOTHER ASKED MR. SMITH TO TAKE ME AS HIS WIFE...
AND MY UNCLE MUST'VE FELT MR. SMITH WAS IN THE WAY...
THAT'S AWFUL!
I CAN HARDLY BELIEVE IT...
WHAT THE HELL IS THAT!?
HE SHOULD BE THE ONE BEING HATED!
HE FALSELY ACCUSED YOU OVER SOMETHING LIKE THAT!? IS HE OUT OF HIS MIND!?

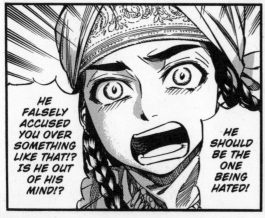

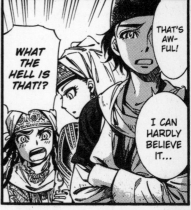

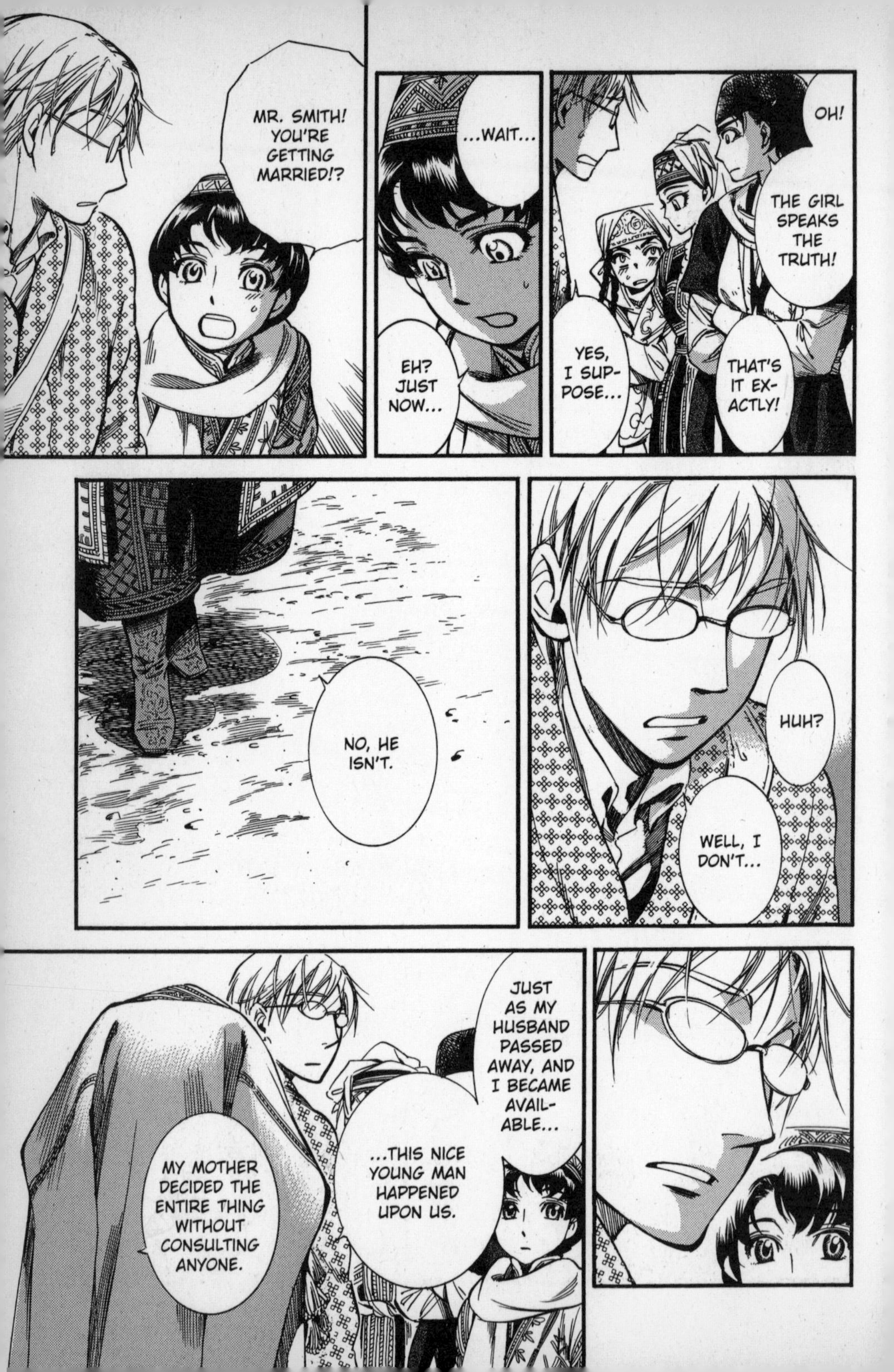
OH!
THE GIRL SPEAKS THE TRUTH!
THAT'S IT EX-ACTLY!
YES, I SUP-POSE...
...WAIT...
EH? JUST NOW...
MR. SMITH! YOU'RE GETTING MARRIED!?
HUH?
WELL, I DON'T...
NO, HE ISN'T.
JUST AS MY HUSBAND PASSED AWAY, AND I BECAME AVAIL-ABLE...
...THIS NICE YOUNG MAN HAPPENED UPON US.
MY MOTHER DECIDED THE ENTIRE THING WITHOUT CONSULTING ANYONE.

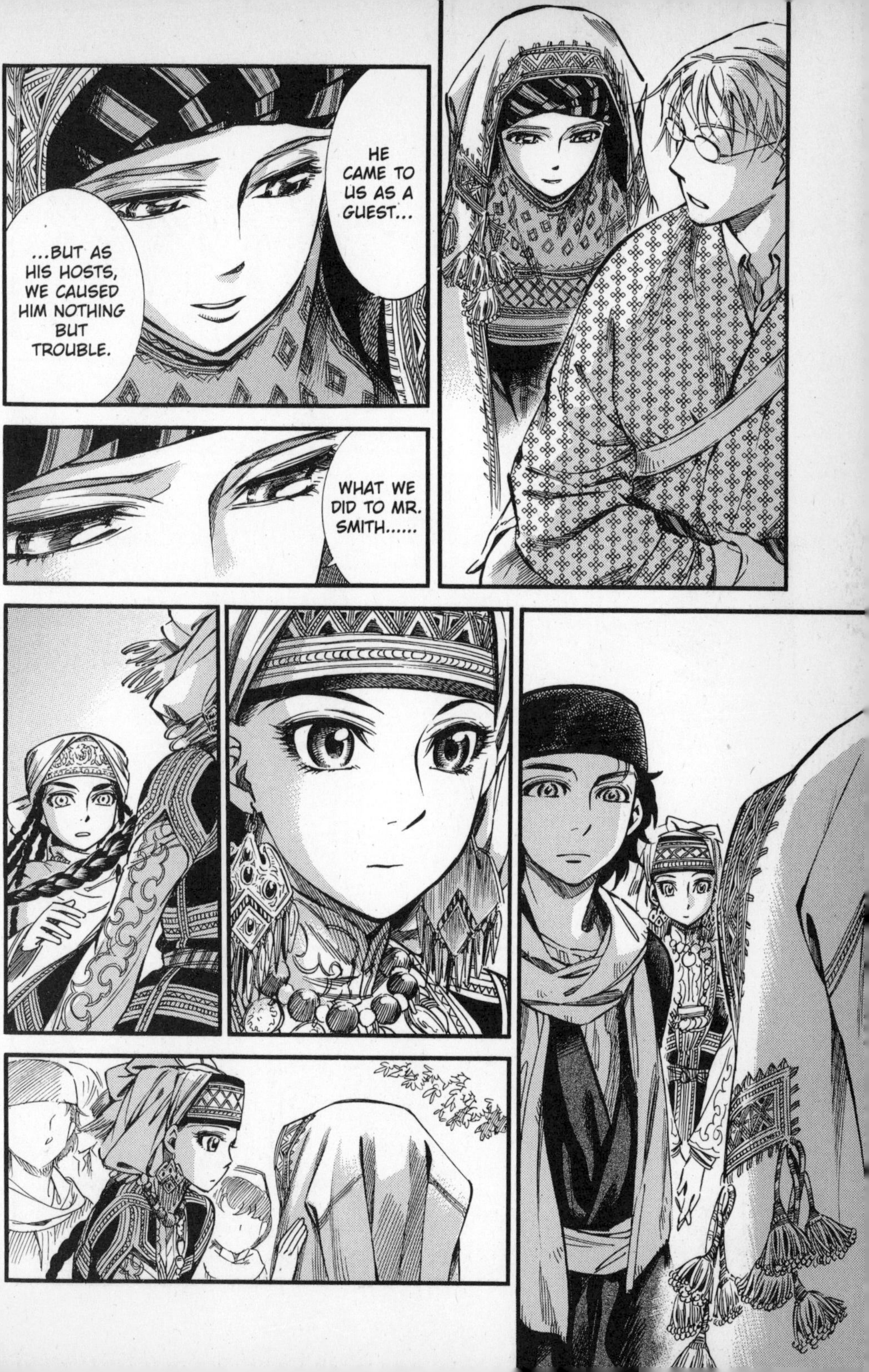
HE CAME TO US AS A GUEST...
...BUT AS HIS HOSTS, WE CAUSED HIM NOTHING BUT TROUBLE.
WHAT WE DID TO MR. SMITH......

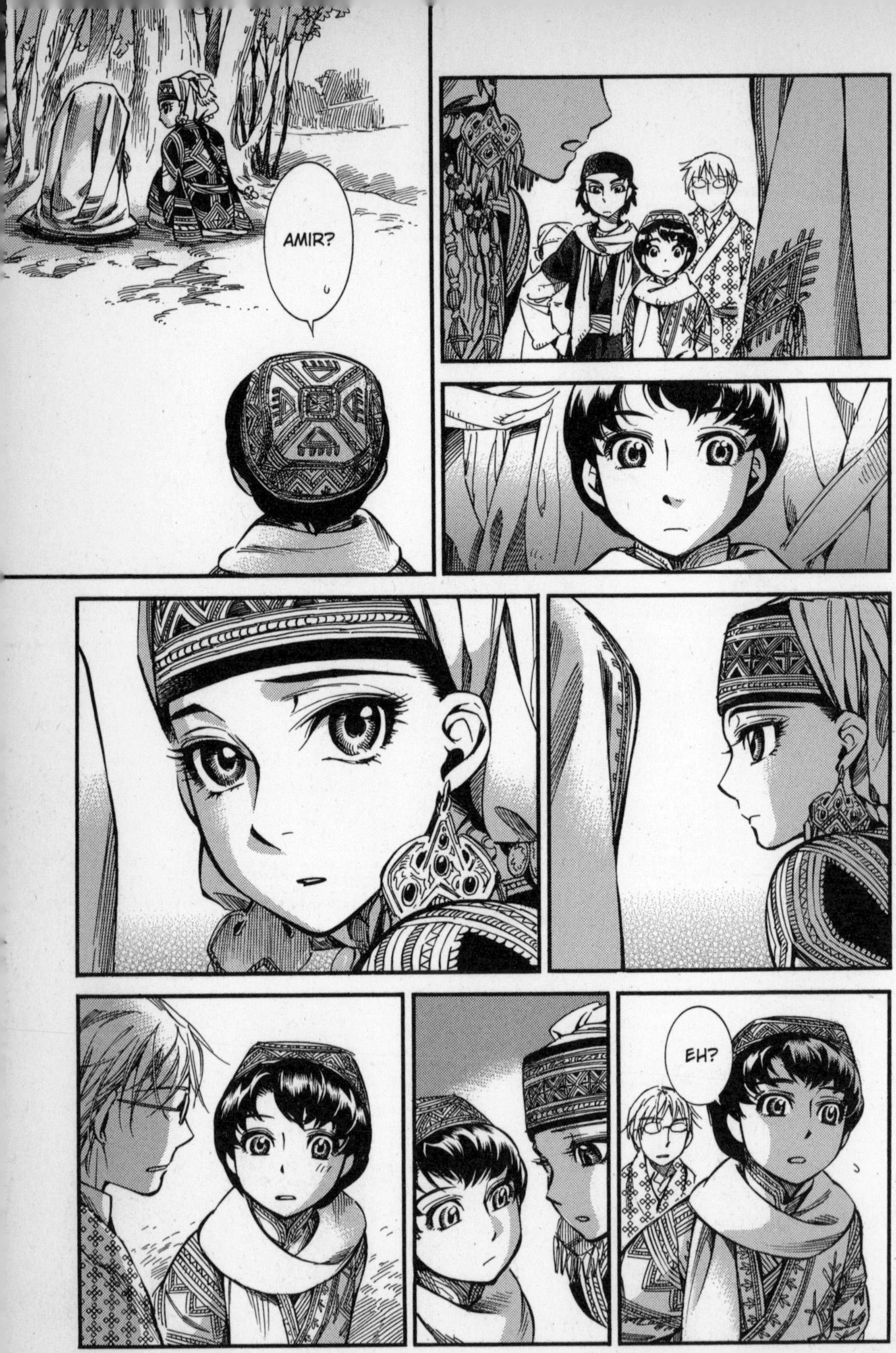
AMIR?
EH?

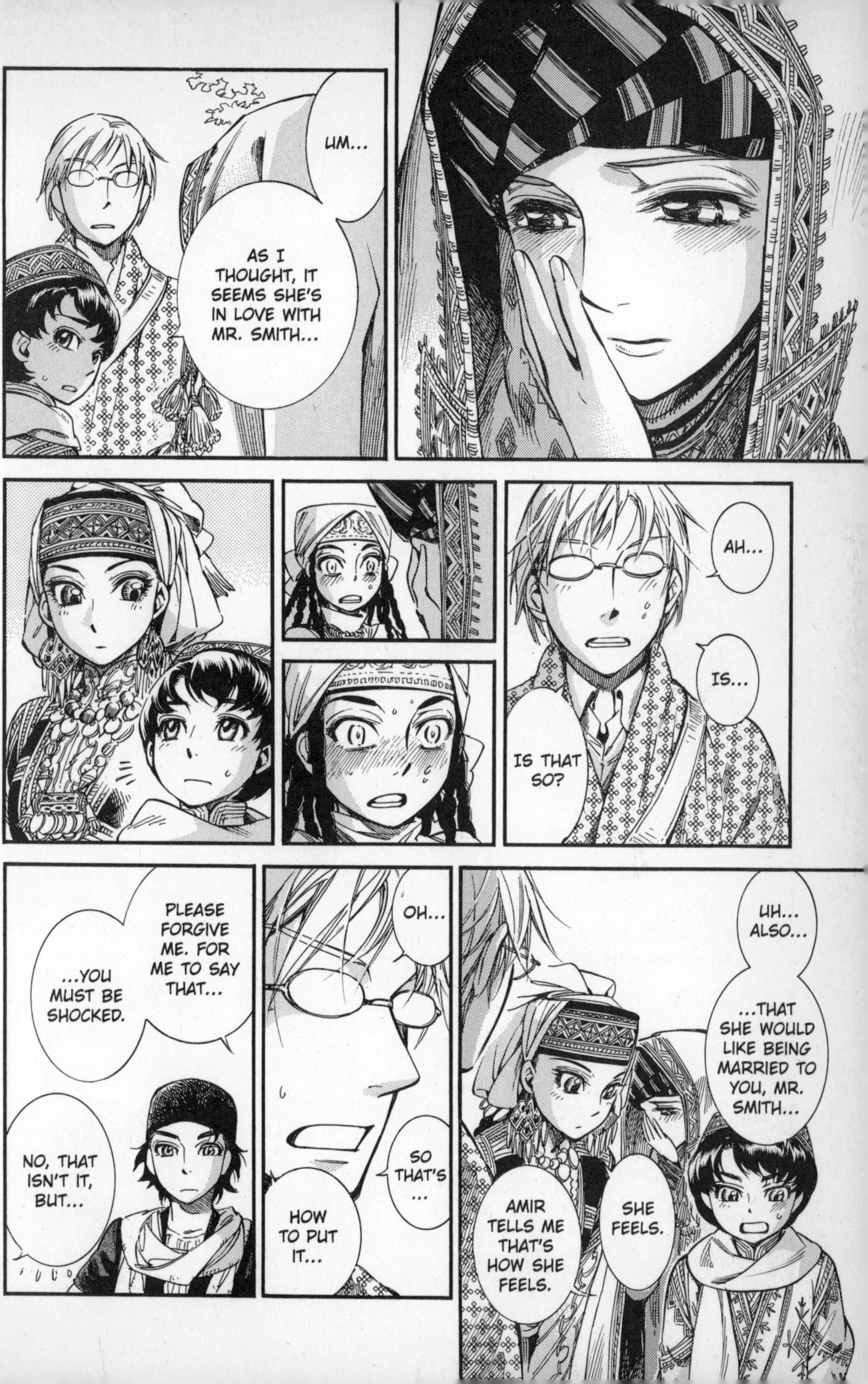
UM...
AS I THOUGHT, IT SEEMS SHE'S IN LOVE WITH MR. SMITH...
AH...
IS...
IS THAT SO?
UH... ALSO...
...THAT SHE WOULD LIKE BEING MARRIED TO YOU, MR. SMITH...
SHE FEELS.
AMIR TELLS ME THAT'S HOW SHE FEELS.
OH...
SO THAT'S ...
HOW TO PUT IT...
PLEASE FORGIVE ME. FOR ME TO SAY THAT...
...YOU MUST BE SHOCKED.
NO, THAT ISN'T IT, BUT...

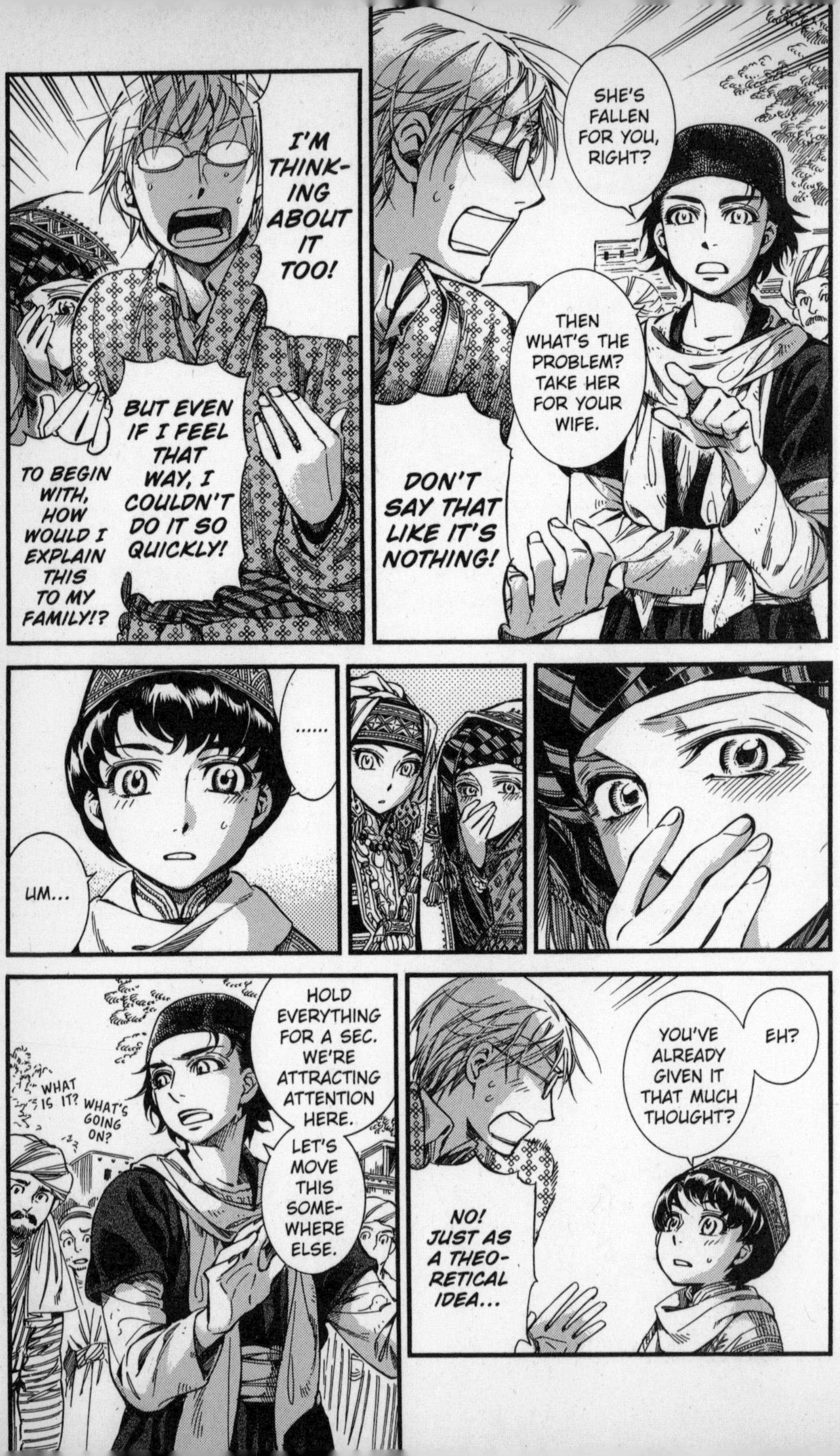
SHE'S FALLEN FOR YOU, RIGHT?
THEN WHAT'S THE PROBLEM? TAKE HER FOR YOUR WIFE.
DON'T SAY THAT LIKE IT'S NOTHING!
I'M THINKING ABOUT IT TOO!
BUT EVEN IF I FEEL THAT WAY, I COULDN'T DO IT SO QUICKLY!
TO BEGIN WITH, HOW WOULD I EXPLAIN THIS TO MY FAMILY!?
......
UM...
EH?
YOU'VE ALREADY GIVEN IT THAT MUCH THOUGHT?
NO! JUST AS A THEORETICAL IDEA...
HOLD EVERYTHING FOR A SEC. WE'RE ATTRACTING ATTENTION HERE.
LET'S MOVE THIS SOMEWHERE ELSE.
WHAT IS IT?
WHAT'S GOING ON?

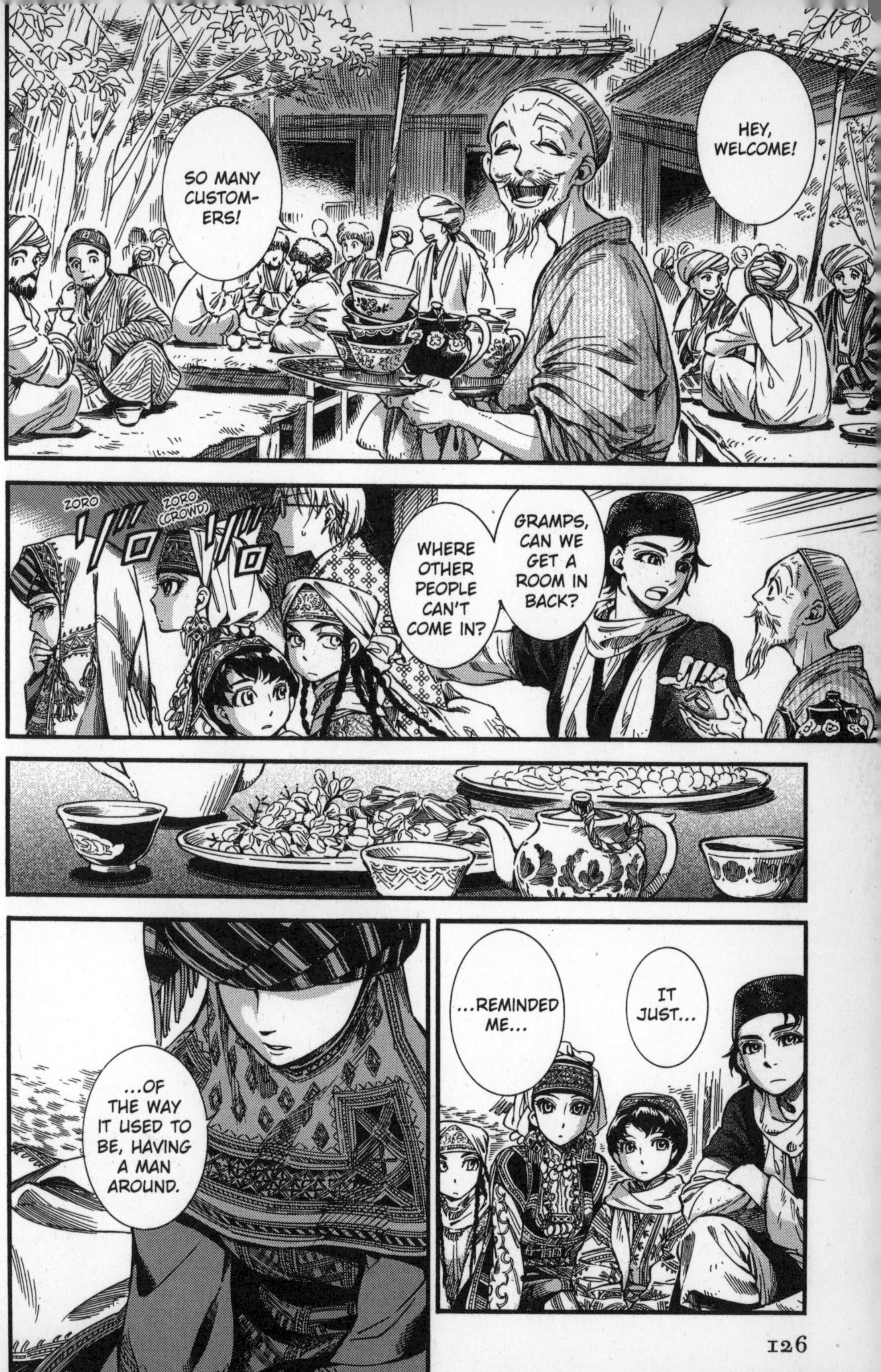
HEY, WELCOME!
SO MANY CUSTOMERS!
GRAMPS, CAN WE GET A ROOM IN BACK?
WHERE OTHER PEOPLE CAN'T COME IN?
ZORO (CROWD)
ZORO
IT JUST...
...REMINDED ME...
...OF THE WAY IT USED TO BE, HAVING A MAN AROUND.

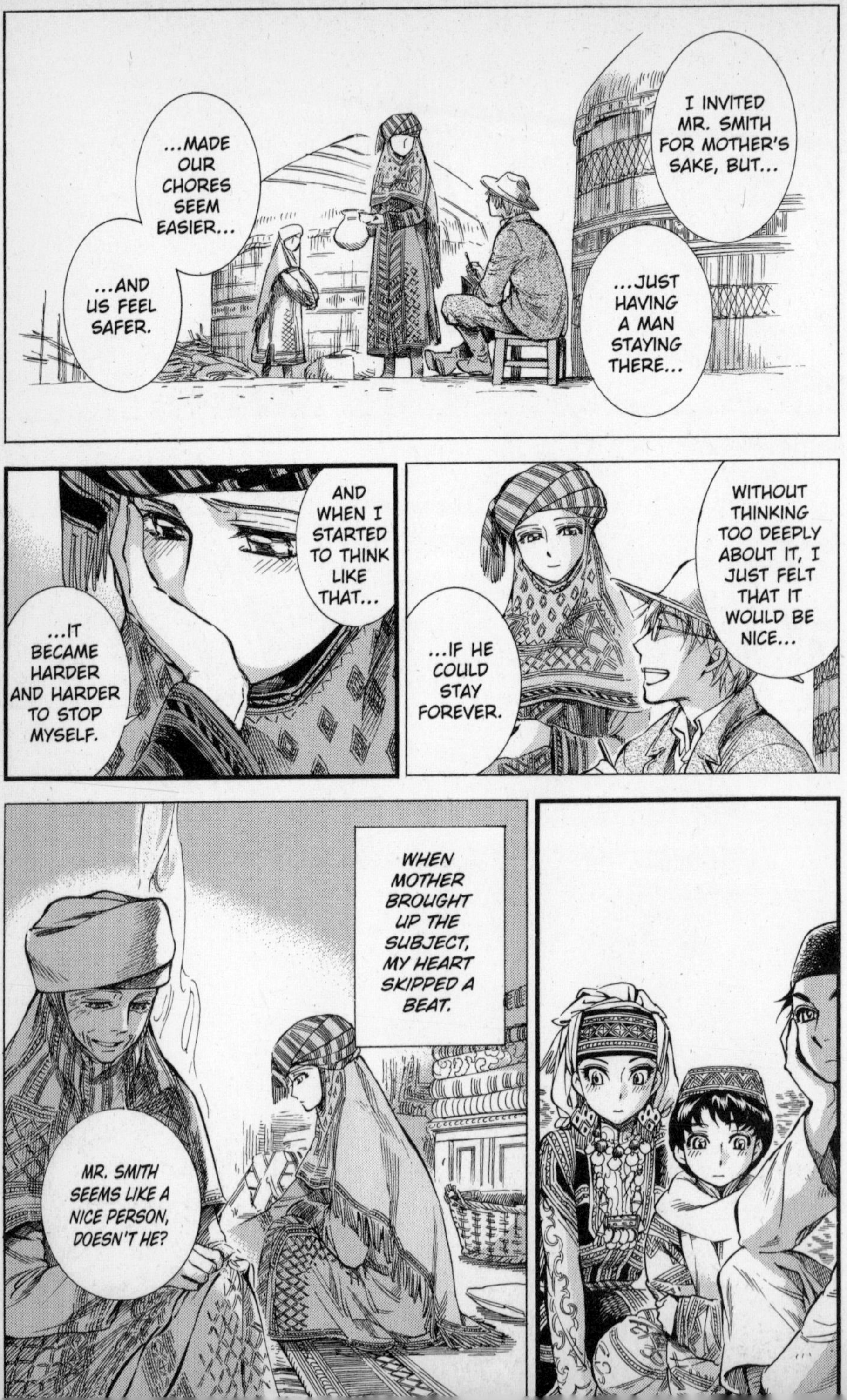
I INVITED MR. SMITH FOR MOTHER'S SAKE, BUT...
...JUST HAVING A MAN STAYING THERE...
...MADE OUR CHORES SEEM EASIER...
...AND US FEEL SAFER.
WITHOUT THINKING TOO DEEPLY ABOUT IT, I JUST FELT THAT IT WOULD BE NICE...
...IF HE COULD STAY FOREVER.
AND WHEN I STARTED TO THINK LIKE THAT...
...IT BECAME HARDER AND HARDER TO STOP MYSELF.
WHEN MOTHER BROUGHT UP THE SUBJECT, MY HEART SKIPPED A BEAT.
MR. SMITH SEEMS LIKE A NICE PERSON, DOESN'T HE?

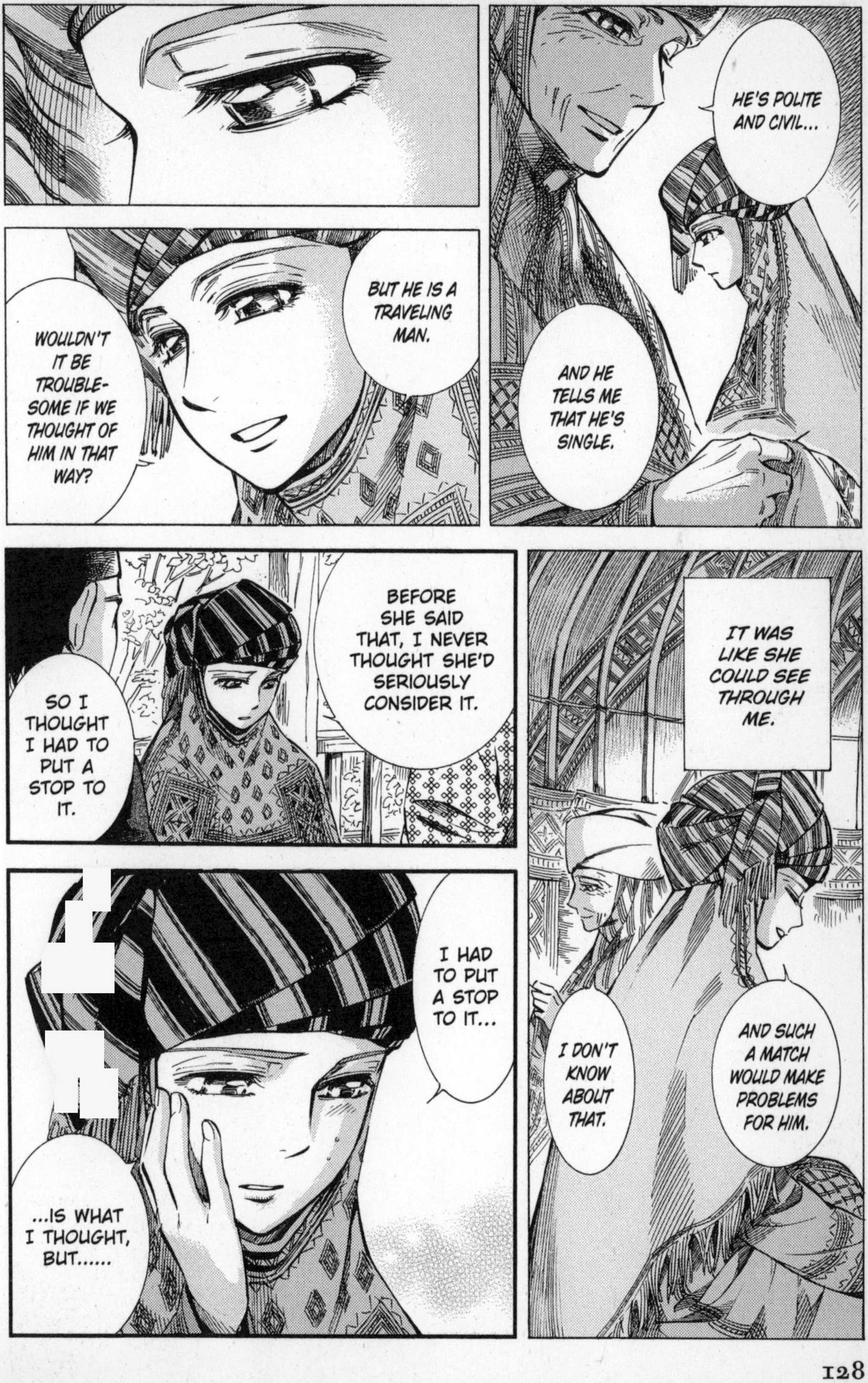
HE'S POLITE AND CIVIL...
AND HE TELLS ME THAT HE'S SINGLE.
BUT HE IS A TRAVELING MAN.
WOULDN'T IT BE TROUBLE-SOME IF WE THOUGHT OF HIM IN THAT WAY?
IT WAS LIKE SHE COULD SEE THROUGH ME.
AND SUCH A MATCH WOULD MAKE PROBLEMS FOR HIM.
I DON'T KNOW ABOUT THAT.
BEFORE SHE SAID THAT, I NEVER THOUGHT SHE'D SERIOUSLY CONSIDER IT.
SO I THOUGHT I HAD TO PUT A STOP TO IT.
I HAD TO PUT A STOP TO IT...
...IS WHAT I THOUGHT, BUT......

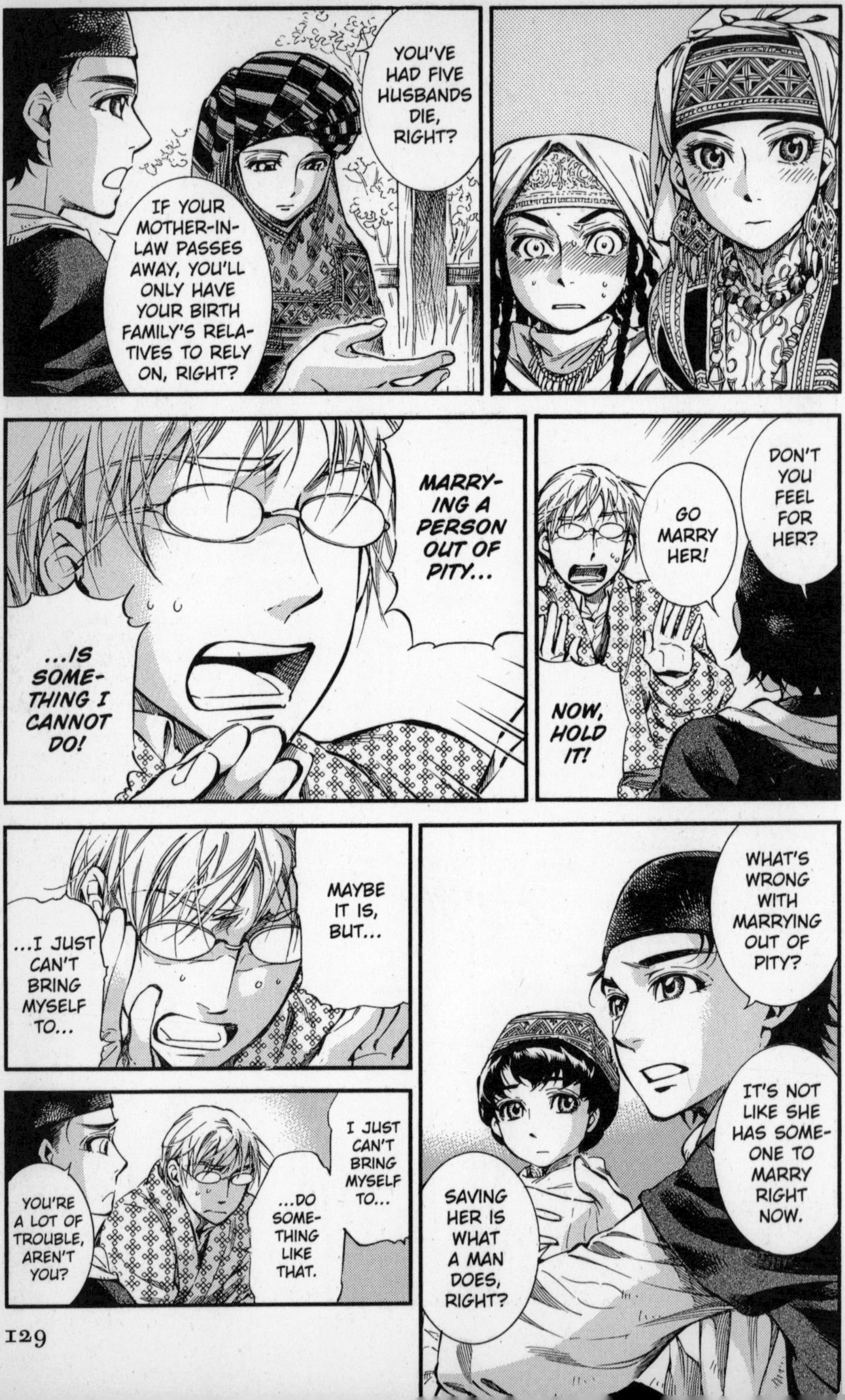

YOU'VE HAD FIVE HUSBANDS DIE, RIGHT?
IF YOUR MOTHER-IN-LAW PASSES AWAY, YOU'LL ONLY HAVE YOUR BIRTH FAMILY'S RELATIVES TO RELY ON, RIGHT?
DON'T YOU FEEL FOR HER?
GO MARRY HER!
NOW, HOLD IT!
MARRYING A PERSON OUT OF PITY...
...IS SOMETHING I CANNOT DO!
WHAT'S WRONG WITH MARRYING OUT OF PITY?
IT'S NOT LIKE SHE HAS SOMEONE TO MARRY RIGHT NOW.
SAVING HER IS WHAT A MAN DOES, RIGHT?
MAYBE IT IS, BUT...
...I JUST CAN'T BRING MYSELF TO...
I JUST CAN'T BRING MYSELF TO...
...DO SOMETHING LIKE THAT.
YOU'RE A LOT OF TROUBLE, AREN'T YOU?

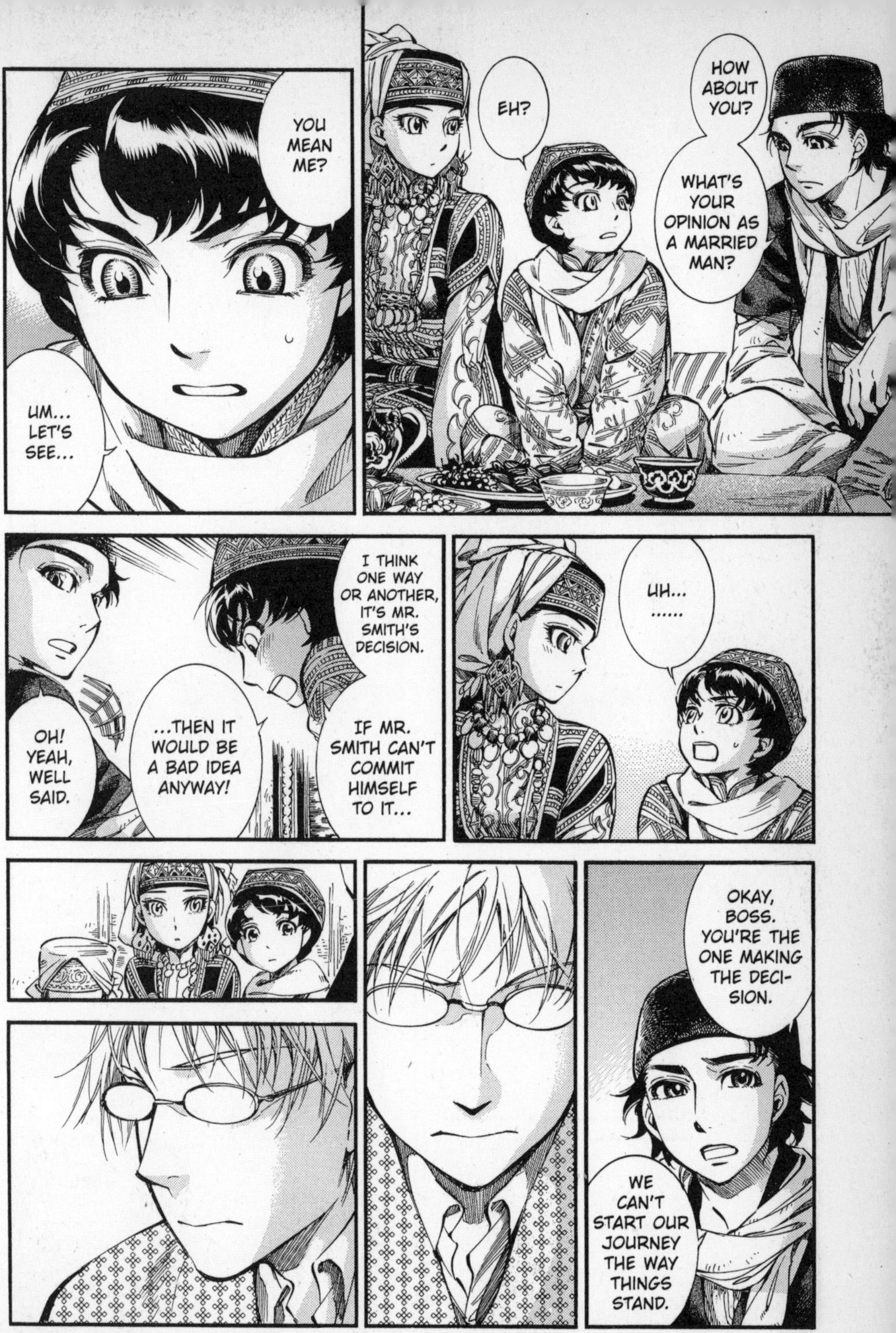
HOW ABOUT YOU?
WHAT'S YOUR OPINION AS A MARRIED MAN?
EH?
YOU MEAN ME?
UM... LET'S SEE...
UH... ......
I THINK ONE WAY OR ANOTHER, IT'S MR. SMITH'S DECISION.
IF MR. SMITH CAN'T COMMIT HIMSELF TO IT...
...THEN IT WOULD BE A BAD IDEA ANYWAY!
OH! YEAH, WELL SAID.
OKAY, BOSS. YOU'RE THE ONE MAKING THE DECISION.
WE CAN'T START OUR JOURNEY THE WAY THINGS STAND.

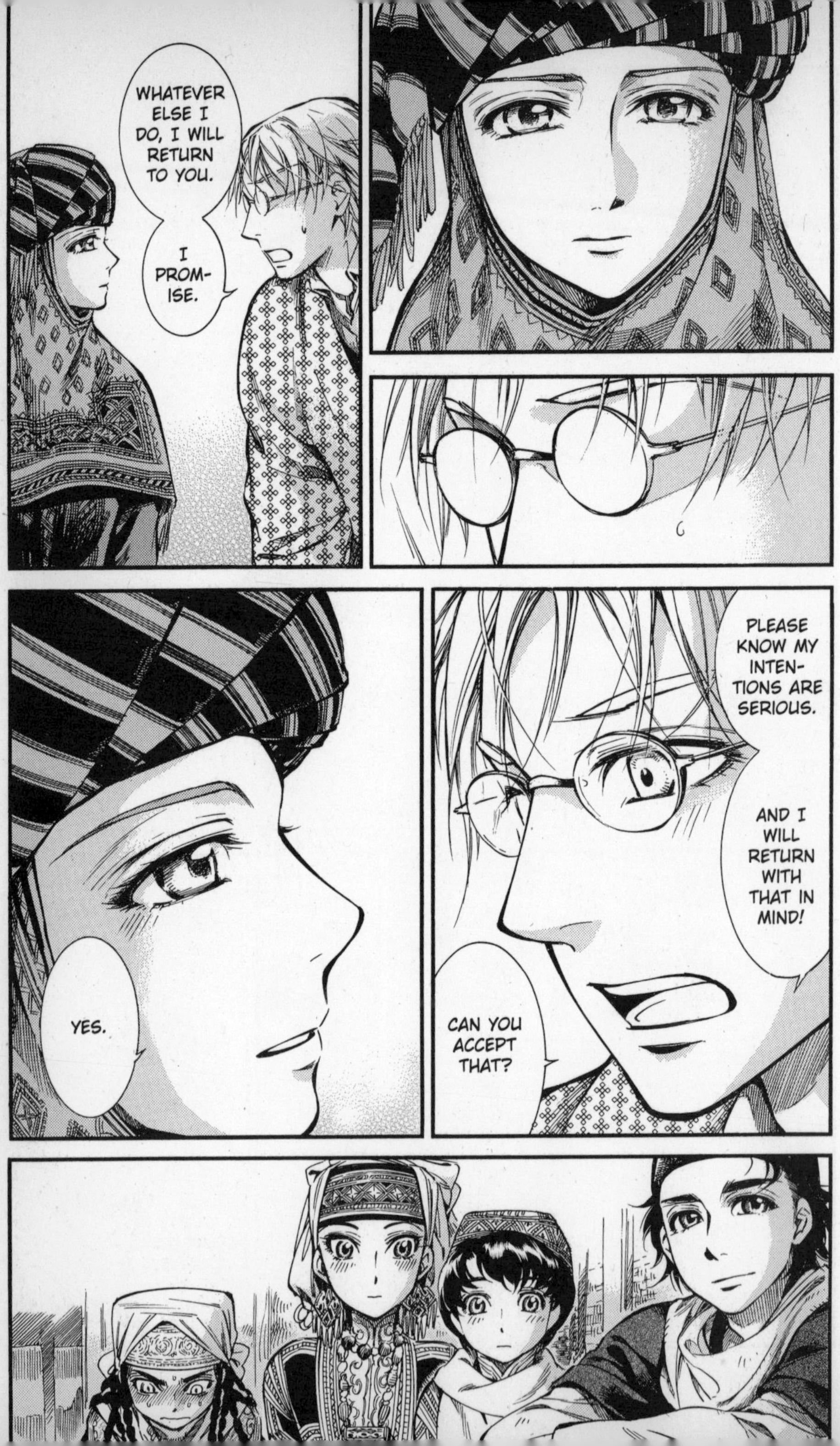
WHATEVER ELSE I DO, I WILL RETURN TO YOU.
I PROM-ISE.
PLEASE KNOW MY INTEN-TIONS ARE SERIOUS.
AND I WILL RETURN WITH THAT IN MIND!
CAN YOU ACCEPT THAT?
YES.

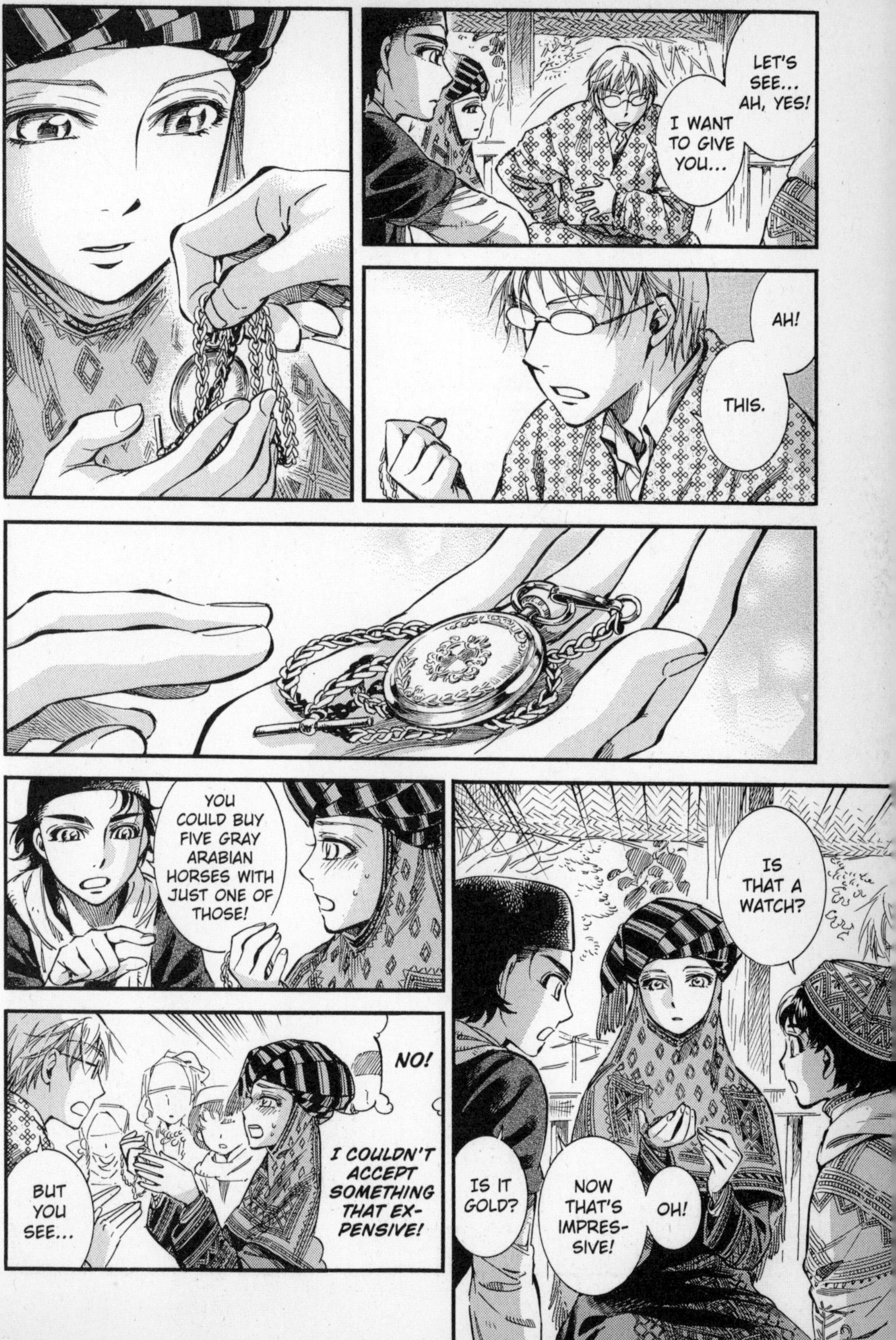

LET'S SEE... AH, YES!
I WANT TO GIVE YOU...
AH!
THIS.
IS THAT A WATCH?
OH!
NOW THAT'S IMPRES-SIVE!
IS IT GOLD?
YOU COULD BUY FIVE GRAY ARABIAN HORSES WITH JUST ONE OF THOSE!
NO!
I COULDN'T ACCEPT SOMETHING THAT EX-PENSIVE!
BUT YOU SEE...

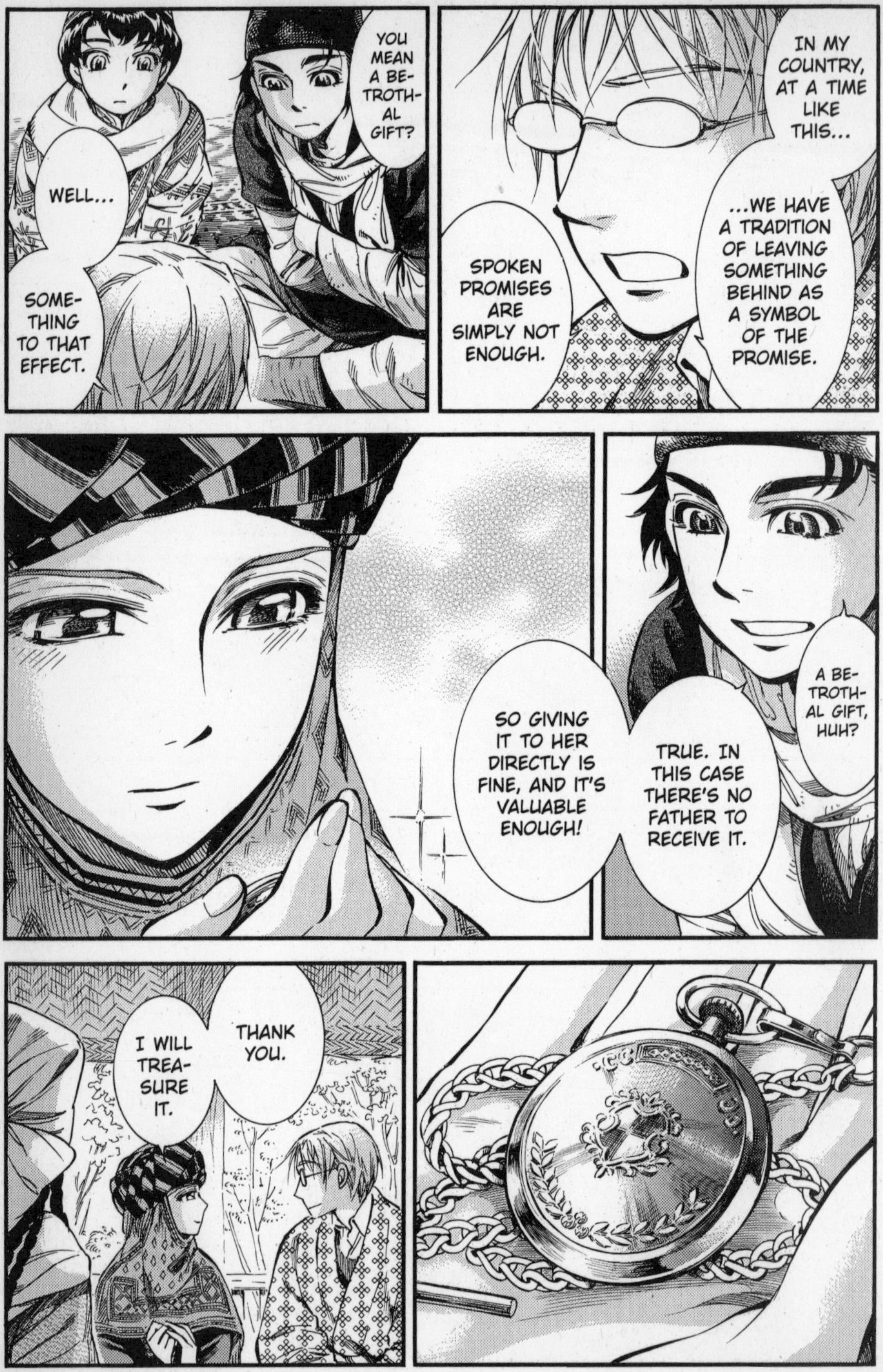
IN MY COUNTRY, AT A TIME LIKE THIS...
...WE HAVE A TRADITION OF LEAVING SOMETHING BEHIND AS A SYMBOL OF THE PROMISE.
SPOKEN PROMISES ARE SIMPLY NOT ENOUGH.
YOU MEAN A BE-TROTH-AL GIFT?
WELL...
SOME-THING TO THAT EFFECT.
A BE-TROTH-AL GIFT, HUH?
TRUE. IN THIS CASE THERE'S NO FATHER TO RECEIVE IT.
SO GIVING IT TO HER DIRECTLY IS FINE, AND IT'S VALUABLE ENOUGH!
THANK YOU.
I WILL TREA-SURE IT.

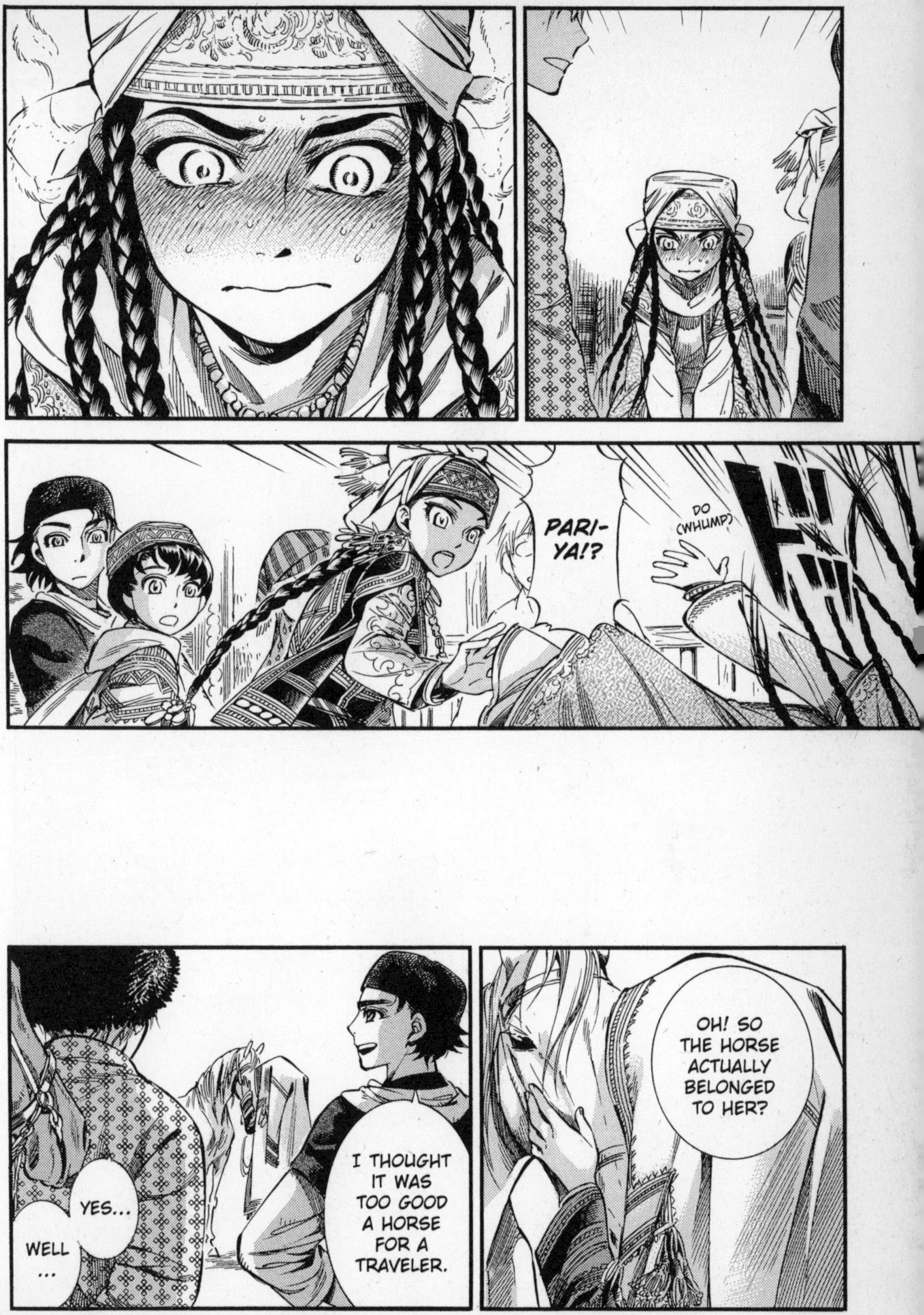
DO (WHUMP)
PARI-YA!?
OH! SO THE HORSE ACTUALLY BELONGED TO HER?
I THOUGHT IT WAS TOO GOOD A HORSE FOR A TRAVELER.
YES...
WELL...

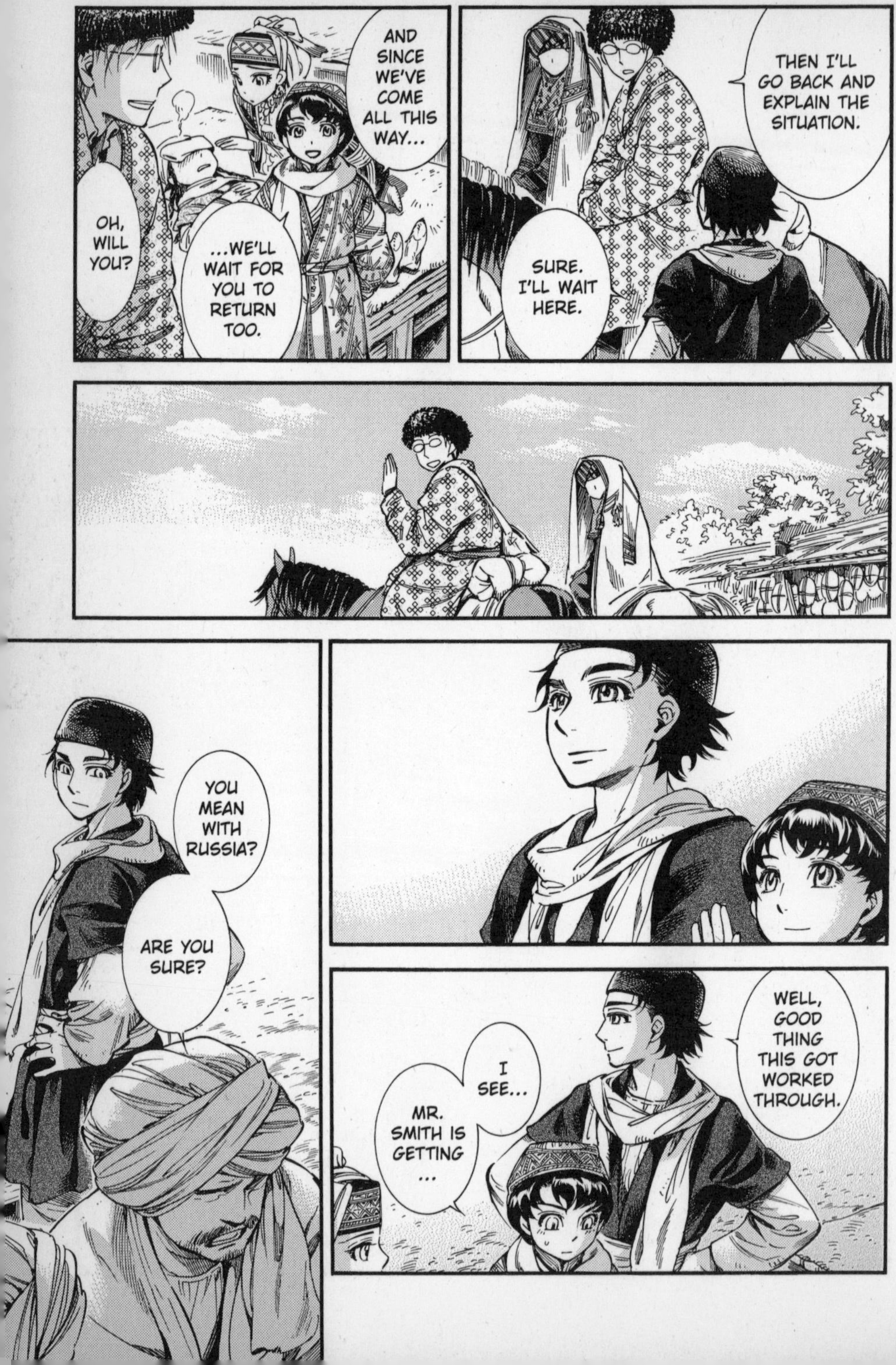
THEN I'LL GO BACK AND EXPLAIN THE SITUATION.
SURE. I'LL WAIT HERE.
AND SINCE WE'VE COME ALL THIS WAY...
...WE'LL WAIT FOR YOU TO RETURN TOO.
OH, WILL YOU?
WELL, GOOD THING THIS GOT WORKED THROUGH.
I SEE...
MR. SMITH IS GETTING ...
YOU MEAN WITH RUSSIA?
ARE YOU SURE?

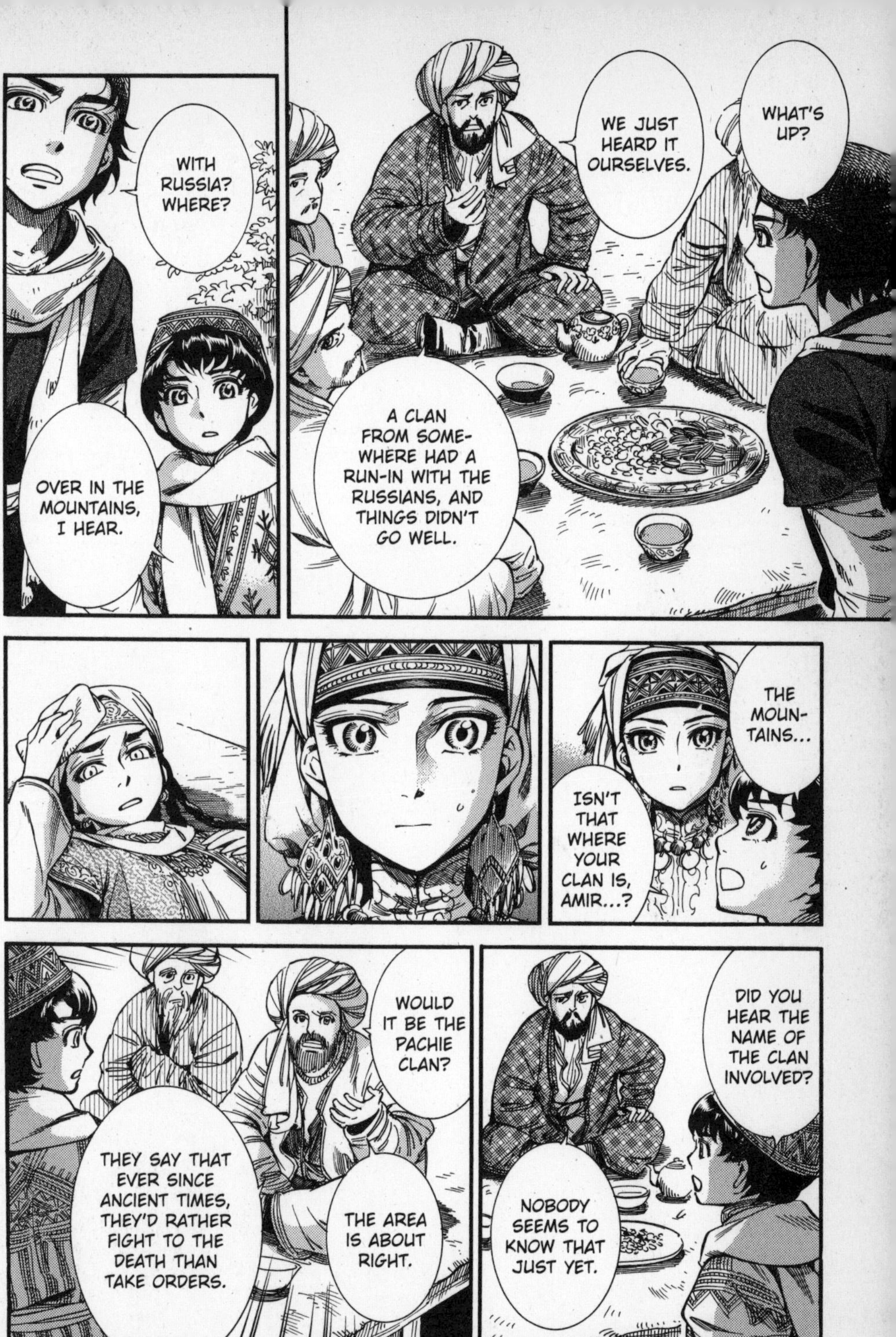
WHAT'S UP?
WE JUST HEARD IT OURSELVES.
A CLAN FROM SOME-WHERE HAD A RUN-IN WITH THE RUSSIANS, AND THINGS DIDN'T GO WELL.
WITH RUSSIA? WHERE?
OVER IN THE MOUNTAINS, I HEAR.
THE MOUN-TAINS...
ISN'T THAT WHERE YOUR CLAN IS, AMIR...?
DID YOU HEAR THE NAME OF THE CLAN INVOLVED?
NOBODY SEEMS TO KNOW THAT JUST YET.
WOULD IT BE THE PACHIE CLAN?
THE AREA IS ABOUT RIGHT.
THEY SAY THAT EVER SINCE ANCIENT TIMES, THEY'D RATHER FIGHT TO THE DEATH THAN TAKE ORDERS.

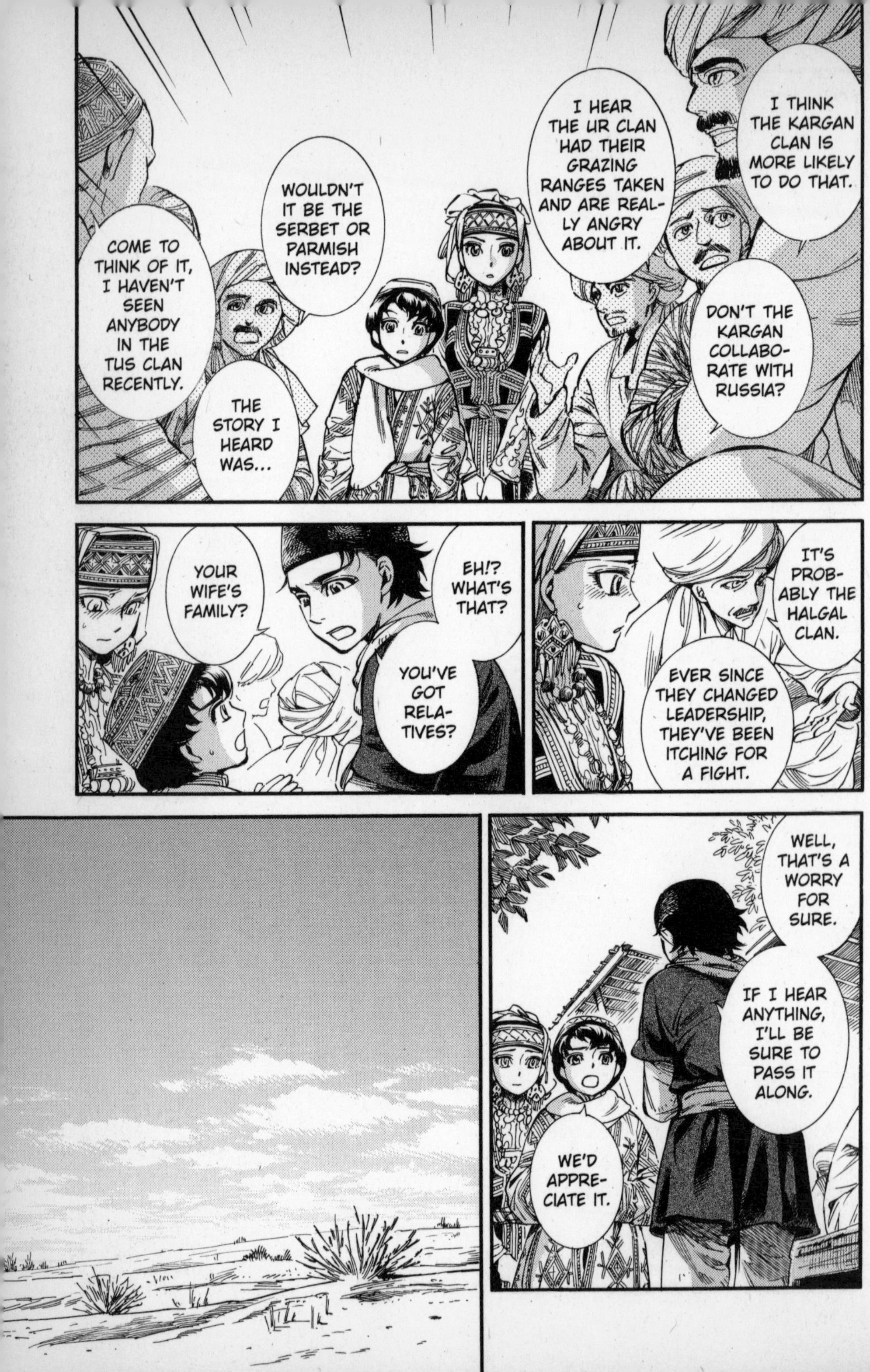
I THINK THE KARGAN CLAN IS MORE LIKELY TO DO THAT.
I HEAR THE UR CLAN HAD THEIR GRAZING RANGES TAKEN AND ARE REALLY ANGRY ABOUT IT.
DON'T THE KARGAN COLLABORATE WITH RUSSIA?
WOULDN'T IT BE THE SERBET OR PARMISH INSTEAD?
COME TO THINK OF IT, I HAVEN'T SEEN ANYBODY IN THE TUS CLAN RECENTLY.
THE STORY I HEARD WAS...
IT'S PROBABLY THE HALGAL CLAN.
EVER SINCE THEY CHANGED LEADERSHIP, THEY'VE BEEN ITCHING FOR A FIGHT.
EH!? WHAT'S THAT?
YOUR WIFE'S FAMILY?
YOU'VE GOT RELATIVES?
WELL, THAT'S A WORRY FOR SURE.
IF I HEAR ANYTHING, I'LL BE SURE TO PASS IT ALONG.
WE'D APPRECIATE IT.

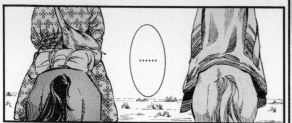

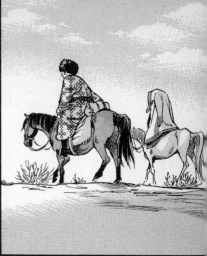

......

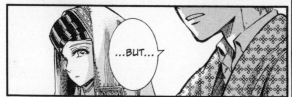

...BUT...

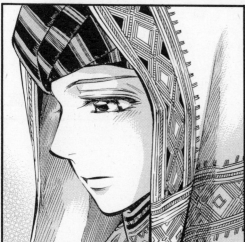

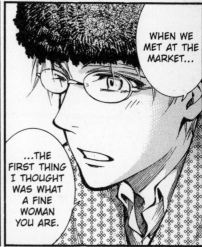

WHEN WE MET AT THE MARKET...

...THE FIRST THING I THOUGHT WAS WHAT A FINE WOMAN YOU ARE.

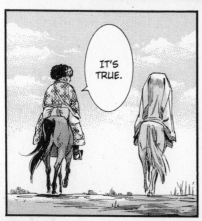

IT'S TRUE.

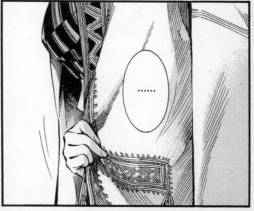

......

◆ CHAPTER FIFTEEN: END ◆

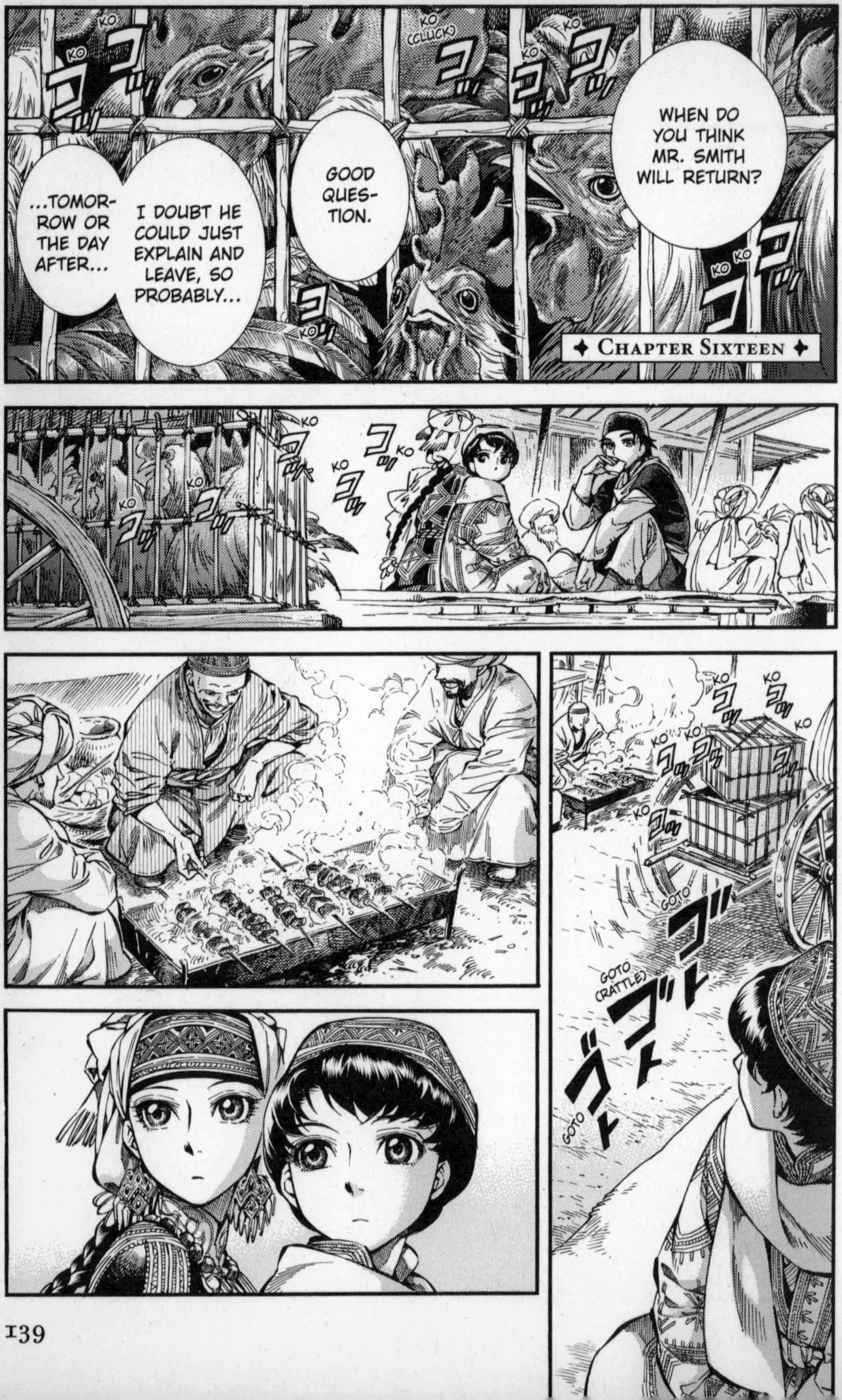
KO KO
WHEN DO YOU THINK MR. SMITH WILL RETURN?
CHAPTER SIXTEEN
KO KO
KO (CLUCK)
GOOD QUES-TION.
KO
KO
I DOUBT HE COULD JUST EXPLAIN AND LEAVE, SO PROBABLY...
...TOMOR-ROW OR THE DAY AFTER...
KO KO
KO KO
KO KO KO
KO KO
GOTO GOTO
GOTO (RATTLE)
GOTO

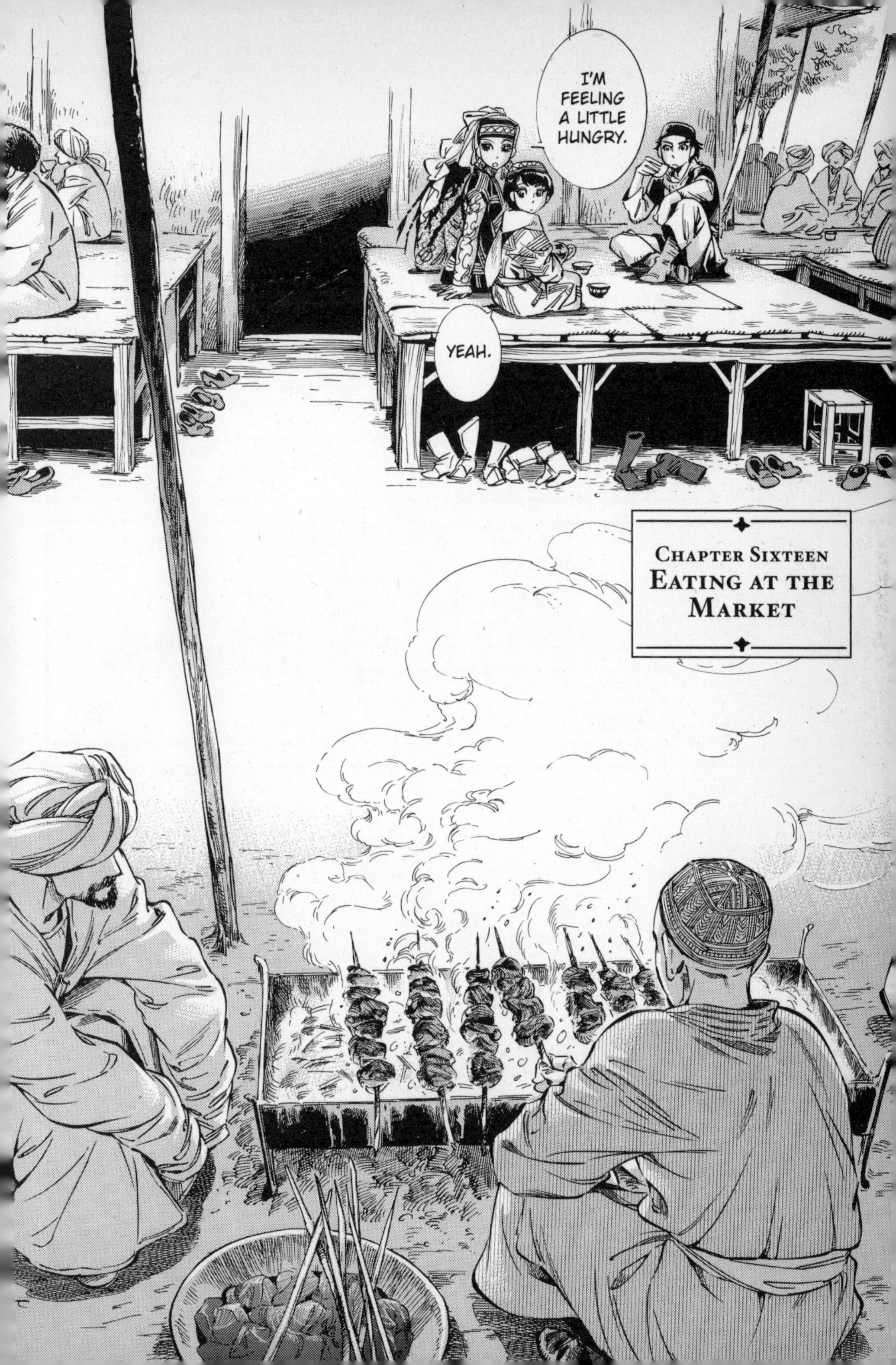
I'M FEELING A LITTLE HUNGRY.
YEAH.
CHAPTER SIXTEEN
EATING AT THE MARKET

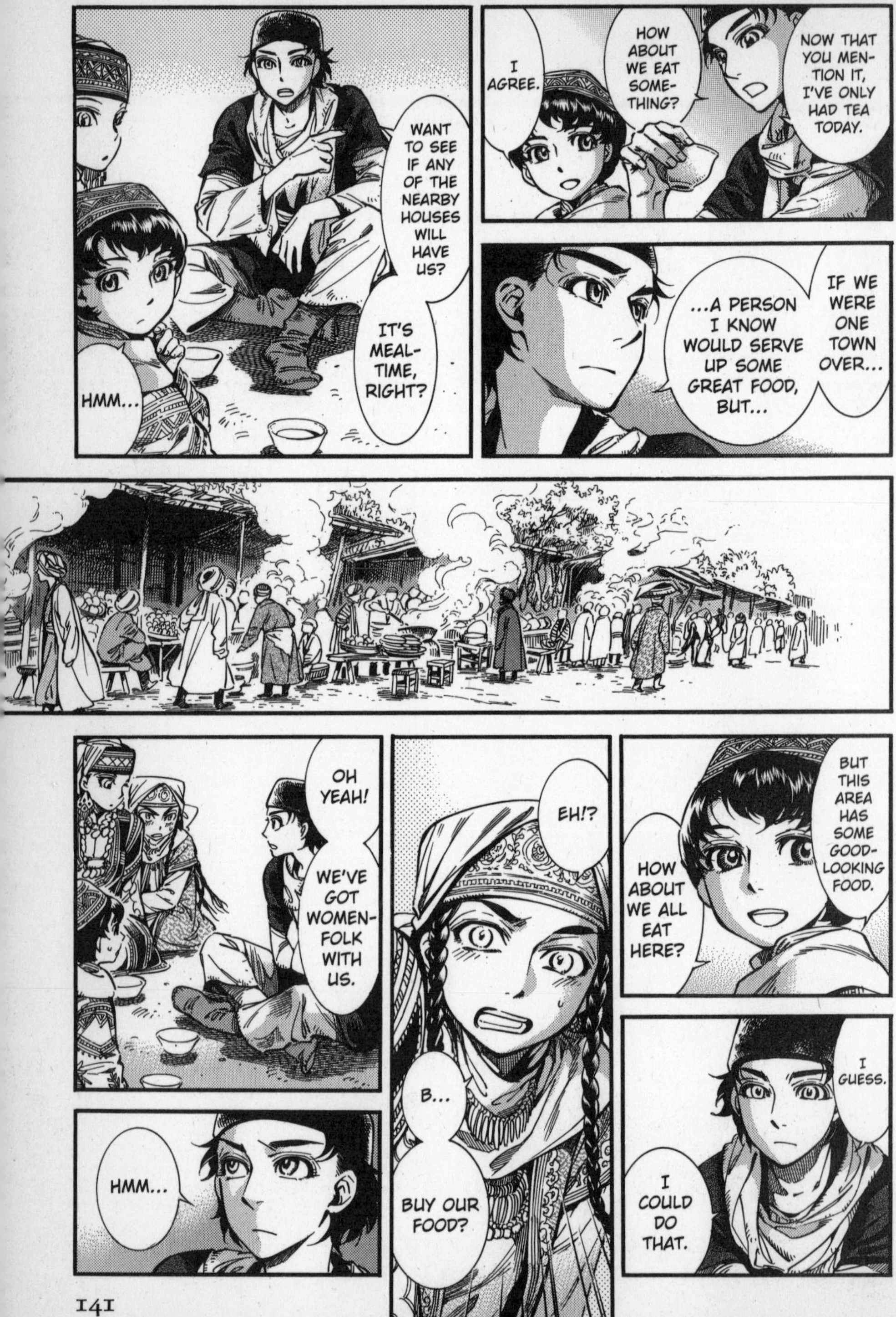
NOW THAT YOU MENTION IT, I'VE ONLY HAD TEA TODAY.
HOW ABOUT WE EAT SOMETHING?
I AGREE.
IF WE WERE ONE TOWN OVER...
...A PERSON I KNOW WOULD SERVE UP SOME GREAT FOOD, BUT...
WANT TO SEE IF ANY OF THE NEARBY HOUSES WILL HAVE US?
IT'S MEALTIME, RIGHT?
HMM...
BUT THIS AREA HAS SOME GOOD-LOOKING FOOD.
HOW ABOUT WE ALL EAT HERE?
I GUESS.
I COULD DO THAT.
EH!?
B...
BUY OUR FOOD?
OH YEAH!
WE'VE GOT WOMENFOLK WITH US.
HMM...

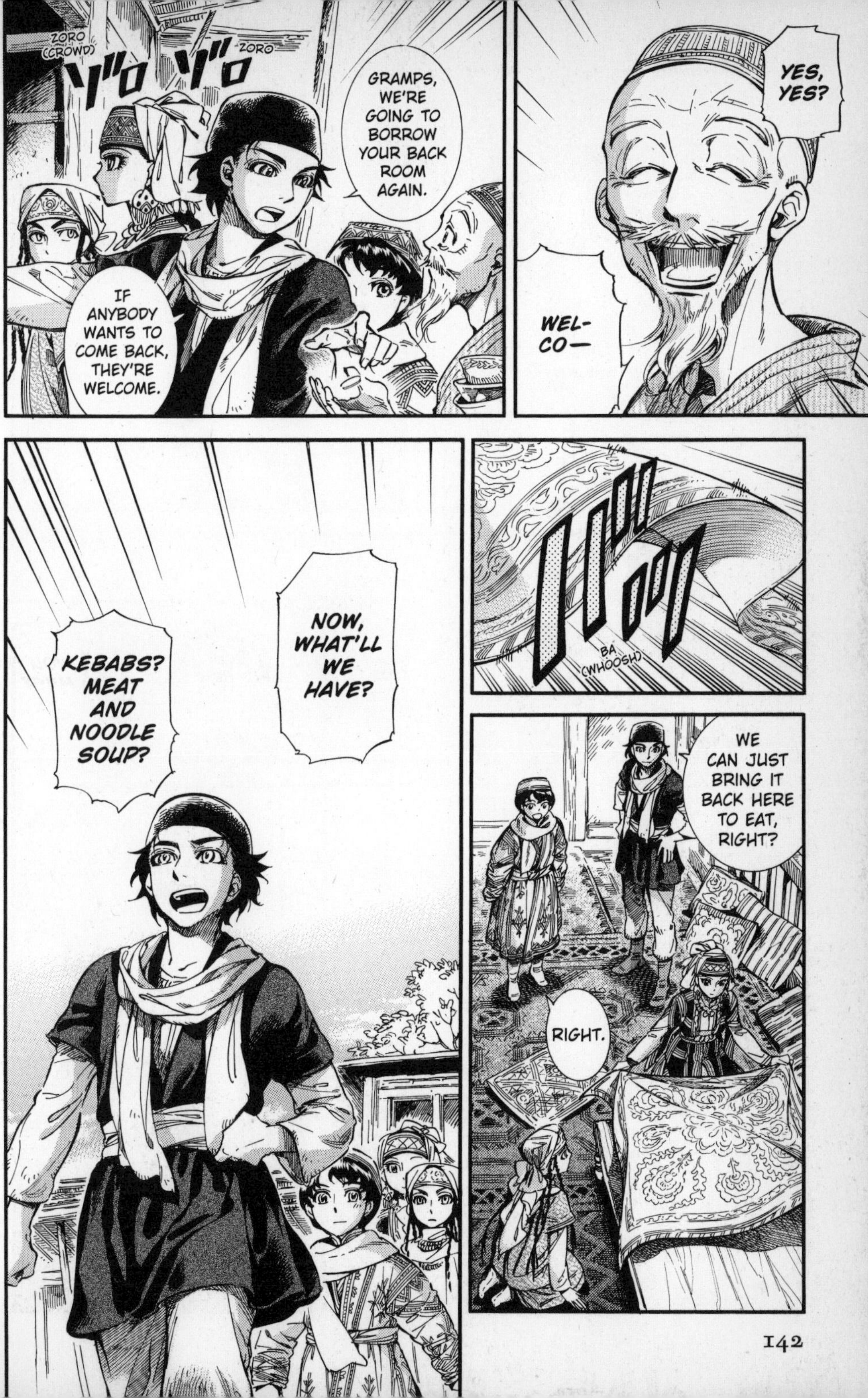
ZORO (CROWD)
ZORO
GRAMPS, WE'RE GOING TO BORROW YOUR BACK ROOM AGAIN.
IF ANYBODY WANTS TO COME BACK, THEY'RE WELCOME.
YES, YES?
WEL-CO—
NOW, WHAT'LL WE HAVE?
KEBABS? MEAT AND NOODLE SOUP?
BA (WHOOSH)
WE CAN JUST BRING IT BACK HERE TO EAT, RIGHT?
RIGHT.

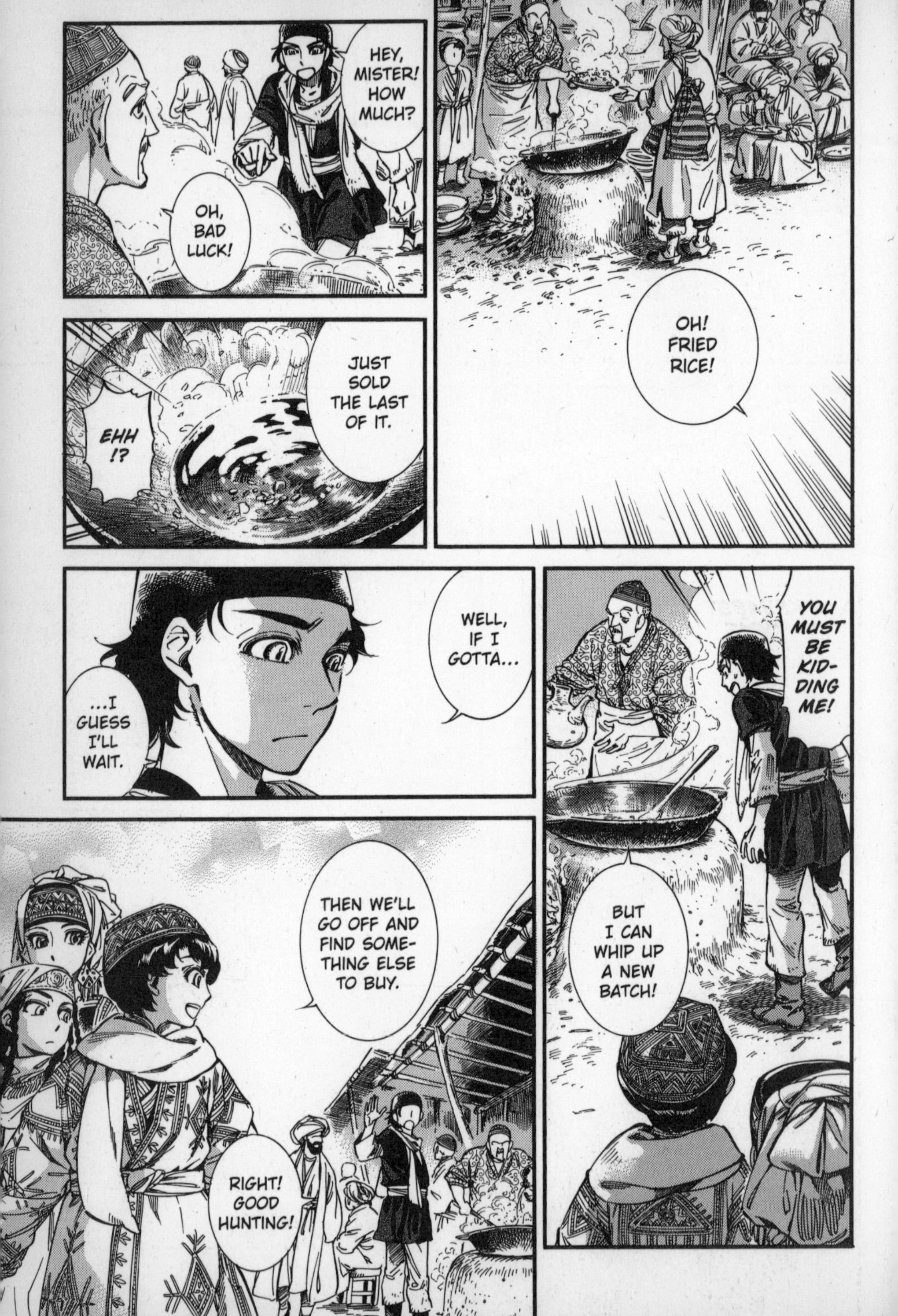
OH! FRIED RICE!
HEY, MISTER! HOW MUCH?
OH, BAD LUCK!
JUST SOLD THE LAST OF IT.
EHH!?
YOU MUST BE KID-DING ME!
BUT I CAN WHIP UP A NEW BATCH!
WELL, IF I GOTTA...
...I GUESS I'LL WAIT.
THEN WE'LL GO OFF AND FIND SOME-THING ELSE TO BUY.
RIGHT! GOOD HUNTING!

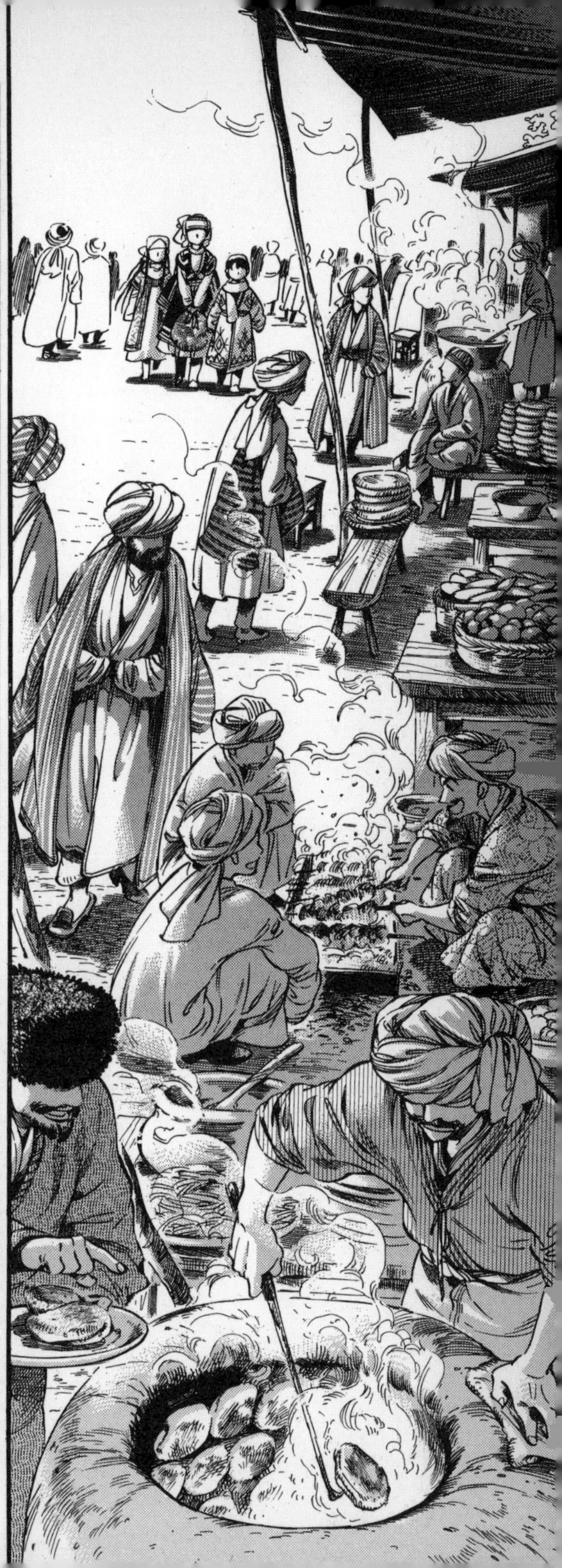
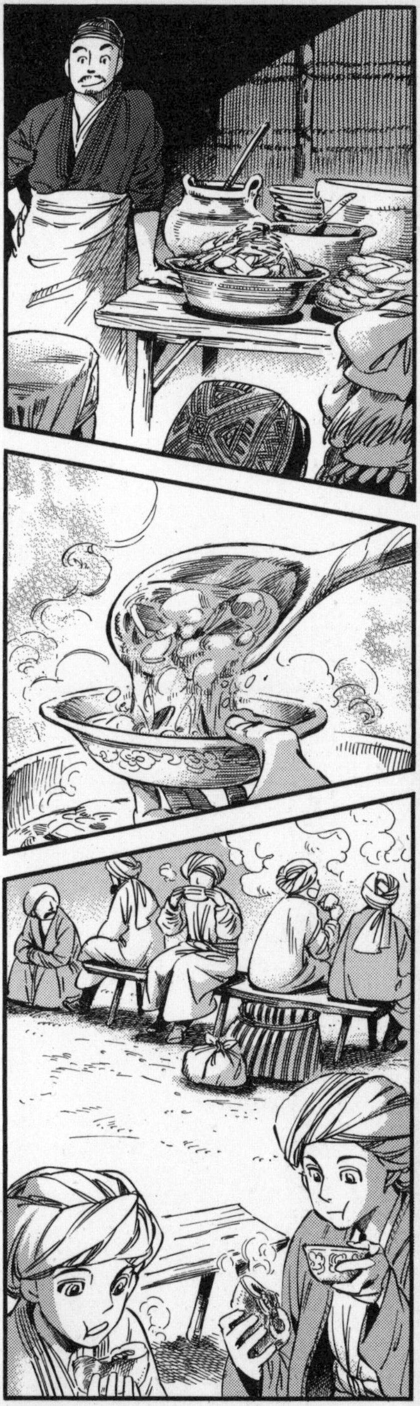

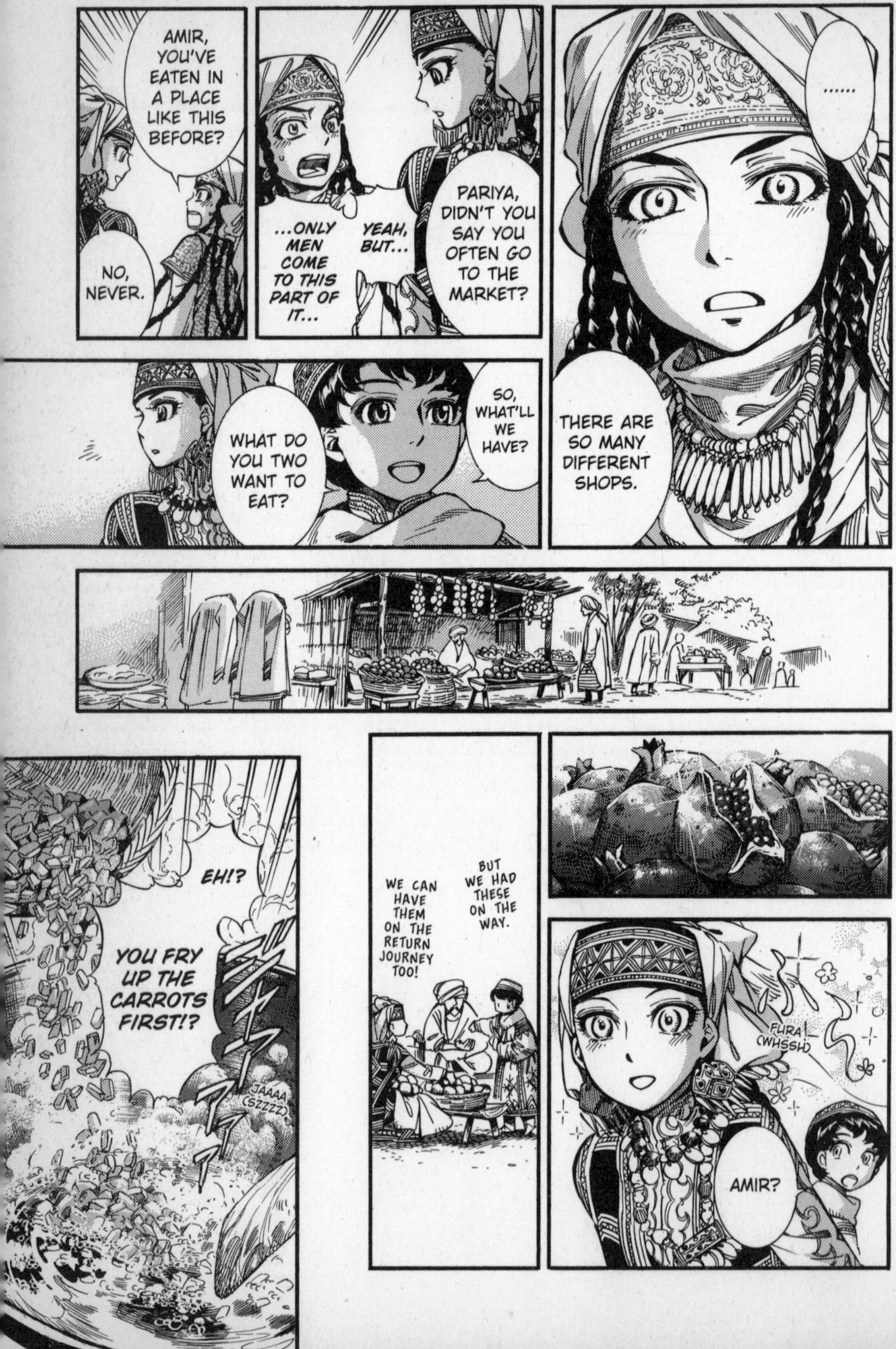
......
THERE ARE SO MANY DIFFERENT SHOPS.
PARIYA, DIDN'T YOU SAY YOU OFTEN GO TO THE MARKET?
YEAH, BUT...
...ONLY MEN COME TO THIS PART OF IT...
AMIR, YOU'VE EATEN IN A PLACE LIKE THIS BEFORE?
NO, NEVER.
SO, WHAT'LL WE HAVE?
WHAT DO YOU TWO WANT TO EAT?
FURA (WHSSH)
AMIR?
BUT WE HAD THESE ON THE WAY.
WE CAN HAVE THEM ON THE RETURN JOURNEY TOO!
EH!?
YOU FRY UP THE CARROTS FIRST!?
JAAAA (SZZZZ)

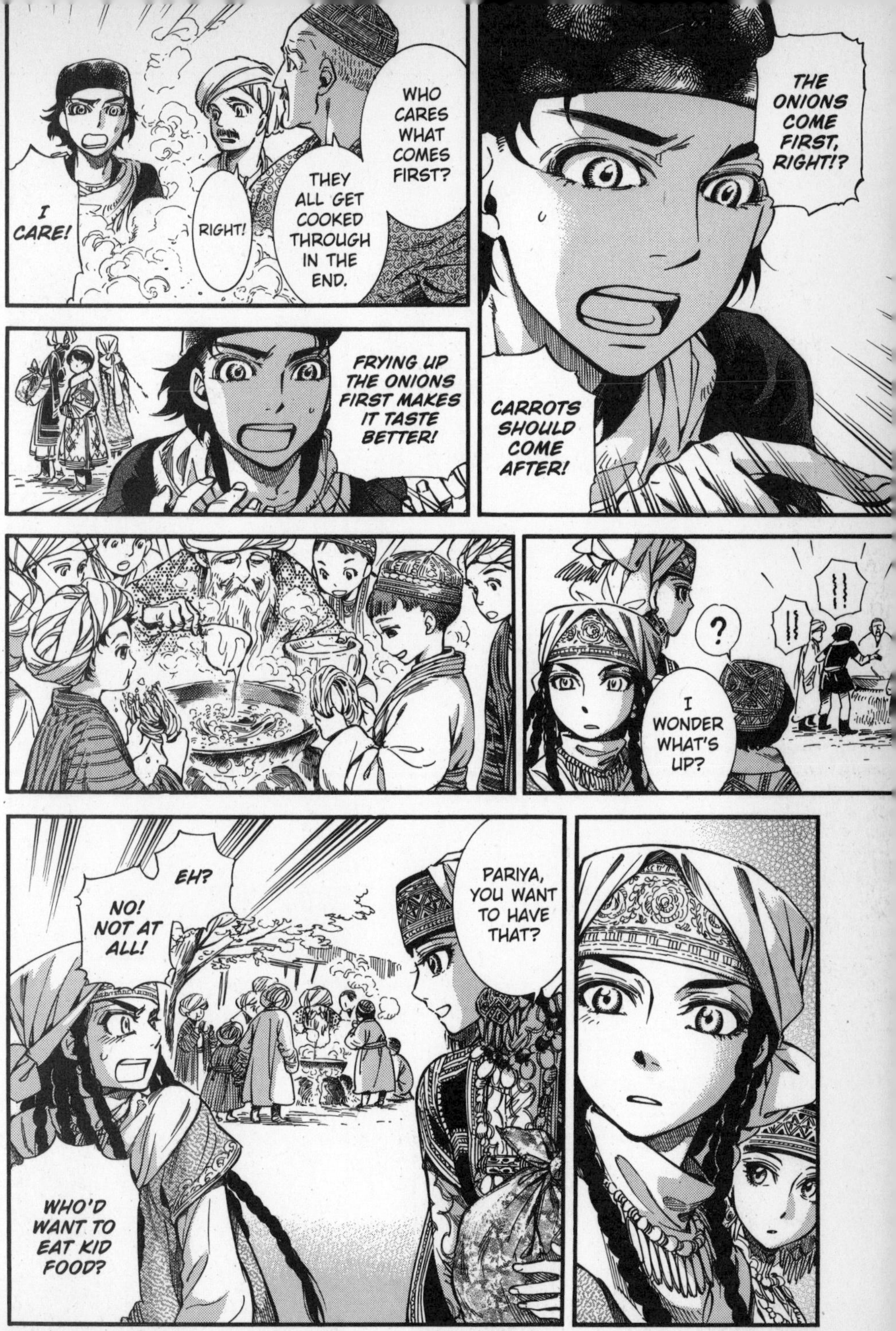

THE ONIONS COME FIRST, RIGHT!?
CARROTS SHOULD COME AFTER!
WHO CARES WHAT COMES FIRST?
THEY ALL GET COOKED THROUGH IN THE END.
RIGHT!
I CARE!
FRYING UP THE ONIONS FIRST MAKES IT TASTE BETTER!
?
I WONDER WHAT'S UP?
PARIYA, YOU WANT TO HAVE THAT?
EH?
NO! NOT AT ALL!
WHO'D WANT TO EAT KID FOOD?

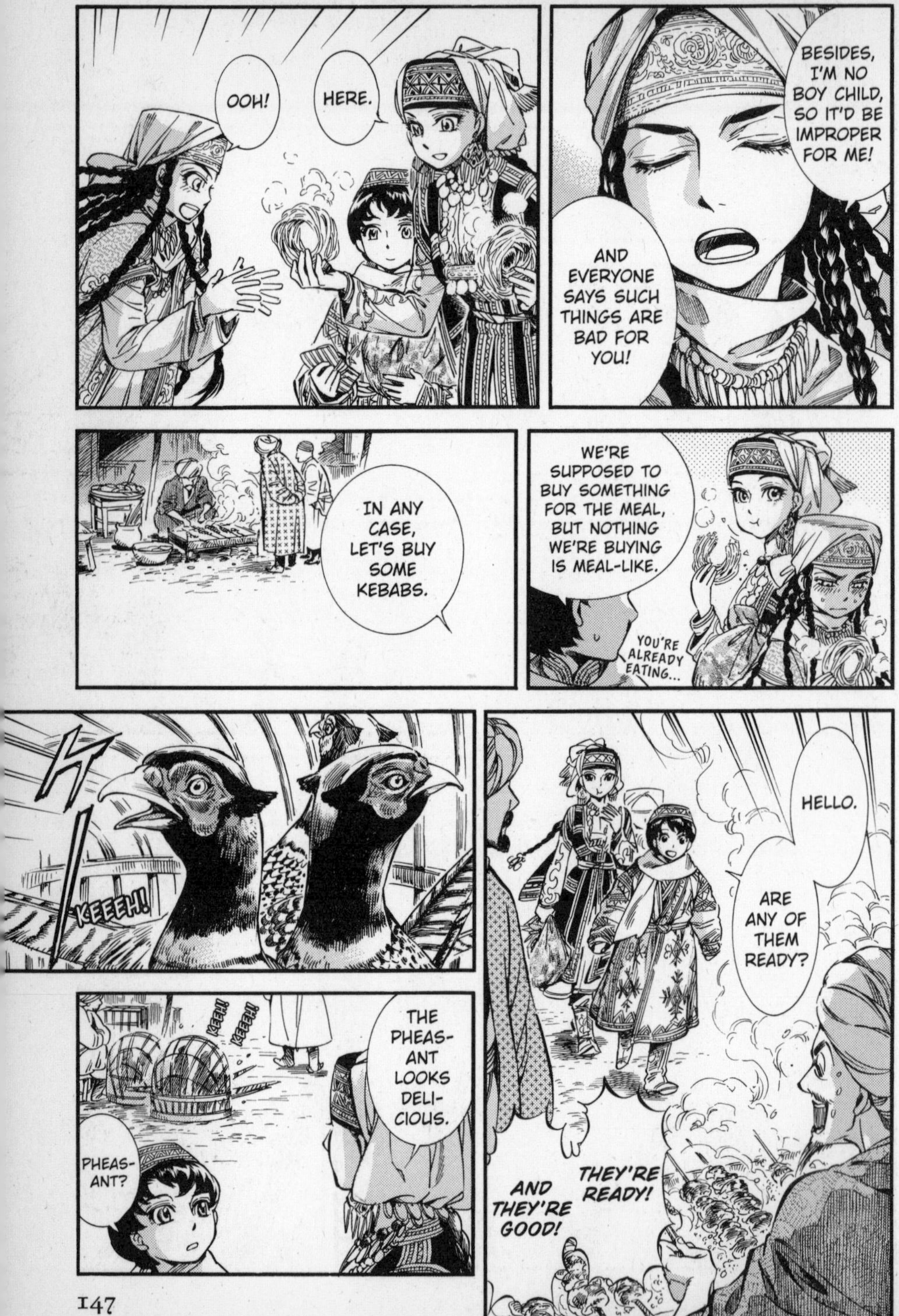
BESIDES, I'M NO BOY CHILD, SO IT'D BE IMPROPER FOR ME!
AND EVERYONE SAYS SUCH THINGS ARE BAD FOR YOU!
HERE.
OOH!
WE'RE SUPPOSED TO BUY SOMETHING FOR THE MEAL, BUT NOTHING WE'RE BUYING IS MEAL-LIKE.
YOU'RE ALREADY EATING...
IN ANY CASE, LET'S BUY SOME KEBABS.
HELLO.
ARE ANY OF THEM READY?
THEY'RE READY!
AND THEY'RE GOOD!
KEEEH!
KEEH!
KEEEH!
THE PHEAS-ANT LOOKS DELI-CIOUS.
PHEAS-ANT?

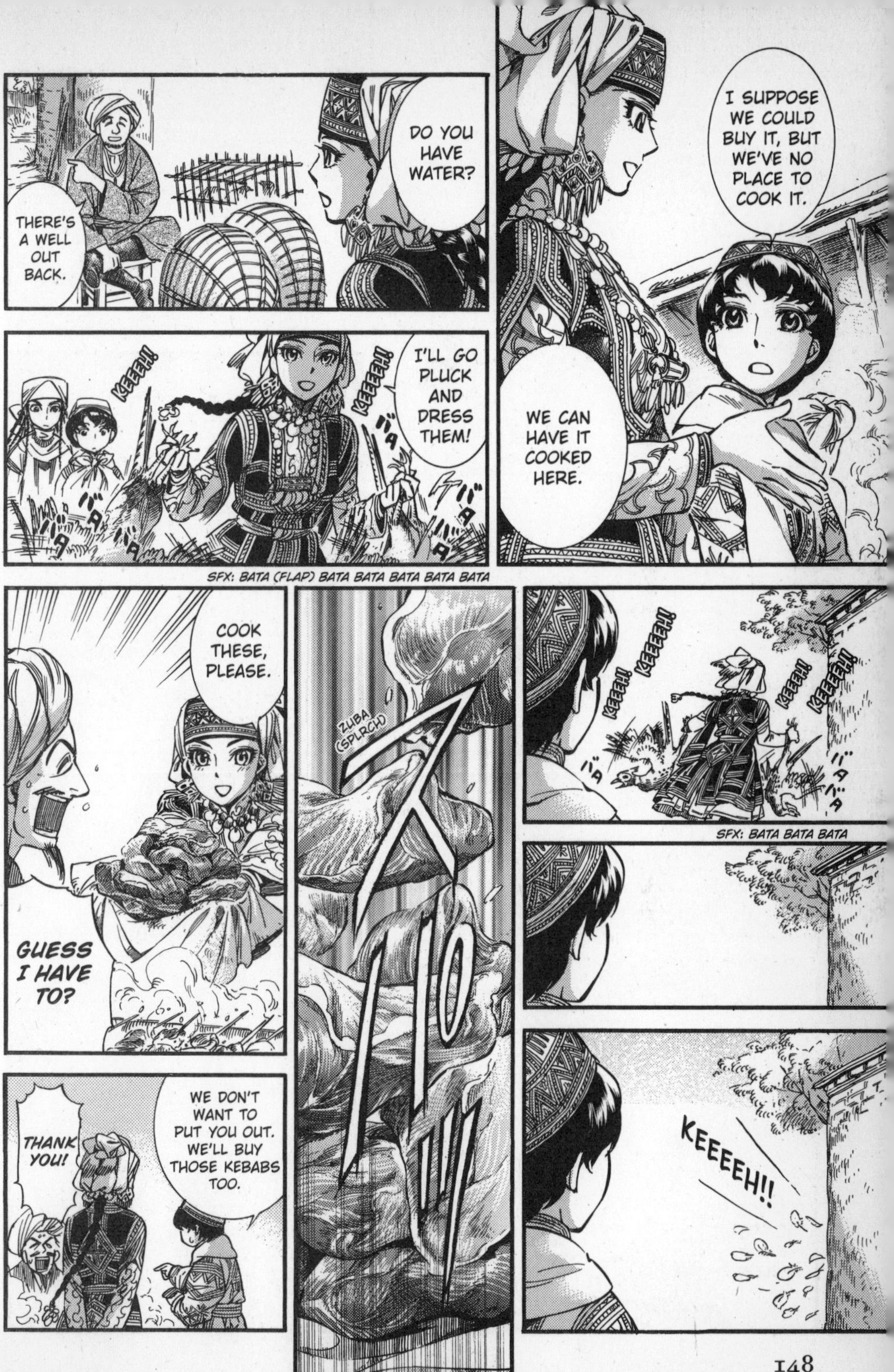
I SUPPOSE WE COULD BUY IT, BUT WE'VE NO PLACE TO COOK IT.
WE CAN HAVE IT COOKED HERE.
DO YOU HAVE WATER?
THERE'S A WELL OUT BACK.
I'LL GO PLUCK AND DRESS THEM!
KEEEEH!
KEEEH!
SFX: BATA (FLAP) BATA BATA BATA BATA BATA
KEEEEH!
KEEEH!
KEEEEH!
KEEEH!
SFX: BATA BATA BATA
KEEEEH!!
ZUBA (SPLRCH)
COOK THESE, PLEASE.
GUESS I HAVE TO?
WE DON'T WANT TO PUT YOU OUT. WE'LL BUY THOSE KEBABS TOO.
THANK YOU!

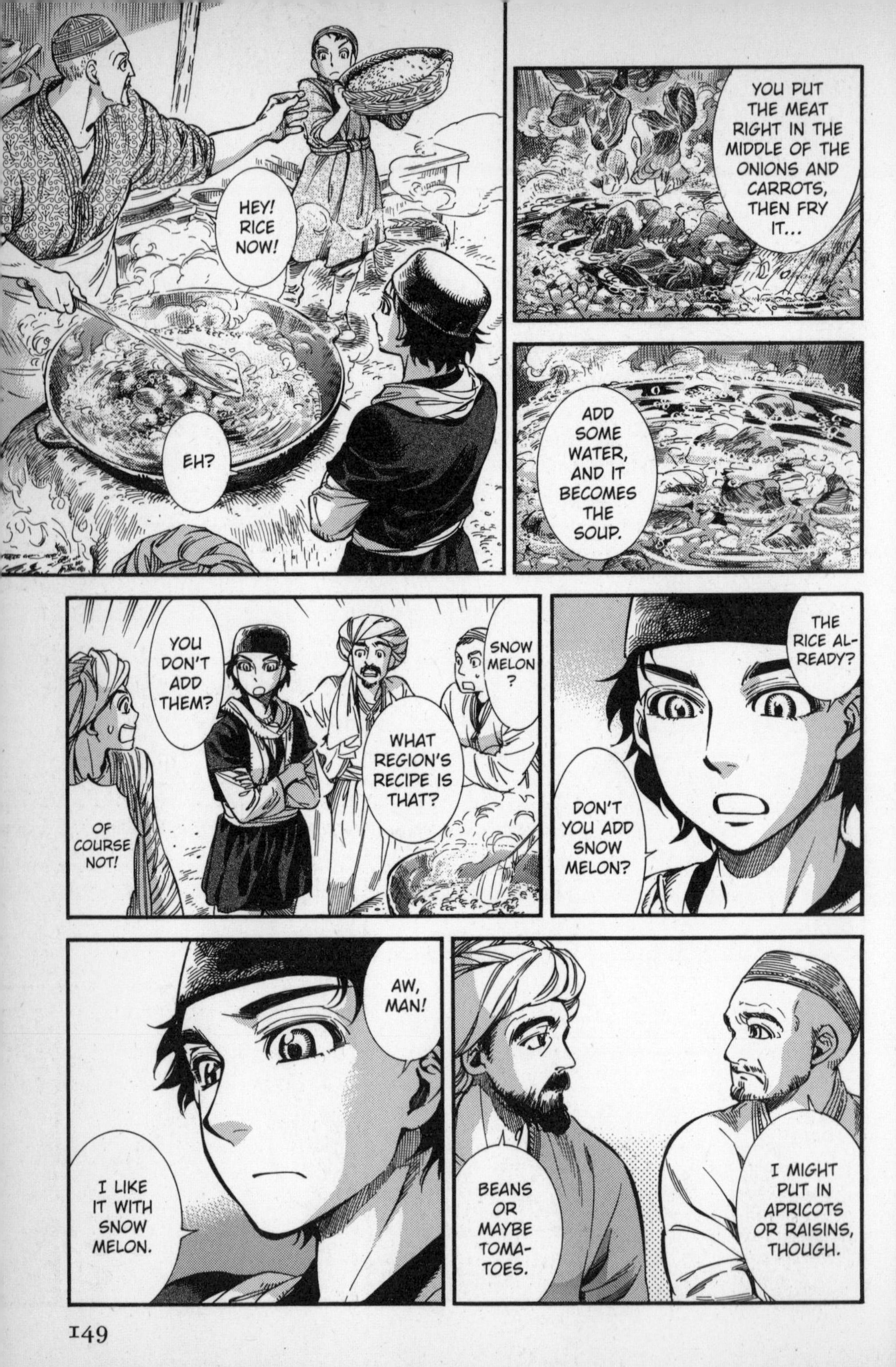
YOU PUT THE MEAT RIGHT IN THE MIDDLE OF THE ONIONS AND CARROTS, THEN FRY IT...
ADD SOME WATER, AND IT BECOMES THE SOUP.
HEY! RICE NOW!
EH?
THE RICE AL-READY?
DON'T YOU ADD SNOW MELON?
SNOW MELON?
WHAT REGION'S RECIPE IS THAT?
YOU DON'T ADD THEM?
OF COURSE NOT!
I MIGHT PUT IN APRICOTS OR RAISINS, THOUGH.
BEANS OR MAYBE TOMA-TOES.
AW, MAN!
I LIKE IT WITH SNOW MELON.

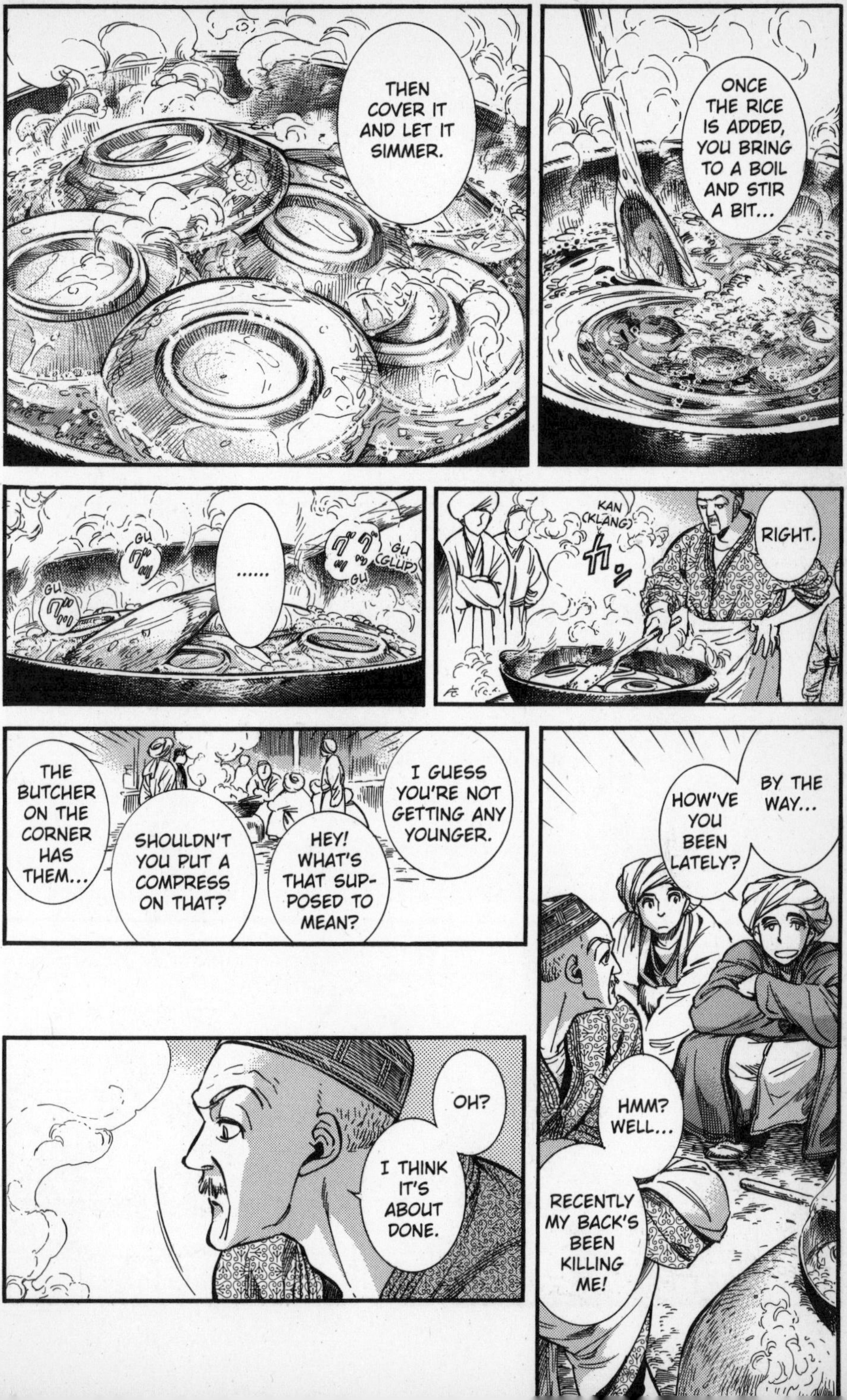
ONCE THE RICE IS ADDED, YOU BRING TO A BOIL AND STIR A BIT...
THEN COVER IT AND LET IT SIMMER.
KAN (KLANG)
カッ
RIGHT.
GU (GLUP)
GU
GU
......
BY THE WAY...
HOW'VE YOU BEEN LATELY?
HMM? WELL...
RECENTLY MY BACK'S BEEN KILLING ME!
I GUESS YOU'RE NOT GETTING ANY YOUNGER.
HEY! WHAT'S THAT SUP-POSED TO MEAN?
SHOULDN'T YOU PUT A COMPRESS ON THAT?
THE BUTCHER ON THE CORNER HAS THEM...
OH?
I THINK IT'S ABOUT DONE.

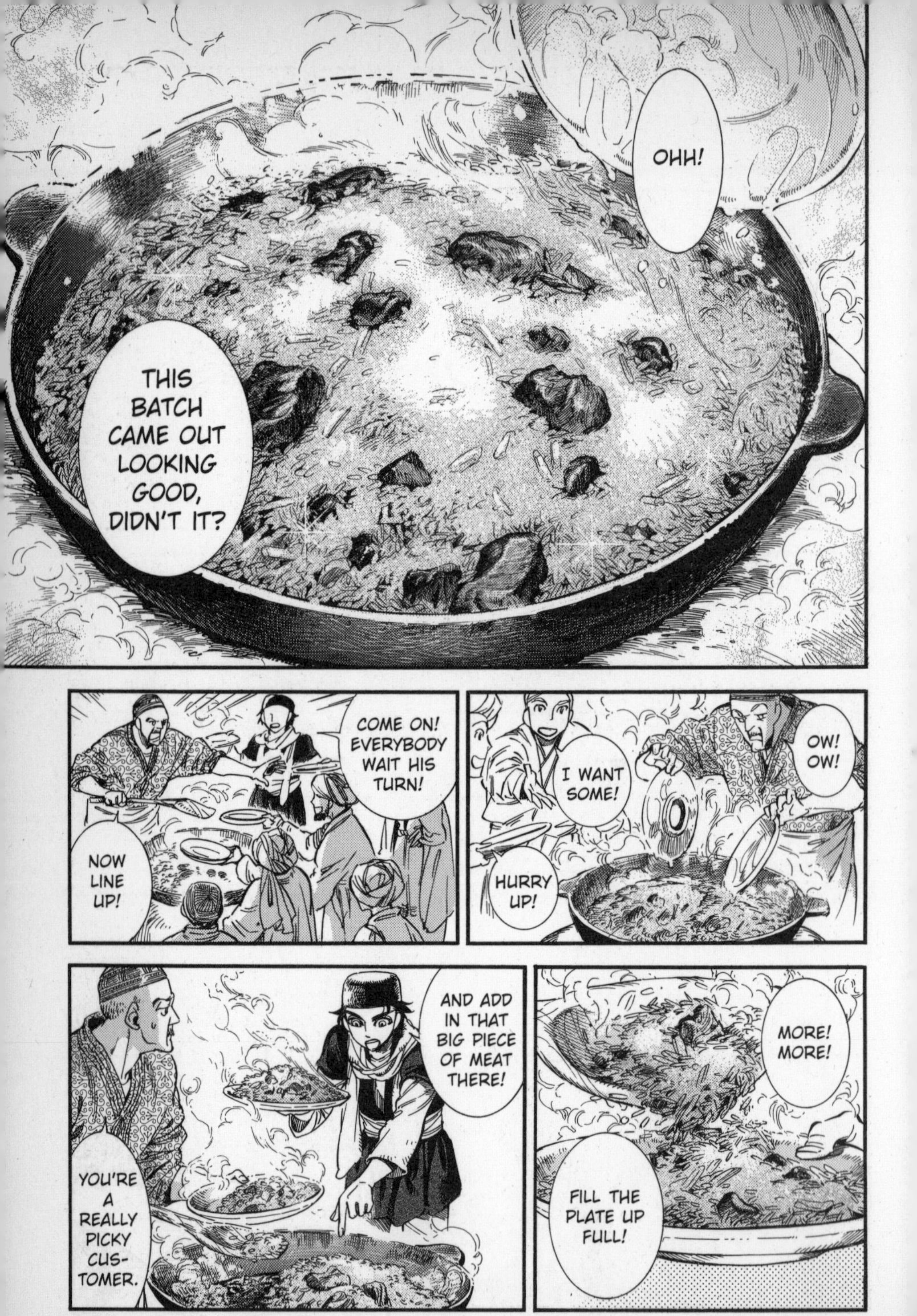
OHH!
THIS BATCH CAME OUT LOOKING GOOD, DIDN'T IT?
OW! OW!
I WANT SOME!
HURRY UP!
COME ON! EVERYBODY WAIT HIS TURN!
NOW LINE UP!
MORE! MORE!
FILL THE PLATE UP FULL!
AND ADD IN THAT BIG PIECE OF MEAT THERE!
YOU'RE A REALLY PICKY CUS-TOMER.

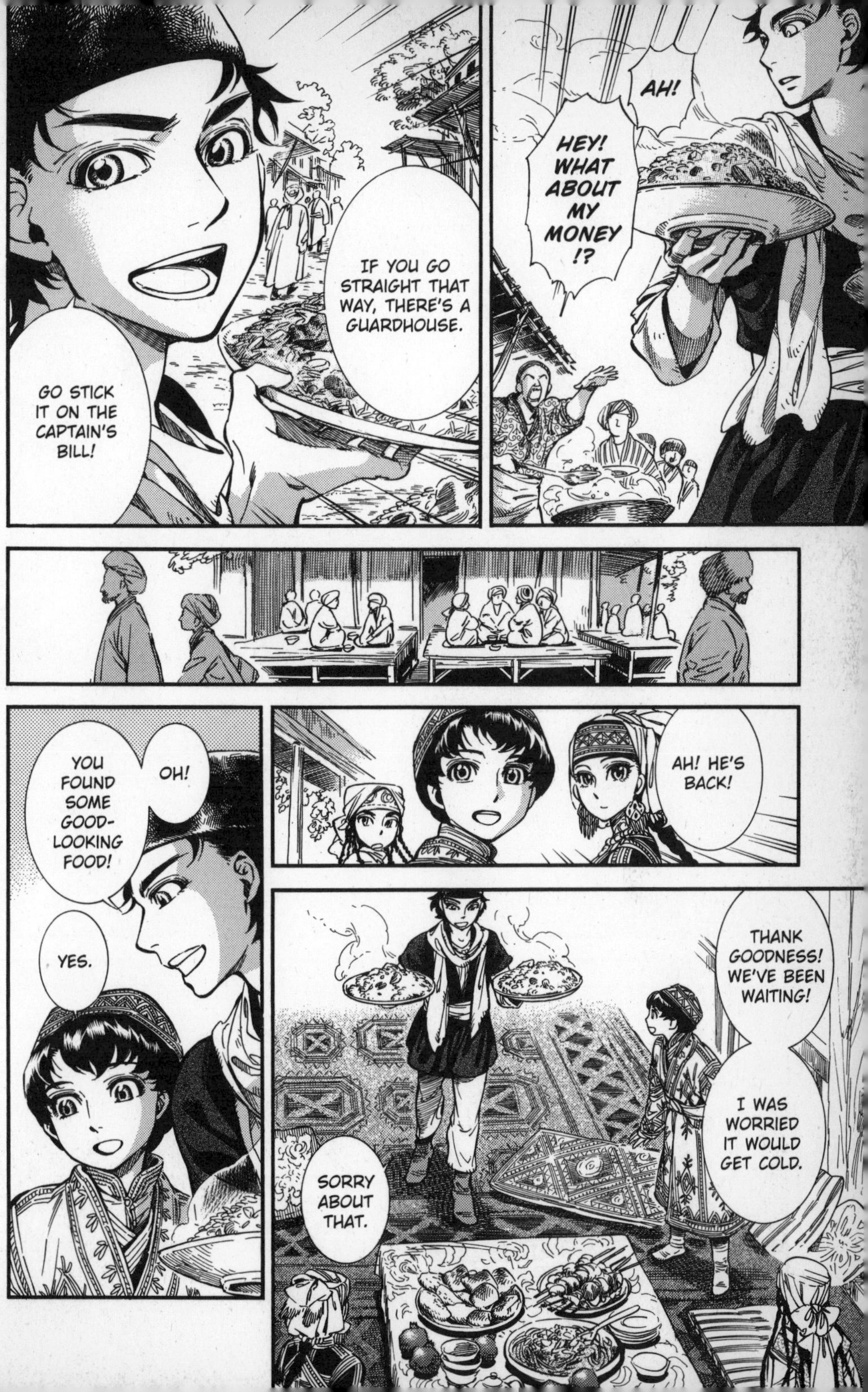
AH!
HEY! WHAT ABOUT MY MONEY !?
IF YOU GO STRAIGHT THAT WAY, THERE'S A GUARDHOUSE.
GO STICK IT ON THE CAPTAIN'S BILL!
AH! HE'S BACK!
THANK GOODNESS! WE'VE BEEN WAITING!
I WAS WORRIED IT WOULD GET COLD.
SORRY ABOUT THAT.
OH!
YOU FOUND SOME GOOD-LOOKING FOOD!
YES.

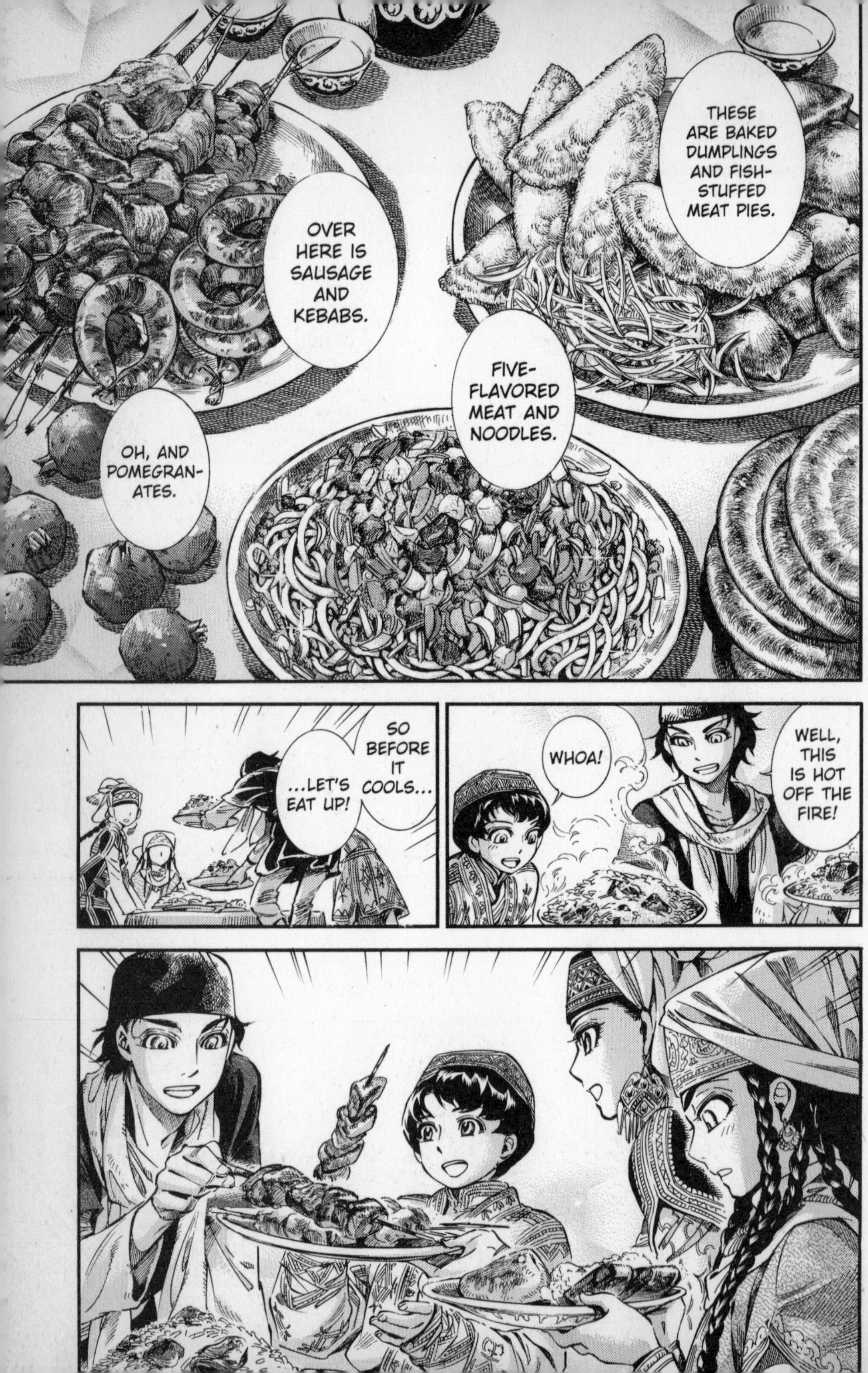
THESE ARE BAKED DUMPLINGS AND FISH-STUFFED MEAT PIES.
OVER HERE IS SAUSAGE AND KEBABS.
FIVE-FLAVORED MEAT AND NOODLES.
OH, AND POMEGRAN-ATES.
WELL, THIS IS HOT OFF THE FIRE!
WHOA!
SO BEFORE IT COOLS...
...LET'S EAT UP!

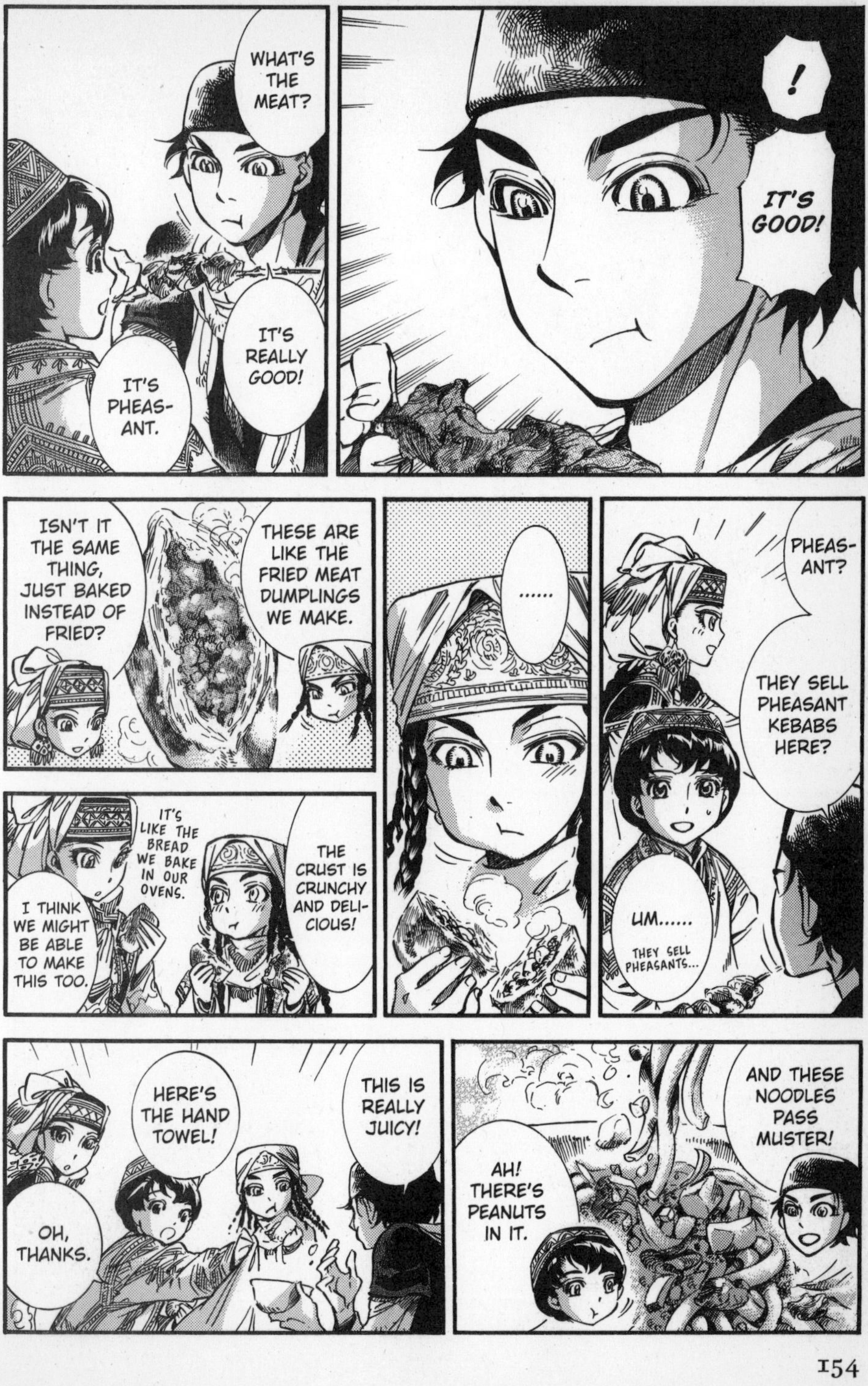
!
IT'S GOOD!
WHAT'S THE MEAT?
IT'S REALLY GOOD!
IT'S PHEAS-ANT.
PHEAS-ANT?
THEY SELL PHEASANT KEBABS HERE?
UM......
THEY SELL PHEASANTS...
......
THESE ARE LIKE THE FRIED MEAT DUMPLINGS WE MAKE.
ISN'T IT THE SAME THING, JUST BAKED INSTEAD OF FRIED?
THE CRUST IS CRUNCHY AND DELI-CIOUS!
IT'S LIKE THE BREAD WE BAKE IN OUR OVENS.
I THINK WE MIGHT BE ABLE TO MAKE THIS TOO.
AND THESE NOODLES PASS MUSTER!
AH! THERE'S PEANUTS IN IT.
THIS IS REALLY JUICY!
HERE'S THE HAND TOWEL!
OH, THANKS.

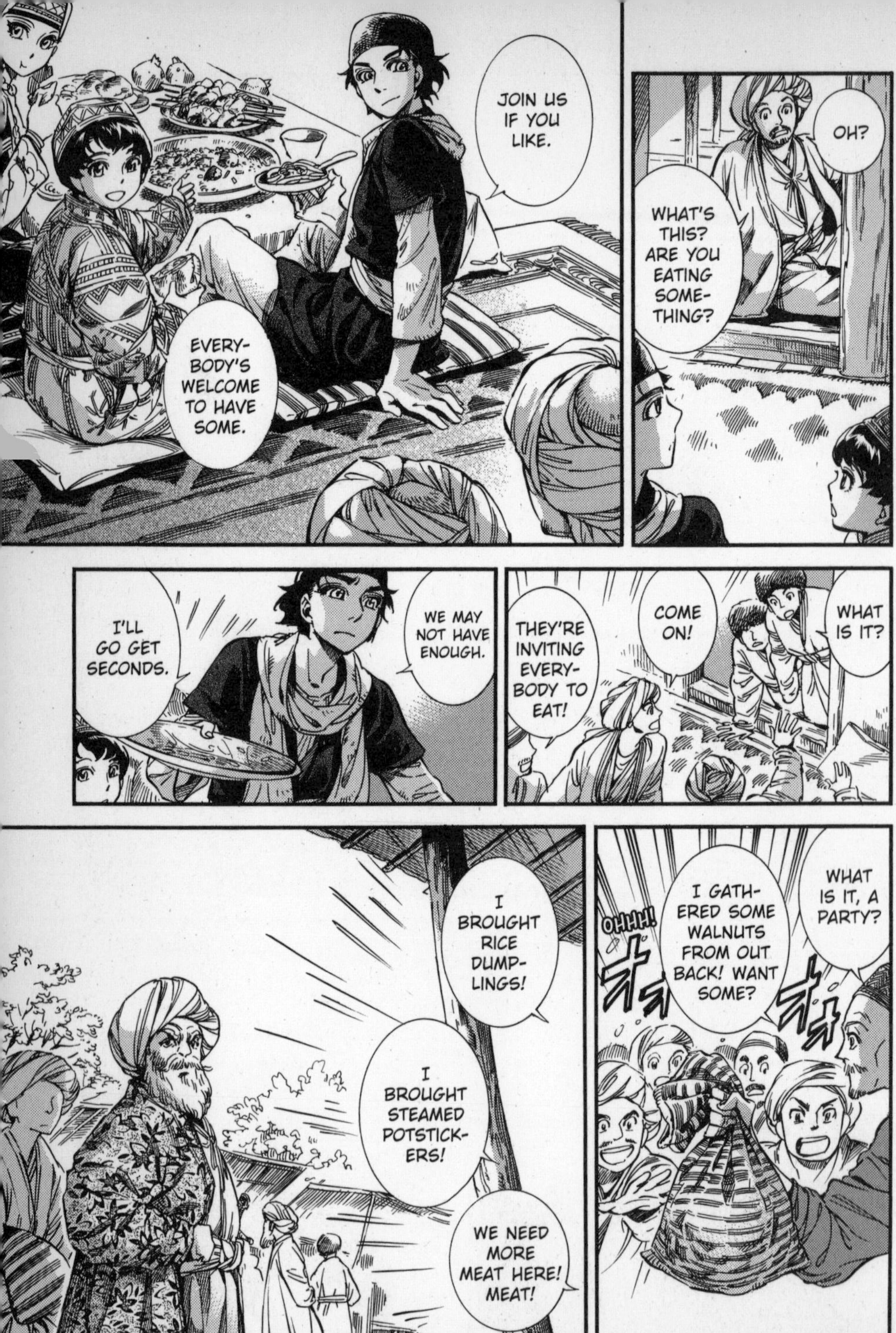
OH?
WHAT'S THIS? ARE YOU EATING SOME-THING?
JOIN US IF YOU LIKE.
EVERY-BODY'S WELCOME TO HAVE SOME.
WHAT IS IT?
COME ON!
THEY'RE INVITING EVERY-BODY TO EAT!
WE MAY NOT HAVE ENOUGH.
I'LL GO GET SECONDS.
WHAT IS IT, A PARTY?
OHHH!
I GATH-ERED SOME WALNUTS FROM OUT BACK! WANT SOME?
I BROUGHT RICE DUMP-LINGS!
I BROUGHT STEAMED POTSTICK-ERS!
WE NEED MORE MEAT HERE! MEAT!

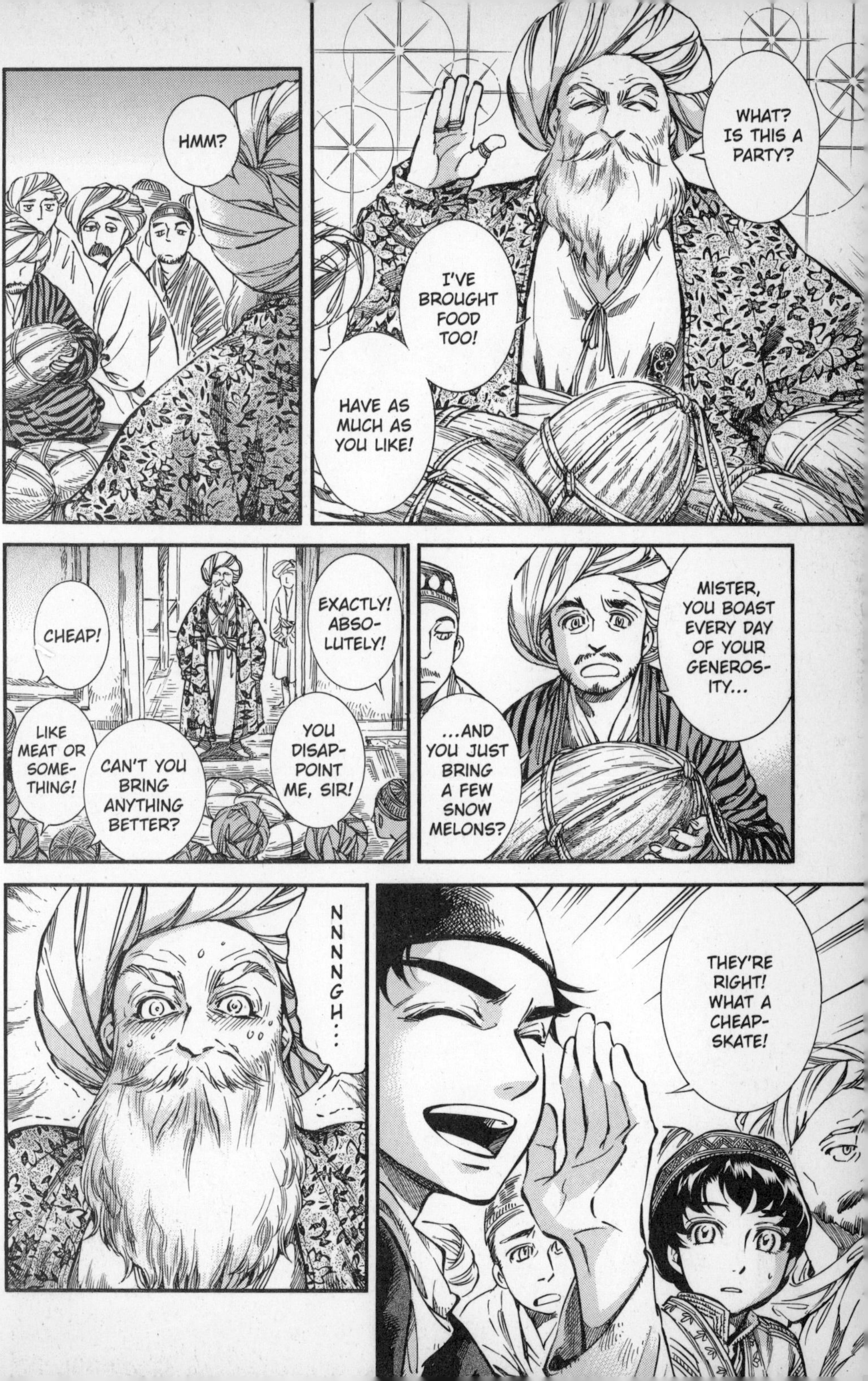
WHAT? IS THIS A PARTY?
I'VE BROUGHT FOOD TOO!
HAVE AS MUCH AS YOU LIKE!
HMM?
MISTER, YOU BOAST EVERY DAY OF YOUR GENEROS-ITY...
...AND YOU JUST BRING A FEW SNOW MELONS?
EXACTLY! ABSO-LUTELY!
YOU DISAP-POINT ME, SIR!
CHEAP!
CAN'T YOU BRING ANYTHING BETTER?
LIKE MEAT OR SOME-THING!
THEY'RE RIGHT! WHAT A CHEAP-SKATE!
NNNNGH...

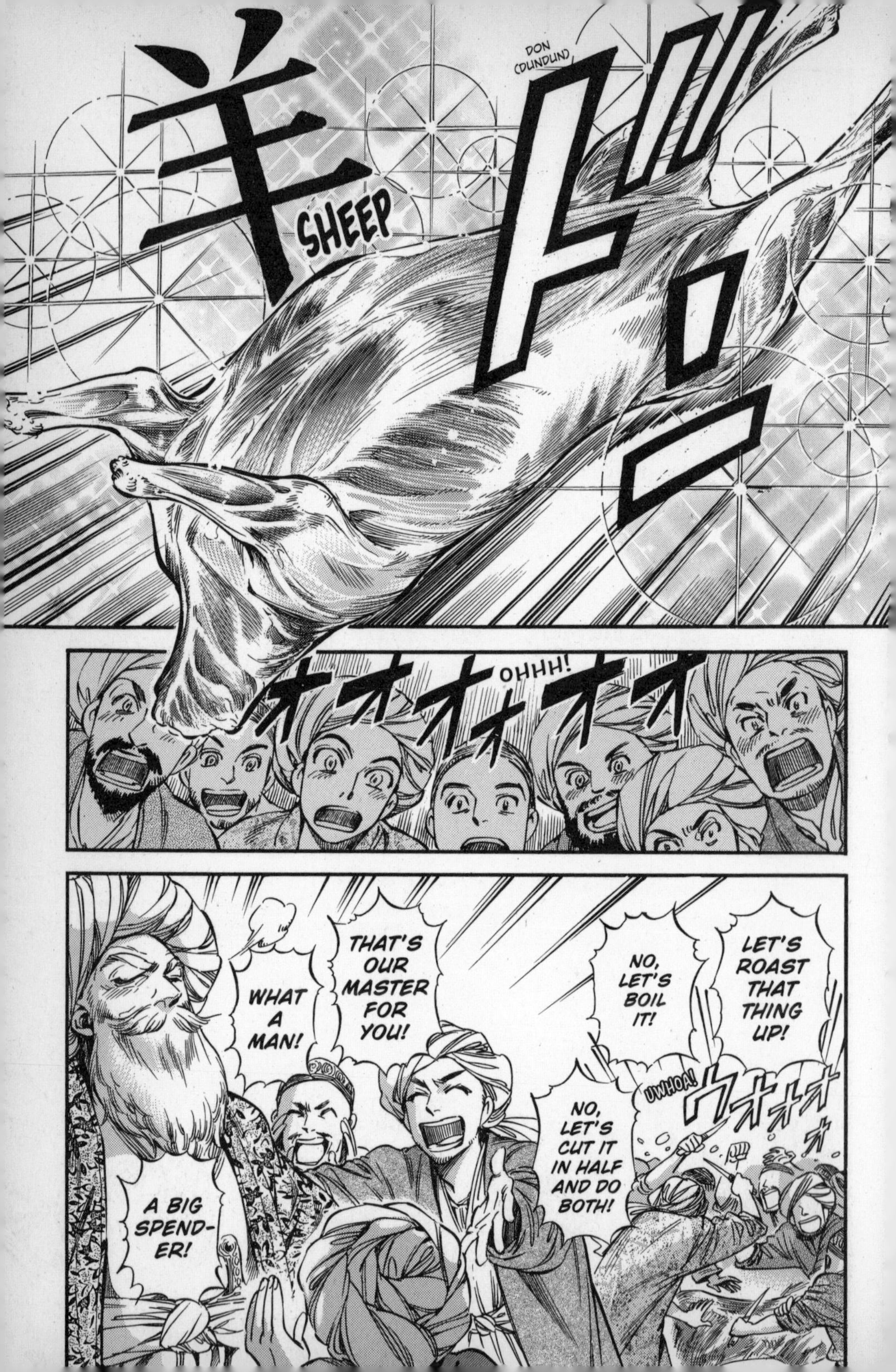

ドン
DON (DUNDUN)
羊
SHEEP
OHHH!
LET'S ROAST THAT THING UP!
NO, LET'S BOIL IT!
UWHOA!
NO, LET'S CUT IT IN HALF AND DO BOTH!
THAT'S OUR MASTER FOR YOU!
WHAT A MAN!
A BIG SPEND-ER!

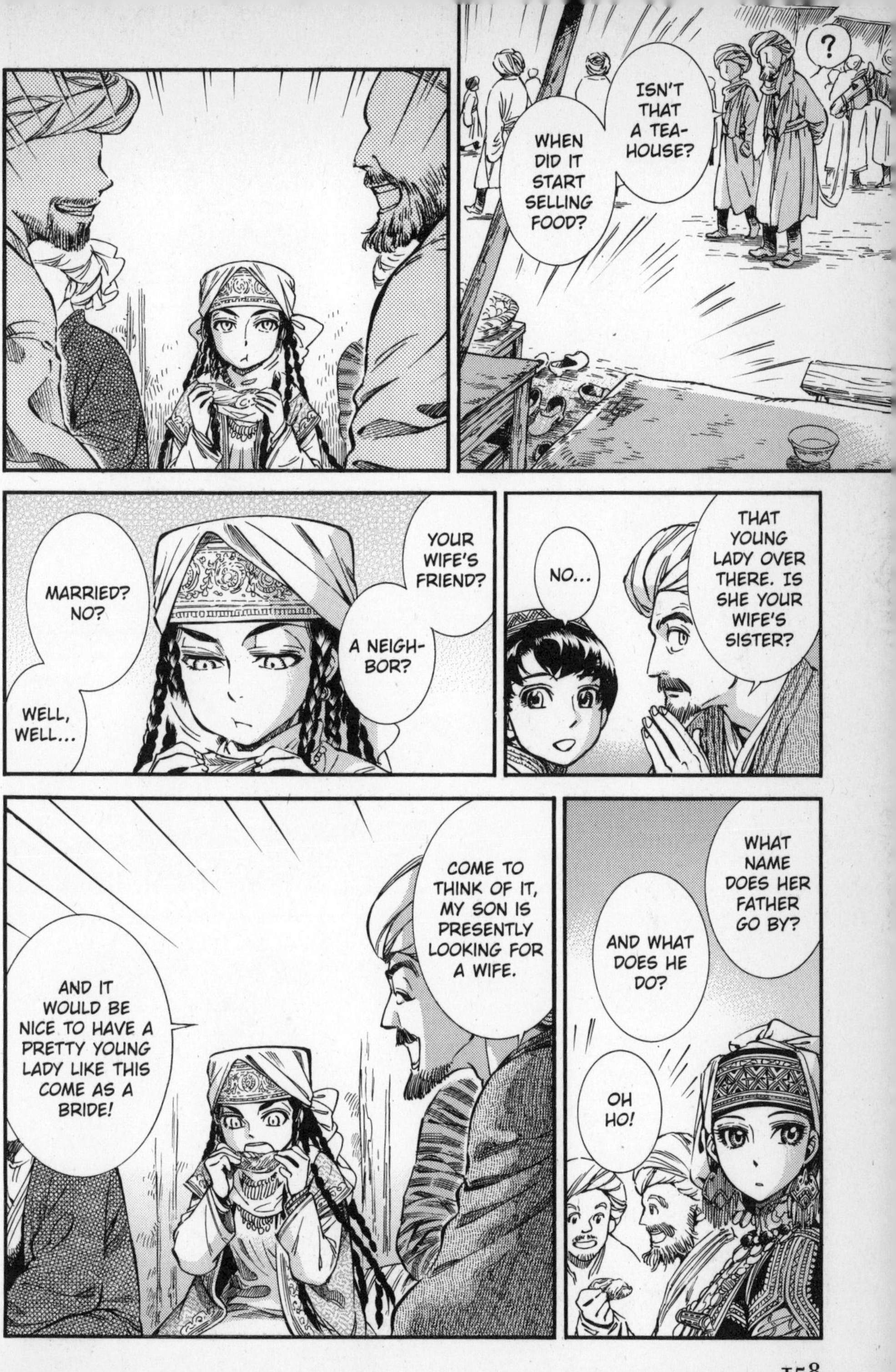
?
ISN'T THAT A TEA-HOUSE?
WHEN DID IT START SELLING FOOD?
THAT YOUNG LADY OVER THERE. IS SHE YOUR WIFE'S SISTER?
NO...
YOUR WIFE'S FRIEND?
A NEIGH-BOR?
MARRIED? NO?
WELL, WELL...
WHAT NAME DOES HER FATHER GO BY?
AND WHAT DOES HE DO?
OH HO!
COME TO THINK OF IT, MY SON IS PRESENTLY LOOKING FOR A WIFE.
AND IT WOULD BE NICE TO HAVE A PRETTY YOUNG LADY LIKE THIS COME AS A BRIDE!

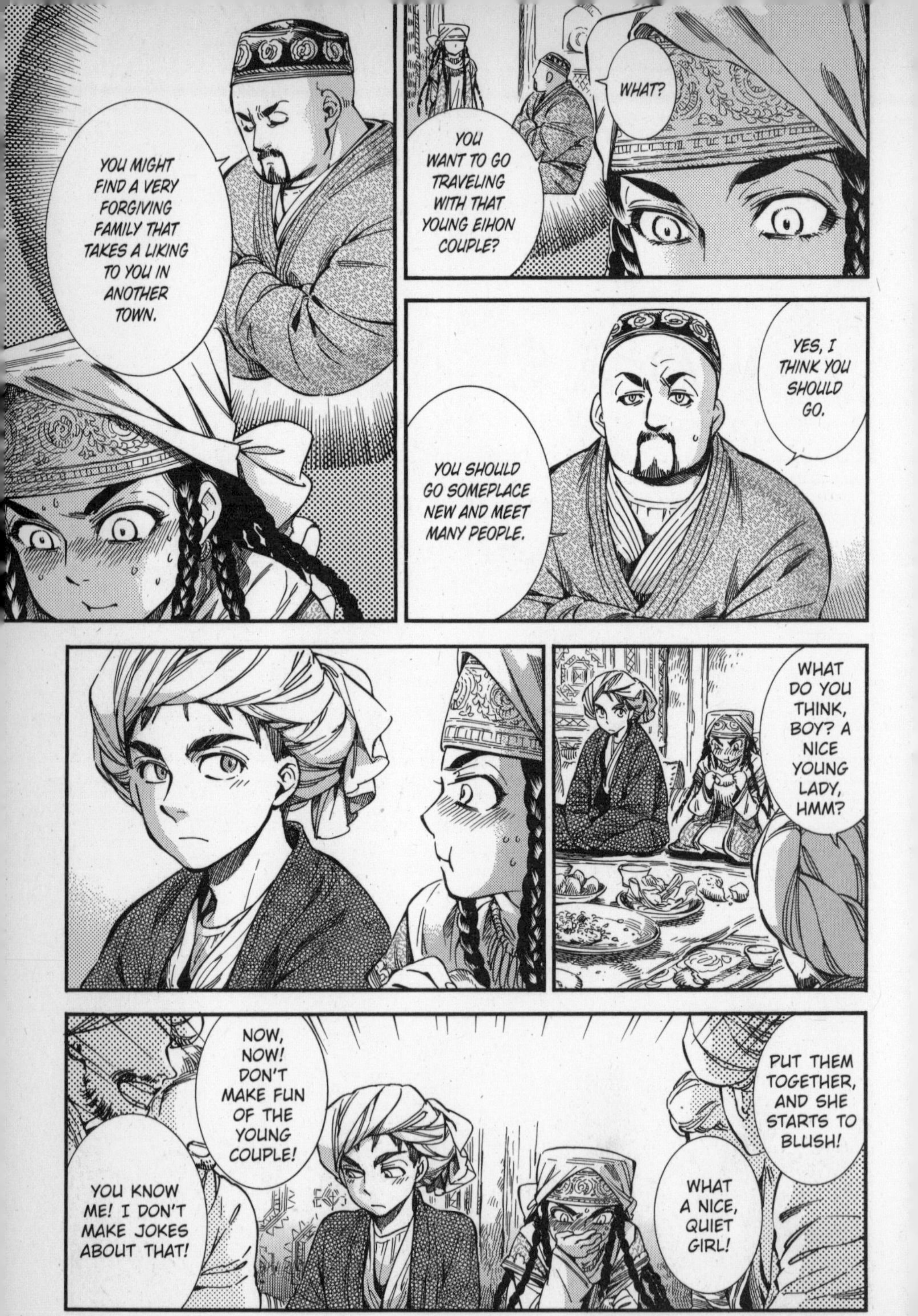
WHAT?
YOU WANT TO GO TRAVELING WITH THAT YOUNG EIHON COUPLE?
YES, I THINK YOU SHOULD GO.
YOU SHOULD GO SOMEPLACE NEW AND MEET MANY PEOPLE.
YOU MIGHT FIND A VERY FORGIVING FAMILY THAT TAKES A LIKING TO YOU IN ANOTHER TOWN.
WHAT DO YOU THINK, BOY? A NICE YOUNG LADY, HMM?
PUT THEM TOGETHER, AND SHE STARTS TO BLUSH!
WHAT A NICE, QUIET GIRL!
NOW, NOW! DON'T MAKE FUN OF THE YOUNG COUPLE!
YOU KNOW ME! I DON'T MAKE JOKES ABOUT THAT!

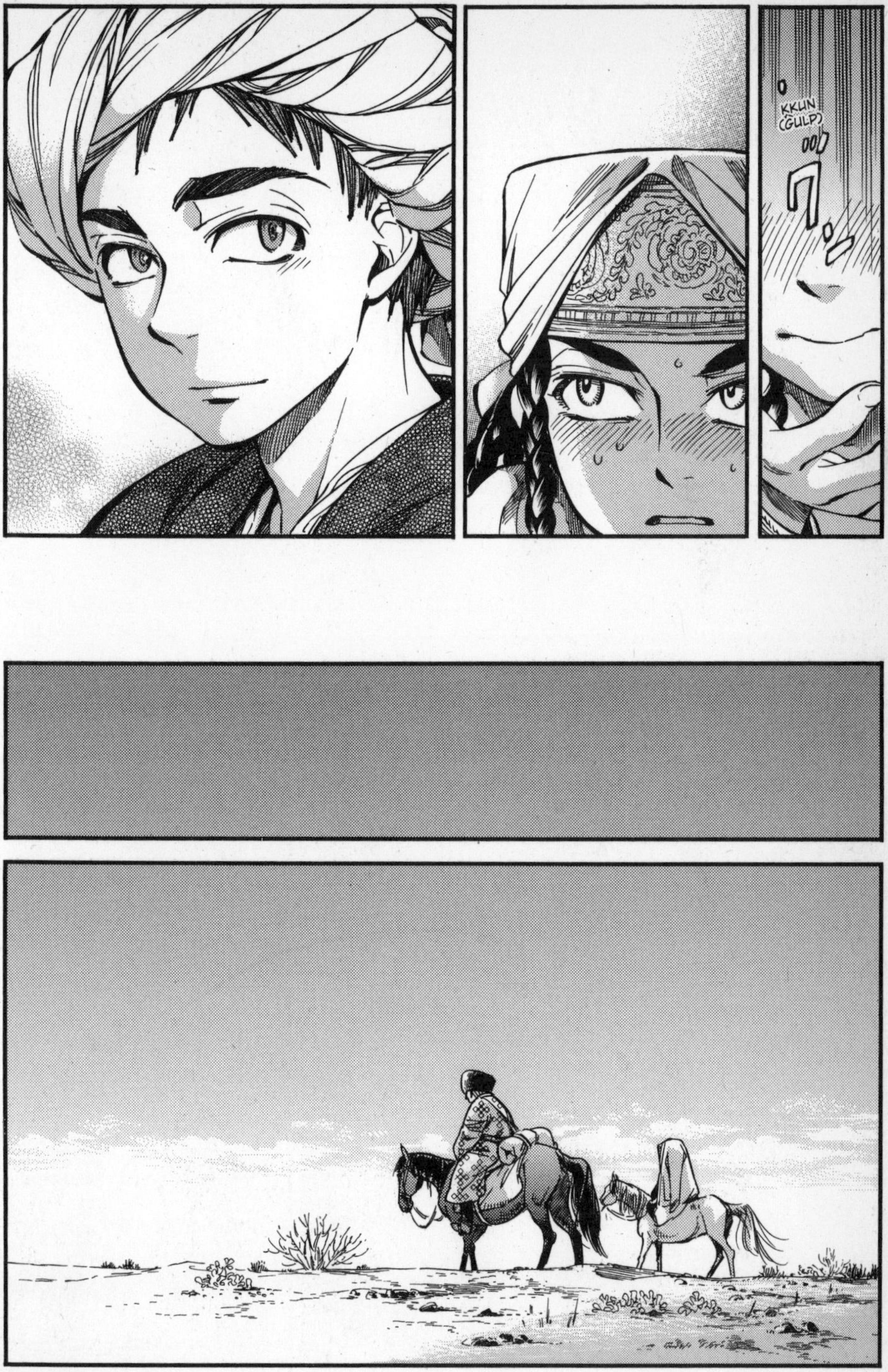
KKUN
(GULP)

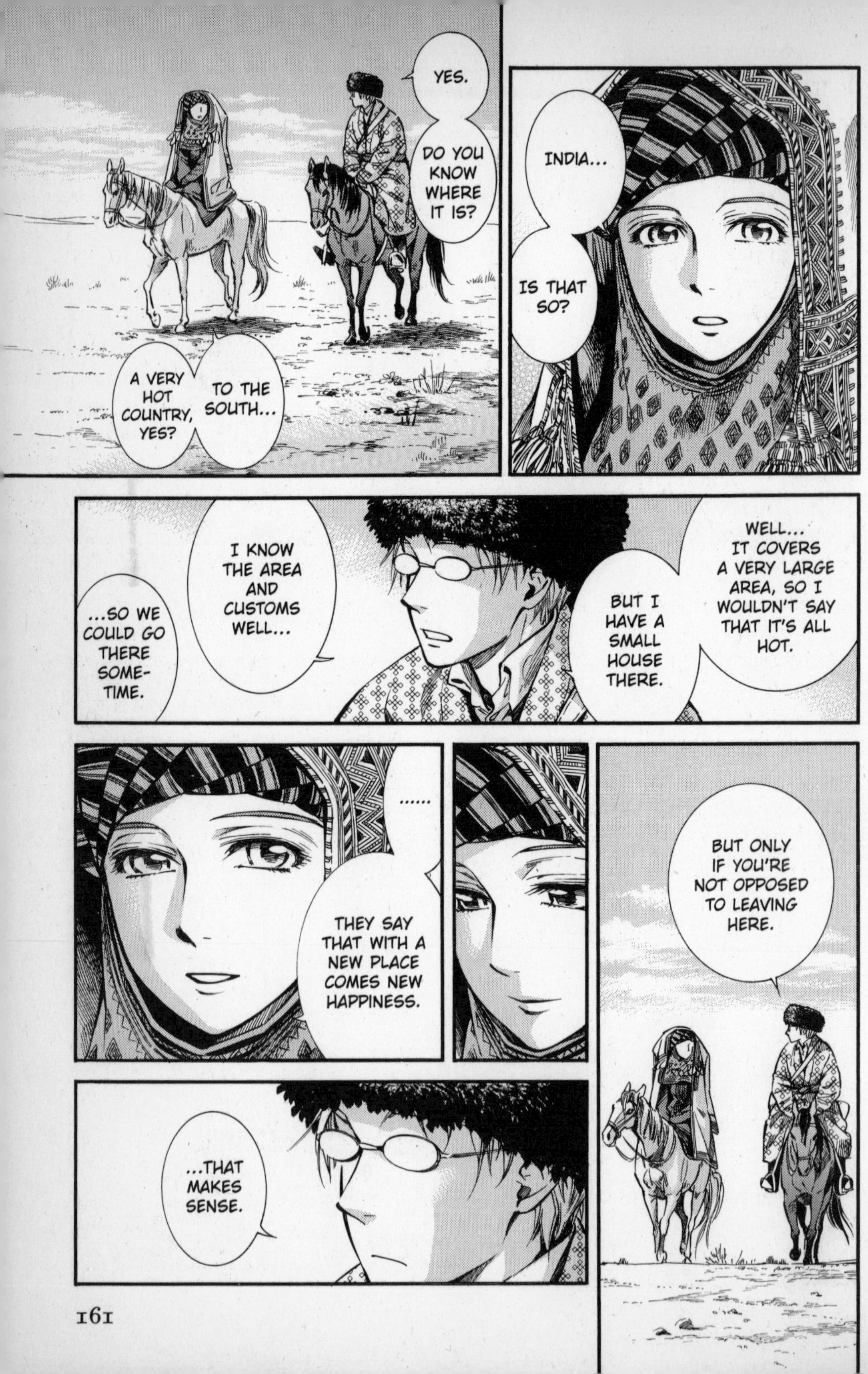
INDIA...
IS THAT SO?
YES.
DO YOU KNOW WHERE IT IS?
TO THE SOUTH...
A VERY HOT COUNTRY, YES?
WELL... IT COVERS A VERY LARGE AREA, SO I WOULDN'T SAY THAT IT'S ALL HOT.
BUT I HAVE A SMALL HOUSE THERE.
I KNOW THE AREA AND CUSTOMS WELL...
...SO WE COULD GO THERE SOME-TIME.
BUT ONLY IF YOU'RE NOT OPPOSED TO LEAVING HERE.
......
THEY SAY THAT WITH A NEW PLACE COMES NEW HAPPINESS.
...THAT MAKES SENSE.

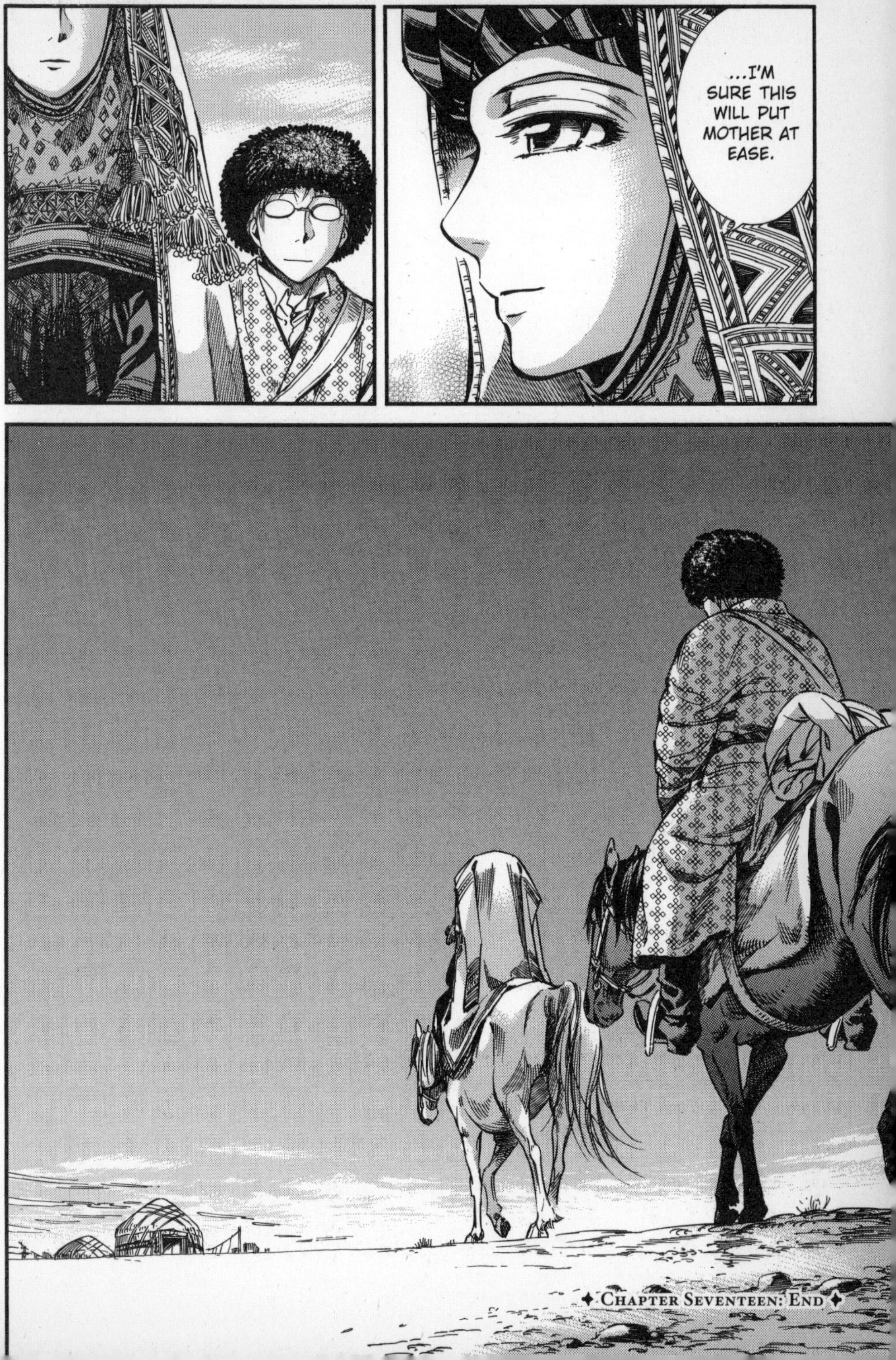
...I'M SURE THIS WILL PUT MOTHER AT EASE.
✦ Chapter Seventeen: End ✦

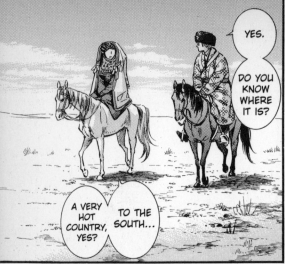

YES.

DO YOU KNOW WHERE IT IS?

INDIA...

IS THAT SO?

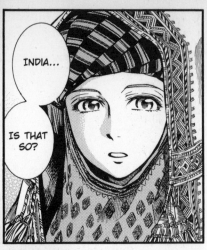

A VERY HOT COUNTRY, YES?

TO THE SOUTH...

...SO WE COULD GO THERE SOMETIME.

I KNOW THE AREA AND CUSTOMS WELL...

WELL... IT COVERS A VERY LARGE AREA, SO I WOULDN'T SAY THAT IT'S ALL HOT.

BUT I HAVE A SMALL HOUSE THERE.

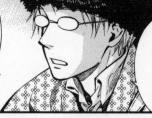

......

THEY SAY THAT WITH A NEW PLACE COMES NEW HAPPINESS.

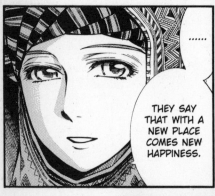

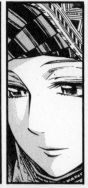

BUT ONLY IF YOU'RE NOT OPPOSED TO LEAVING HERE.

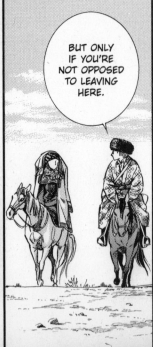

...THAT MAKES SENSE.

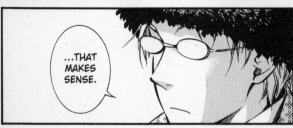

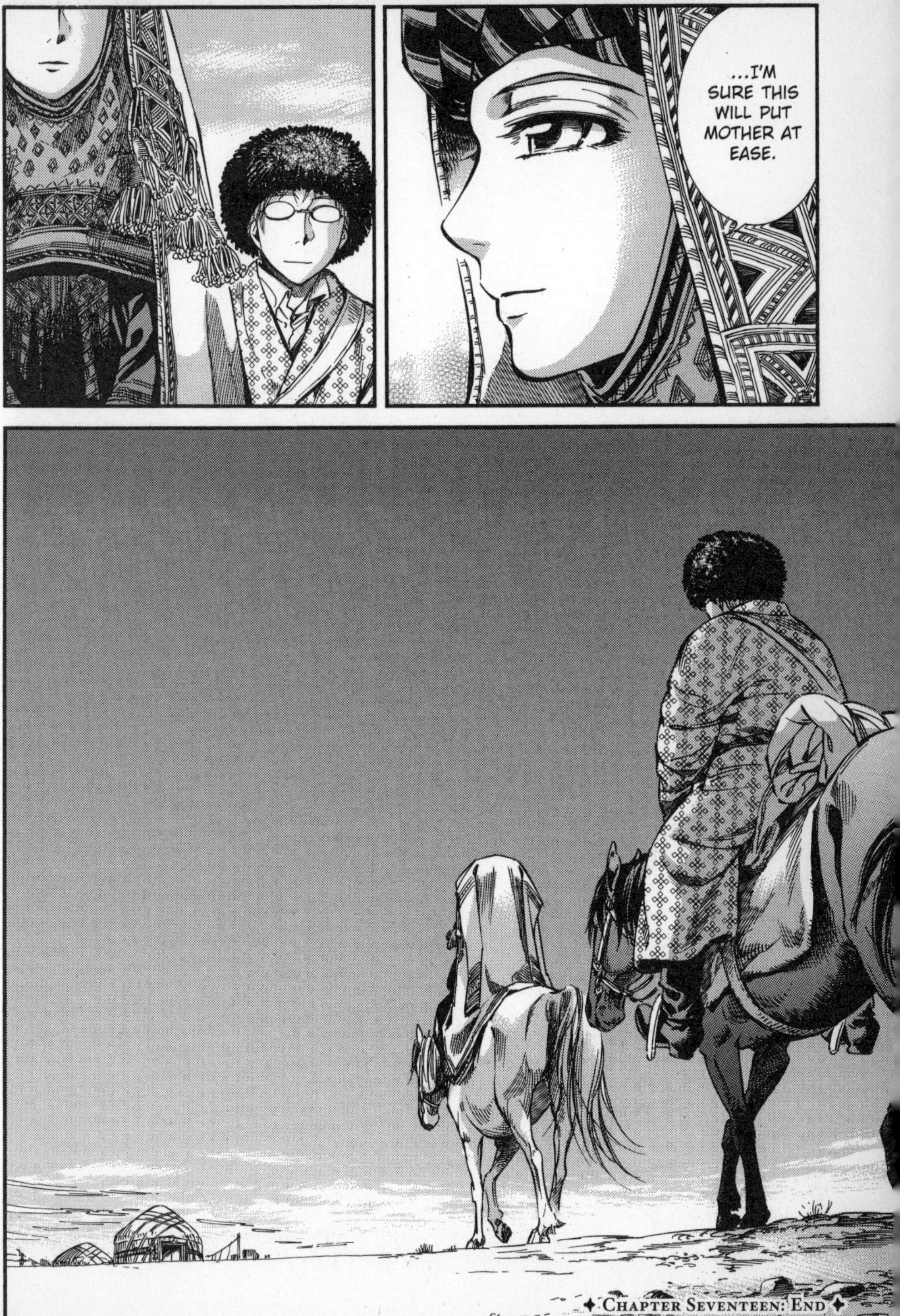
...I'M SURE THIS WILL PUT MOTHER AT EASE.
✦ CHAPTER SEVENTEEN: END ✦

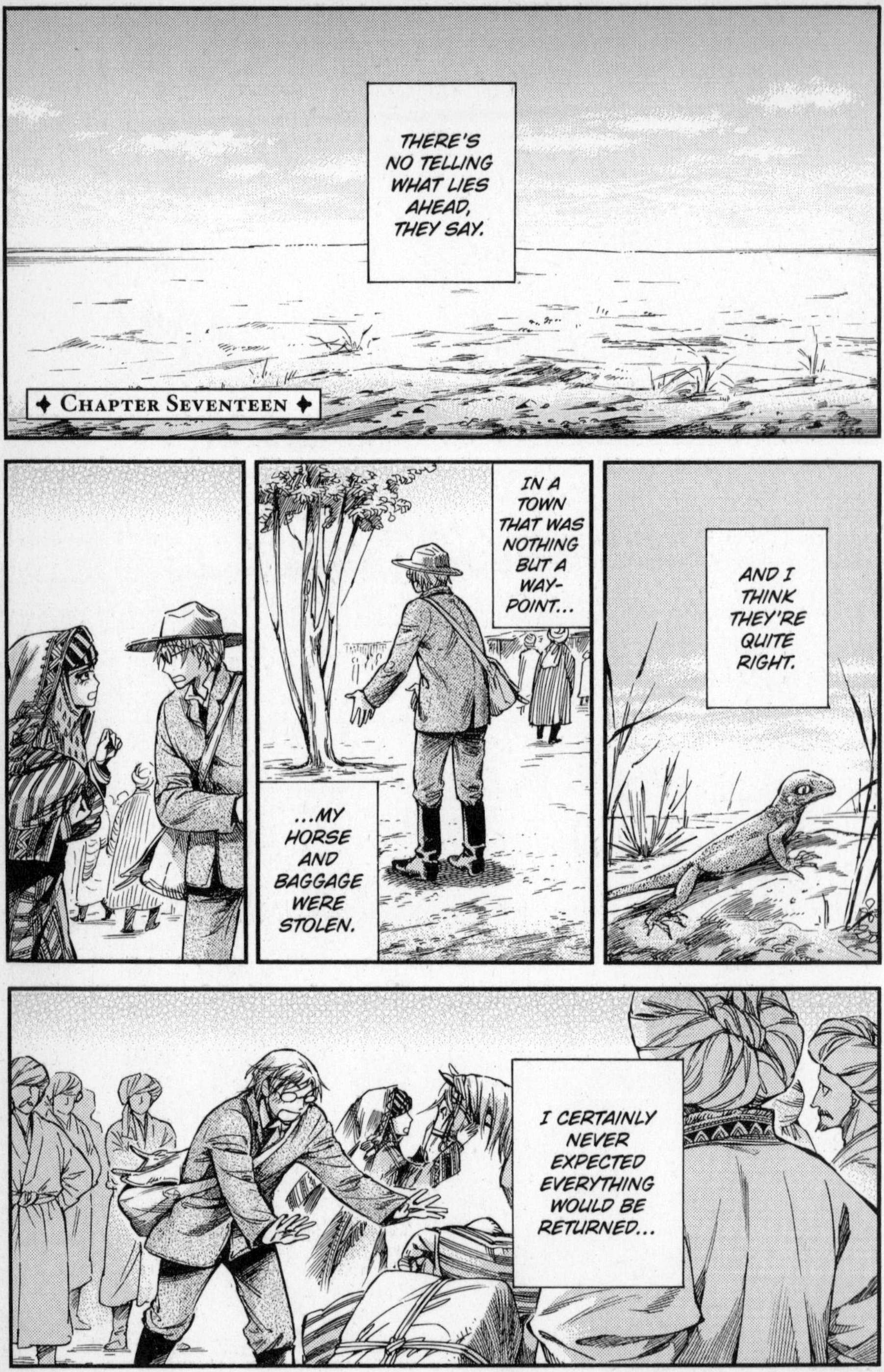
Chapter Seventeen
THERE'S NO TELLING WHAT LIES AHEAD, THEY SAY.
AND I THINK THEY'RE QUITE RIGHT.
IN A TOWN THAT WAS NOTHING BUT A WAY-POINT...
...MY HORSE AND BAGGAGE WERE STOLEN.
I CERTAINLY NEVER EXPECTED EVERYTHING WOULD BE RETURNED...

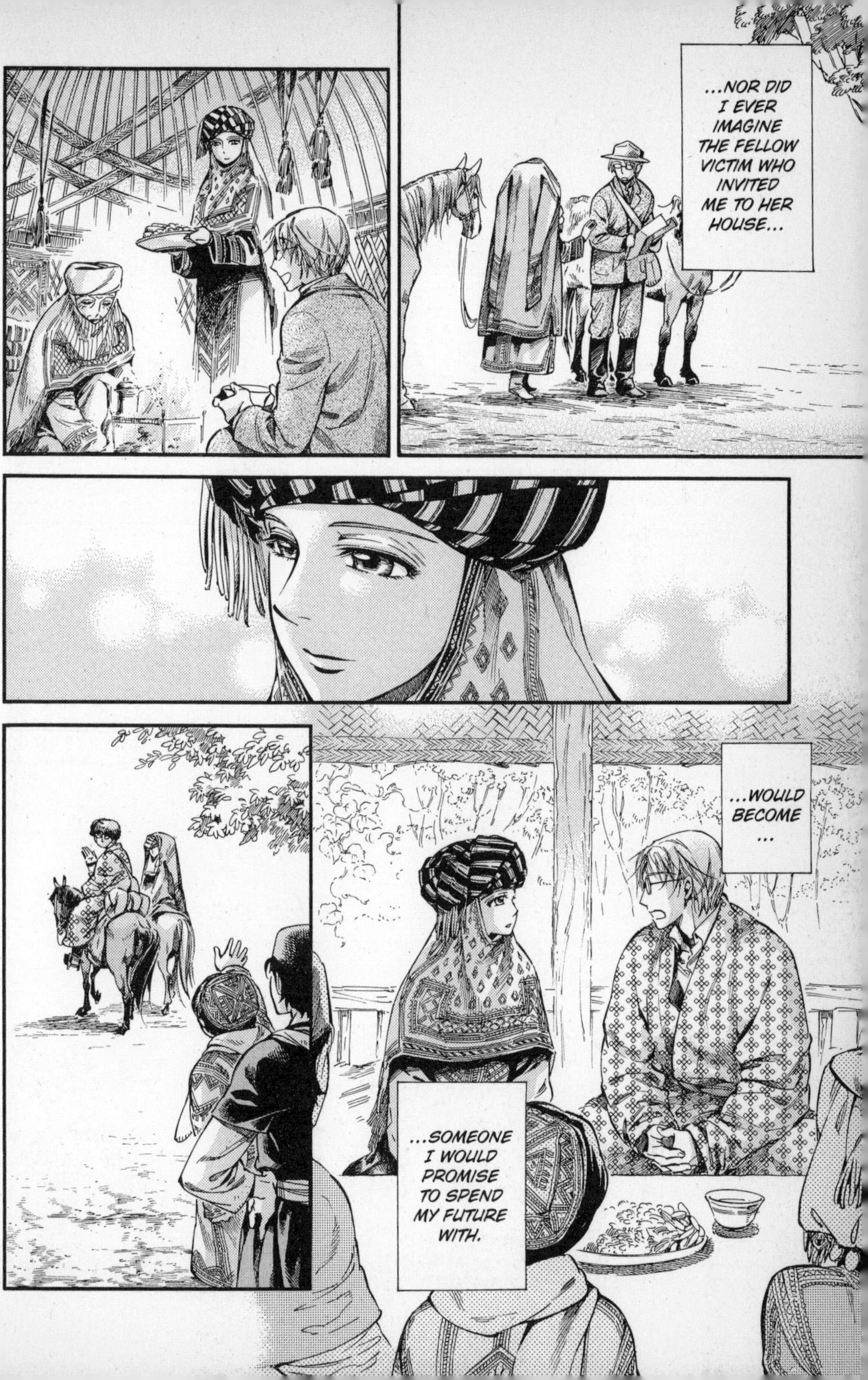
...NOR DID I EVER IMAGINE THE FELLOW VICTIM WHO INVITED ME TO HER HOUSE...
...WOULD BECOME ...
...SOMEONE I WOULD PROMISE TO SPEND MY FUTURE WITH.

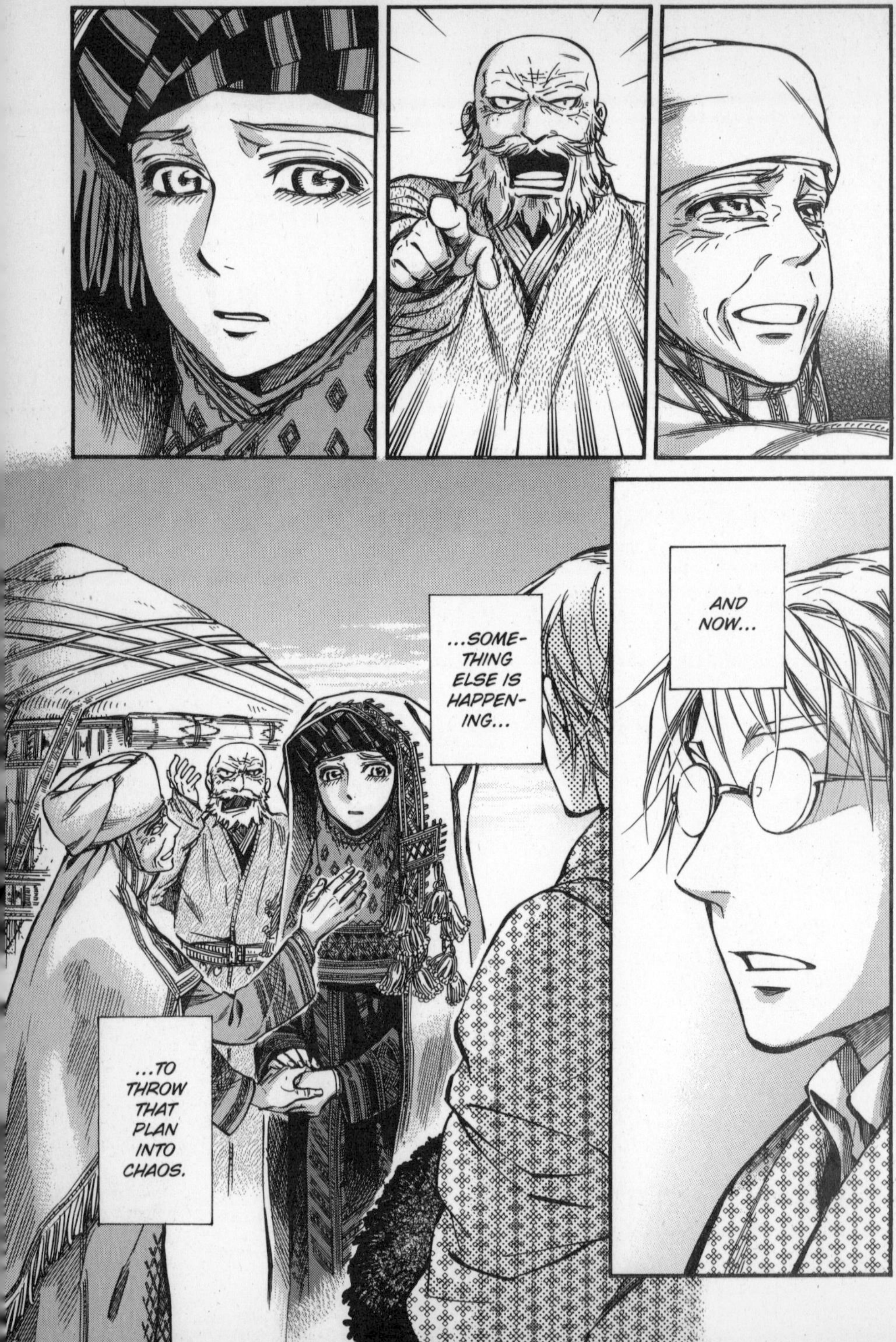
AND NOW...
...SOMETHING ELSE IS HAPPENING...
...TO THROW THAT PLAN INTO CHAOS.

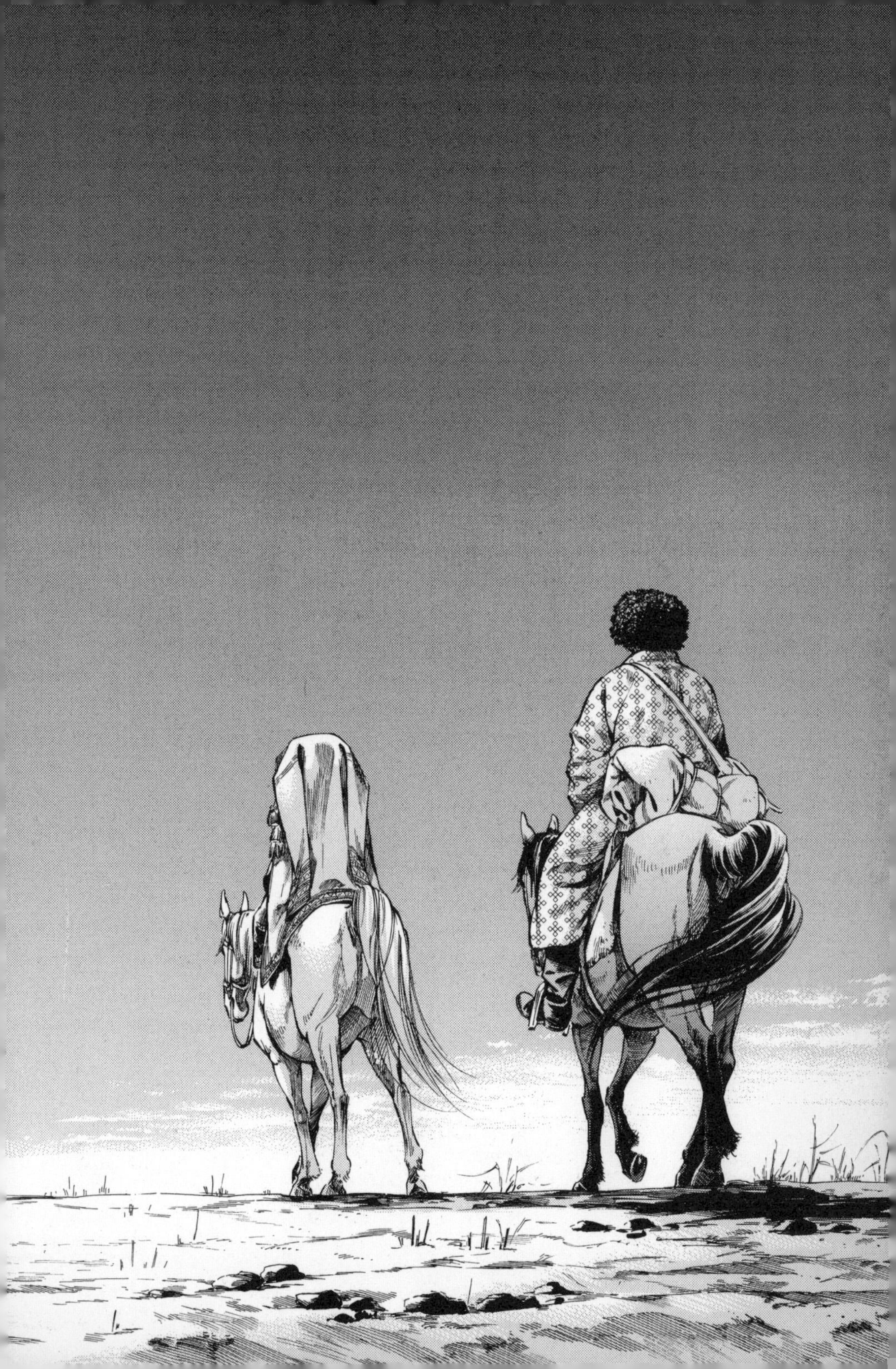

Chapter Seventeen
Heading to Ankara

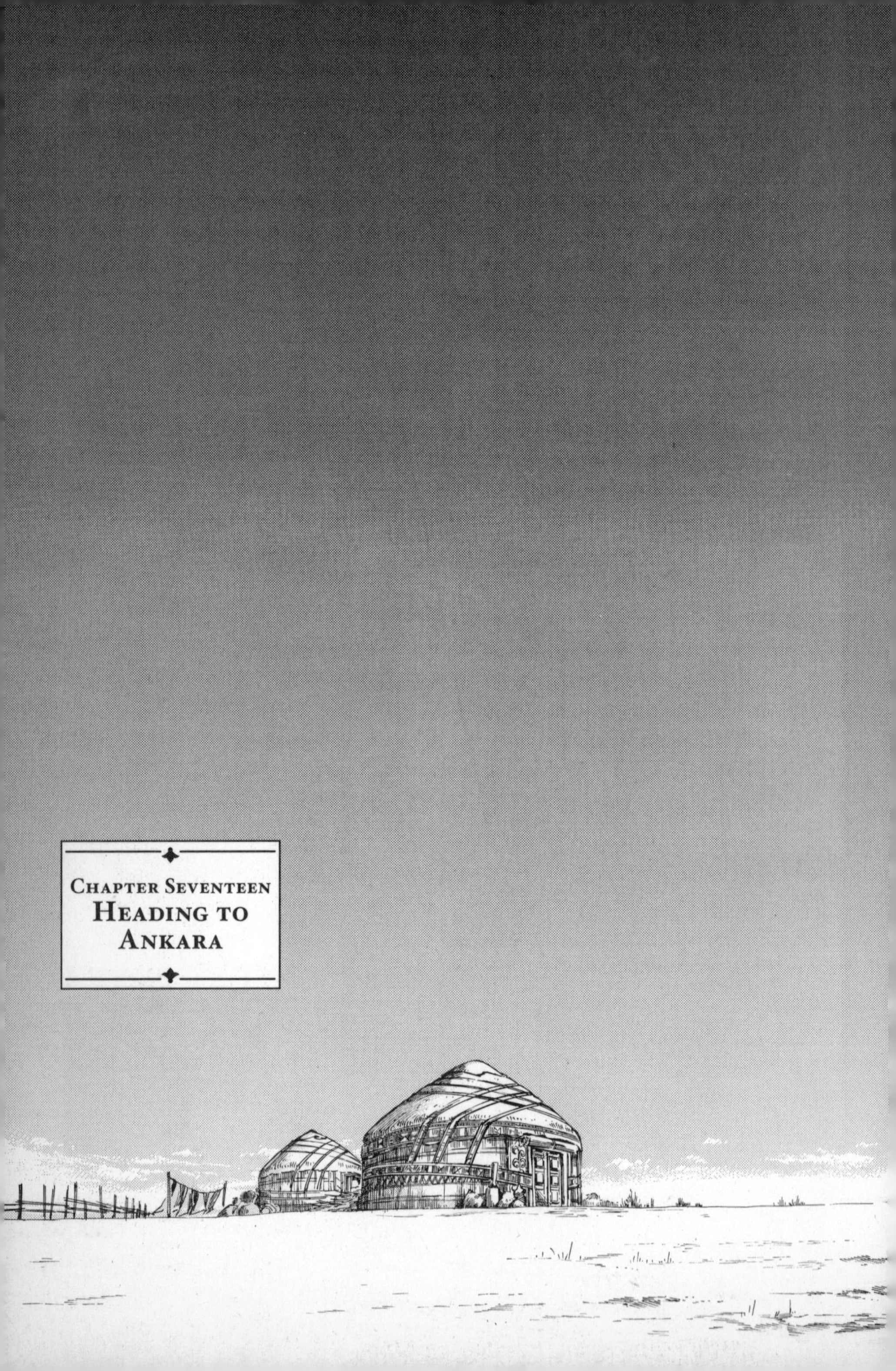

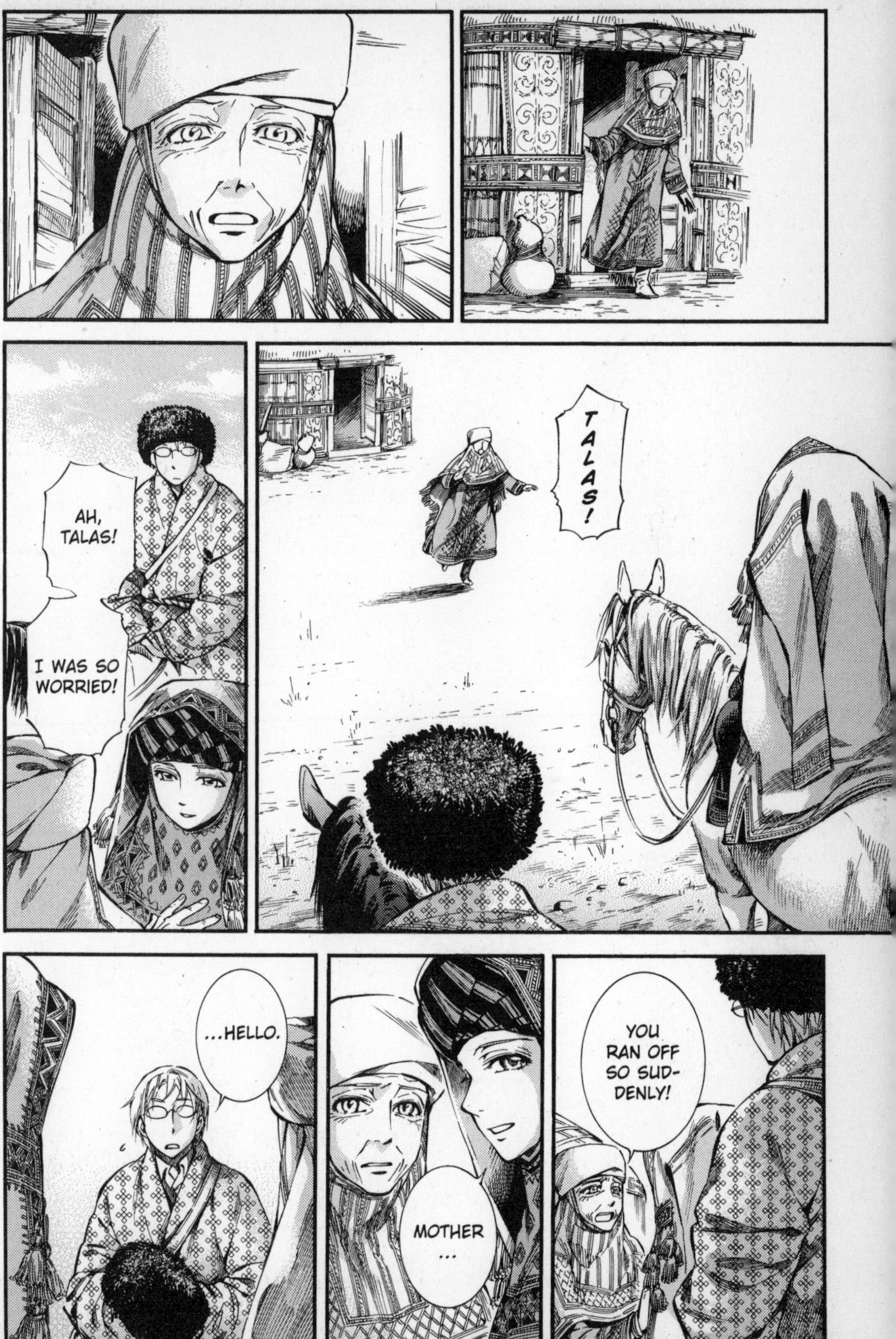
TALAS!
AH, TALAS!
I WAS SO WORRIED!
YOU RAN OFF SO SUD-DENLY!
MOTHER ...
...HELLO.

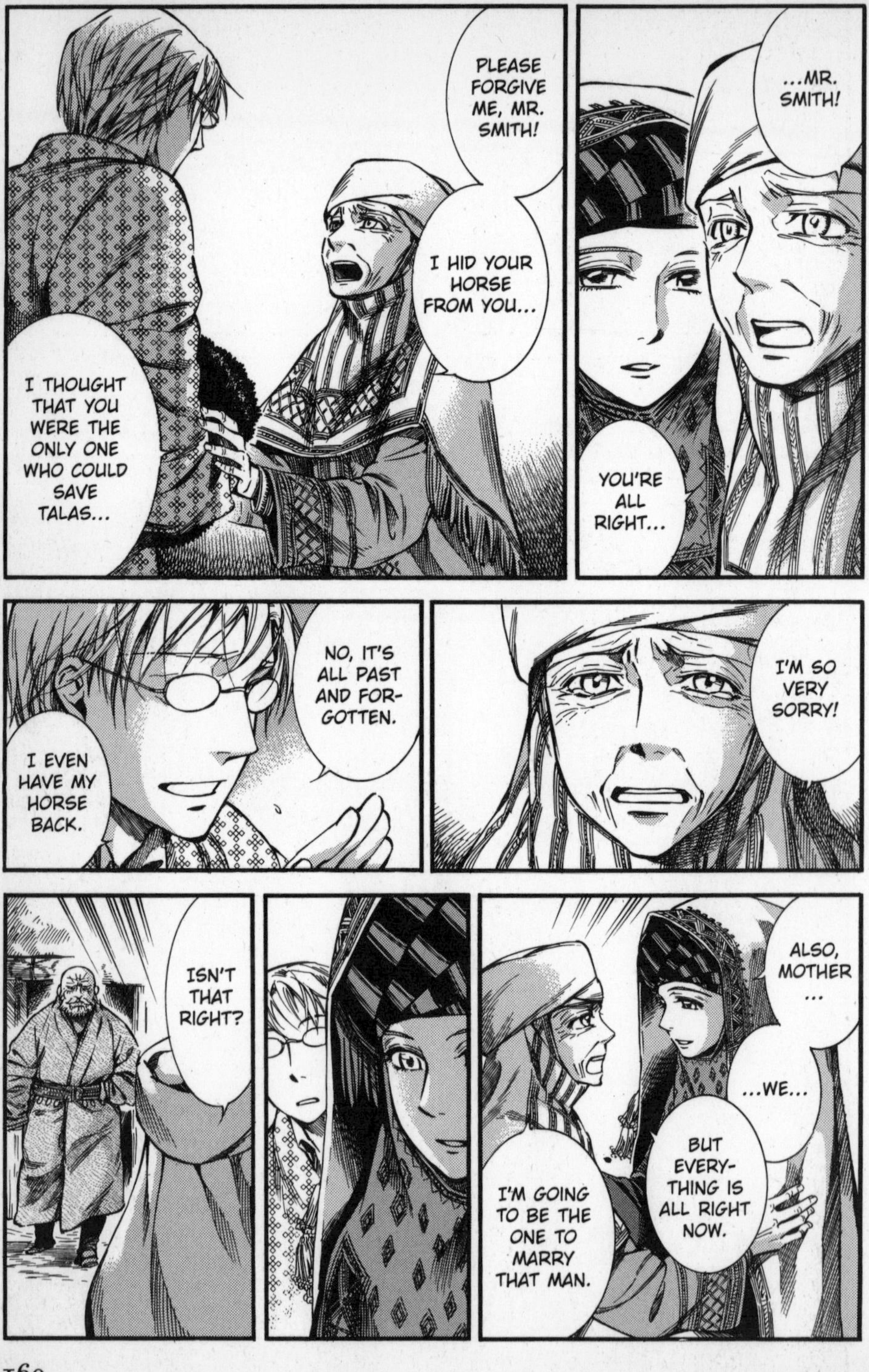
...MR. SMITH!
YOU'RE ALL RIGHT...
PLEASE FORGIVE ME, MR. SMITH!
I HID YOUR HORSE FROM YOU...
I THOUGHT THAT YOU WERE THE ONLY ONE WHO COULD SAVE TALAS...
I'M SO VERY SORRY!
NO, IT'S ALL PAST AND FOR-GOTTEN.
I EVEN HAVE MY HORSE BACK.
ALSO, MOTHER ...
...WE...
BUT EVERY-THING IS ALL RIGHT NOW.
I'M GOING TO BE THE ONE TO MARRY THAT MAN.
ISN'T THAT RIGHT?

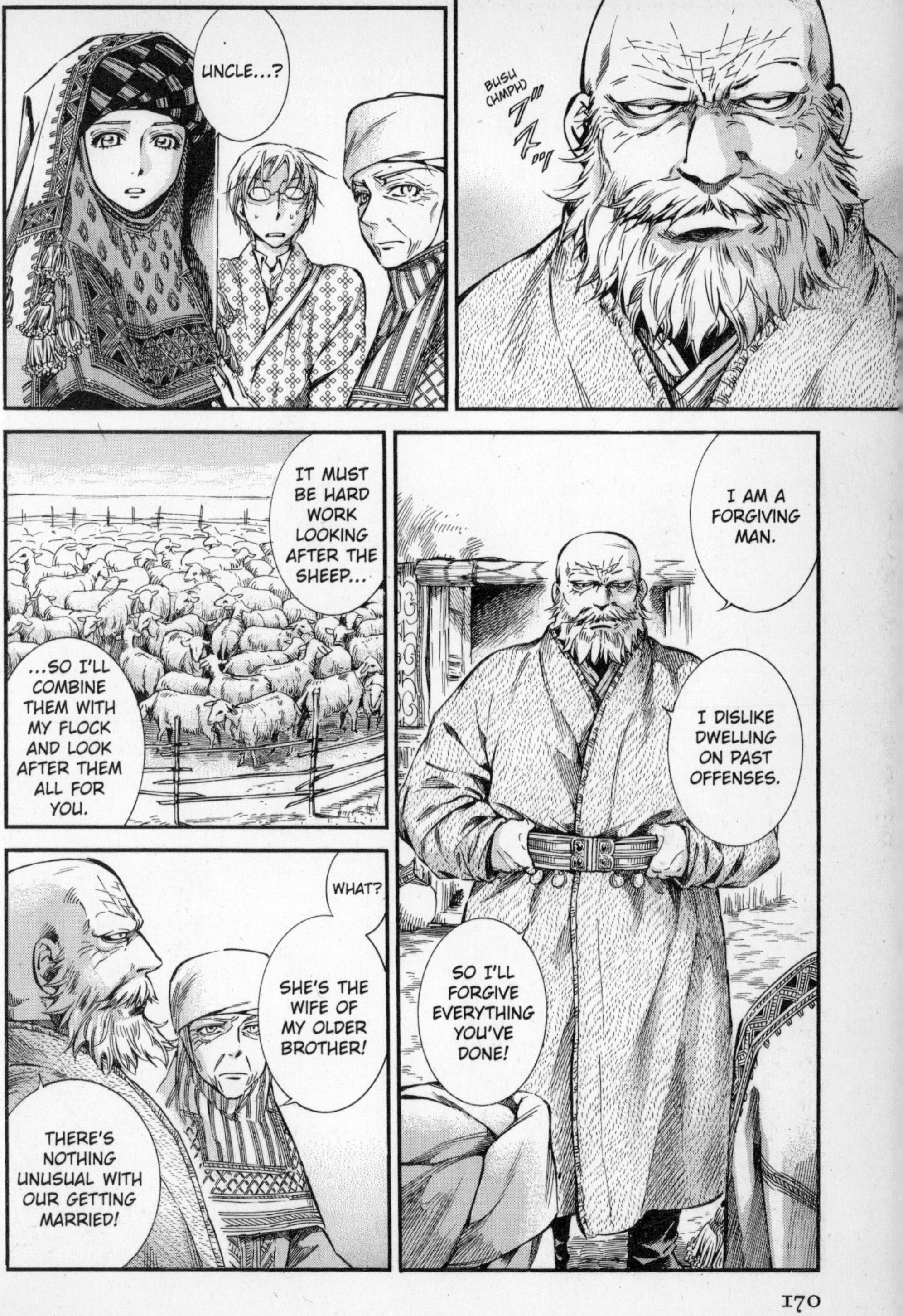
BUSU (HMPH)
UNCLE...?
I AM A FORGIVING MAN.
I DISLIKE DWELLING ON PAST OFFENSES.
SO I'LL FORGIVE EVERYTHING YOU'VE DONE!
IT MUST BE HARD WORK LOOKING AFTER THE SHEEP...
...SO I'LL COMBINE THEM WITH MY FLOCK AND LOOK AFTER THEM ALL FOR YOU.
WHAT?
SHE'S THE WIFE OF MY OLDER BROTHER!
THERE'S NOTHING UNUSUAL WITH OUR GETTING MARRIED!

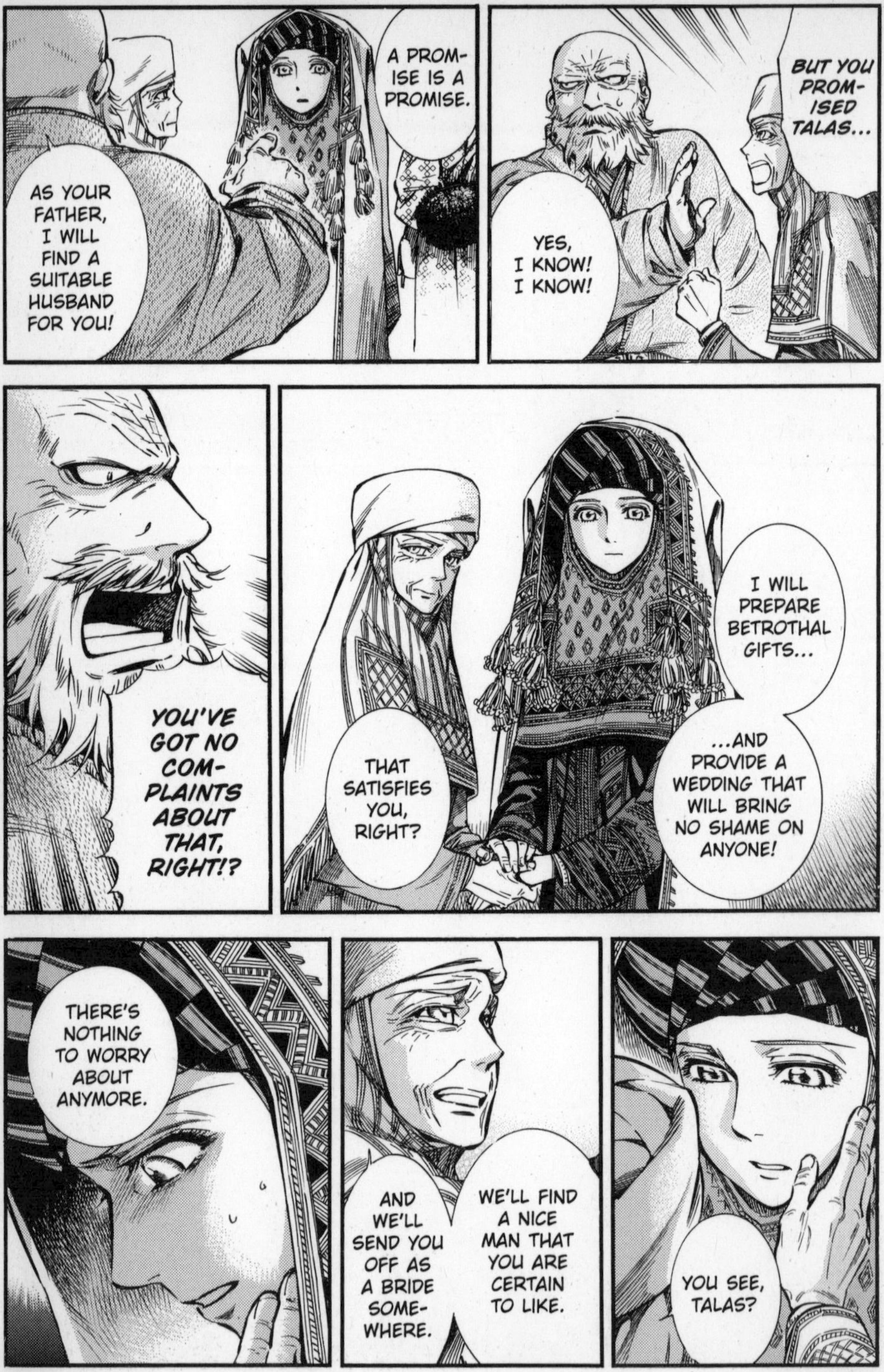
BUT YOU PROMISED TALAS...
YES, I KNOW! I KNOW!
A PROMISE IS A PROMISE.
AS YOUR FATHER, I WILL FIND A SUITABLE HUSBAND FOR YOU!
I WILL PREPARE BETROTHAL GIFTS...
...AND PROVIDE A WEDDING THAT WILL BRING NO SHAME ON ANYONE!
THAT SATISFIES YOU, RIGHT?
YOU'VE GOT NO COMPLAINTS ABOUT THAT, RIGHT!?
YOU SEE, TALAS?
WE'LL FIND A NICE MAN THAT YOU ARE CERTAIN TO LIKE.
AND WE'LL SEND YOU OFF AS A BRIDE SOMEWHERE.
THERE'S NOTHING TO WORRY ABOUT ANYMORE.

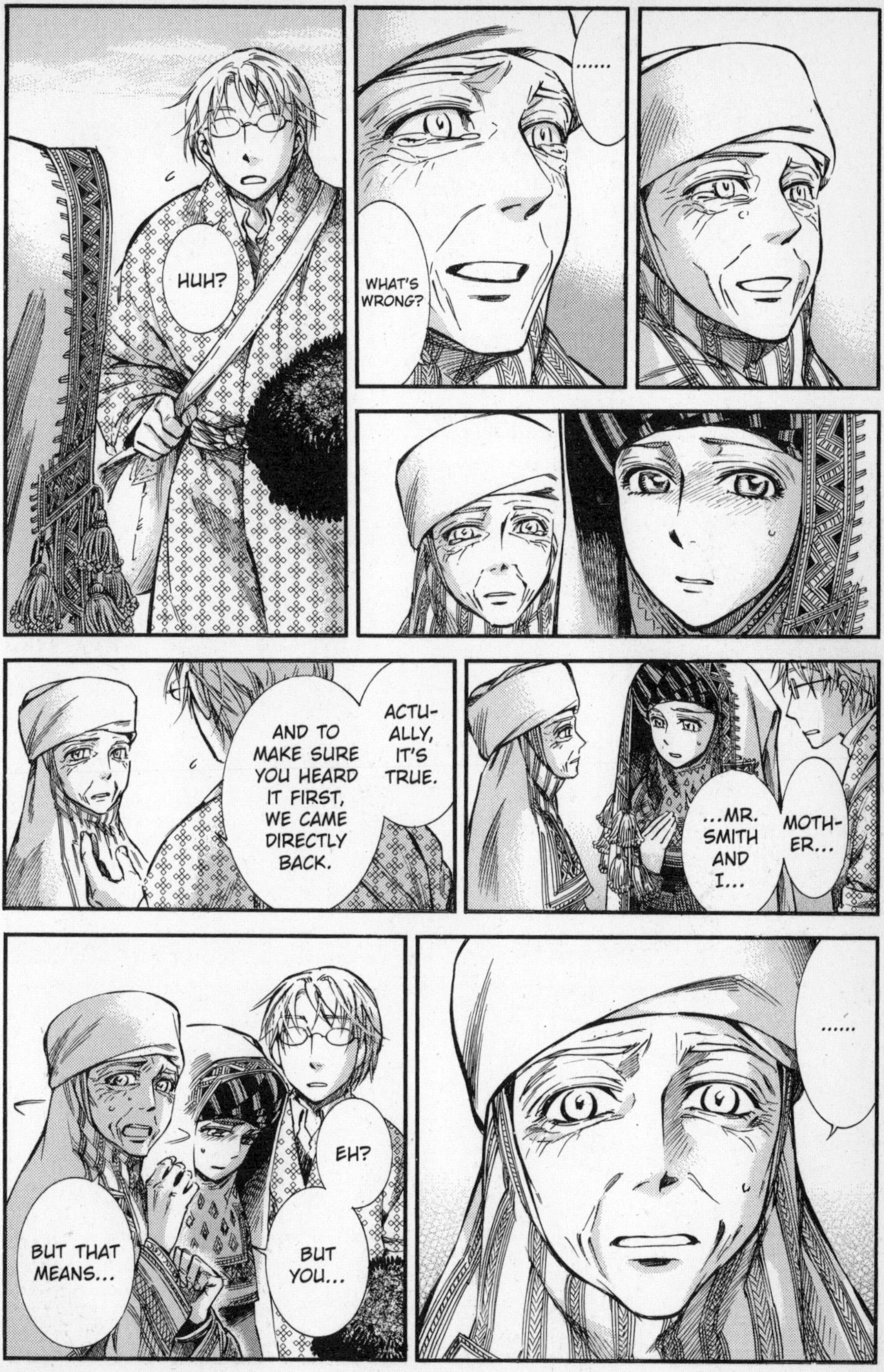

......
WHAT'S WRONG?
HUH?
MOTHER...
...MR. SMITH AND I...
ACTUALLY, IT'S TRUE.
AND TO MAKE SURE YOU HEARD IT FIRST, WE CAME DIRECTLY BACK.
......
EH?
BUT YOU...
BUT THAT MEANS...

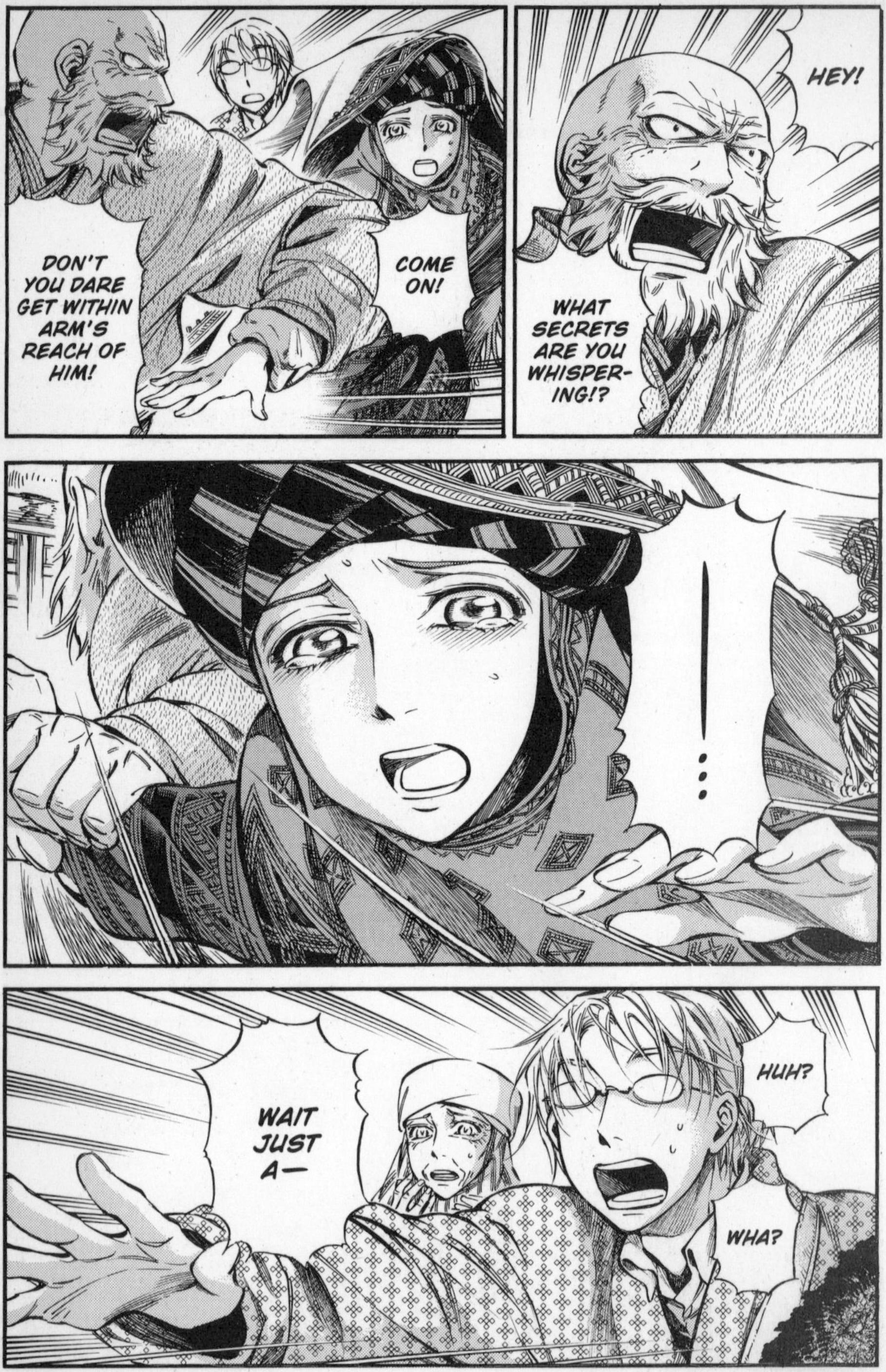
HEY!
WHAT SECRETS ARE YOU WHISPERING!?
COME ON!
DON'T YOU DARE GET WITHIN ARM'S REACH OF HIM!
!...
HUH?
WHA?
WAIT JUST A—

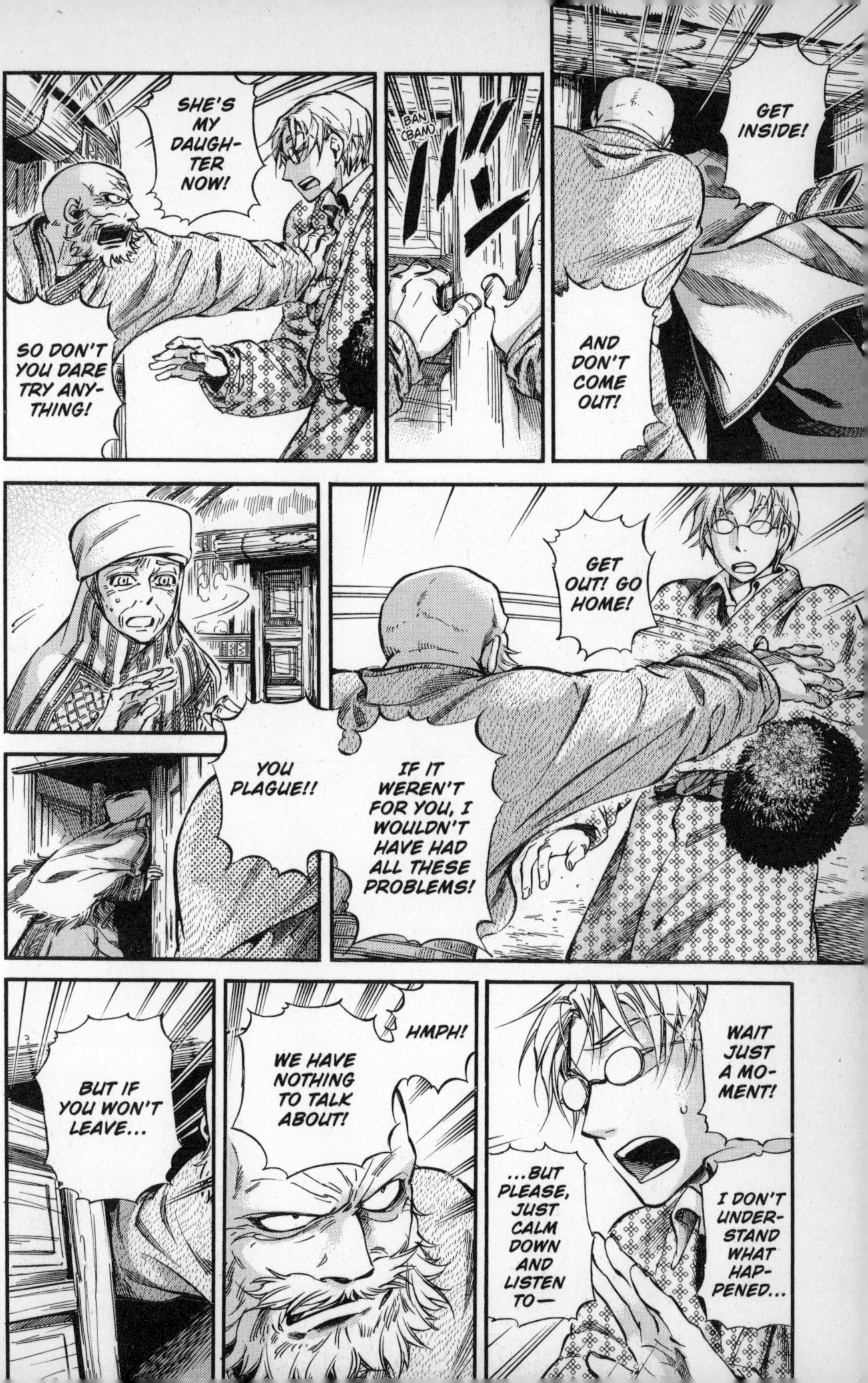
GET INSIDE!
AND DON'T COME OUT!
BAN (BAM)
SHE'S MY DAUGHTER NOW!
SO DON'T YOU DARE TRY ANYTHING!
GET OUT! GO HOME!
IF IT WEREN'T FOR YOU, I WOULDN'T HAVE HAD ALL THESE PROBLEMS!
YOU PLAGUE!!
WAIT JUST A MOMENT!
I DON'T UNDERSTAND WHAT HAPPENED...
...BUT PLEASE, JUST CALM DOWN AND LISTEN TO—
HMPH!
WE HAVE NOTHING TO TALK ABOUT!
BUT IF YOU WON'T LEAVE...

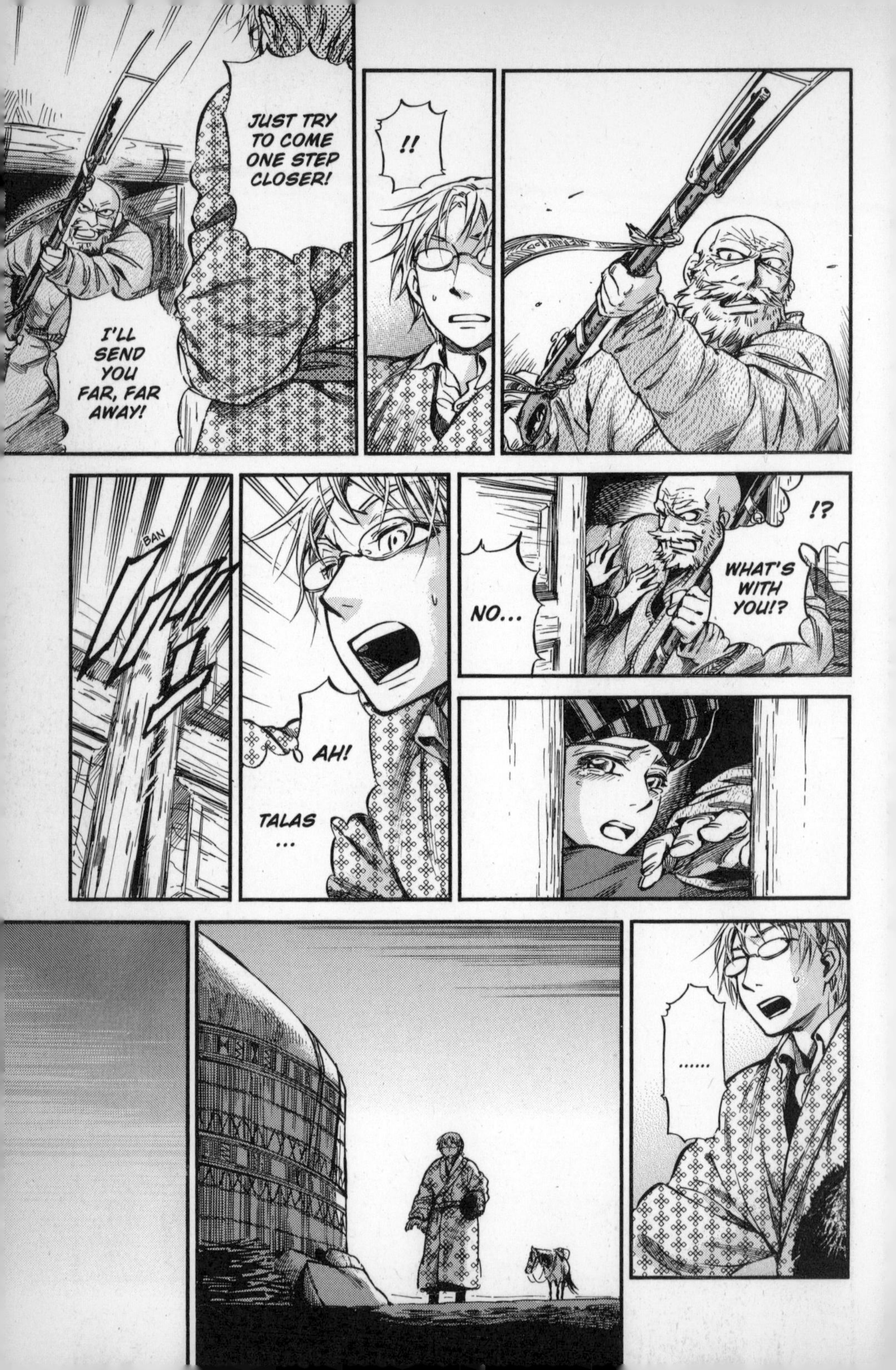
!!
JUST TRY TO COME ONE STEP CLOSER!
I'LL SEND YOU FAR, FAR AWAY!
!?
WHAT'S WITH YOU!?
NO...
AH!
TALAS ...
BAN
......

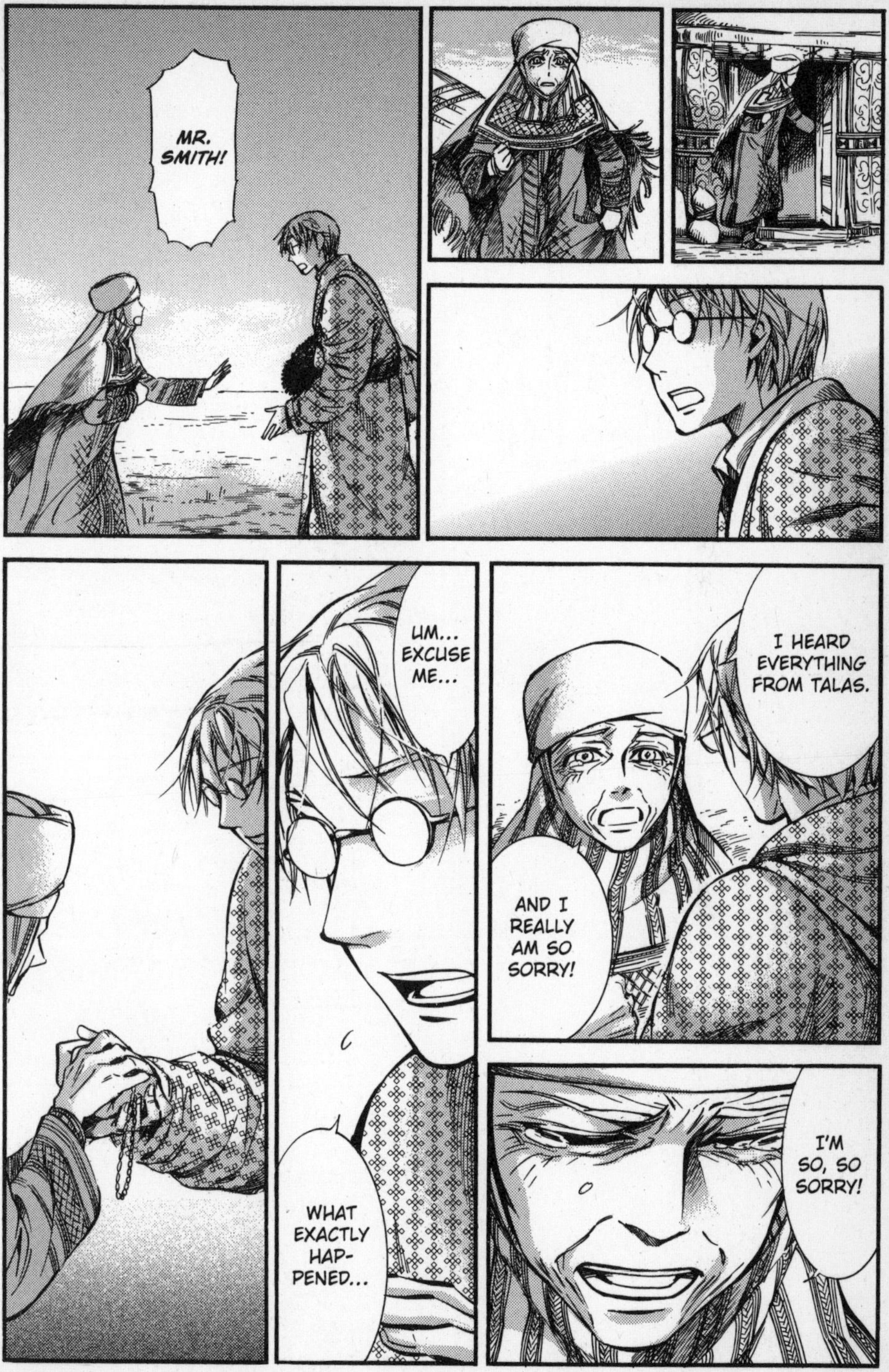
MR. SMITH!
I HEARD EVERYTHING FROM TALAS.
AND I REALLY AM SO SORRY!
I'M SO, SO SORRY!
UM... EXCUSE ME...
WHAT EXACTLY HAP-PENED...

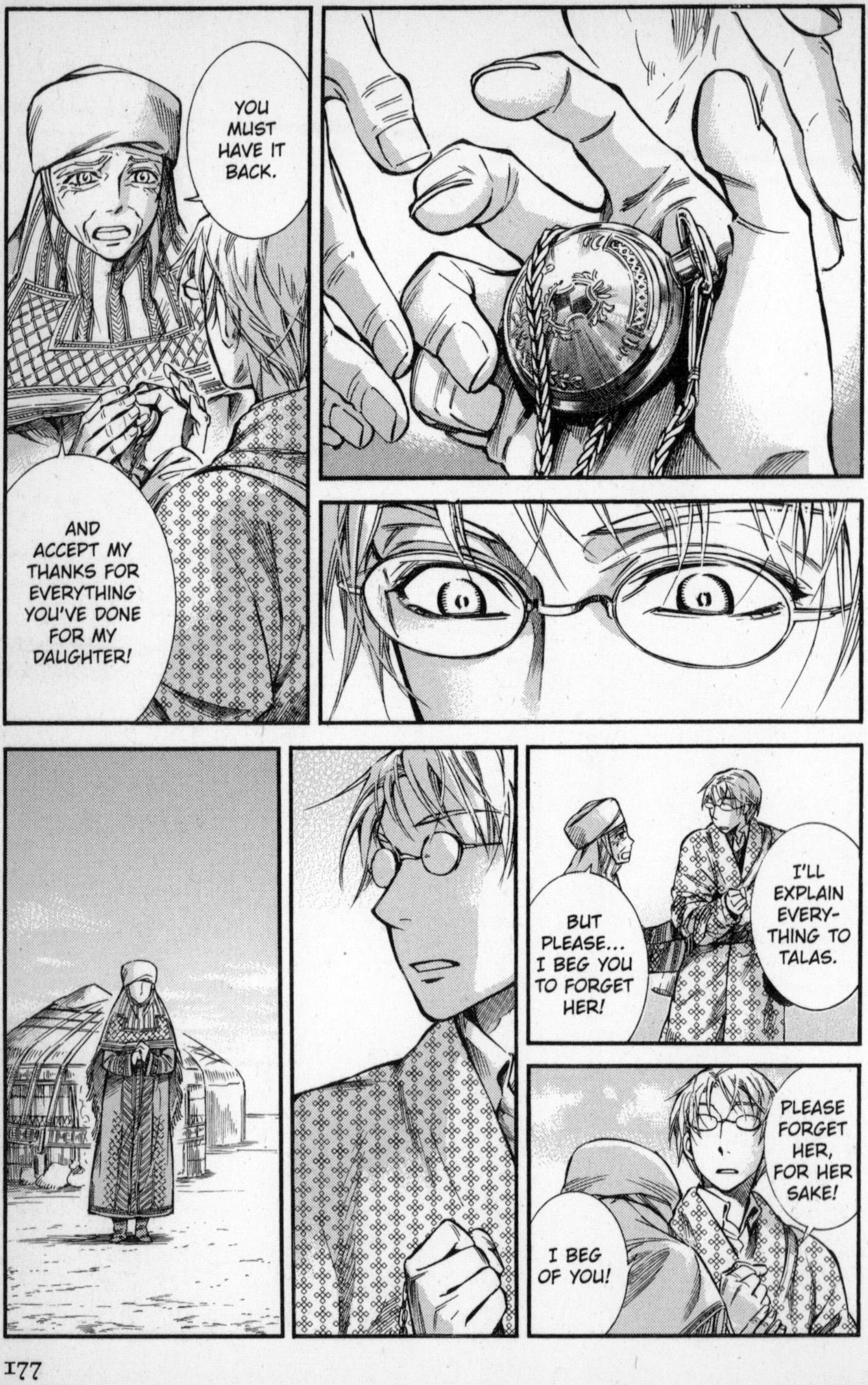
YOU MUST HAVE IT BACK.
AND ACCEPT MY THANKS FOR EVERYTHING YOU'VE DONE FOR MY DAUGHTER!
I'LL EXPLAIN EVERY-THING TO TALAS.
BUT PLEASE... I BEG YOU TO FORGET HER!
PLEASE FORGET HER, FOR HER SAKE!
I BEG OF YOU!

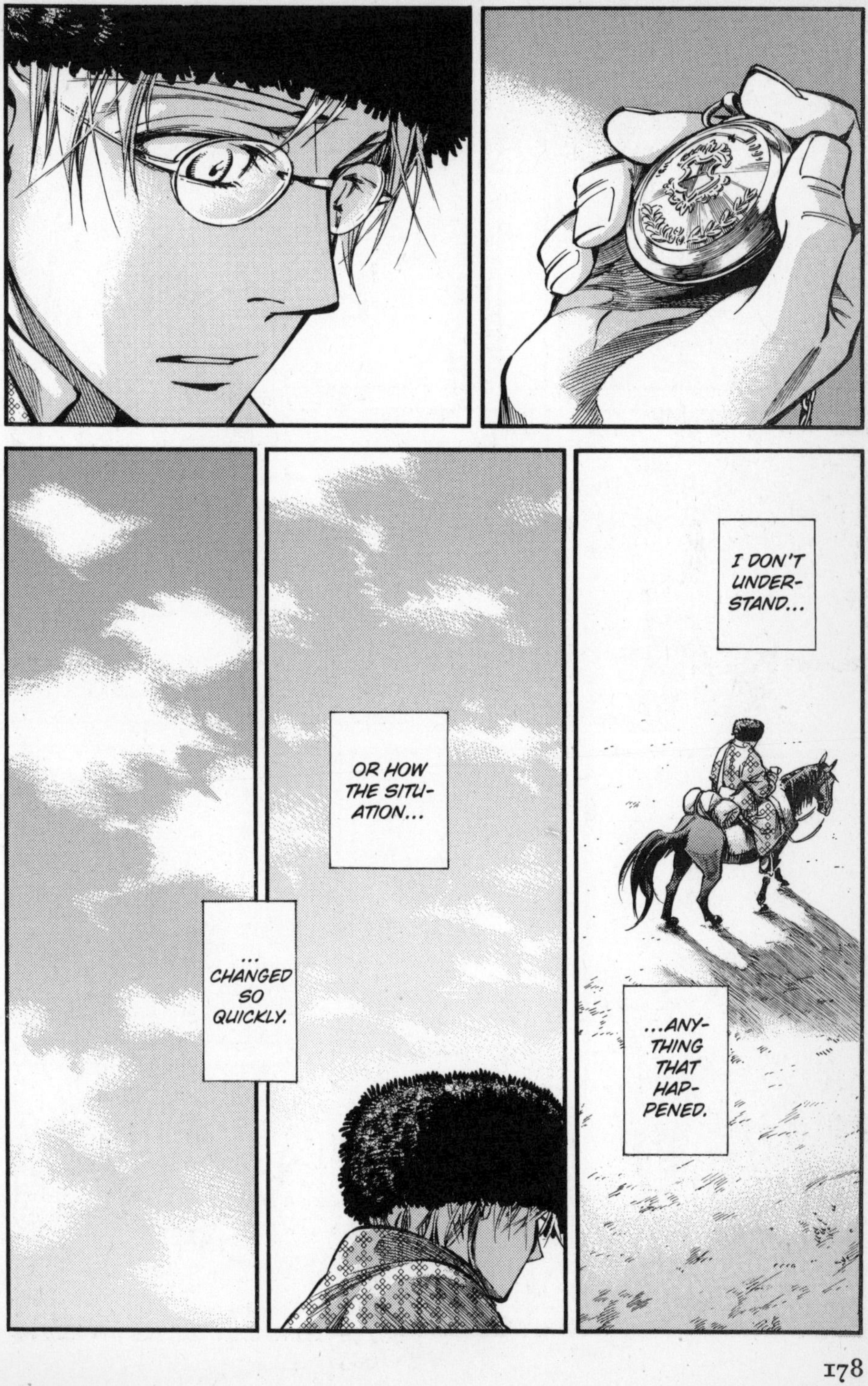
I DON'T UNDERSTAND...
...ANYTHING THAT HAPPENED.
OR HOW THE SITUATION...
...CHANGED SO QUICKLY.

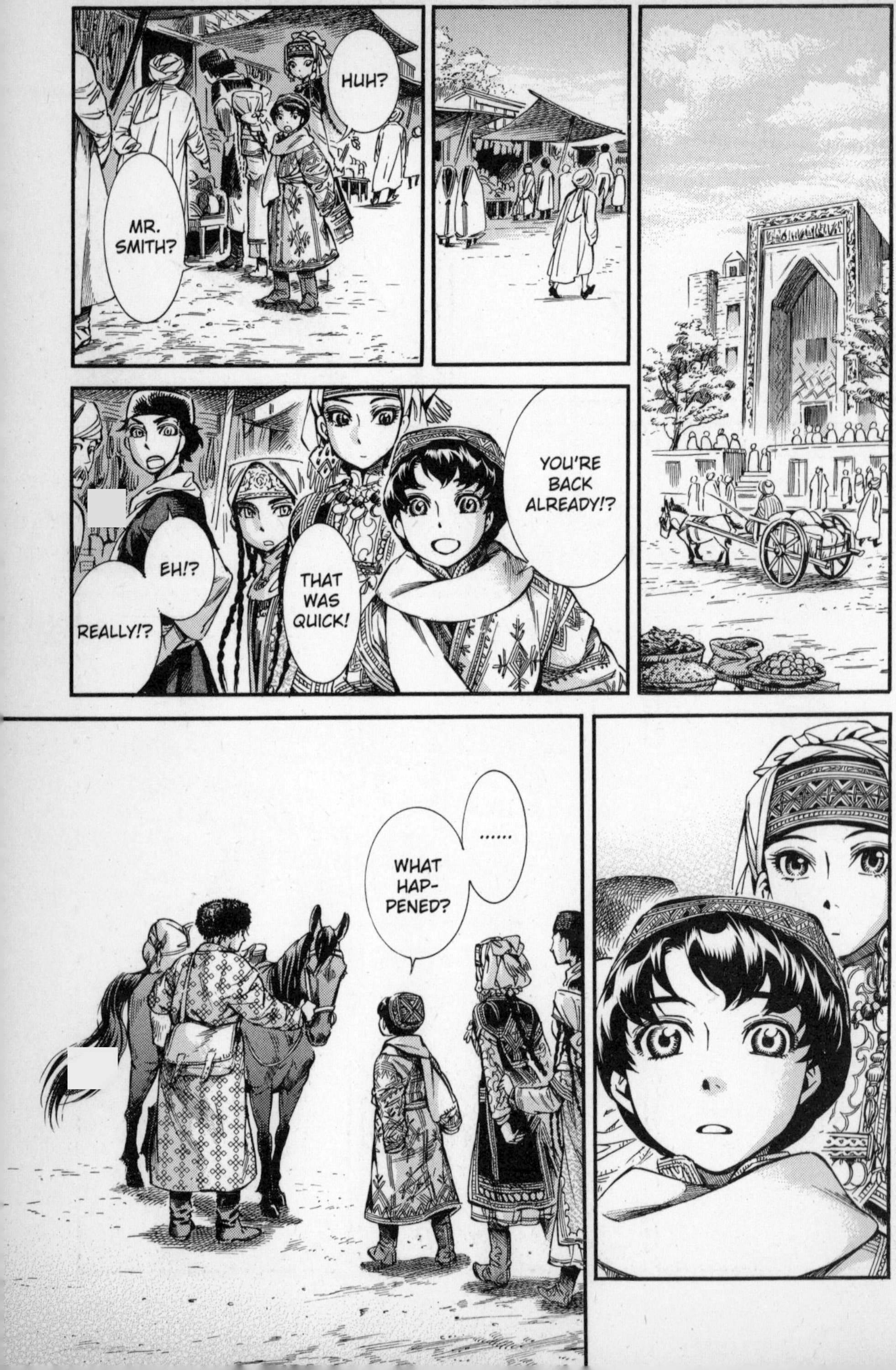
HUH?
MR. SMITH?
YOU'RE BACK ALREADY!?
THAT WAS QUICK!
EH!?
REALLY!?
......
WHAT HAP-PENED?

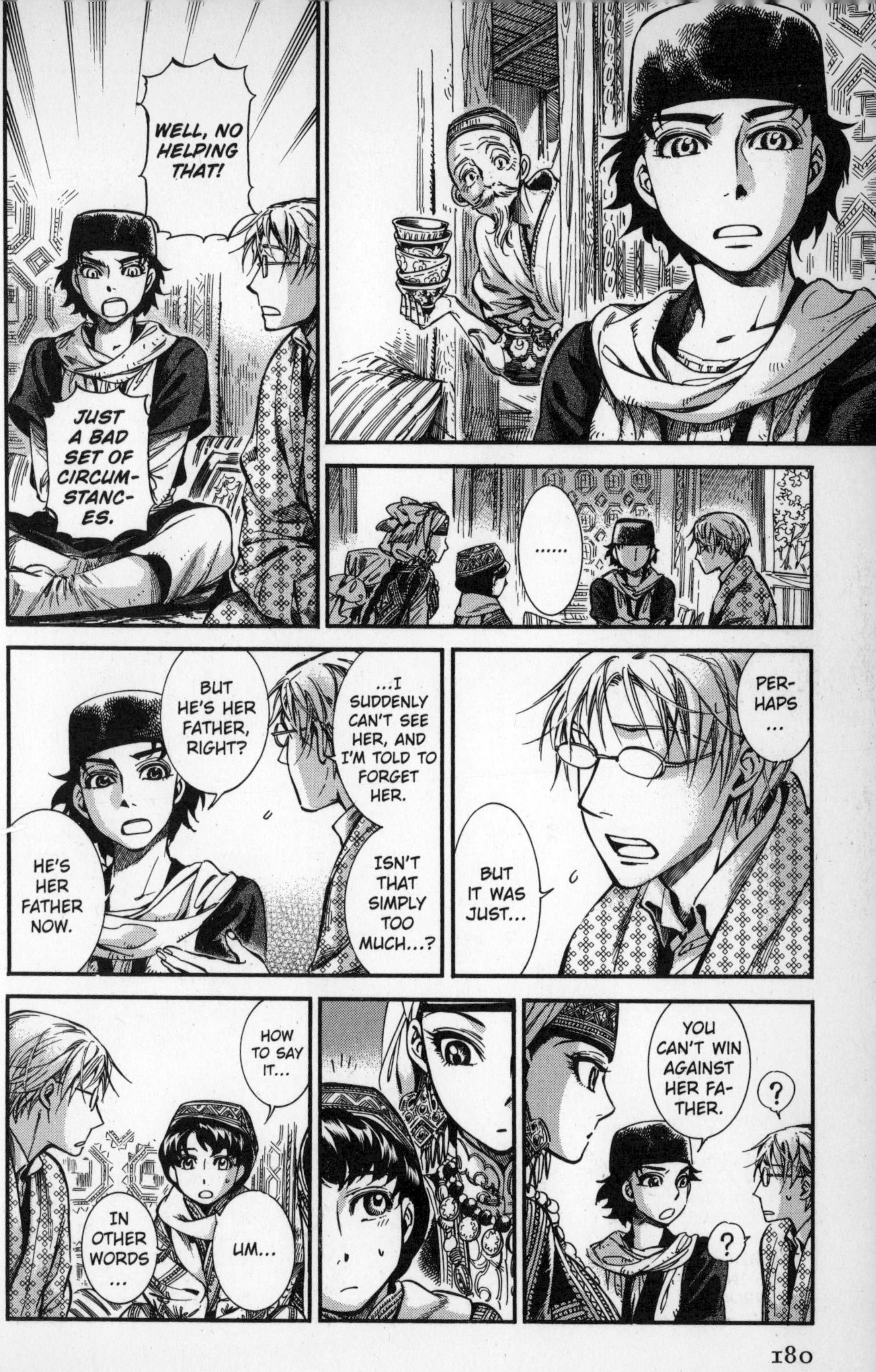
......
WELL, NO HELPING THAT!
JUST A BAD SET OF CIRCUM-STANCES.
PER-HAPS...
BUT IT WAS JUST...
...I SUDDENLY CAN'T SEE HER, AND I'M TOLD TO FORGET HER.
ISN'T THAT SIMPLY TOO MUCH...?
BUT HE'S HER FATHER, RIGHT?
HE'S HER FATHER NOW.
YOU CAN'T WIN AGAINST HER FA-THER.
?
?
HOW TO SAY IT...
UM...
IN OTHER WORDS...

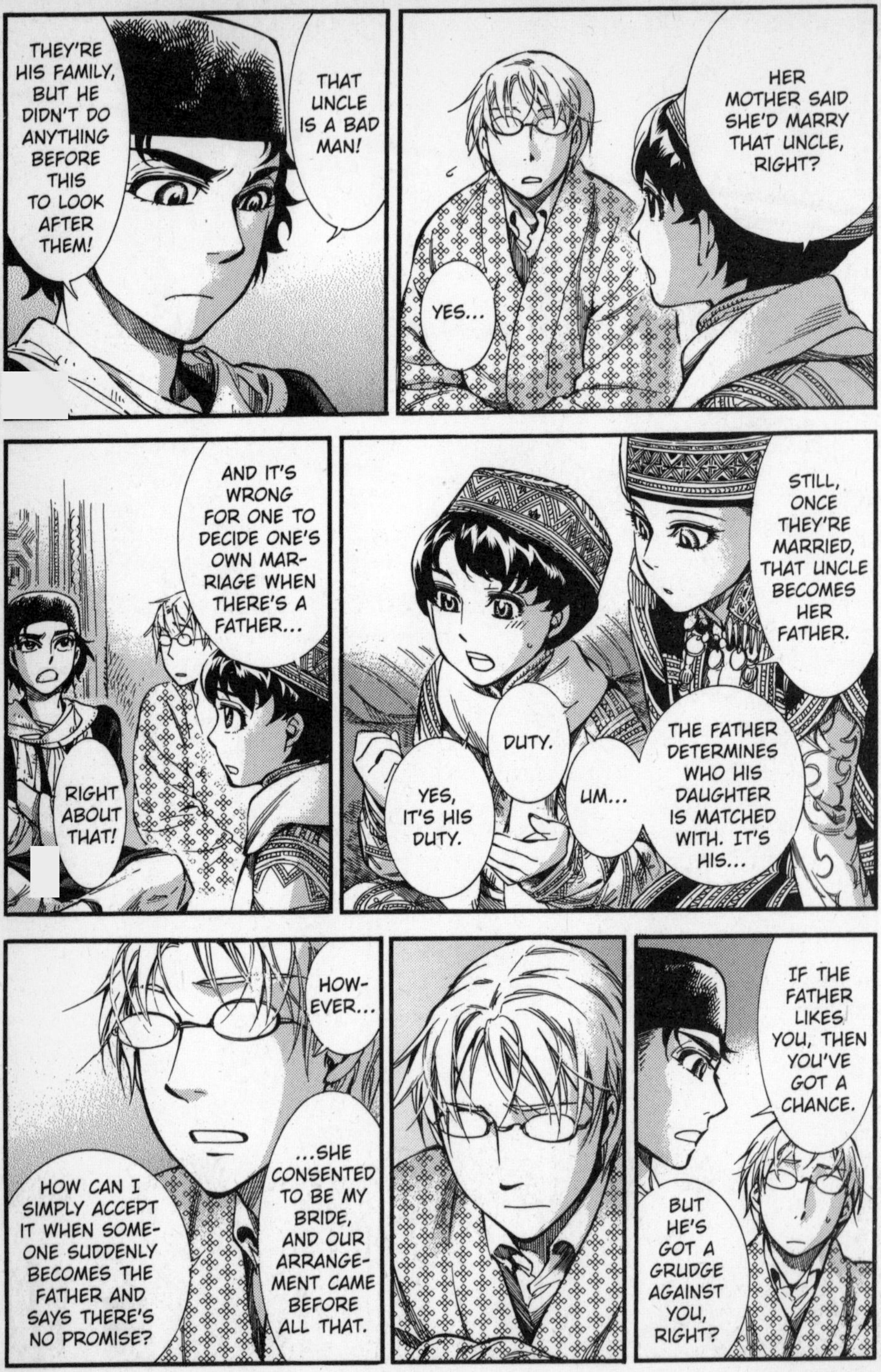
HER MOTHER SAID SHE'D MARRY THAT UNCLE, RIGHT?
YES...
THAT UNCLE IS A BAD MAN!
THEY'RE HIS FAMILY, BUT HE DIDN'T DO ANYTHING BEFORE THIS TO LOOK AFTER THEM!
STILL, ONCE THEY'RE MARRIED, THAT UNCLE BECOMES HER FATHER.
THE FATHER DETERMINES WHO HIS DAUGHTER IS MATCHED WITH. IT'S HIS...
UM...
DUTY.
YES, IT'S HIS DUTY.
AND IT'S WRONG FOR ONE TO DECIDE ONE'S OWN MARRIAGE WHEN THERE'S A FATHER...
RIGHT ABOUT THAT!
IF THE FATHER LIKES YOU, THEN YOU'VE GOT A CHANCE.
BUT HE'S GOT A GRUDGE AGAINST YOU, RIGHT?
HOWEVER...
...SHE CONSENTED TO BE MY BRIDE, AND OUR ARRANGEMENT CAME BEFORE ALL THAT.
HOW CAN I SIMPLY ACCEPT IT WHEN SOMEONE SUDDENLY BECOMES THE FATHER AND SAYS THERE'S NO PROMISE?

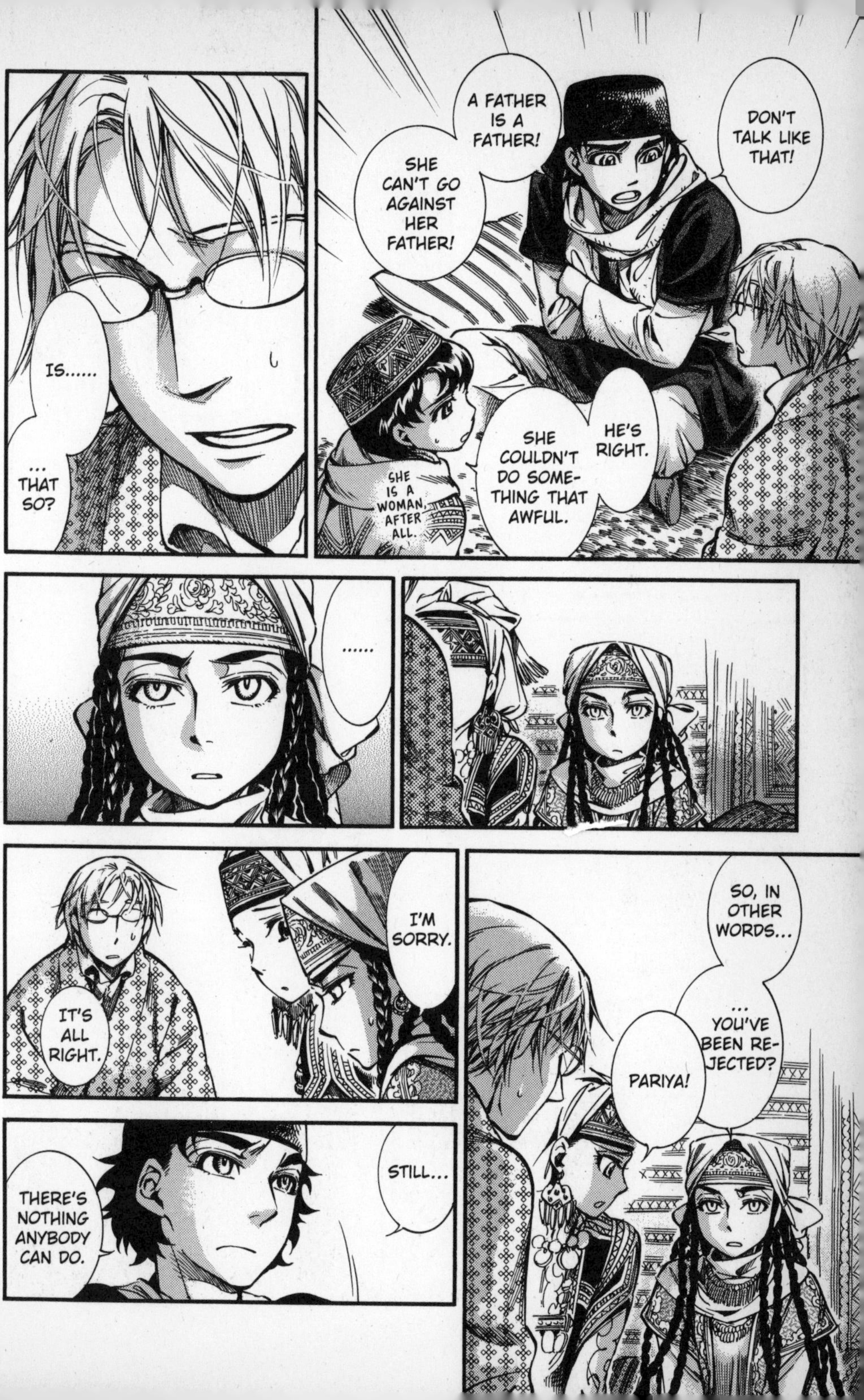
DON'T TALK LIKE THAT!
A FATHER IS A FATHER!
SHE CAN'T GO AGAINST HER FATHER!
HE'S RIGHT.
SHE COULDN'T DO SOME-THING THAT AWFUL.
SHE IS A WOMAN, AFTER ALL.
IS......
...THAT SO?
......
SO, IN OTHER WORDS...
...YOU'VE BEEN RE-JECTED?
PARIYA!
I'M SORRY.
IT'S ALL RIGHT.
STILL...
THERE'S NOTHING ANYBODY CAN DO.

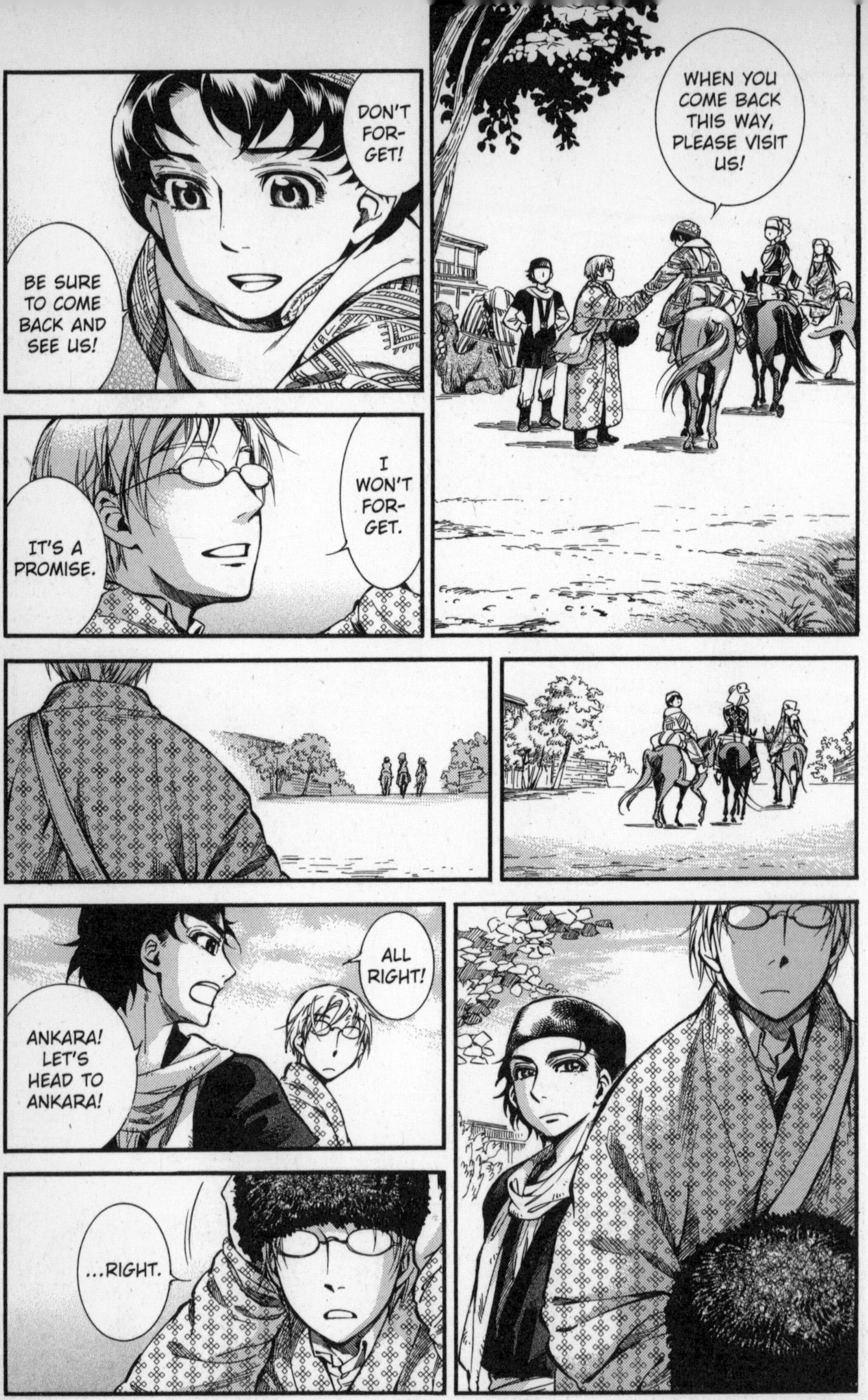
WHEN YOU COME BACK THIS WAY, PLEASE VISIT US!
DON'T FOR-GET!
BE SURE TO COME BACK AND SEE US!
I WON'T FOR-GET.
IT'S A PROMISE.
ALL RIGHT!
ANKARA! LET'S HEAD TO ANKARA!
...RIGHT.

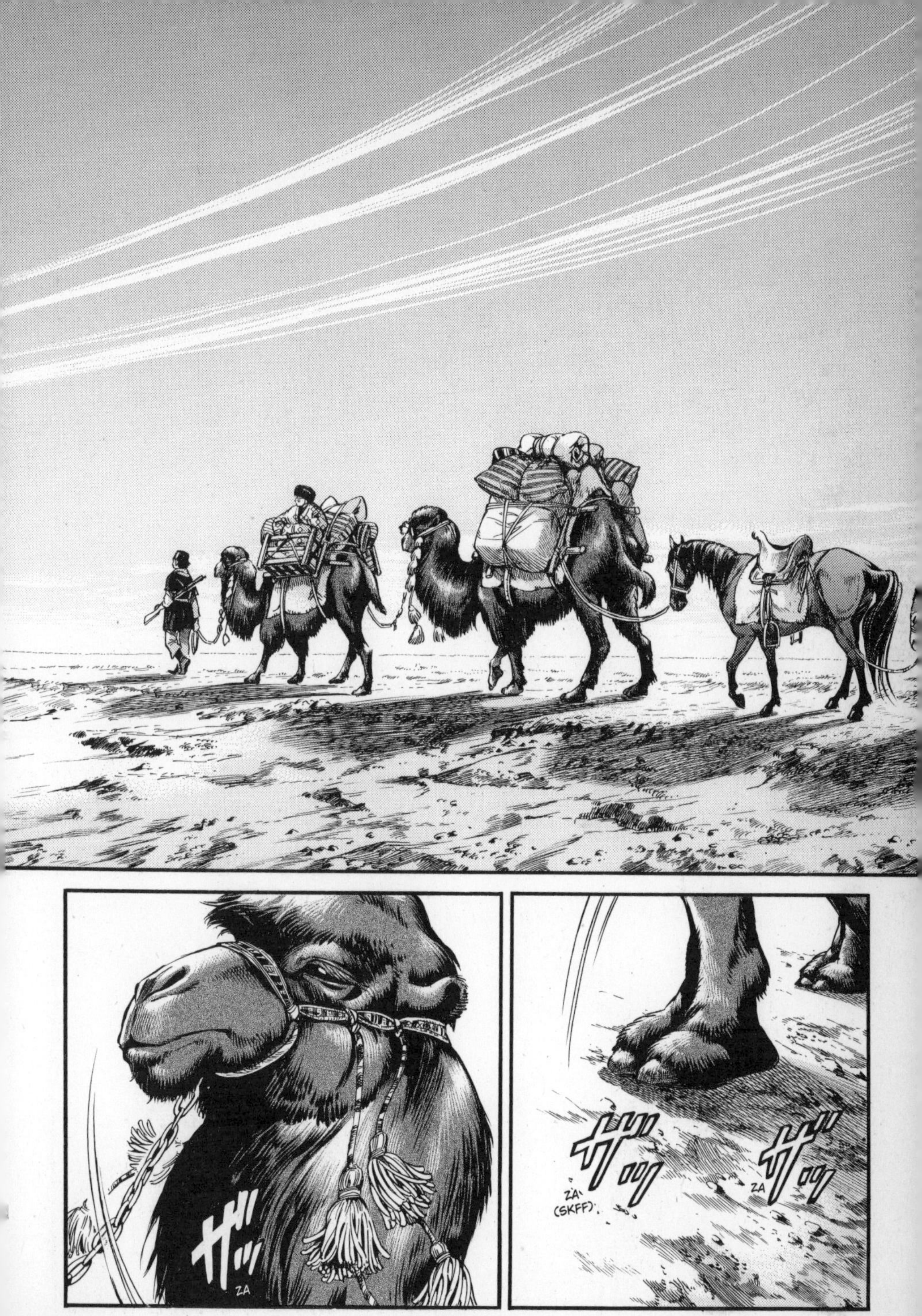
ザッ
ZA
ザッ
ZA
(SKFF)
ザッ
ZA

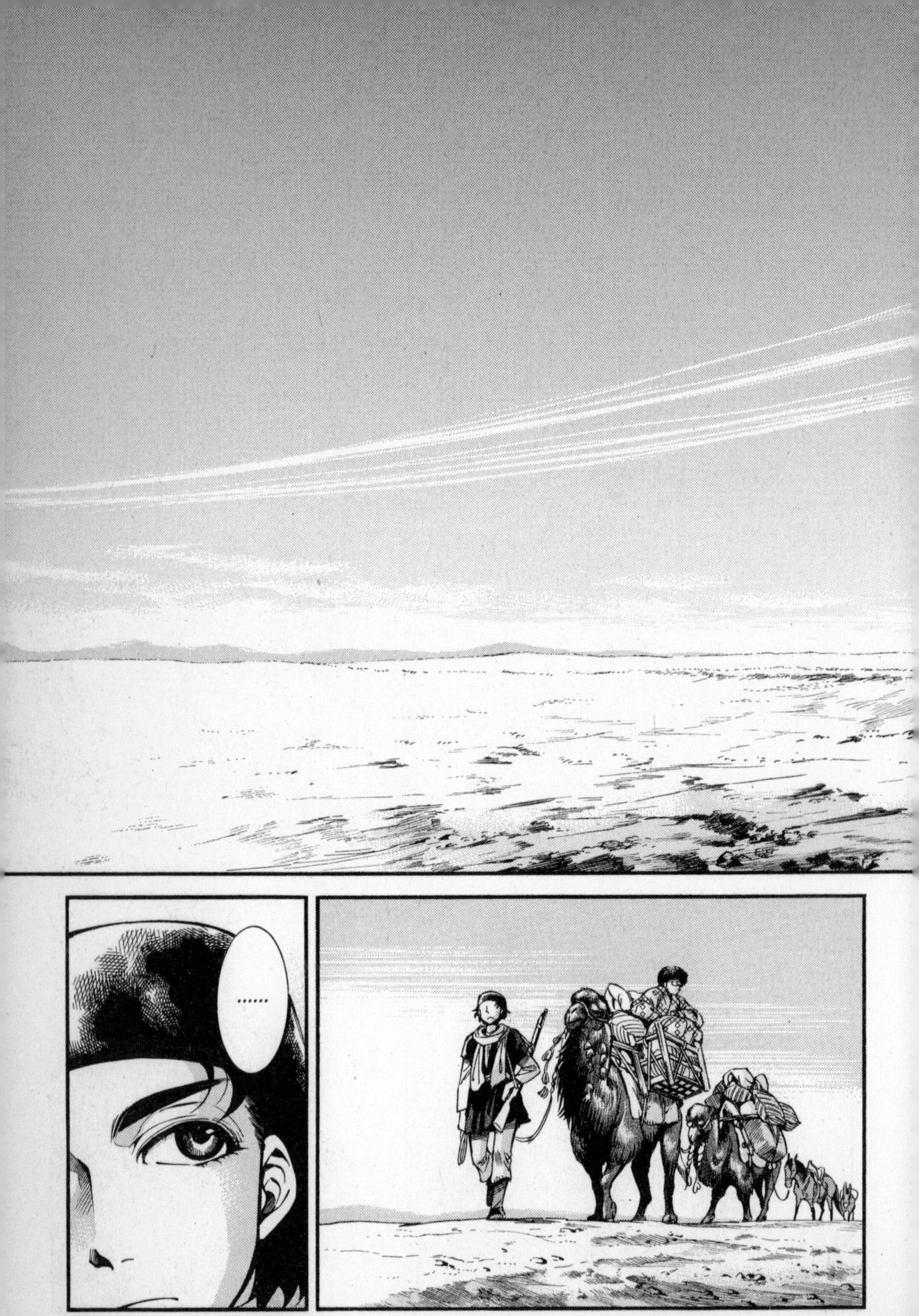
......

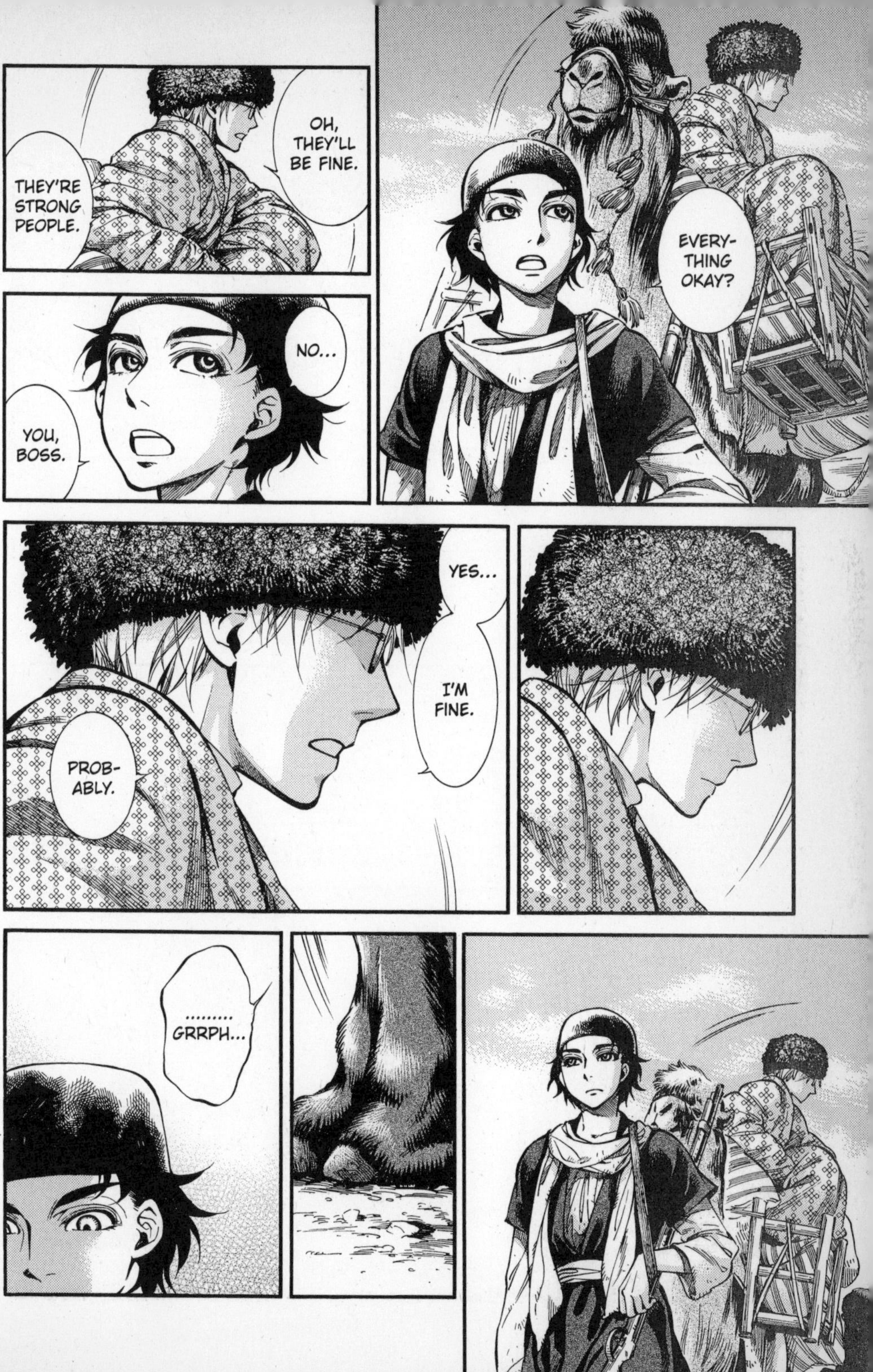
EVERY-THING OKAY?
OH, THEY'LL BE FINE.
THEY'RE STRONG PEOPLE.
NO...
YOU, BOSS.
YES...
I'M FINE.
PROBABLY.
.........GRRPH...

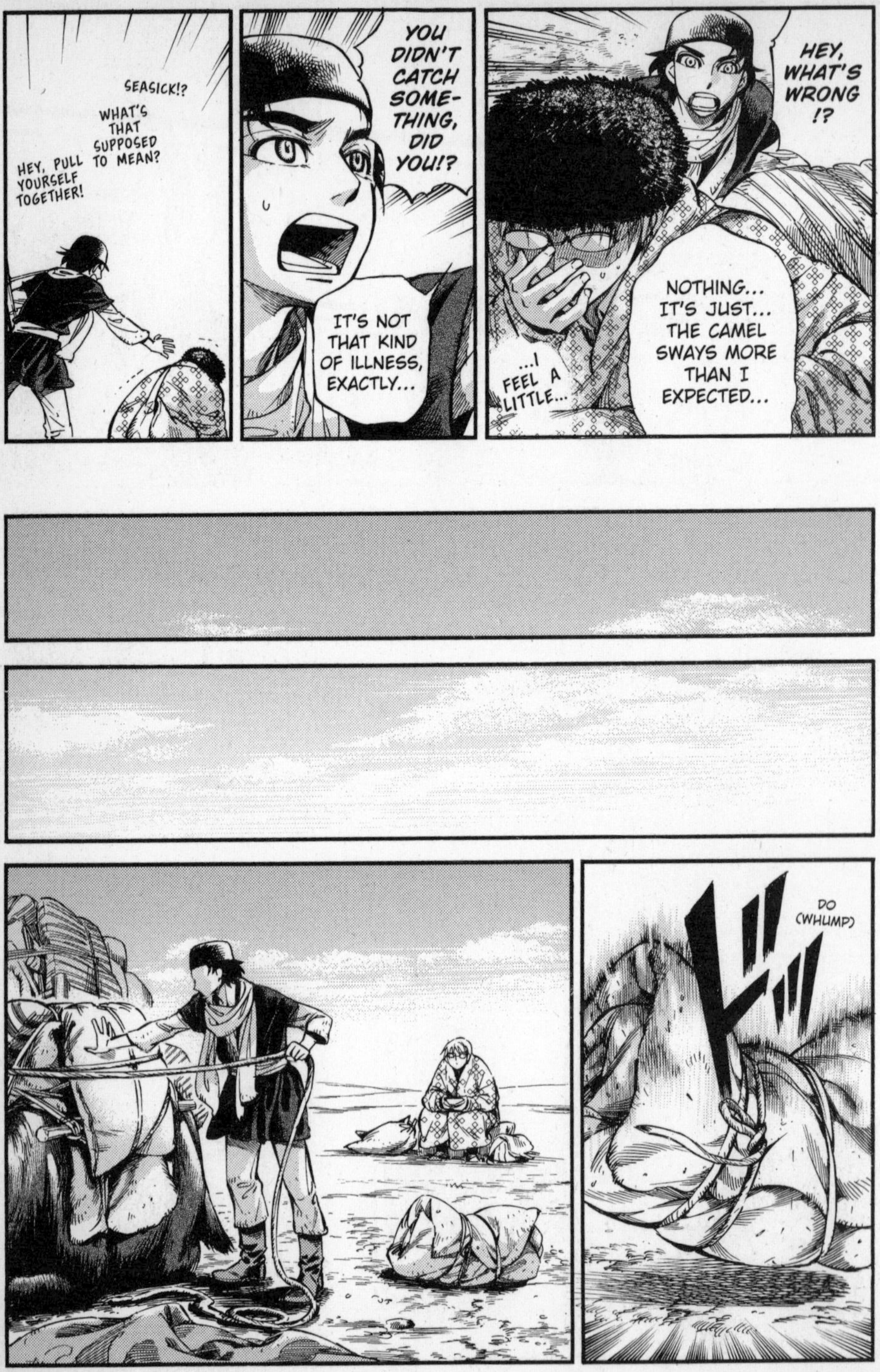
HEY, WHAT'S WRONG !?
NOTHING... IT'S JUST... THE CAMEL SWAYS MORE THAN I EXPECTED...
...I FEEL A LITTLE...
YOU DIDN'T CATCH SOME-THING, DID YOU!?
IT'S NOT THAT KIND OF ILLNESS, EXACTLY...
SEASICK!?
WHAT'S THAT SUPPOSED TO MEAN?
HEY, PULL YOURSELF TOGETHER!
DO (WHUMP)

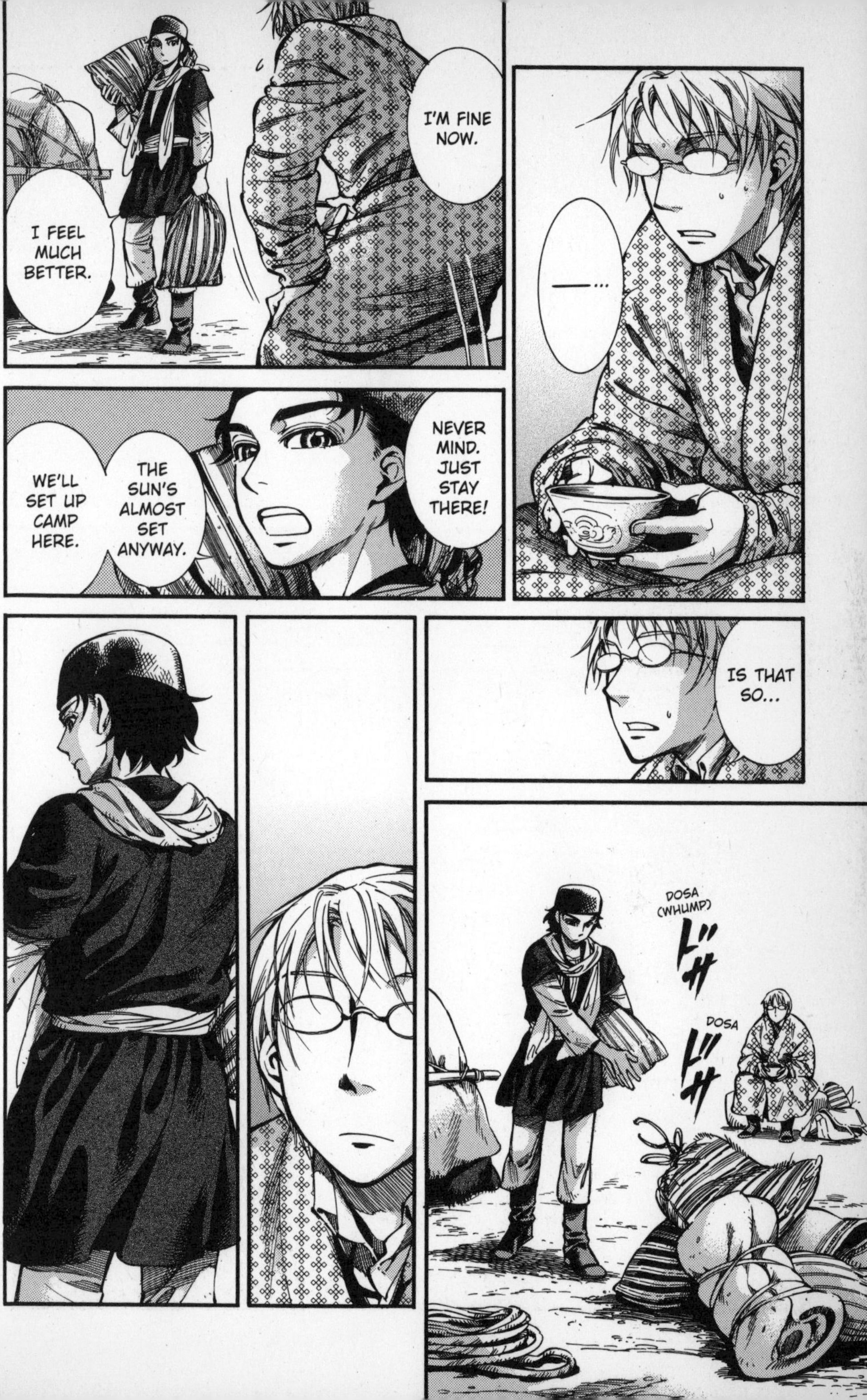
——...
I'M FINE NOW.
I FEEL MUCH BETTER.
NEVER MIND. JUST STAY THERE!
THE SUN'S ALMOST SET ANYWAY.
WE'LL SET UP CAMP HERE.
IS THAT SO...
DOSA (WHUMP)
DOSA

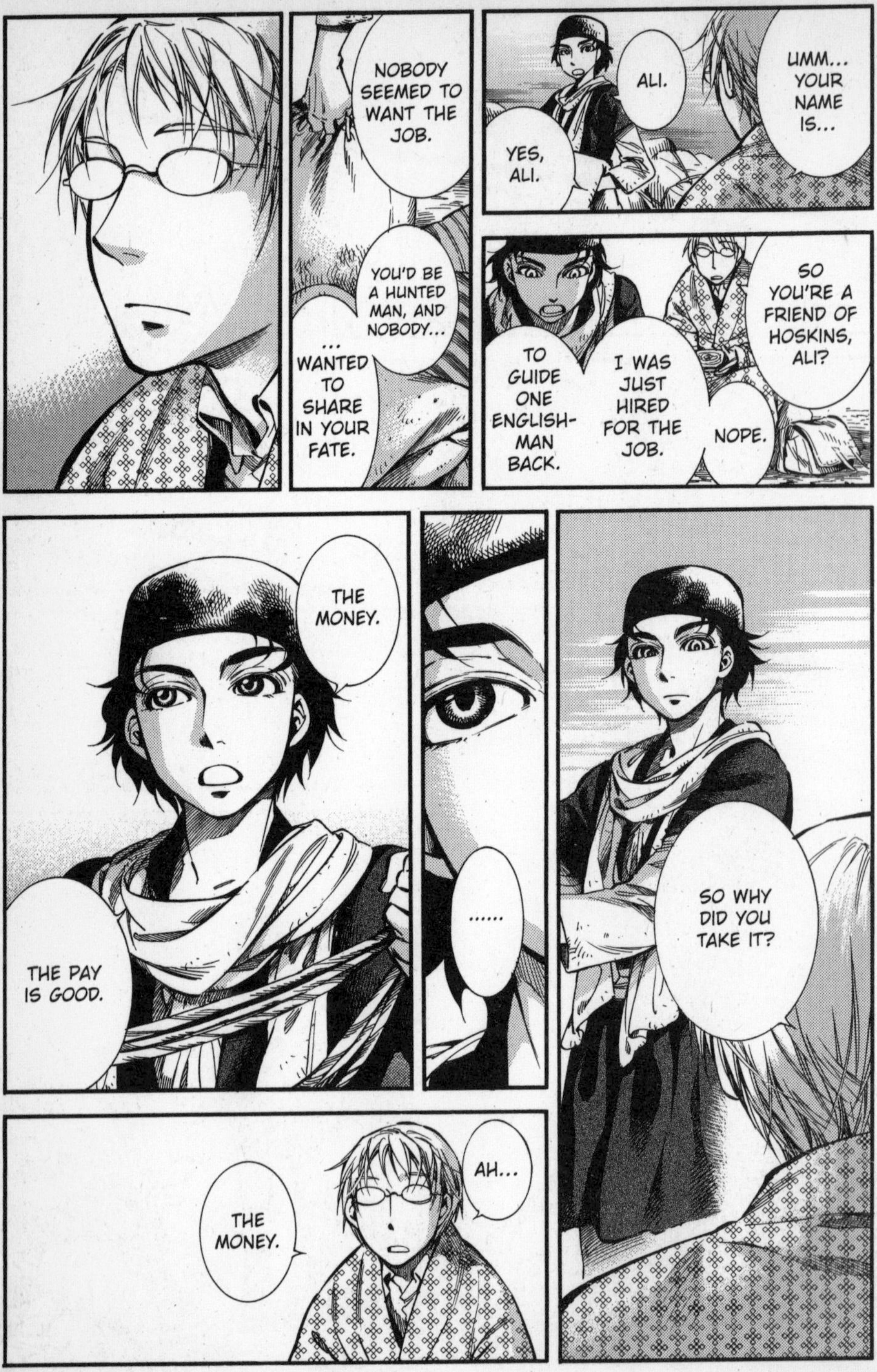
UMM... YOUR NAME IS...
ALI.
YES, ALI.
SO YOU'RE A FRIEND OF HOSKINS, ALI?
NOPE.
I WAS JUST HIRED FOR THE JOB.
TO GUIDE ONE ENGLISH-MAN BACK.
NOBODY SEEMED TO WANT THE JOB.
YOU'D BE A HUNTED MAN, AND NOBODY...
...WANTED TO SHARE IN YOUR FATE.
SO WHY DID YOU TAKE IT?
......
THE MONEY.
THE PAY IS GOOD.
AH...
THE MONEY.

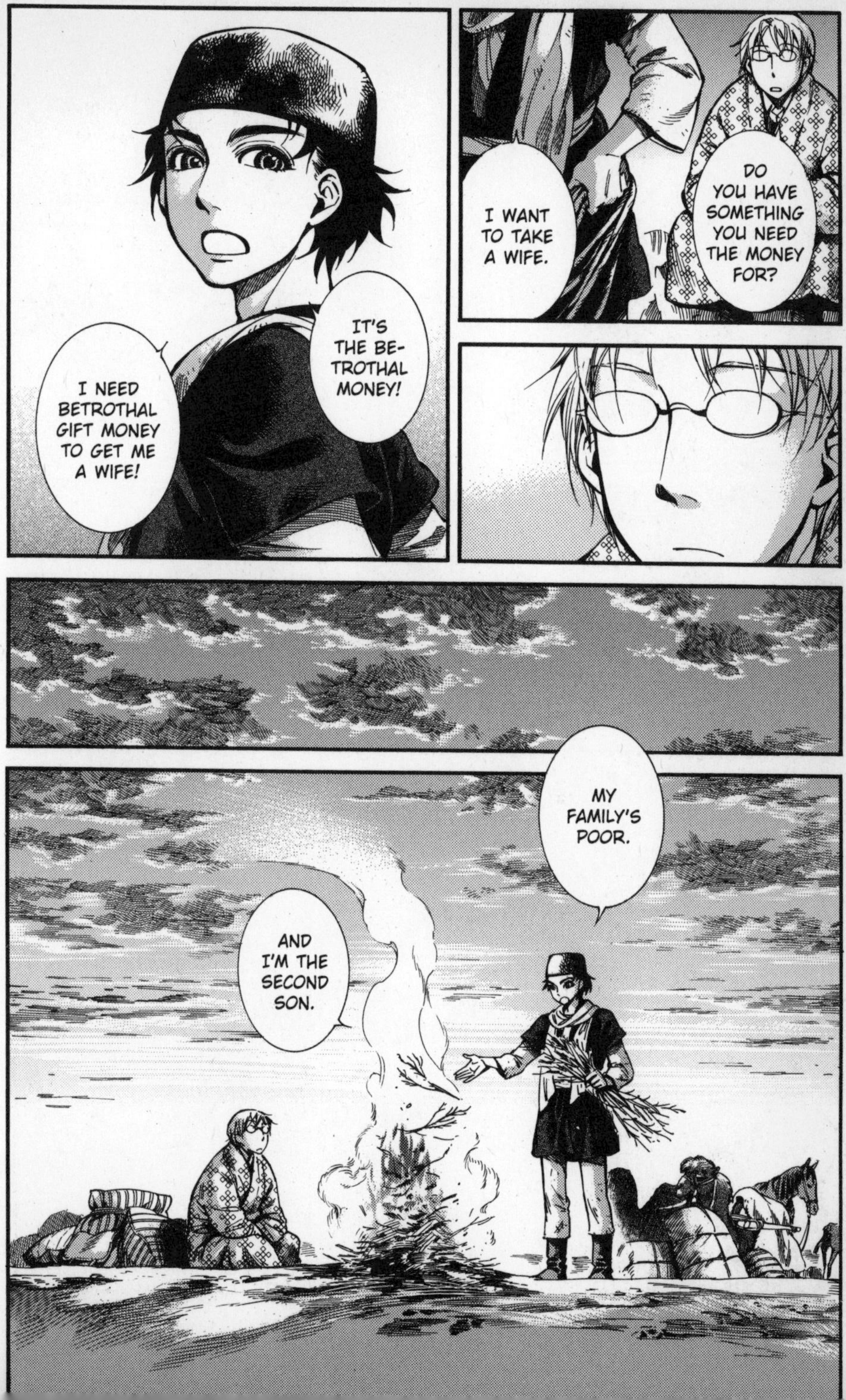
DO YOU HAVE SOMETHING YOU NEED THE MONEY FOR?
I WANT TO TAKE A WIFE.
IT'S THE BE-TROTHAL MONEY!
I NEED BETROTHAL GIFT MONEY TO GET ME A WIFE!
MY FAMILY'S POOR.
AND I'M THE SECOND SON.

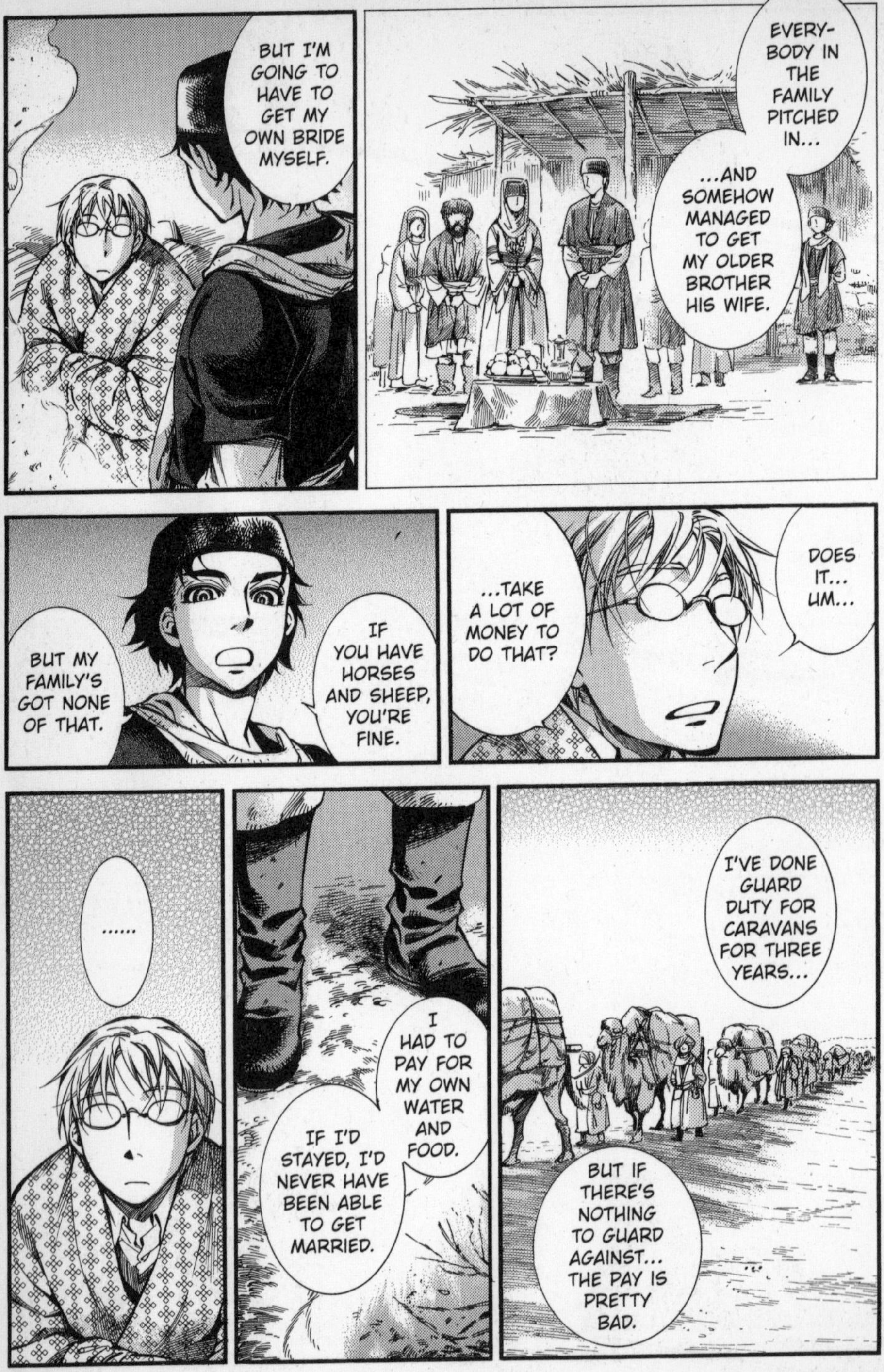
EVERY-BODY IN THE FAMILY PITCHED IN...
...AND SOMEHOW MANAGED TO GET MY OLDER BROTHER HIS WIFE.
BUT I'M GOING TO HAVE TO GET MY OWN BRIDE MYSELF.
DOES IT... UM...
...TAKE A LOT OF MONEY TO DO THAT?
IF YOU HAVE HORSES AND SHEEP, YOU'RE FINE.
BUT MY FAMILY'S GOT NONE OF THAT.
I'VE DONE GUARD DUTY FOR CARAVANS FOR THREE YEARS...
BUT IF THERE'S NOTHING TO GUARD AGAINST... THE PAY IS PRETTY BAD.
I HAD TO PAY FOR MY OWN WATER AND FOOD.
IF I'D STAYED, I'D NEVER HAVE BEEN ABLE TO GET MARRIED.
......

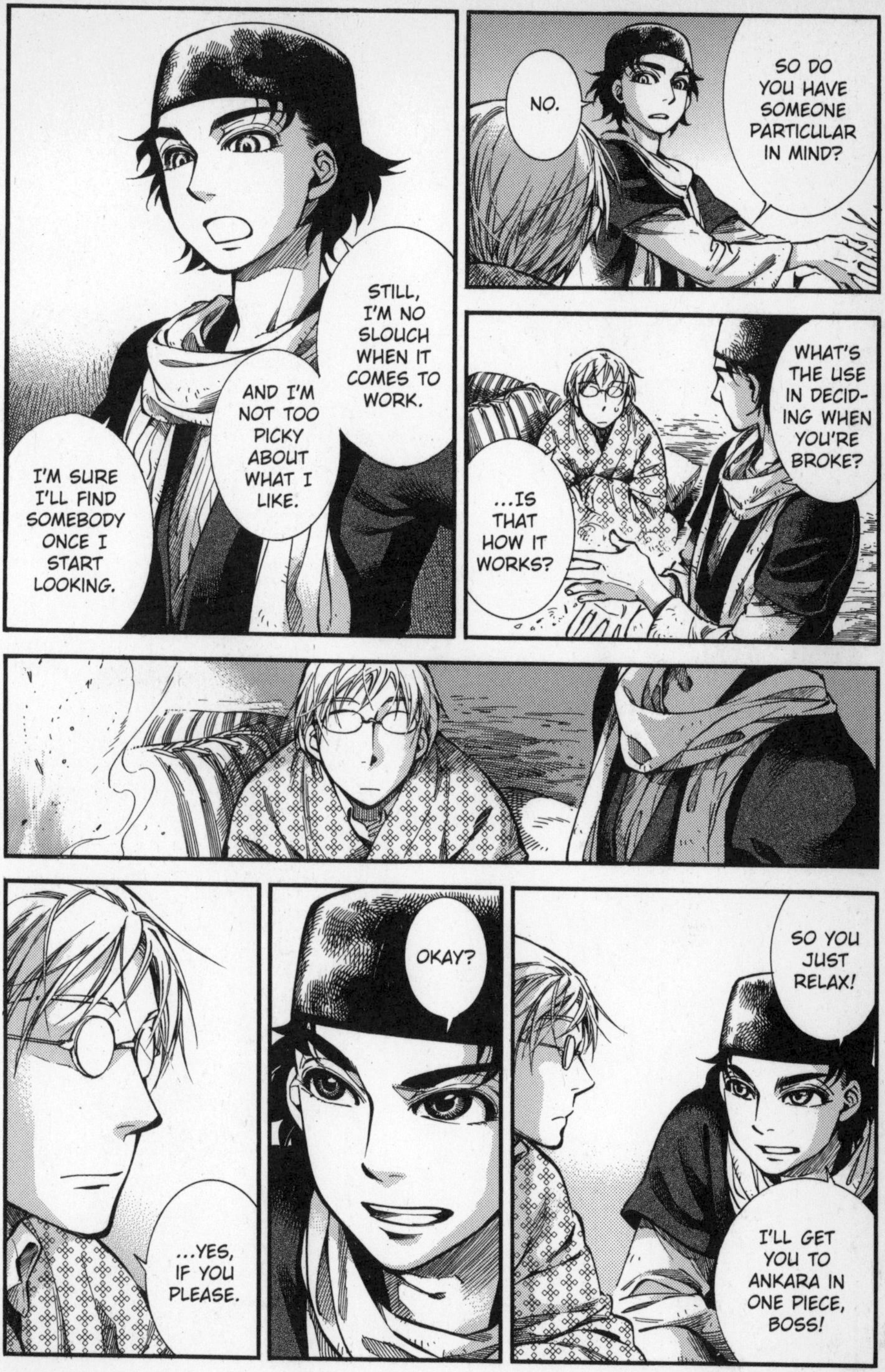
SO DO YOU HAVE SOMEONE PARTICULAR IN MIND?
NO.
WHAT'S THE USE IN DECIDING WHEN YOU'RE BROKE?
...IS THAT HOW IT WORKS?
STILL, I'M NO SLOUCH WHEN IT COMES TO WORK.
AND I'M NOT TOO PICKY ABOUT WHAT I LIKE.
I'M SURE I'LL FIND SOMEBODY ONCE I START LOOKING.
SO YOU JUST RELAX!
I'LL GET YOU TO ANKARA IN ONE PIECE, BOSS!
OKAY?
...YES, IF YOU PLEASE.

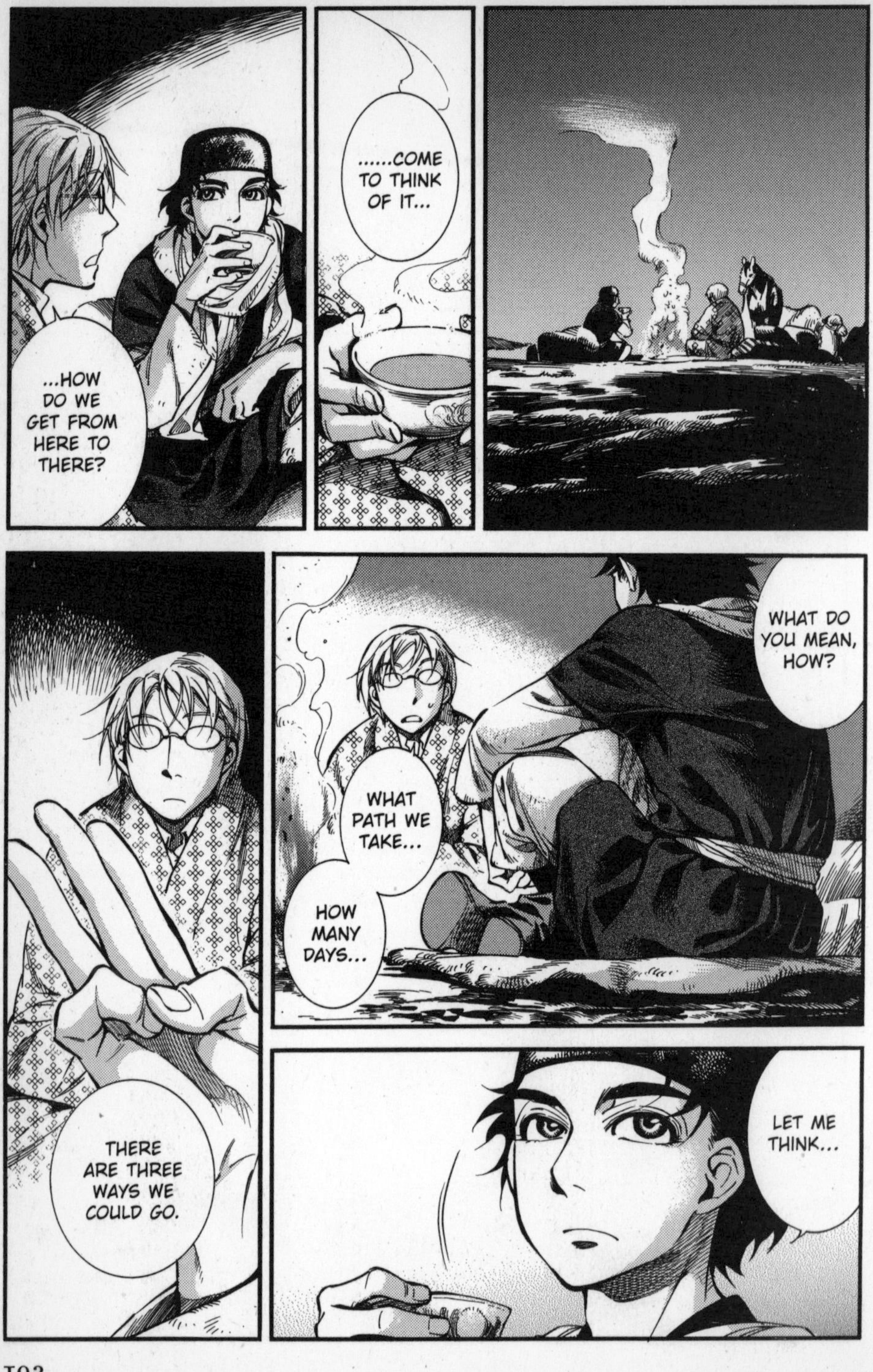
......COME TO THINK OF IT...
...HOW DO WE GET FROM HERE TO THERE?
WHAT DO YOU MEAN, HOW?
WHAT PATH WE TAKE...
HOW MANY DAYS...
LET ME THINK...
THERE ARE THREE WAYS WE COULD GO.

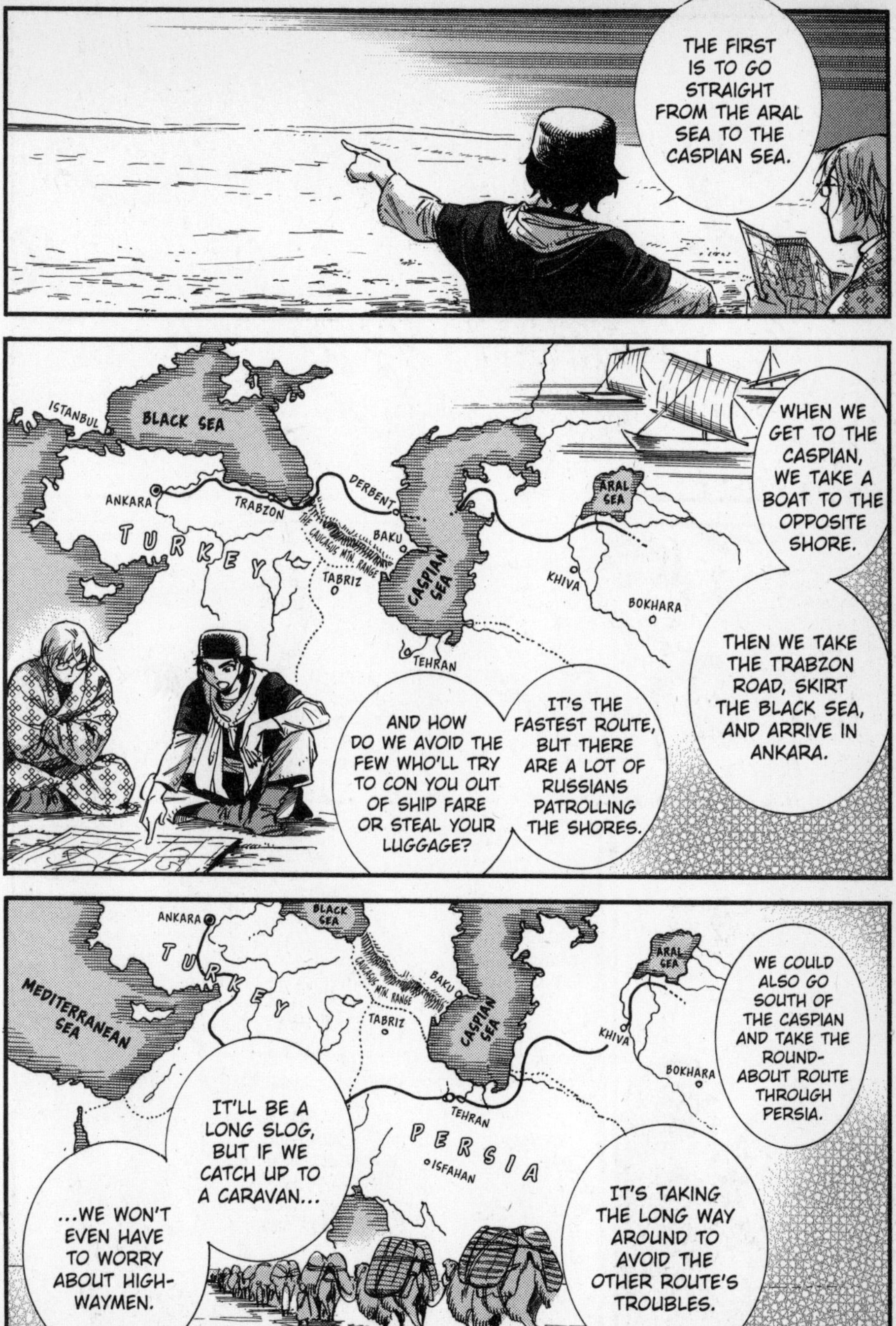
THE FIRST IS TO GO STRAIGHT FROM THE ARAL SEA TO THE CASPIAN SEA.
WHEN WE GET TO THE CASPIAN, WE TAKE A BOAT TO THE OPPOSITE SHORE.
THEN WE TAKE THE TRABZON ROAD, SKIRT THE BLACK SEA, AND ARRIVE IN ANKARA.
ISTANBUL
BLACK SEA
ANKARA
TRABZON
DERBENT
TURKEY
THE CAUCASUS MTN. RANGE
BAKU
TABRIZ
CASPIAN SEA
ARAL SEA
KHIVA
BOKHARA
TEHRAN
IT'S THE FASTEST ROUTE, BUT THERE ARE A LOT OF RUSSIANS PATROLLING THE SHORES.
AND HOW DO WE AVOID THE FEW WHO'LL TRY TO CON YOU OUT OF SHIP FARE OR STEAL YOUR LUGGAGE?
WE COULD ALSO GO SOUTH OF THE CASPIAN AND TAKE THE ROUND-ABOUT ROUTE THROUGH PERSIA.
ANKARA
BLACK SEA
TURKEY
MEDITERRANEAN SEA
CAUCASUS MTN. RANGE
BAKU
TABRIZ
CASPIAN SEA
ARAL SEA
KHIVA
BOKHARA
TEHRAN
PERSIA
ISFAHAN
IT'S TAKING THE LONG WAY AROUND TO AVOID THE OTHER ROUTE'S TROUBLES.
IT'LL BE A LONG SLOG, BUT IF WE CATCH UP TO A CARAVAN...
...WE WON'T EVEN HAVE TO WORRY ABOUT HIGH-WAYMEN.

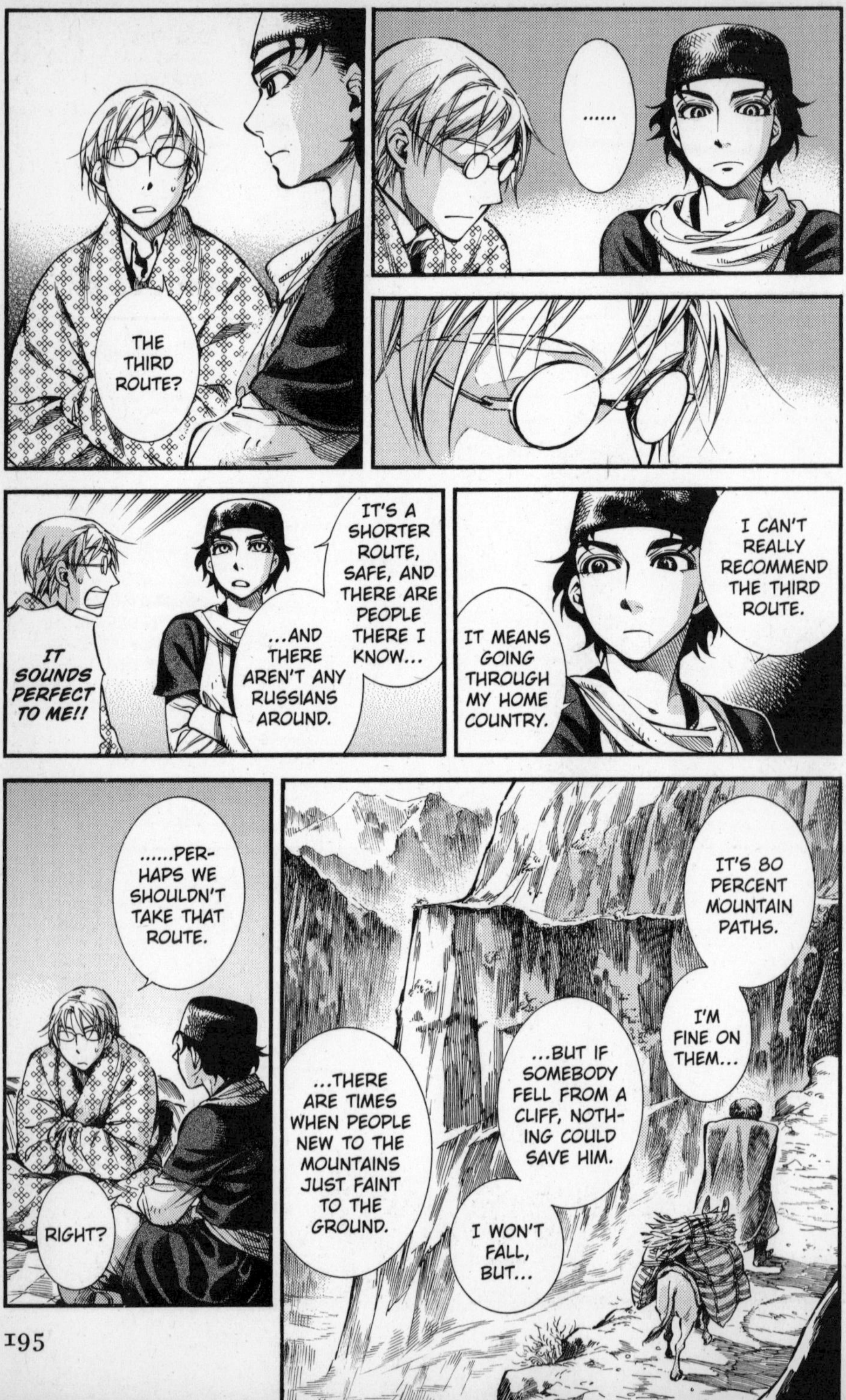
......
THE THIRD ROUTE?
I CAN'T REALLY RECOMMEND THE THIRD ROUTE.
IT MEANS GOING THROUGH MY HOME COUNTRY.
IT'S A SHORTER ROUTE, SAFE, AND THERE ARE PEOPLE THERE I KNOW...
...AND THERE AREN'T ANY RUSSIANS AROUND.
IT SOUNDS PERFECT TO ME!!
IT'S 80 PERCENT MOUNTAIN PATHS.
I'M FINE ON THEM...
...BUT IF SOMEBODY FELL FROM A CLIFF, NOTH-ING COULD SAVE HIM.
I WON'T FALL, BUT...
...THERE ARE TIMES WHEN PEOPLE NEW TO THE MOUNTAINS JUST FAINT TO THE GROUND.
......PER-HAPS WE SHOULDN'T TAKE THAT ROUTE.
RIGHT?

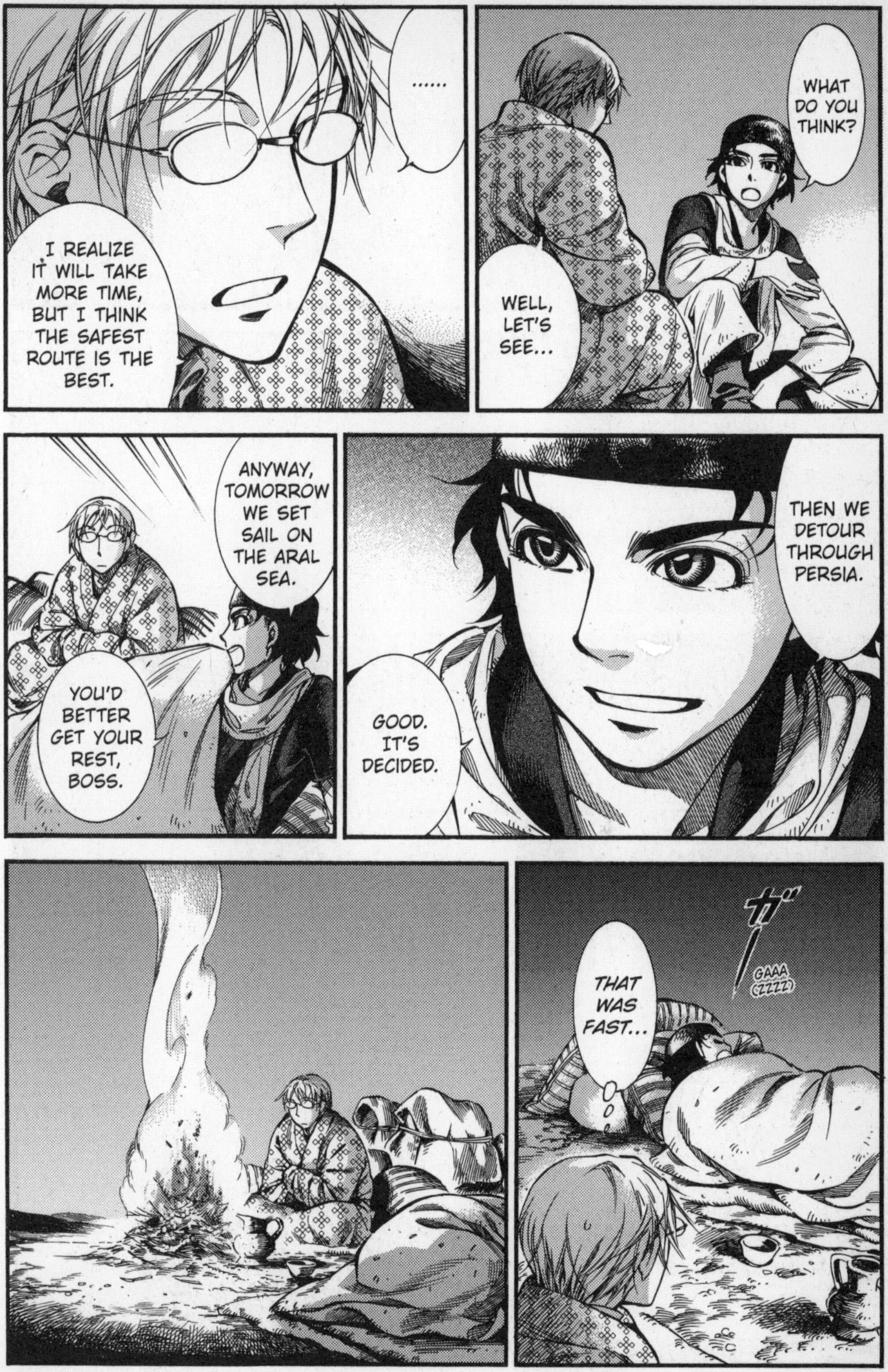
WHAT DO YOU THINK?
WELL, LET'S SEE...
......
I REALIZE IT WILL TAKE MORE TIME, BUT I THINK THE SAFEST ROUTE IS THE BEST.
THEN WE DETOUR THROUGH PERSIA.
GOOD. IT'S DECIDED.
ANYWAY, TOMORROW WE SET SAIL ON THE ARAL SEA.
YOU'D BETTER GET YOUR REST, BOSS.
ガ
GAAA (ZZZZ)
THAT WAS FAST...

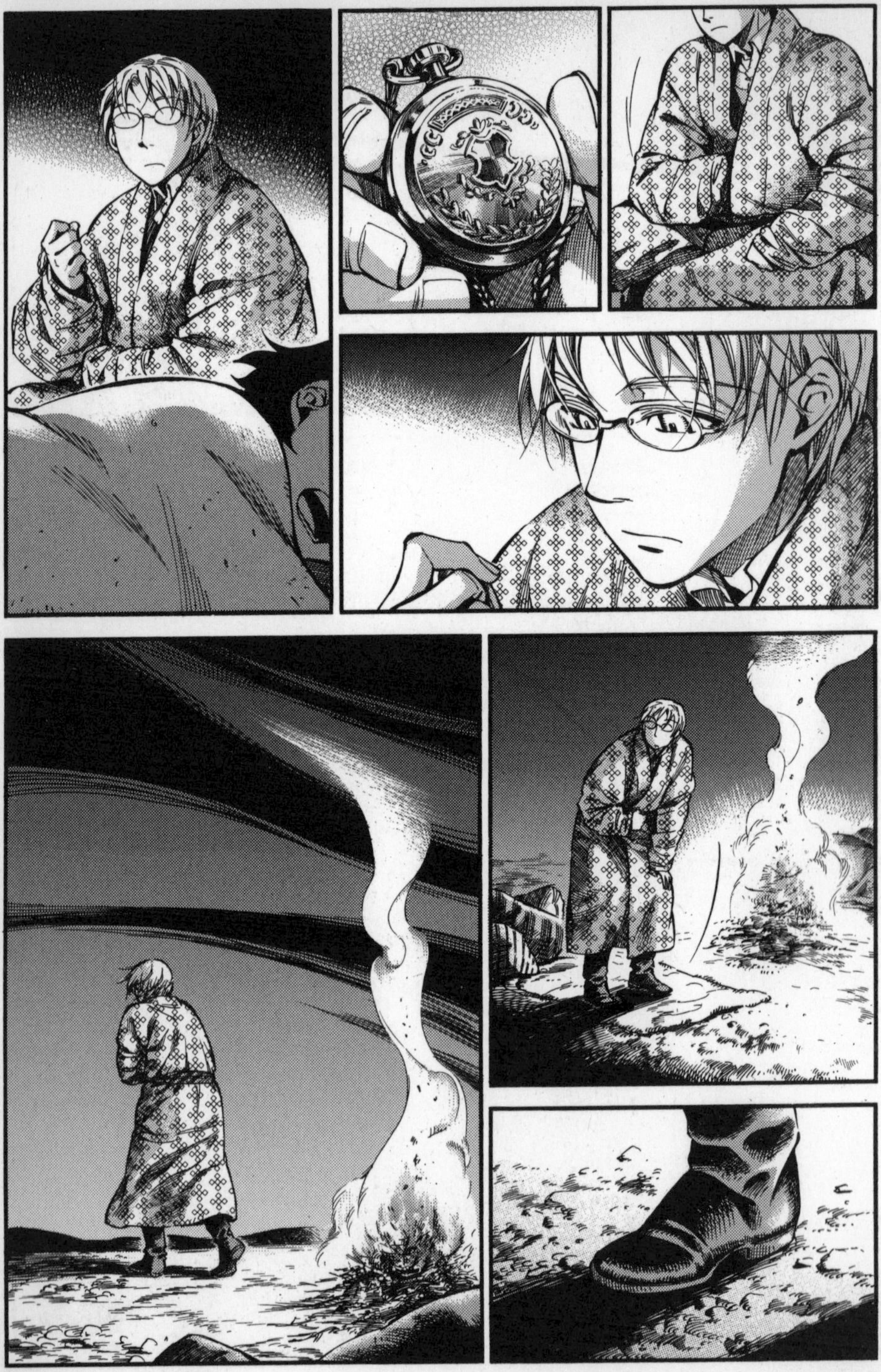

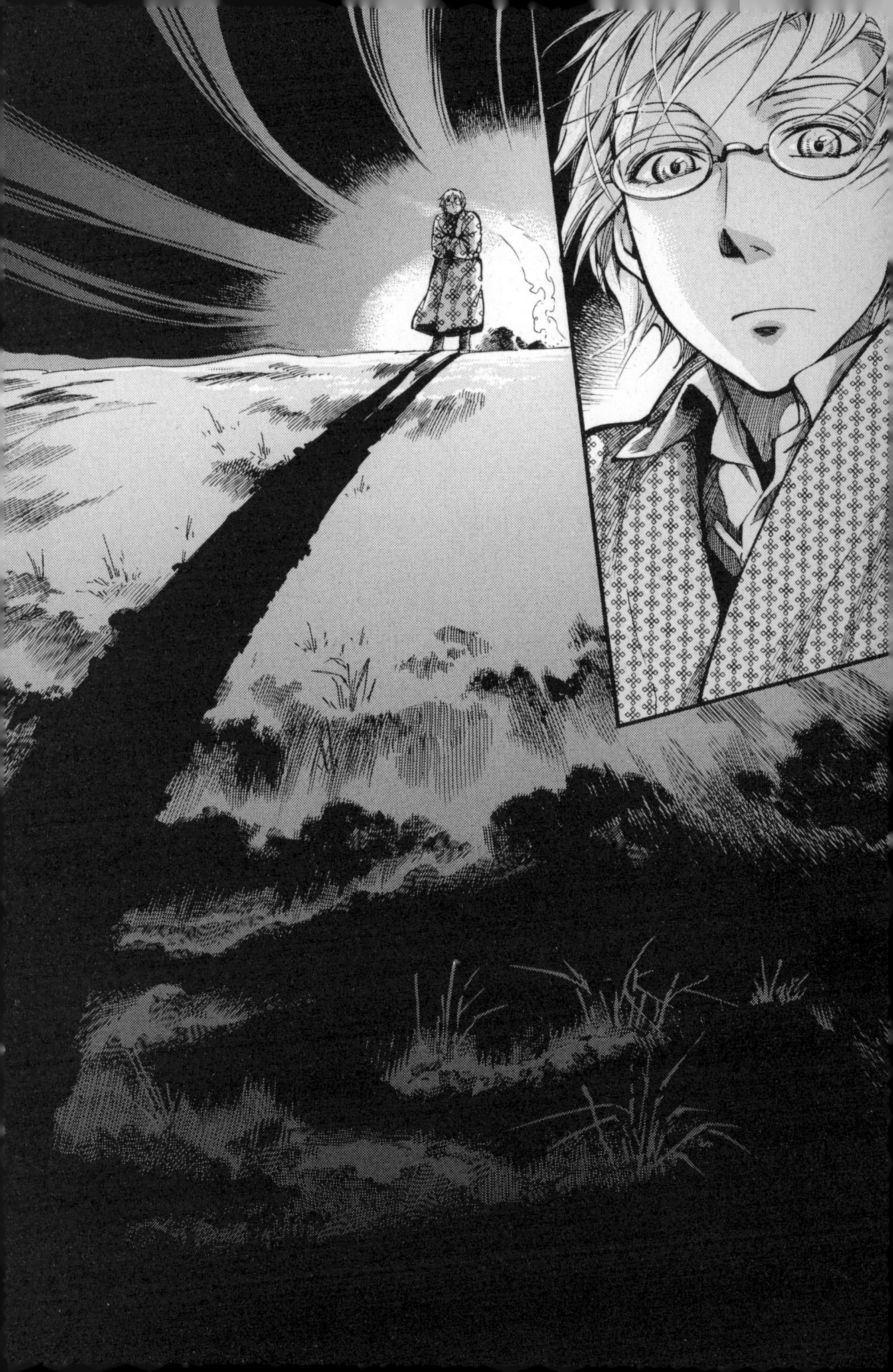

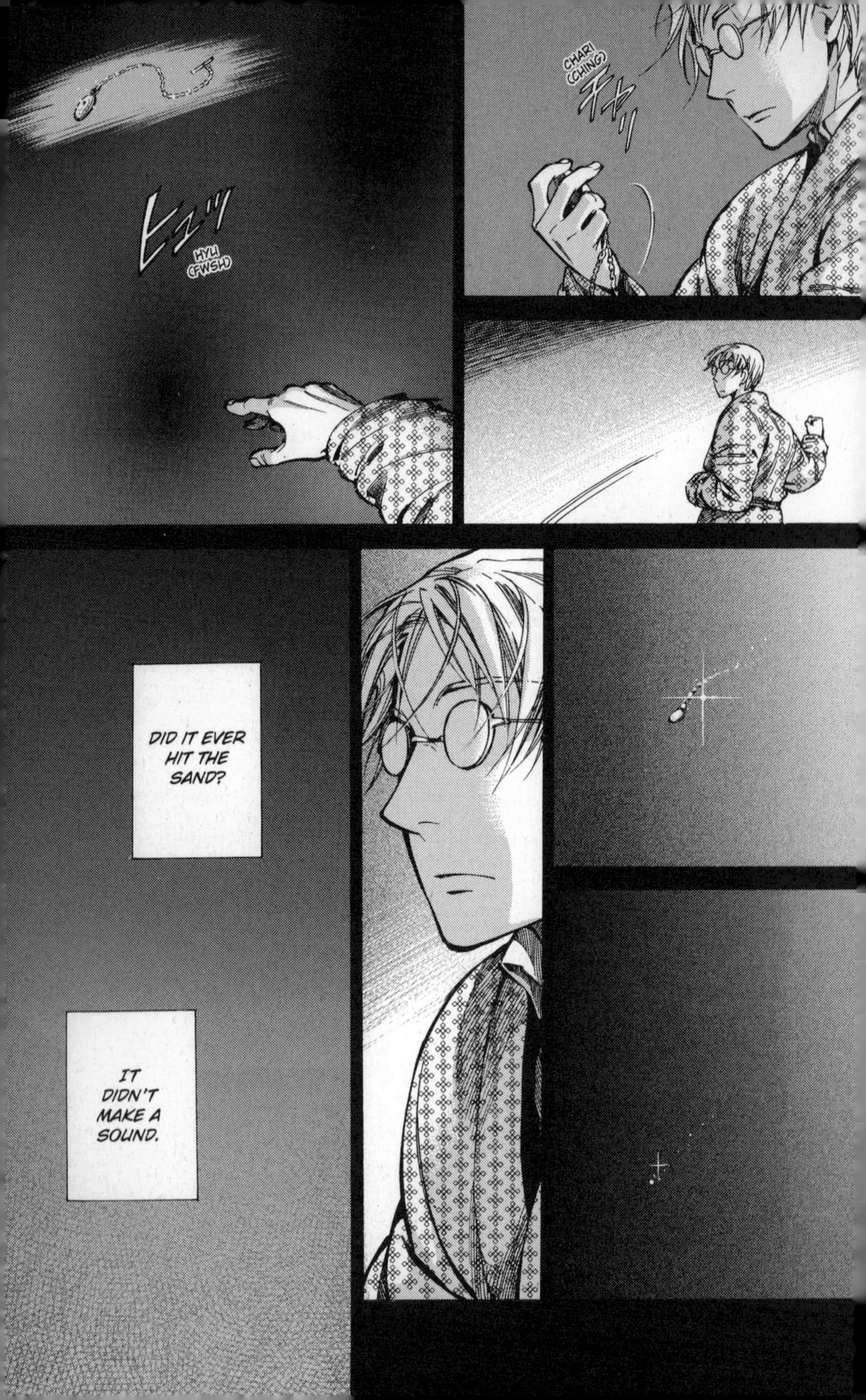
CHARI (CHING)
HYU (FWSH)
DID IT EVER HIT THE SAND?
IT DIDN'T MAKE A SOUND.

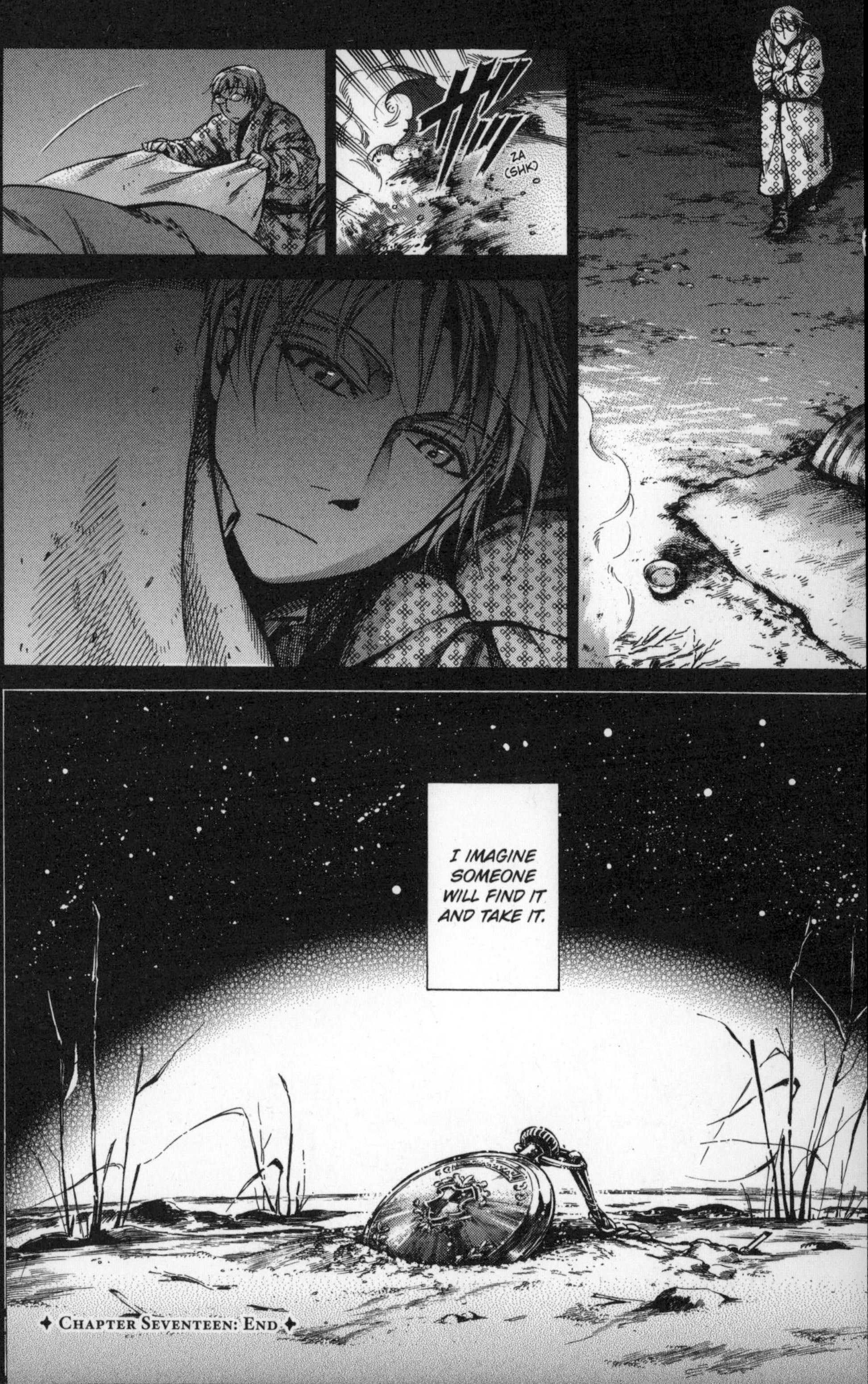
ZA (SHK)
I IMAGINE SOMEONE WILL FIND IT AND TAKE IT.
✦ Chapter Seventeen: End ✦

AFTERWORD

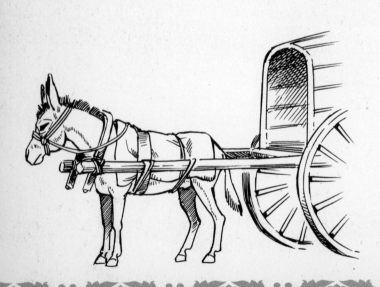

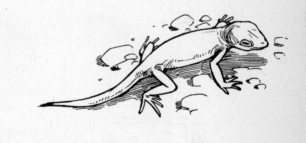

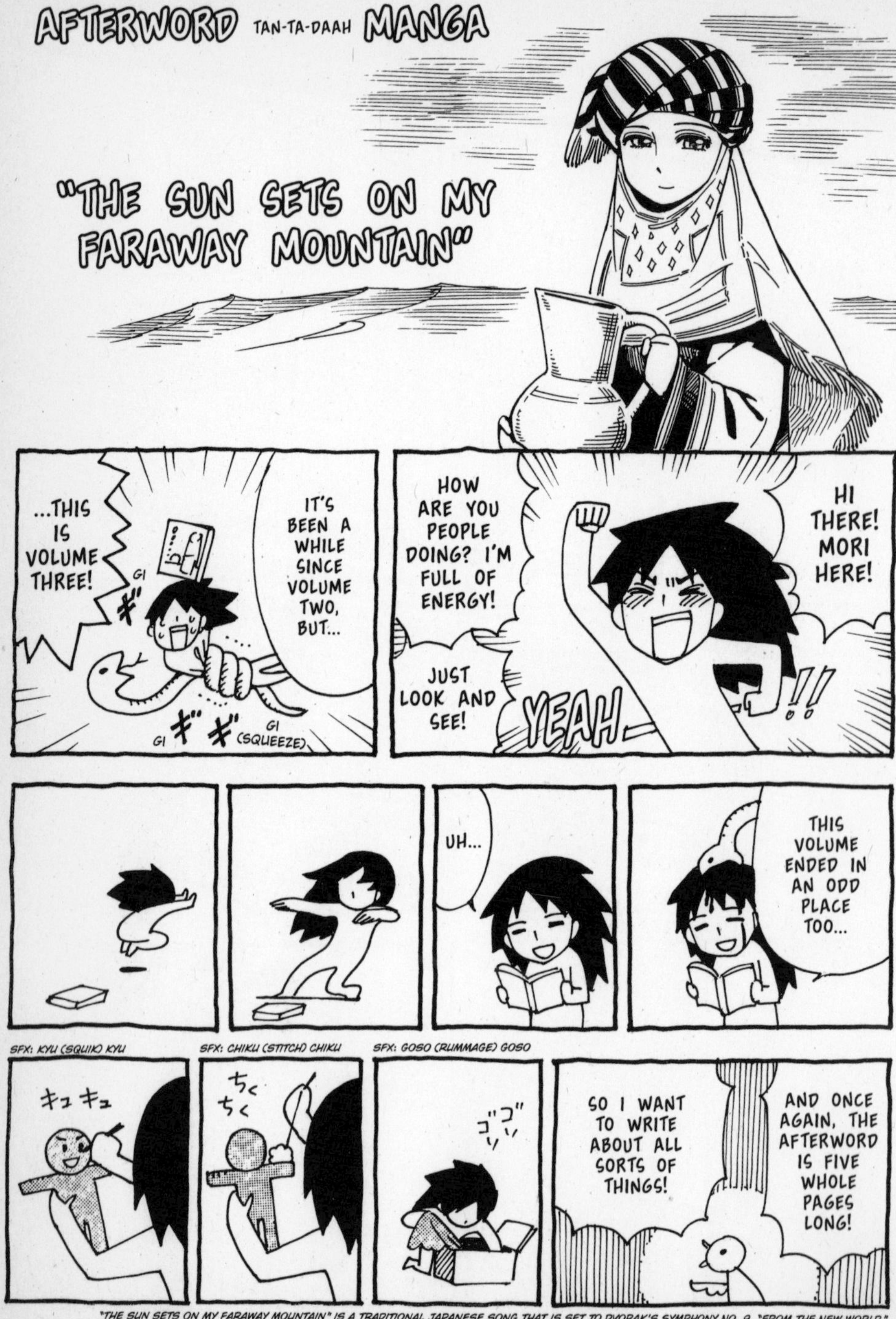
AFTERWORD TAN-TA-DAAH MANGA
"THE SUN SETS ON MY FARAWAY MOUNTAIN"
HI THERE! MORI HERE!
HOW ARE YOU PEOPLE DOING? I'M FULL OF ENERGY!
YEAH!!
JUST LOOK AND SEE!
IT'S BEEN A WHILE SINCE VOLUME TWO, BUT...
...THIS IS VOLUME THREE!
GI ギ
GI ギ ギ GI (SQUEEZE)
THIS VOLUME ENDED IN AN ODD PLACE TOO...
UH...
AND ONCE AGAIN, THE AFTERWORD IS FIVE WHOLE PAGES LONG!
SO I WANT TO WRITE ABOUT ALL SORTS OF THINGS!
SFX: GOSO (RUMMAGE) GOSO
ゴソゴソ
SFX: CHIKU (STITCH) CHIKU
ちくちく
SFX: KYU (SQUIK) KYU
キュキュ

"THE SUN SETS ON MY FARAWAY MOUNTAIN" IS A TRADITIONAL JAPANESE SONG THAT IS SET TO DVORAK'S SYMPHONY NO. 9, "FROM THE NEW WORLD," SUPPOSEDLY WRITTEN BY DVOŘÁK IN A TIME OF HOMESICKNESS. IN THE EARLY 1900s, LYRICS WERE ADDED AND THE PIECE WAS TITLED, "GOIN' HOME." NOT LONG AFTERWARD, KEIZO HORIUCHI LOOSELY ADAPTED THE LYRICS OF "GOIN' HOME" TO JAPANESE, TAKING THE SAME NOSTALGIC TONE OF THE PIECE BUT REWRITING IT FOR THE JAPANESE SCENERY (MOUNTAINS) AND SENSIBILITY. THE SONG HAS SINCE BECOME A JAPANESE STANDARD.

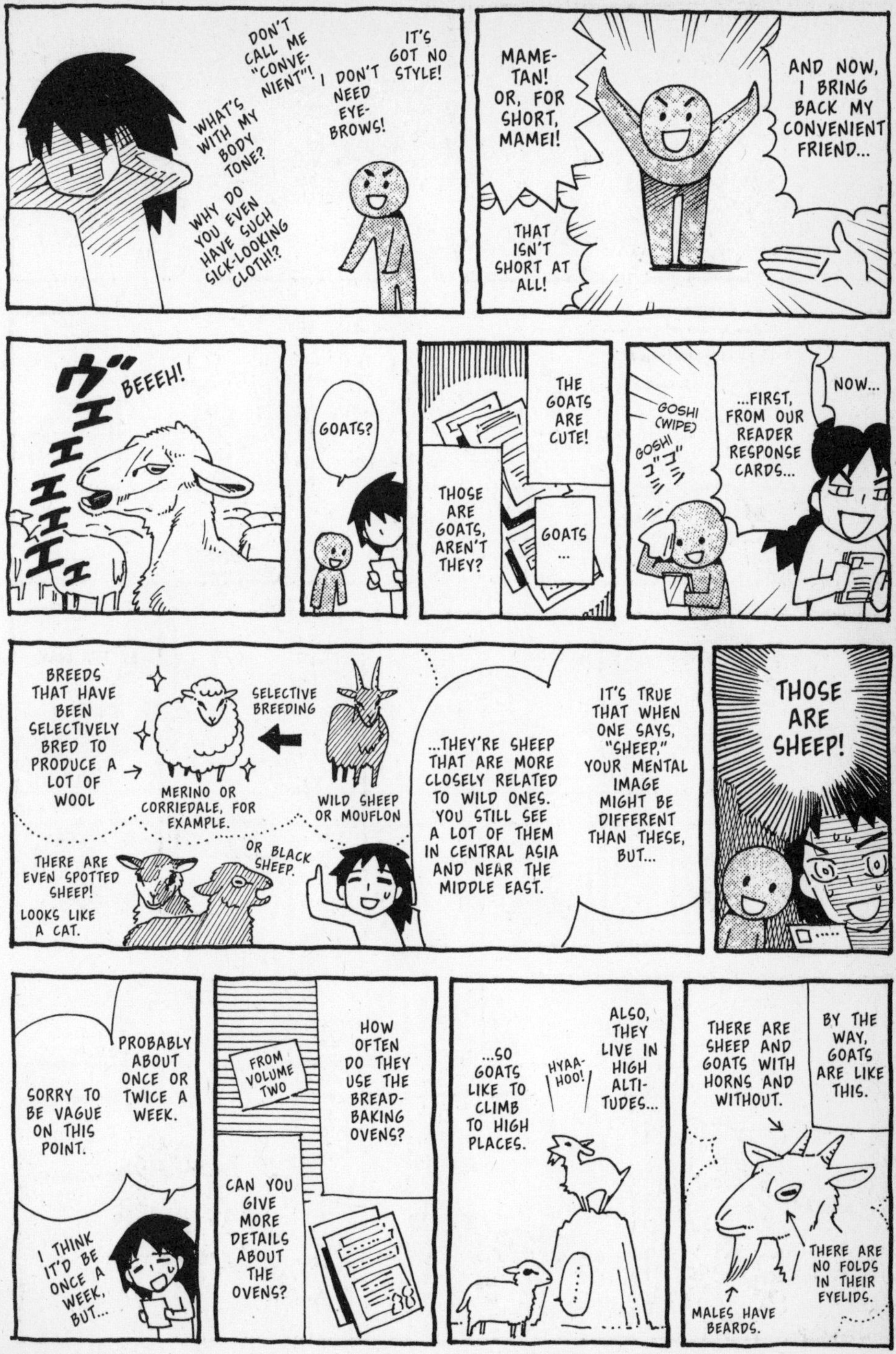
AND NOW, I BRING BACK MY CONVENIENT FRIEND...
MAME-TAN! OR, FOR SHORT, MAMEI!
THAT ISN'T SHORT AT ALL!
IT'S GOT NO STYLE!
DON'T CALL ME "CONVENIENT"!
I DON'T NEED EYE-BROWS!
WHAT'S WITH MY BODY TONE?
WHY DO YOU EVEN HAVE SUCH SICK-LOOKING CLOTH!?
NOW...
...FIRST, FROM OUR READER RESPONSE CARDS...
GOSHI (WIPE)
GOSHI
THE GOATS ARE CUTE!
THOSE ARE GOATS, AREN'T THEY?
GOATS...
GOATS?
BEEEH!
THOSE ARE SHEEP!
IT'S TRUE THAT WHEN ONE SAYS, "SHEEP," YOUR MENTAL IMAGE MIGHT BE DIFFERENT THAN THESE, BUT...
...THEY'RE SHEEP THAT ARE MORE CLOSELY RELATED TO WILD ONES. YOU STILL SEE A LOT OF THEM IN CENTRAL ASIA AND NEAR THE MIDDLE EAST.
WILD SHEEP OR MOUFLON
SELECTIVE BREEDING
MERINO OR CORRIEDALE, FOR EXAMPLE.
BREEDS THAT HAVE BEEN SELECTIVELY BRED TO PRODUCE A LOT OF WOOL
OR BLACK SHEEP.
THERE ARE EVEN SPOTTED SHEEP!
LOOKS LIKE A CAT.
BY THE WAY, GOATS ARE LIKE THIS.
THERE ARE SHEEP AND GOATS WITH HORNS AND WITHOUT.
THERE ARE NO FOLDS IN THEIR EYELIDS.
MALES HAVE BEARDS.
ALSO, THEY LIVE IN HIGH ALTI-TUDES...
HYAA-HOO!
...SO GOATS LIKE TO CLIMB TO HIGH PLACES.
HOW OFTEN DO THEY USE THE BREAD-BAKING OVENS?
FROM VOLUME TWO
CAN YOU GIVE MORE DETAILS ABOUT THE OVENS?
PROBABLY ABOUT ONCE OR TWICE A WEEK.
SORRY TO BE VAGUE ON THIS POINT.
I THINK IT'D BE ONCE A WEEK, BUT...

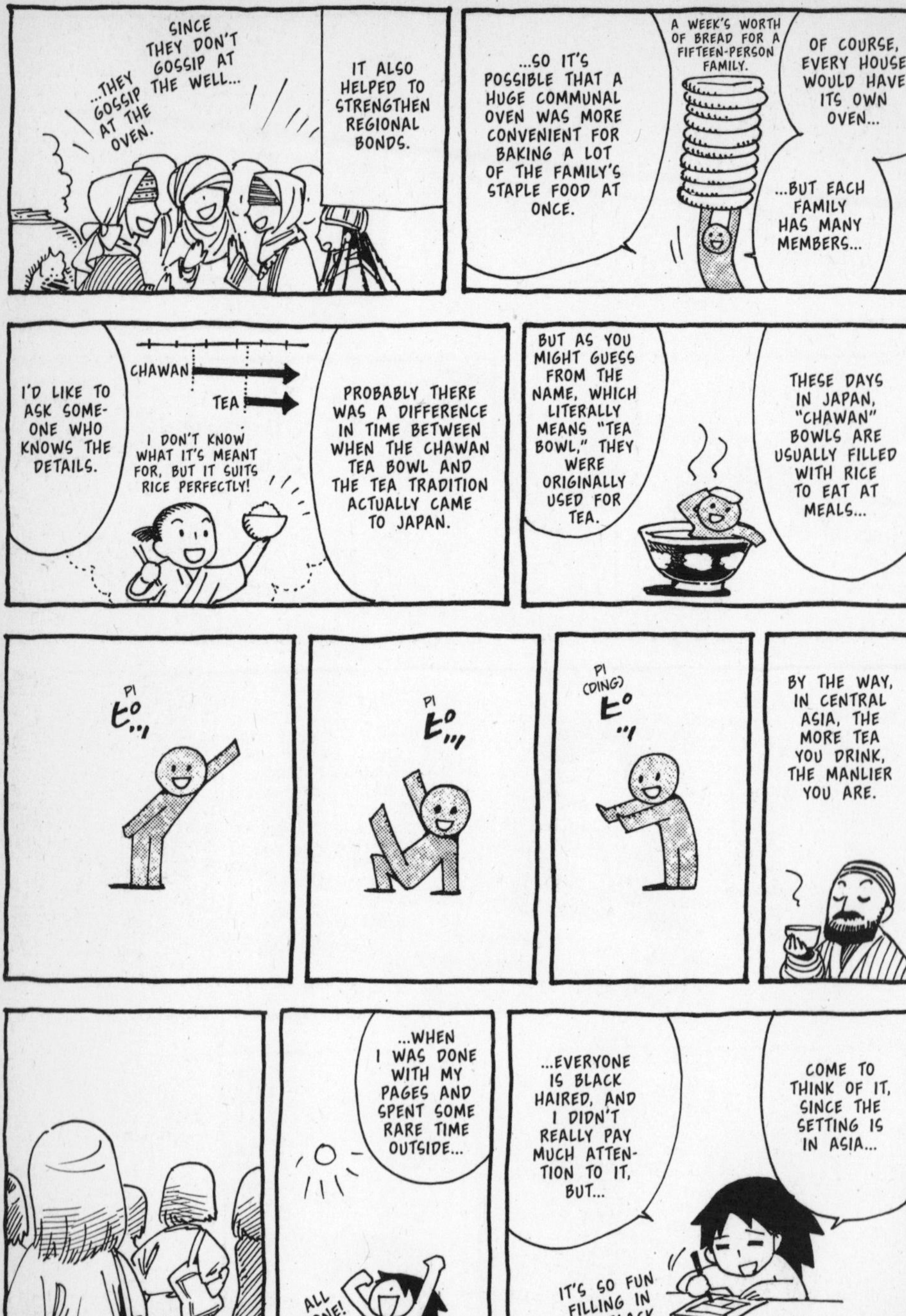
OF COURSE, EVERY HOUSE WOULD HAVE ITS OWN OVEN...
...BUT EACH FAMILY HAS MANY MEMBERS...
A WEEK'S WORTH OF BREAD FOR A FIFTEEN-PERSON FAMILY.
...SO IT'S POSSIBLE THAT A HUGE COMMUNAL OVEN WAS MORE CONVENIENT FOR BAKING A LOT OF THE FAMILY'S STAPLE FOOD AT ONCE.
IT ALSO HELPED TO STRENGTHEN REGIONAL BONDS.
SINCE THEY DON'T GOSSIP AT THE WELL...
...THEY GOSSIP AT THE OVEN.
THESE DAYS IN JAPAN, "CHAWAN" BOWLS ARE USUALLY FILLED WITH RICE TO EAT AT MEALS...
BUT AS YOU MIGHT GUESS FROM THE NAME, WHICH LITERALLY MEANS "TEA BOWL," THEY WERE ORIGINALLY USED FOR TEA.
PROBABLY THERE WAS A DIFFERENCE IN TIME BETWEEN WHEN THE CHAWAN TEA BOWL AND THE TEA TRADITION ACTUALLY CAME TO JAPAN.
CHAWAN
TEA
I DON'T KNOW WHAT IT'S MEANT FOR, BUT IT SUITS RICE PERFECTLY!
I'D LIKE TO ASK SOME-ONE WHO KNOWS THE DETAILS.
BY THE WAY, IN CENTRAL ASIA, THE MORE TEA YOU DRINK, THE MANLIER YOU ARE.
ピッ PI (DING)
ピッ PI
ピッ PI
COME TO THINK OF IT, SINCE THE SETTING IS IN ASIA...
...EVERYONE IS BLACK HAIRED, AND I DIDN'T REALLY PAY MUCH ATTEN-TION TO IT, BUT...
IT'S SO FUN FILLING IN THE BLACK SPACES!
...WHEN I WAS DONE WITH MY PAGES AND SPENT SOME RARE TIME OUTSIDE...
ALL DONE!

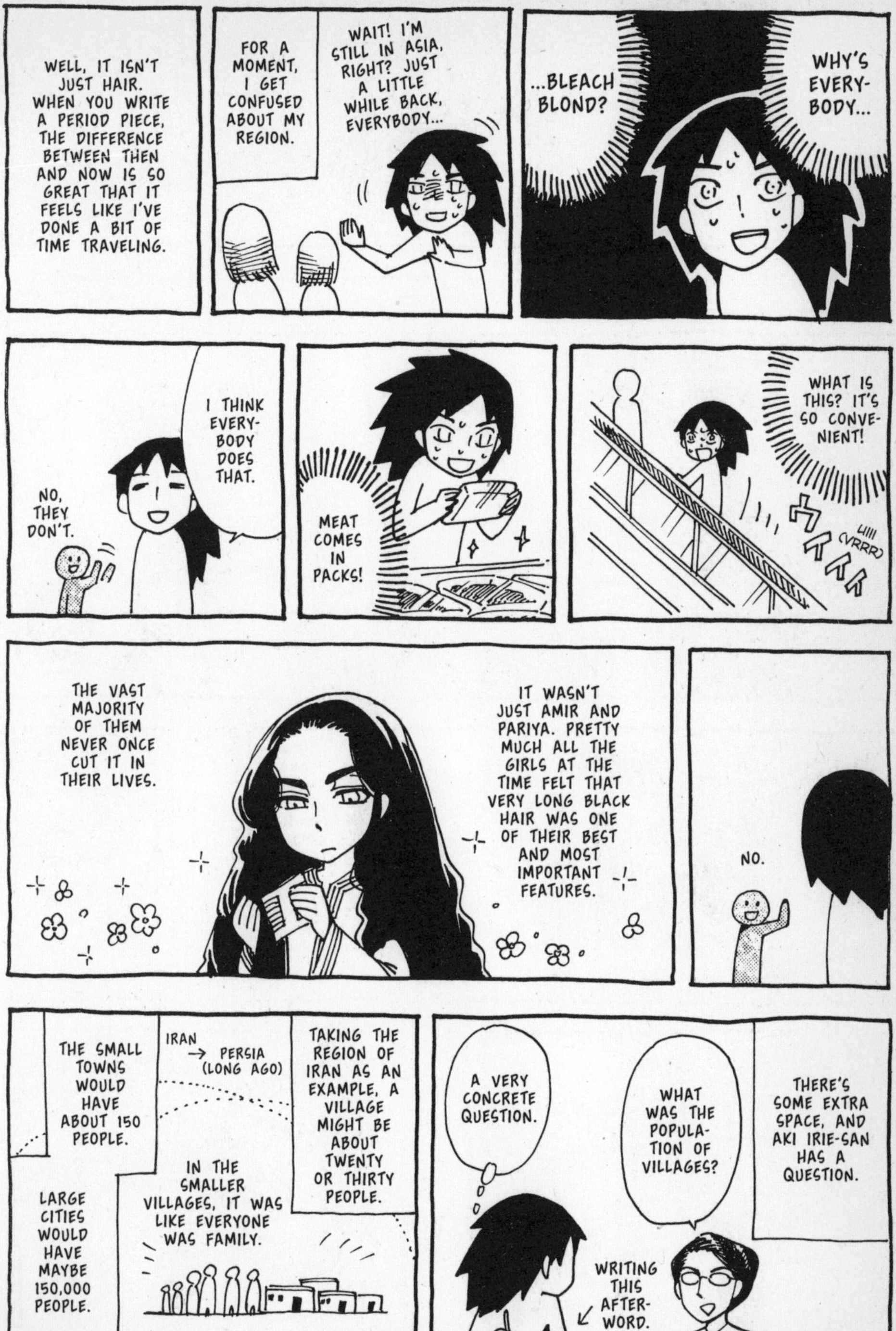
WHY'S EVERY-BODY...
...BLEACH BLOND?
WAIT! I'M STILL IN ASIA, RIGHT? JUST A LITTLE WHILE BACK, EVERYBODY...
FOR A MOMENT, I GET CONFUSED ABOUT MY REGION.
WELL, IT ISN'T JUST HAIR. WHEN YOU WRITE A PERIOD PIECE, THE DIFFERENCE BETWEEN THEN AND NOW IS SO GREAT THAT IT FEELS LIKE I'VE DONE A BIT OF TIME TRAVELING.
WHAT IS THIS? IT'S SO CONVE-NIENT!
ウィィィ
UIII (VRRR)
MEAT COMES IN PACKS!
I THINK EVERY-BODY DOES THAT.
NO, THEY DON'T.
NO.
IT WASN'T JUST AMIR AND PARIYA. PRETTY MUCH ALL THE GIRLS AT THE TIME FELT THAT VERY LONG BLACK HAIR WAS ONE OF THEIR BEST AND MOST IMPORTANT FEATURES.
THE VAST MAJORITY OF THEM NEVER ONCE CUT IT IN THEIR LIVES.
THERE'S SOME EXTRA SPACE, AND AKI IRIE-SAN HAS A QUESTION.
WHAT WAS THE POPULA-TION OF VILLAGES?
A VERY CONCRETE QUESTION.
WRITING THIS AFTER-WORD.
TAKING THE REGION OF IRAN AS AN EXAMPLE, A VILLAGE MIGHT BE ABOUT TWENTY OR THIRTY PEOPLE.
IRAN → PERSIA (LONG AGO)
THE SMALL TOWNS WOULD HAVE ABOUT 150 PEOPLE.
IN THE SMALLER VILLAGES, IT WAS LIKE EVERYONE WAS FAMILY.
LARGE CITIES WOULD HAVE MAYBE 150,000 PEOPLE.

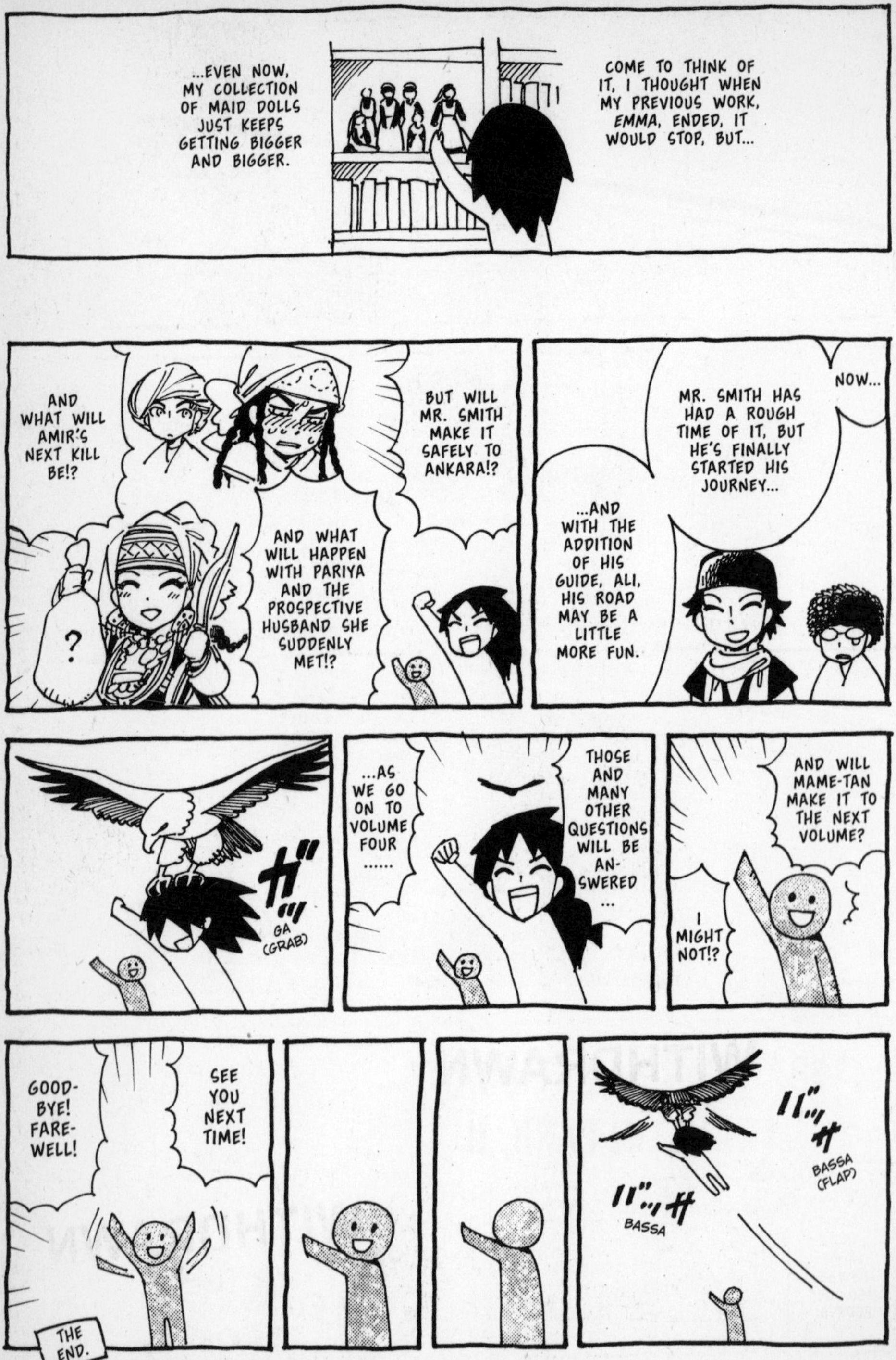
COME TO THINK OF IT, I THOUGHT WHEN MY PREVIOUS WORK, EMMA, ENDED, IT WOULD STOP, BUT...
...EVEN NOW, MY COLLECTION OF MAID DOLLS JUST KEEPS GETTING BIGGER AND BIGGER.
NOW...
MR. SMITH HAS HAD A ROUGH TIME OF IT, BUT HE'S FINALLY STARTED HIS JOURNEY...
...AND WITH THE ADDITION OF HIS GUIDE, ALI, HIS ROAD MAY BE A LITTLE MORE FUN.
BUT WILL MR. SMITH MAKE IT SAFELY TO ANKARA!?
AND WHAT WILL AMIR'S NEXT KILL BE!?
AND WHAT WILL HAPPEN WITH PARIYA AND THE PROSPECTIVE HUSBAND SHE SUDDENLY MET!?
?
AND WILL MAME-TAN MAKE IT TO THE NEXT VOLUME?
I MIGHT NOT!?
THOSE AND MANY OTHER QUESTIONS WILL BE AN-SWERED ...
...AS WE GO ON TO VOLUME FOUR ......
ガッ
GA (GRAB)
バッサ
BASSA (FLAP)
バッサ
BASSA
SEE YOU NEXT TIME!
GOOD-BYE! FARE-WELL!
THE END.

A BRIDE'S STORY ③

Kaoru Mori

Translation: William Flanagan

Lettering: Abigail Blackman

A BRIDE'S STORY Volume 3 © 2011 Kaoru Mori All rights reserved. First published in Japan in 2011 by ENTERBRAIN, INC., Tokyo. English translation rights arranged with ENTERBRAIN, INC. through Tuttle-Mori Agency, Inc., Tokyo.

Translation © 2012 by Hachette Book Group

Yen Press
Hachette Book Group
237 Park Avenue, New York, NY 10017

www.HachetteBookGroup.com • www.YenPress.com

Yen Press is an imprint of Hachette Book Group, Inc. The Yen Press name and logo are trademarks of Hachette Book Group, Inc.

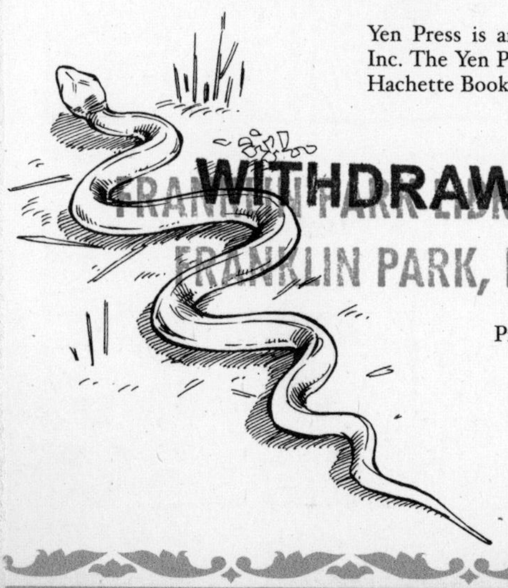

First Yen Press Edition: March 2012

ISBN: 978-0-316-21034-8

10 9 8 7 6 5 4 3 2

BVG

Printed in the United States of America